The Rules

S J Thomsett

The characters and events portrayed in this book are fictitious. Any similarity to real persons, living or dead is coincidental and not intended by the author.

First paperback edition August 2024

Cover Design by Julie Adams

ISBN 978-1-0686-9421-9 (paperback)
ISBN 978-1-0686-9420-2 (ebook)

1

Autumn 2014

The first time he saw her, he was sparring, matching mock blows with another regular, Alan Kirby. She had walked into the boxing club like she knew the place, had been there before. After taking a look around, she walked directly to a table where the old man was sitting, said something to him and sat.

Kirby was taller than Anton and carried no fat, he took things seriously and didn't usually say much. This time however, his sparring partner was annoyingly distracted,

'Are we doing this or what?'

Anton looked back at him and tried to focus.

'Sorry'.

They got back to it, finding a rhythm, Anton thinking about how he looked and trying to catch the girl's eye when he had a chance. He and Kirby had an understanding and put on a good show, trading feints, light taps, blocked punches, beating out a tempo on the practice ring floor. He made sure they kept moving round the ring, allowing himself regular glimpses of the girl. She was talking a lot with the old guy, but she was checking the two of them out as well.

When they took a breather, Anton leant back on the ropes, letting them take some of his weight, his back to her. She got a view of his shoulders and the back of his head and would have seen him stretch his neck and flex, loosening up nicely now.

When they started back up, he had a little swagger about him, he was fired up and ready to go. Kirby gave him a look that said *what's the matter with you today?*

Anton was bouncing and he kept her in his peripheral vision, knew when she was looking over.

When a gap opened up in front of Kirby's face, Anton let go a punch that carried real force. Kirby wasn't ready, he had no reason to be, and it took him off his feet. He flew back, hit the ropes, and slumped to the canvas.

Barney looked up from nearby, muttered 'What the fuck?' and took off before anyone else had noticed, reaching the ring in a few steps then ducking through the ropes, kneeling down, and lifting Kirby's head to check he was conscious. The others stopped what they were doing to watch.

'What are you doing?' he looked round at Anton, 'Get out of here.'

'He's okay, right?' Anton trying to be confident, keep his swagger; she was watching.

'Deano, get over here and look after him.' Kenny Dean was on his way already, two of the other trainers in his wake. Anton made a move to try and go to Kirby to help in some way but Barney pushed him back and brought his face up close. 'I said get the fuck out of here'.

'Barney, I'm sorry, I didn't-' but Barney was on him now and put a hand to his throat.

'What do you think you're doing? The rules don't apply to you?' Anton shook his head and went to speak but had no chance. 'No, that's right, they do,' he held his throat for just a second more to make sure he'd made his point. 'I told you what to do.' He let him go and turned back to the group around the still prone Kirby.

Anton dropped his hands, breathed out and climbed down, avoiding her gaze but knowing she was still watching. As the noise in the gym started up again, he could hear her talking with the old man,

'Why is he so angry?' she asked.

'He shouldn't talk to them like that, it's too much, they're kids… in front of ladies,' he said.

'It's okay Uncle Nico, I can cope… so why?'

'The short one-'

'-He's not short…' she said, and Anton knew she was watching him as he stepped out of the ring and walked over to the bench by the wall where he had a kit bag. He didn't change, just picked the bag up and walked back around the ring, taking the longer route to reach the door, one that took him past the girl. The older man was talking again,

'…they were supposed to be practicing, this is training, not competition… no discipline.'

Anton stopped to lift his kit bag over his shoulder, adjust his posture, catch a little more of the conversation.

'Why don't you speak to Rosa anymore?' she asked.

'You shouldn't call your mother by her name.'

'It's what names are for, Uncle Nico, that is the point of having a name, so that we can use it to identify each other… I'm not a child now and I just can't call her Mummy or Mother…or Mama, she's okay that I use her name, and anyway, you don't answer my question...'

'It's difficult for me.'

'What's difficult…?'

Anton let the door close behind him and stood for a moment in the cold, breathing the fresh air deep into his lungs, then started for home.

It was two weeks before Anton saw her again. He was standing at the counter of Purely Pizza one evening, waiting for his takeaway order and suddenly she was there beside him. He looked round at her, almost looked away but stopped himself. She smiled and leant forward on the counter.

'Hi.'

Anton tried to smile back as naturally as he could, instead his mouth twitched and he grimaced, he stepped back, tried to speak but his throat was dry. He took a moment to straighten up, get control, and finally manage to smile normally enough back at her.

'Hi. The gym…?'

'Yes. You were drawing quite a bit of attention to yourself.' Anton blushed, she smiled. 'It was fun. You want to come and sit with us?' She stepped back and he saw another girl standing next to her, she was about the same age and didn't look at all like she wanted him to come and sit with them.

Anton's pizza arrived and he reached over the counter to take it.

'No, it's okay, thanks, I've got a takeaway…'

'It's alright, you could stay and talk to us for a while, couldn't he Marcello?' she called out to the kitchen at the back. Marcello, whose real name was Justin but who felt he ought to sound Italian, looked around when he heard her and waved his hand to indicate indifference. *No way out.*

She ordered a large one with just about everything on it, picked a table and led him and her reluctant friend to it.

'Is that all for you?' Eyeing his pizza.

'I'm sharing it with my brother, Nev…he's back-'

'Can we have a slice? While we're waiting? You can have some of ours when it comes… we're starving… please?' Anton nodded, not feeling as if he really had a choice. 'What's your name?'

'Anton. Anton,' second time for clarity.

'I'm Franca, this is Sally,' Sally looked up at him, gave him a look that said that none of this was cool, 'I saw Anton knock a boy out up at the boxing club, there was blood everywhere, he broke his nose.' Sally made a face to make it clear she didn't like the idea of blood everywhere.

'It was an accident. I think it looked worse than it was,' he said.

Franca leaned over and started to tear a slice of his pizza, she looked up at him and he took his first close look into her dark green eyes.

'You sure this is alright?' He nodded and smiled and briefly considered that he had known Franca for about five minutes and submitted to her will twice already.

'How can you eat this much pizza if you're a boxer?' Franca asked him.

'Are you a boxer?' asked Sally, catching on very slowly.

'Amateur. It's okay, I don't eat pizza every day.' By now Franca had torn two slices and handed one to Sally.

'I don't like boxing,' said Sally which earned her a toe-poke from Franca, '…except amateur boxing…'

'You should give it a try,' he said, 'it's just a good way to keep fit really.' Sally looked at him then went back to the stolen pizza slice.

'Have you been back? Since… you know,' asked Franca.

'No, not yet, I have to work out how to do it. The boss, the one who was shouting at me, he's not happy, I have to find a way to get back in his good books. He needs a bit of time.'

Marcello called over to say that Franca's pizza was ready, and she went to the counter. Anton looked at Sally and thought to himself how miserable she seemed to be, not to mention ungrateful, given that she was eating his food. She looked back like she'd worked out what he was thinking, and she didn't care.

Franca was true to her word and tore him a slice of her pizza once she had sat back down. They relaxed a little and joked, Sally looking on.

Once the food was finished, Franca ditched Sally with not much subtlety and suggested Anton walk her home. Getting up to leave, she pulled her leather jacket around herself, zipped up the front, tipped her head forward and swept her hand up the back of her neck to free her long, black hair, shaking it one last time to make sure it fell over the collar. It wasn't hard for him to be smitten with Franca.

They left together, Anton holding the door for her, Franca then leading the way, both of them hunched up against the cold, their hands in their pockets.

'You *want* to go back though?' she asked, Anton nodded in reply. 'Are you actually barred?' Despite the cold, Franca was ambling, she lived close by but was making the walk last.

'Yes, of course.'

'You just have to go and say sorry. You shouldn't give it up if you enjoy it. Couldn't you let the other boy hit you one in the gob in return?' Anton stopped and stared in mock horror.

'I beg your pardon? I'm not stupid, and anyway, that's not how it works.'

Franca smiled and saw his nose was turning red in the chill. She reached out and gently brushed it with her fist. He smiled at her, and she did it again, connecting this time, very gently, just a playful push; as she did it, she said, 'Bosh!'

Anton fell to the ground theatrically, breaking his fall with skill, but landing flat out in front of her. She looked down at him for a moment then looked around, there were only a few people about, but one older couple had seen it and were watching, keeping their distance, not wanting to be involved.

'Oy, get up,' she moved closer to him and leant down, his eyes were shut.

'Anton, get up, what are you doing? Stop it. Get up….' She crouched down now, closer, touched his forehead, put the back of her hand gently against his cheek. 'Anton… don't….' She was holding her breath when suddenly his eyes opened, and he let out a low roar which made her lose her balance and fall back onto the freezing pavement. Anton laughed now as he took in her startled look and got quickly to his feet as she gathered herself.

He could out-run her, which was no surprise, but he was a little shocked by the stream of obscenities that came from her as she chased him. After a few seconds she called out,

'Wait, we're going the wrong way.' He turned and went back to her, warily, but she seemed to have forgiven him. 'Tosser.'

'Didn't realise you had a punch on you.'

'Tosser.' She took his arm, turned him, and started down a side street.

'So why were you there? In the gym?'

'My Uncle owns it,' she said.

'The boxing club?' She nodded. 'Barney?' She shook her head. 'George?'

'No, they're managers, my Uncle Nico owns the building, the freehold.' He was a little put out that she knew something he didn't about the club, *his* club. Before he could get too caught up in that thought his phone rang. He looked at the screen.

'Fuck… Its Nev.'

'Don't answer.'

'I have to, he'll think I'm dead or something…'

'Really?'

'No, not really, but I don't have a reason not to answer him.'

'Yes you do, we're home,' she pointed down the road, 'the one on the corner.'

Anton carefully put the phone back in his pocket, letting it ring out, keeping options open for later when he had to explain all this. He had a vision of Neville sitting at home in front of the television, wondering where his promised half-pizza was and getting annoyed. Franca stopped and clutched Anton's arm, pulling him closer. He looked up at the house.

'Come in for a moment.'

The house was typical late Victorian design, three storeys, end of terrace and on the corner. It had been looked after and stood out next to its neighbours.

'It used to be three separate flats, there's still a kitchen on each level. It means I can be self-contained. Come on.' Franca pulled his arm.

'I'd better get back,' he said, but Franca was having none of it. She was strong too, they were at the door, and she had her keys ready before he could work out a way to leave. Once inside, the sudden warmth of the hallway felt good. There were cooking smells too: garlic, tomatoes, fried onions... and something else, something less pleasant. They looked at each other, then lifted their feet one by one and checked each other's shoe soles.

'Clear,' said Anton.

'Yours too,' said Franca 'but there's definitely dog shit somewhere nearby.'

Anton reached behind into his hair and flinched as his hand found a soft smudge where his head had hit the pavement. He brought his hand round to look at it, realisation dawning as a woman appeared at the far end of the corridor, emerging from the kitchen.

'Where's the toilet?' he asked, beginning to panic. Franca pointed to the stairs.

'First landing, go left then first door on the left.' The woman was halfway down the corridor as Anton started up the stairs.

'This is my mother… Anton this is Rosa,' Anton stopped on the stairs, smiled at Rosa, hoping that would do for now. 'This is Anton.' Rosa held out a hand and Anton almost shook it with his right hand but made a late and awkward switch to his clean left, managing only a clumsily fumbled clasp rather than a handshake which confused Rosa. Franca tried to fan him away, 'He needs the loo,' then to Anton, 'up there, on the left.'

Anton took the cue and raced up the stairs. He looked back for a moment and saw Rosa watching him, wondering, he presumed, why her sweet daughter had brought home a boy who had apparently soiled himself. She raised an eyebrow.

Once inside the bathroom, Anton breathed out and shut the door behind him. *Fuck, no lock.* The room was sparkling clean, everything looked new and there was a bidet.

Even afterwards, Anton couldn't really explain why he had thought the bidet was the answer to his problem, it might have been the novelty of it, he'd never seen one in someone's house before, but somehow he decided that was where he would clean himself off.

He turned the water on and dunked his head in it, kneading it and rinsing the dog shit away as best he could. The murky water drained away, and he ran a new, clean supply. As he dunked his head into the spray for a second time, he heard the door handle turn, and he extended his left leg just far enough to reach the door and stop it opening.

'Someone in here,' and a bit of the dirty water went in his mouth; he spat.

'Who is it?' A child's voice.

'Friend of Franca's.' That seemed to do it for a couple of seconds, then,

'I need to go to wee.'

'Just a moment,' he pulled his leg back, regaining his balance and went back to the bidet head-bath. He shook his head around in there one more time and came up, reaching out for a towel. As he put it to his head, he opened his eyes and was face to face with a small boy.

'Why did you have your head in the bidet?' The boy was staring at him, looking puzzled.

'It's a secret,' said Anton, without any back up story. The boy was unimpressed and turned around to the toilet, dropped his trousers, and emptied his bladder noisily and without inhibition. Anton carried on rubbing his hair with the towel.

The boy finished, shook, and zipped up, went to the sink and washed his hands, dried them on another towel and left without looking again at Anton.

Anton gave his head one last rub and looked down at the towel. The thing with shit is that it's really hard to get every last bit out and it will inevitably show up badly on a white towel. But the smell was gone.

He'd been missing now for a few minutes, so it was definitely time to go back downstairs. He folded the towel to hide the stain and put it back on the rail then looked in the mirror and ran his hands through his hair a couple of times. *Best I can do,* he thought and got ready to go and talk to Rosa. *Oh God.*

Franca and Rosa were standing and talking as he walked into the kitchen. The boy was there too, sitting at a table and eating a sandwich, watching the newcomer as he walked in. Anton smiled and nodded to Rosa, trying to be relaxed and friendly but feeling nervous and insecure.

'This is Gregory, my brother,' said Franca, pointing at the boy. 'This is Anton, Greg.' He didn't seem to care.

'We met,' said Anton as a drop of water from his still quite wet hair dripped down his cheek. Rosa was watching him.

'My eyes…I had dust in my eyes from outside, splashed water over them, got it everywhere… not on the floor, on me, everywhere on me.' He could see that Rosa wasn't sure what to make of him yet, but the bad smell had gone so that was one thing. Franca took control.

'We'll go to my room with the coffee,' she had poured two cups and now handed one to Anton, guiding him out of the kitchen as little Gregory looked up,

'I thought the bidet was for washing your bottom.'

'It is darling,' said Rosa, looking up at Anton who was not looking forward to wherever this was going.

'Anton put his head in it.'

'Shut it and mind your own business,' said Franca and pushed Anton out of the kitchen, back down the hallway and to the stairs. 'Second floor.'

When they reached the first floor, Anton stopped and went into the bathroom. He grabbed the towel he had used and folded up and came back out. Rosa was at the bottom of the stairs.

'I'm out early tomorrow, remember Franca...' looking up and seeing Anton clutching the towel.

'I remember,' they carried on up the stairs, Anton offering Rosa an awkward, rather fey wave with his free hand as he turned to go.

In the sanctuary of Franca's room, Anton explained about the bidet, and she helped him clean up.

'I'll explain it all to her tomorrow,' she said and started to laugh.

'Can't I just disappear and never ever have to see her again?' The humiliation was hard to bear.

'Of course you can,' she said with a smile that made his hand unsteady, almost spilling his coffee, 'unless you think you might want to see me some more.'

2

Arriving home, Anton had some explaining to do. He was late, for a start, by a couple of hours. He also brought no pizza.

His brother Neville, who was a little more than two years older than Anton, had been worried, of course, but more importantly, had been hungry. Now, finally his brother walked through the door, looking a little different: something about his hair.

'The happy wanderer. Where you been and where's my pizza?'

'I got distracted, sorry.'

'I'm starving, like literally starving,' Neville lied.

'I met a girl,' Neville stared at him and shrugged his shoulders, 'seriously.'

'Nice for you. That's great news. I pretty much starved to death, we lost a saucepan and nearly burnt the house down, but you met a bird, that's brilliant. Good for you.' Neville started moving out to the kitchen. 'Come and look at this…'

'Nev, listen… what do you mean we lost a saucepan?' he followed Neville into the kitchen, immediately aware of an acrid smell.

'I nearly set the house on fire,' Neville picked up a blackened saucepan. Blasted baked bean remains coated the bottom of it, 'look…'

'I'm sorry, I'll go back and get another pizza in a minute-'

'I don't care about that, anyway it's too late and that's not what I'm talking about,' still waving the saucepan in the air, 'what's this? Eh? Tell me what this is,' Anton shrugged, not able to understand the question well enough to provide the obviously required answer. 'What is it?'

'It's a saucepan,' Anton went for the literal truth. Neville shook his head,

'Ah, no, no…it *was* a saucepan. Now it's a bollocksed saucepan isn't it?'

'Yes,' *just agree and this will pass*; confession and penance were called for. 'I'll get another one tomorrow.'

'What if I want to cook something in it? What if I want to cook something tonight?'

'But you don't, Nev.'

'What if I did though?'

'Forget the flipping saucepan, Nev, let me tell you about this girl…'

Neville raised his eyes to the ceiling, muttered something Anton didn't catch but guessed was an insult, looked around the kitchen until he found a half-finished bottle of beer and went back into the living room and sat down. Anton followed him, waiting for his brother to calm down.

'You'd better have a good story.'

'I have-'

'Because that was a bloody good saucepan.'

'Nev, listen-'

'Okay, as you're asking: I gave you an hour which is usually the longest it takes there and back and thought we'd have some beans with them, so I put them on low and you didn't turn up and I forgot about them. That is until the smoke alarm went off.'

'Alright. Once more, I'm sorry. But this girl…'

'Alright. What's her name?'

'Franca.'

'This is a woman, right? Frank...'

'...*a*. Franca, yes. She's Italian, a bit... she looks Italian... black hair, dark eyes, she's gorgeous.' With that, Neville got a little more interested, and Anton told him the whole story, playing down the part about sharing the pizza.

It was close to midnight when their father, Malcolm, arrived home from snooker night. Every Wednesday and Friday it was snooker night, every week, without fail. As far as they knew, it was always at the same pub; they'd gone along once, to hang out and see what it was like. What it was like was the most boring possible night in a pub. From that point on, the brothers decided to leave Malcolm alone to his snooker nights.

When he got back, he was usually worn out and went straight up to bed; this time he walked in on the conversation about Franca which meant that Anton had to tell it all over again and, of course, he was happy to do so, Franca gaining a few degrees of glamour and desirability with the second telling.

When eventually they decided they'd heard enough and it was time to turn in, there was a lightness to the house: Anton was simply excited by the prospect of someone like Franca wanting to see him again; his brother and father were content with the vicarious thrill of an emerging romance, a new story starting up.

'When are you seeing her again?' Malcolm had asked, but Anton hadn't planned that far ahead, and he just shrugged. 'Not tomorrow, remember, it's the First.'

Before going to bed, Anton bathed and washed his hair, this time with shampoo and whilst doing so discovered a sizeable lump where his head had hit the pavement, the dog shit having failed to provide even the small consolation of some cushioning.

By the time he put his light out, he had decided he needed to find a way back into the gym, which meant first of all making peace with Barney, and that would be more difficult than it might have sounded. But more than anything, he wanted to impress Franca and thought his best chance of that would be back in the gym. After all, it was where he had first seen her, and his memory of that moment and his subsequent expulsion was painfully humiliating and needed putting right.

He relaxed his limbs, enjoying the smoothness of the sheets against his clean skin and began to compose an elaborate and suitable apology for Barney, the effort of which sent him gently off to sleep where he dreamt of Franca's eyes and that hair…

The way to get round Barney was to be serious and humble. Next morning, hot coffee in front of him, Anton called the gym. Barney answered the phone, he always did if it was first thing.

'George's,' no clue to his mood.

'Barney? Its Anton,' he paused, hoping for a friendly cue.

'So?' *Thanks Barney, thanks for making it easy.*

'I wanted to talk to you…'

'Go on then.'

'I wanted to say that I'm sorry. For what happened.'

'Go on then.'

'So, I want to do it properly. To your face.' Silence. 'I owe you a proper apology.'

'I'd say you owe young Kirby one of them as well.'

'I agree. I know. Can I come over then?' More silence, then: 'Three o'clock.'

'Can I make it two? I'm working later on…' as he spoke, he winced, *no,* he shouldn't have tried that.

'If you want to come over, come over at three,' as if there had ever been any doubt.

'I'll be there. Thanks.' He hung up. His father had appeared in the kitchen and was looking for a clean, or clean enough mug in the sink.

'First today, don't forget,' said Malcolm.

'I'll be back for five, don't worry.'

'Otherwise, you just wind Neville up, you know how he is.'

'I know, I'll be back in time.' Anton tried to sound reassuring but was clearly tense and uncertain. He had other things on his mind.

'You gonna call her?' said Malcolm.

'I don't know, yes, I suppose.'

'You should. And we need a picture next time you see her.' He looked round at Anton, 'Go on then, tell me what she's like again.'

'She's too good for me Dad. No, she really is too good for me.'

Anton arrived at the gym at three. He stood on the step outside for a moment and took a long deep breath before reaching out to open the door. As he did so, one of the new recruits to the Boys Club who Anton was fairly sure was called Jason arrived and walked past him. The boy hesitated, unsure about pushing in front but Anton gestured to let him go first and followed him inside. Everything looked the same as before and it was invitingly warm. There was a smell to the place that was familiar and comforting, the smell of physical work, of leather and lotions, floor polish and old mops.

At first no-one really noticed him as he walked as casually as he could manage across the floor towards Barney who was on the far side with his back to the room, counting time for two of the boys who were skipping, twirling ropes gradually faster and faster.

Then a few of the others saw him and went quiet, stopped what they were doing and watched to see what would happen. He walked past Kirby who was speed punching a bag. Kirby looked up, saw him, and went back to pummelling the bag.

Although Barney was turned away, he must have been aware of the gradual silencing of the background babble. The boys he was working with were too caught up in the exercise to notice until Anton had almost reached them. Barney turned to look at him, poker faced, giving nothing away. The skipping boys stopped.

'Barney,' he tried a smile but there was no point, 'I just want to say that I'm sorry. I'm truly sorry for what happened.' Barney nodded slightly and tilted his head back,

'Are you now?' Barney was staring him out now.

'Yes, I'm sorry for what I did. I behaved…like a…' Barney raised an eyebrow encouraging Anton to find the right word. '…like an idiot.'

'Like a what?' wanting just a bit more.

'Like a complete fucking idiot. And I'm sorry,' without looking away, Barney called out,

'Kirby, son. Get over here.' Anton looked over at Kirby who had carried on punishing the bag even when everyone else had stopped to watch. He stopped when he heard his name, steadied the bag and stopped it swinging. He was slow to let the bag go, like he hadn't finished whatever business it had been that he had with it. Eventually he straightened; he'd sweated up and after a casual wipe of his brow, he turned and walked towards them. It was all but silent in the room now.

Anton watched his slow walk, ambling, like his balls were too big to allow him to walk normally. He had time to take in his pale, sallow skin, his skin fade haircut, and he thought: *ugly fucker*. But every ugly fucker has his day.

'Kirby…' said Anton, '… I want to say I'm sorry.' Kirby didn't know what to do or whether he should say something, so he just rocked back and forth on his feet for a while, still wired from the punchbag, and stared at him. Barney spoke,

'You gonna shake his hand then?' Kirby took a glove off and extended a hand towards Anton. He didn't move any closer to him though, so Anton had to take two steps forward to reach him. He shook his hand and Kirby tightened his grip, just to let him know.

'Okay, we're going to have a vote.' Barney now back in charge, the master of ceremonies, 'Gentlemen… and lady… maybe, if she's here, I want to know if you want to let our friend here back into the club? Is he back in?' Hands started to rise, one by one, everyone checking each other out to see if there was any kind of consensus emerging. They all joined in, all except Kirby.

'Kirby, son… if you say no then that's how it is. It has to be everyone. Everyone else is saying yes though.' Kirby waited a little longer then raised his hand, it was his moment, everyone looking over at him.

Barney looked back at Anton and got in close. 'Alright. You're lucky… this time.'

'I know,' said Anton, 'thank you. Thanks Kirby.' But he'd turned away and gone back to finish what he'd started with the bag.

Everyone else went back to doing whatever it was they had been doing before. Anton crossed over to a spare bag and changed down to his shorts and a sweatshirt. *That could have been a lot worse.* The others were keeping away from him but that was to be expected, *they'll be fine next time.*

He worked out alone for an hour or so then got dressed and ready to leave. On his way out, he stopped by Kirby who was still pumping: working pads with Kenny Dean, ducking, punching, honing his footwork. When he saw Anton, he stopped and gave him a look.

'Listen, I really meant it when I said sorry, okay? It's not just because I had to for Barney's sake, okay?' Kirby nodded and grunted something which didn't sound entirely unfriendly and went back to his exercise. Anton left, *step one out of the way.*

3

Anton was home in time to shower, change and grab a couple of biscuits before Neville appeared, limping, and looking sorry for himself.

'You alright?'

'I'm gonna sue the council,' said Neville.

'Because you can't walk properly?'

'Funny. You have to drive.'

Anton made a face, 'Oh come on, you do the driving, you always do.'

'I've fucked my ankle up, I can't drive,' said Neville, looking sorry for himself.

'What happened?'

'I was running, I keep myself fit too, you know… anyway, there's this loose paver which gave way when I stepped on it, and I fell over on my ankle. My foot's gone black…' he started to take his sock off, Anton tried to stop him, but his brother was keen to show just how bad the injury was. 'Look at that, look.' Anton looked. His brother had a point, his whole foot was alarmingly discoloured, there were bands of deep dark grey and ruddy bruising that looked as if he'd been set upon. He probably couldn't drive.

'Hang on then.' Anton left him there, sprinted up the stairs to his room and came back a few moments later holding a brown spectacle case. 'Glasses. I need them for driving if we're gonna get through it alive. You got the key?'

Neville held the key up to show him he had everything under control.

'Way ahead of you,' he said as Anton took out his phone and wallet and put them on the kitchen table, 'and we have to stay away from the North Circular, there's tailbacks… I checked.'

Anton nodded, grabbed another biscuit, and led the way out of the house, Neville hobbling behind him.

They walked out to the street where the Outlander was parked. They'd bought the car second hand the previous year, Neville was particularly fond of it and wouldn't have been in the passenger seat out of choice. Keeping it clean and polished was the one task Neville took on without complaint and under his care it always looked ready to roll. Once they were inside, Anton took out the glasses and put them on, feeling self-conscious.

'I'll try and get us through this in one piece then,' he said, looking over at his brother who, he knew, still found it weird to see him in spectacles. Neville fidgeted and looked back at him, not saying anything, just eager to get on with it.

The first of the month was rent day and they followed a set routine. The brothers would visit and collect rent from the eight different properties that Malcolm owned, all within twenty minutes' drive. The tenants were mostly easy to deal with. Rents were collected in person and paid in cash, simple and clean. It was a two-man job, for security's sake although the round was usually trouble free: same faces, same people, mostly organised so the money was counted out and ready.

The first stop was Neville's favourite, a group of three young women who, he felt sure, were secretly impressed by his charm.

Anton stopped the car outside the building, and they looked up. The flat was on the top floor of a three-storey house. He took off the glasses, put them back in the case and followed Neville out.

'You supposed to wear those all the time?' asked Neville.

'Just for driving… to be safe, you know…'

They climbed the stairs quickly, Neville lagging behind a little, adjusting his collar and tousling his hair on the way. The one they knew as Lucy answered the door and let them in. The money was in an envelope on the mantelpiece, tucked behind a framed photograph of a group of young women who seemed to be having a whale of a time in the sun somewhere. Anton got up close to study the picture while Neville counted out the money and signed the rent book. This one always took a bit longer due to Neville starting conversations about who-knows-what, Anton not listening but waiting to get going again.

The next stop was close by, a small, terraced house and a couple with a child who had just started walking and demanded their attention. They worried Anton, it seemed to him that they were having to scrape by. He'd notice when things changed in the house, if it looked clean or not, if there was food out for cooking, washing draped over radiators or in piles on the floor ready to be dealt with sometime later. These people were doing their best to get by, he believed, and he tended to pay attention to whatever they said; if there was something needed repairing or replacing, Anton would see to it.

The route was the same each month, planned out to avoid any doubling back. Anton usually took the lead, did the small talk (except for the women in the first stop, that was Neville's domain) whilst Neville stood around being a silent presence, just in case anyone ever got an idea.

The next two stops were in the same block: student flat shares and the low point of the round. The first was always in a state of chaos and full of random junk: discarded clothing, bits of electronic equipment and carrier bags full of who-knows-what. On top of it all, there was a kind of musty smell, a mixture of stale food and damp. They always paid up without trouble though which was not the case with their neighbours.

One floor below was a family sized flat but shared by two couples who kept it neater than might be expected but who never had the right money ready. The young man who answered the door was their least favourite client, they didn't know his name, just that he had a way of making everything more painful than it needed to be. After letting them in, his first words were,

'I don't think we've got it…' Anton and Neville didn't say anything, just stood and looked at him. 'Can't you sort out a card machine or something? It's really hard getting this much cash together.'

'It's not though, is it? We come round every month, you have four weeks to get it together, it's not difficult,' said Anton, Neville looking on, looking a bit pissed off, strong and silent.

'Why can't we do it by card?'

'Because we don't take cards, that's the rule. You knew it when you took the flat.'

The young man took an envelope out of his back pocket and handed it to Anton who handed it on to Neville. 'Here's some of it,' Neville counted it out, twice.

'You're four hundred and ten short,' said Neville.

'Can't I do the rest on a card?' The brothers were now running out of patience, and it was Neville who spoke,

'Don't make us have to come back tomorrow, that really would be annoying.' *Neville was good at that,* thought Anton, *not saying much but sounding like you shouldn't push your luck.* The young man said they should wait there, he'd come back, and he left them standing in the hall. 'Why d'you think he doesn't want us to go through into the back?' wondered Neville, but before Anton had a chance to reply, he was back, holding a handful of cash. He counted out £400, slowly, like it was an imposition then took a £10 note from his wallet and handed it all to Neville who recounted just to be sure.

Neville nodded to confirm the amount was correct, 'You got the book?'

'Wait here.' The young man left again; Anton paced around, shaking his head in frustration. A few moments later he came back and handed the rent book to Neville.

'Thank you,' said Neville and signed it. 'Now, what you should do is start putting some cash away ready for next time, so it doesn't get all fucked up like this.'

'Are you dodging the tax?' The young man said.

'Tell you what, you mind your own business, and we'll do the same. If you're not happy here, you can go and live somewhere else. Shall we just go and have a look round, make sure there's no damage to the property that we should be getting concerned about… in case we have to let it out to someone new?'

'Its fine, we're busy, so…' standing in Neville's way, stopping him walking any further. 'We'll have it ready next time.' Neville smiled at him, and they left.

Back at the car, they opened the boot and put the money in a mini safe that was bolted to the floor, Anton looking round, feeling uneasy, this particular stop always left him on edge. They didn't speak until they were back inside and buckling up to move on.

'What a wanker,' said Neville. *Sums it up*, thought Anton.

The next two stops were easier: two middle aged men who shared one of their bigger flats and who they thought might be running a business out of it, the whole place just *looked* like an office; and a young woman who was a solicitor or some such who had sole use of a top floor flat with a south facing balcony that she populated with exotic pot plants; both had everything ready and in order.

There were just two more stops to make.

'Off to your girlfriend then…' said Neville, knowing the response.

'She's not my girlfriend,' said his brother, putting the glasses back on and easing the Outlander out into the road.

Paul and Carol occupied a second floor flat in a four-level converted Victorian terraced house and were never any trouble. As always, Carol answered the door and as always she gave Anton a kiss on the cheek, something which never failed to amuse his brother. After the book was signed and Neville was handing it back to her, she said they were being bothered by noise from the flat above and asked if they could have a word. Neville said they would, and they left. As he started down the stairs, Anton stopped him.

'Aren't we going to talk to the upstairs?'

Neville shook his head and carried on heading down. 'Nah, it's probably nothing, just a one-off, we can check it out next time if it carries on.'

The last stop was a house shared by a couple and two male friends of theirs who may or may not have also been a couple, no fuss and no problems. They were done and back home for nine.

Malcolm greeted them with a grin and a message for Anton.

'I answered your phone. It was that bird of yours. She said, are you gay?'

'No, she didn't… did she call?' asked Anton.

'Yep,' not looking up.

'Come on, what did she say?'

Neville had brought the inner box from the safe in from the

car and Malcolm had started counting out the contents. 'I can't really remember much about it but what she meant was: are you gay and is that why you haven't called her?'

Anton sighed, picked up his phone and went to his room. He called her but she didn't answer, and he didn't know what message to leave so he rang off and went back downstairs. Malcolm had finished the count and handed him and his brother each a bundle of twenties,

'She sounds nice.'

'She is,' said Anton.

Half an hour later, she called him back. Malcolm had made a stew, and they were eating. Anton looked at the number and left the table to go into the next room.

'Hi, you okay?' She sounded older on the phone, more mature somehow, a bit posh even.

'Yeah, I'm good. Sorry I missed the call. I called you back just now.'

'I know. I spoke to your dad earlier. He seems nice.'

'He's okay, a bit nosey.'

'He was alright. How come he answered your phone?'

'I don't take it with me on the rent rounds. Nev and I leave our stuff at home when we go out on the round, better not to have distractions. There's a phone in the car for emergencies.' There was a pause.

'See you tomorrow?'

Anton answered immediately, 'Yes. Definitely. I could come round… in the afternoon?'

'That would be nice. After five… I'm working.'

Anton hesitated then asked, 'You haven't told me what you do… have you?'

'You haven't asked… I'm a dental assistant.'

'Right. So, what does that entail?'

'It's very complicated. I assist a dentist.'

'I'll be there for five past five.'

'I told Rosa. About… you know. Didn't want her to think you were a weirdo.'

'Appreciate that. I'll see you tomorrow.' He was sure he heard her blow a kiss as she hung up.

The next morning, Anton was at the gym by ten o'clock. It had opened an hour earlier, and the place was buzzing. This visit was always going to be a whole lot more straightforward than the last time, but he was aware he was still in the process of being accepted back.

Entrance was straight off the street. There was no reception area or lobby, once inside the door you were in the thick of it. In itself, that could be intimidating to first timers; George, who had set it all up in the first place hadn't intended it that way, he just hadn't thought about it, hadn't seen a need for anything other than the main business of the gym.

Anton too, hadn't given it any thought since the first time he'd walked in years ago. This time however, he noticed it again, along with the familiar smell; this was home, he knew he'd miss it badly if he was ever really shut out.

And, of course, he had friends there, people he knew and liked, and those friends greeted him, all in the same basic way as he walked in and past them.

'Alright?'

'Alright Anton?'

'Alright mate?'

'You alright…?' and on and on, Anton returning the greeting with an added nod to confirm things were definitely alright.

He caught a glimpse of Kirby, on the far side, doing circuits along with one of the regulars, Tyrone, who Anton had known since he'd joined the club a couple of years ago. It was possible that Kirby hadn't seen him, or he might just be pretending not to have seen him. It occurred to him that Kirby was always here, he wondered if he ever went home.

He went out to the back and changed, came back in, and started to warm up. He could see Kirby in his peripheral vision, stopping what he was doing, stretching a bit then gathering up his stuff and walking slowly out to the back, leaving without acknowledging Anton.

Oh well, he's not my mate anymore. I'll live with it.

It was exactly 5.05pm when he reached Franca's front door. He was holding a bunch of flowers comprising the broadest spectrum of colours that he had been able to find in the shop. The mad flourish of reds, pinks, blues, greens, yellows and purples had cost him more than a night out, but the effect was dazzling.

Rosa answered the door and, although she smiled when she saw him, he had the impression that she was still a bit wary of his apparent shiftiness. He smiled back and said,

'These are for you.'

She took the flowers, not breaking eye contact with him. Behind her, Franca appeared from the kitchen.

'I know you know about last time, because Franca told me how she told you…' he paused to check the logic of his sentence, decided it was alright and carried on, 'I just wanted to say I was sorry…'

Rosa put the flowers to her nose, still holding his gaze, and breathed in. She leant back, her eyes widened, and she suppressed a sneeze by pinching her nose.

'Dear God, Anton, this is some bunch of flowers,' she said

and held them away from her face to look at them properly. Her smile widened, she declared them to be absolutely lovely and moved aside to let him in. Franca greeted him with warmth and ushered him away to her room on the first floor.

Once inside, she grabbed him and kissed him. She was eager and strong, her arm was around his neck, and she pulled him in. It was all happening a bit fast for Anton.

She broke off from the kiss, took his hand and led him to sit beside her on the bed,

'The flowers are really nice and very thoughtful,' she said. He smiled back and began to ask whether he'd made the right choices, but Franca kissed him again, this time slowly and with purpose. As he sank into the kiss, he felt her hand on his jeans, on his leg, then higher until she was wrestling with his belt. He eased himself back to make it easier as she unzipped the fly and helped him push his jeans down a little way enough for her to take him in her hand. He knew he wouldn't last long and with little ceremony she finished him off, he held on to her as he came in her hand and tried to keep up.

By the time he got his breath back, Franca had left the room and returned with two glasses of some kind of sparkling wine.

'Are we going out then?' he asked, then laughed at himself, at his slightly missing-the-point question.

'Looks like it,' she said and ran her fingers through his hair, 'I like it better when you don't have dog shit in your hair.' Anton looked away, still embarrassed by the memory of last time. Franca waited for a moment then said, 'if you want to, of course…'

'I do want to, yes.'

'I mean, you did bring flowers for my mum which kind of made me think.'

'I want to,' he drew her back to him, a little clumsily, and kissed her as gently as he could although his heart was still racing. She slowed things down as her mouth made contact with his and cut the kiss short by pulling back to look him in the eye.

'Good.'

4

Bright yellow light formed a fringe around the edges of the heavy red velvet curtains as Anton woke slowly. He turned to see Franca lying on her back. Her hair was everywhere: over her face and the pillows and close enough for a few strays to go up his nose when he breathed in. He brushed them away and Franca groaned, turned to him, slightly opened one eye and smiled. She touched his face gently with the back of her hand. With his fingers, he gently lifted aside a bundle of black hair from her face and lightly traced a line from her cheek bone down her neck and along her arm.

''You okay?' he asked.

'Mmmm…' she stretched out, '…how about you?'

'Yeah, I'm great. What time is it?' He reached out to the side of the bed, searching along the floor, hoping to find his watch which must have been somewhere.

'Who cares?' And she entangled him with arms and legs, so that he was held helpless before her, then looked at him, into him, deep dark green eyes now open but still dreamy. She moved forward and put her head on his shoulder, relaxing her grip just enough to allow him to turn onto his back.

'I have to train in the mornings…' his hand still sweeping the floor beside the bed, 'what about Rosa?'

'Rosa's fine. I promise, I'm a big girl now, don't worry. What are you doing?'

'Trying to find my watch, I don't know what I did with it,'

but whatever he had done with it the night before remained a mystery for a little longer. Franca was not interested in the time nor where his watch might be and instead put her tongue in his ear which distracted him from his fumbling around and made him tense up pleasurably. He felt her hand between his legs and without protest he watched her move over and position herself on top of him. He slid inside her easily and thoughts of training receded as Franca's hair once more swept over his face.

'I suppose this is training, kind of… you use up calories when you do this. I'm sure I read that,' he said.

'You do…' she was in control and that was fine by Anton. '… not entirely sure how much you burn up in the lie-flat-on-your-back-and-do-fuck-all position though.'

Later, when she got out of bed to walk to the bathroom, Anton watched her make her way slowly, with all the time in the world. Her long black hair fell down below her neck, and she shook it out and stretched her arms. She was relaxed, beautiful, at ease with herself. Nothing else in the world mattered.

He stretched out in the bed, content and warm, the fresh sheets and the perfumed air holding him there, he had no wish to be anywhere else. In less than two days she had become a vital part of his life. *This is where I want to be, in this room, her room.*

She came back a few minutes later, smiling, covered now in a white cotton gown, barefoot; as far as he was concerned, she looked like a film star.

'Bathroom's free,' she flopped back on the bed and Anton got up, grabbed his clothes which were mostly slung over a nearby chair, found his jacket which was on the floor by the door and checked the pockets for his phone which he quickly checked for the time and headed out to the shower.

She waited for him to return, held his watch up in front of

her, answered his question by saying it had been under the bed and cajoled him to go downstairs with her to breakfast. She had to persuade him, he wasn't altogether keen to see Rosa at that moment, he just didn't know how to handle that.

In the event, Rosa was nowhere to be seen. Franca made coffee which he accepted and offered him cereal which he declined. He found an apple and a banana however which did the trick.

'I'm still pretty full from last night, what was it, Indian?' He watched her sip her coffee.

'Thai. I love Thai, you get a lot for your money,' she smiled, enjoying his gaze.

'I've got to train. Thanks for all this… for, you know…'

Anton had brought his phone downstairs and thought it was probably alright to check it. He studied it for a moment then called his voicemail. He listened as Franca cleared things away, then made a face, groaned, and hung up. 'I have to make a call, I'll just be a moment,' he pressed a button and sat back. The volume was high enough for Franca to hear both sides of the conversation.

'Where you been?' his father sounded irritated.

'I told you I was coming over to see Franca, we went out and… came back and that's where I am. I'm leaving now, I'll come back and change before I go back out.'

'Before you do, I need you to get round to see your friend at Beulah Mansions…' Anton took the phone away from his ear for a moment and found the tiny volume button which he pressed a couple of times to bring it down and pressed the phone to his ear. '… she was on first thing this morning complaining about noise from the flat above.'

'Have I got to, can't Nev do it?'

'He's over at the students, sorting out their rad's so yeah, you have to. She said that she already told you about it.'

'Yeah, they did but it didn't sound like much. What are we supposed to do about it?'

'I don't know, use your loaf, have a friendly word, we have to look like we've done something.'

'Alright, I'll go there first, let you know what happens. See you later.'

'Hey.'

'What?'

'So, you stayed over?'

'Yes. What?'

'I think it's time you introduced me.'

'All in good time Dad.'

'Like soon.'

'I will, don't worry. See you.' He put the phone in his pocket and moved behind Franca who was standing at a cupboard putting cereal boxes away. He held her round her waist and pulled her towards him, breathing in her perfume, feeling her pushing back against him. They arranged to meet later, and Anton decided he would jog to Beulah Mansions.

He had the wrong shoes on but thought that he should take the opportunity for some light exercise.

Generally, he found it pleasurable to run in the streets but not so much when it was wet, and the drizzle that day didn't ease like he hoped it would, but gradually built so that it was proper rain by the time he was halfway there and too far from anywhere to make a stop and wait for it to pass. By the time he reached Beulah Mansions he was sodden.

He pressed the bell for Flat C, Carol answered and buzzed him in. He ran up the stairs to the second floor, cooling down now and starting to really feel the clammy damp as his clothes sank back onto him.

She answered the door, leaning in for a kissed greeting.

'You're soaked…'

'I'm sorry,' said Anton, 'I jogged here, I wasn't far away but it started pouring.'

'Do you want a towel or something?'

'I'm okay, thanks, don't worry,' but he thought about it and said, 'Yeah, actually, do you mind?' She left him there just inside the door, really regretting not having gone back for the car. Carol returned a few moments later with just about the biggest towel he'd ever seen.

'Here you are… if you want to take your trousers off, feel free. I can lend you one of Paul's track bottoms,' and she was gone again. Anton hesitated for a moment, mildly embarrassed but his jeans were heavy and dripping rainwater and getting colder. He took them off and managed to wrap the towel around himself, then took his jacket off and hung it on a hook by the door.

When Carol returned there was an awkward moment as she handed him a pair of Polo track suit bottoms and put her hand out to take his jeans. 'I'll wash them for you, you can pick them up on rent day.' He took his wallet out from the pocket and handed the jeans over; she threw them onto the floor in the kitchen.

Before he followed her into the flat, Anton went through a clumsy routine of putting the track bottoms on whilst doing his best to hold the towel around himself. Carol turned and came back, gesturing for him to give her the towel which he did with some trepidation, and she held it out in front of him and looked away, allowing him a little bit of privacy while he pulled the dry track bottoms on.

'Thank you,' said Anton, relieved to be fully clothed again. Carol led him into the living room, no sign of Paul.

'Thanks for getting here so quickly…' Anton smiled and waited for her to tell him whatever it was. '…upstairs, I don't know…something's wrong. We're not unreasonable people, we all play music, watch TV but… God knows when he sleeps or maybe he just sleeps with it all on, but it goes on so late. He has visitors, a lot of visitors. He doesn't always let them in so sometimes they just press our bell instead, trying to get us to open the door. It's not our business so we don't let them in, they make a fuss, press our bell for minutes at a time. Paul went down once and had to physically push this girl back out who was trying to force her way past him.'

Anton nodded, in a way he thought looked sympathetic. 'Thing is, the flat upstairs isn't one of ours, he's not *our* tenant.'

'I know,' said Carol, 'but… last night, he came back about two o'clock. We heard the door go and he was drunk I think, crashing around when he passed our door. He put on a sixties compilation, really loud. In the end Paul went up and banged on the door. He didn't answer but after a few minutes the music was turned down. We just can't live like this, we work; Paul has to go to work early and we're afraid of what might happen if it turns into a row. I'm on my own here a lot.'

'Okay, I'll have a word, a gentle word, see what I can do. I'll come round later on and try and catch him,' Anton was doing his best to be reassuring. He was going to sort this.

'I'm pretty sure he's up there now, I haven't heard him go out,' she smiled rather weakly. *These people are a bit obsessed with this guy,* thought Anton.

'Okay.'

'You're still wet through, your hair's soaking. Hold on a moment,' she was still holding the towel and before he could do much about it she was drying his hair with it, fussing, mothering him. 'There, that's a bit better,' and she ran her fingers through his hair, straightening it, 'I've got a brush somewhere-'

'-No, that's fine,' he said, 'only going to get wet again when I go back outside, thank you.' He stepped back and ran his own fingers through his hair, tidying it after a fashion, 'Thanks for these, though,' he gestured at the track bottoms, 'I'll drop them back when we come round,' he moved to leave, and Carol moved with him.

'I'll put yours through the wash before rent day,' she said, then leant in for the customary kiss. 'Don't make a fuss or anything please, we don't want trouble.'

'I know. Don't worry,' he reached the door and gave her what he hoped was a reassuring smile. Carol closed the door behind him, and he looked up the stairs to the door of Flat D. *Okay, keep it simple, polite, strong posture, stand straight, move towards him a little, keep it subtle.* He took a couple of deep breaths. By the time he reached the door of the flat, he had it worked out, how to say it.

There was no answer to his knock. He tried again but still nothing. He waited for a few moments then went back down to the street door where he pressed the bell for 'D'. Still no response. As he closed the front door behind him and sprinted to a nearby bus stop, he convinced himself he would try again tomorrow, maybe return the track bottoms, except he should wash them first so that might have to wait until rent day; but definitely come back tomorrow, or the next day, come back with Neville, just to make the point, nothing heavy, just make the point that she, *they* have friends.

Malcolm was there when he got back. 'How was Beulah?'

'Bloke upstairs is a bit weird, noisy. I said I'd say something, but he wasn't in,' said Anton.

'Don't get involved. Neighbours. Like domestics, don't get involved.'

'You asked me to go round. Either you want me to do it, or you don't.'

'Alright, enough of the lip. Just do as little as needed is all I'm saying.'

'Fine by me. She scares me anyway.'

'Oh, yeah, that's right, she fancies you, doesn't she?'

'Dad, no, that's just Neville's little fantasy, she doesn't fancy me. She does insist on kissing me hello and goodbye though which is all a bit…'

'All a bit…?'

'You know,' and he blushed. 'Who is he anyway? The upstairs,' Anton trying to change the subject.

'Don't know, its rented though, same as ours. I'll look it up, it's a shared freehold, I'll have the details somewhere…' Malcolm went to the two-drawer steel filing cabinet that never seemed to be inadequate for their business even when he had bought new properties over the years. He pulled a cardboard wallet from one of the files and looked through the papers inside it,

'Here you go: Egerton. I don't think I've ever met him, he's a pain, always late with his share of the service charge, here's his address…' he wrote on a notepad, tore off the sheet and handed it to Anton. '… go and see him, see if he's helpful. Give him the problem, keeps us a step away from it all.'

'Good idea,' said Anton, not exactly relishing the task.

'Bloody poshies. Always want you to sort their problems out eh?'

That evening, Anton arranged to meet Franca in a wine bar that had just opened and was close by, more intimate than the pub he knew rather better, and they could be anonymous. It was quiet when he arrived, plenty of space, a few low-lit corners where some privacy was possible. He chose a table in sight of the door and waited. When she walked in, she saw him immediately and made her way to the table. He watched her approach, stood, and kissed her, tried to be cool but in truth was in awe of her, her beauty just seemed to be effortless.

They moved to one of the corners and drank and talked and made no effort to keep their hands off each other. It wasn't a busy night anyway and they were mostly ignored while they sat there, absorbed in each other and their own care-free pleasure.

Anton tried hard not to talk too much about himself but somehow ended up doing so: his work with his brother as they looked after their father's properties and his enthusiasm for boxing, for the club, for staying in physical shape. He told her he was working out just a bit harder now in the run up to a regional tournament, a one-nighter event: Army versus local lads, all in the name of charity but taken seriously by those involved. It was why he thought he should get back home tonight, get rested, be ready for an early start on training.

'It's fine,' said Franca, 'we just take all this as it happens.'

'It feels really good, and I definitely want to be with you, to stay over again… soon, last night was…' he tried to find the right word, settled for, '…amazing. You know what I mean.'

Franca smiled. 'Yes, I do. Same for me. We take it all as it comes, no rush.'

They were naturally at ease with each other, simply enjoying each other's company. Anton was learning to trust her and trust his feelings. She was wise and cool, he didn't need to be anxious, she seemed to want the same things as he did. They didn't need to know where this was all going.

Anton walked with her back to her home and when the time came, they kissed goodbye, taking an age to do so, working themselves up in anticipation of next time, assured that there would be a next time.

Next time was the next day. He called around after five and this time they got no further than Franca's bedroom.

It was after midnight when Franca was sent on a raid to the kitchen, returning with salad in a bowl and two different types of ham.

'It's called Speck,' she said, feeding a piece to him, 'not sure what the other one is, try it,' and she broke a piece off to feed him, 'Rosa loves this stuff.'

'This is playing havoc with my training programme,' he said, looking pretty pleased with the fact and leaning forward to kiss her knee as she sat on the bed in front of him. 'I just want to be like this for ever, can we do that?'

5

A few days later, on Wednesday morning, Anton arrived back from a run and walked in on a row taking place in the kitchen. Malcolm was pacing around the table, rubbing his balding head with the palm of his hand, and getting into a lather, it looked like it was all to do with Neville who was leaning against the sink.

'Don't get us involved, get the landlord to do something – I gave your brother the address,' Anton poured himself a tall glass of water and downed it in one, making himself gasp for air in the process,

'Beulah?' he asked.

'Yeah,' said Malcolm, snappily. 'They called again, just now, him this time, calling from his office. I put the phone down and next thing I know, *she* calls, same thing,' he looked at Anton, 'can you go and talk to Egerton, like, now please?' Anton nodded but Neville had a different idea.

'Look, we'll go round, Ant and me, go round there and see the geezer upstairs, he won't argue if there's two of us. We could go now, just as soon as Rocky here's had a shower...' Malcolm looked unconvinced, but Neville had made a plan and that was usually something that was hard to talk him out of. He turned his attention to Anton, 'Put a clean shirt on, you'll probably get a snog from the bird downstairs.'

'Oh yeah,' said Malcolm, 'you've reminded me, when she called, she said she's got your trousers.' Anton started to say something but gave up and Malcolm just smirked.

Neville was even more amused, 'Back of the net, son,' he said.

'Anyway… best not to be snogging our tenants, eh? It's against the rules really,' said Malcolm who was calming down and coming round to Neville's plan. 'Just a quiet word then, if you must, nice and gentle.'

'Of course,' said Neville, 'nice and gentle.'

'So, what happened?' asked Anton.

'Bloke upstairs; was playing music, loud 'til about three o'clock this morning, same tracks over and over again…' said Malcolm.

'He's a nutter, that's the problem,' Anton added.

'…then someone started ringing the bells, some hysterical bird apparently, he wouldn't let her in, so she rang all the bells, including our tenants'. In the end she got in, no idea how, maybe he let her in or the people on the ground floor maybe just got fed up with it and opened the door. So, she goes up the stairs, bangs on his door, screaming out to be let in, he shouts back at her to fuck off, she's not going anywhere, so eventually he lets her in and they have some kind of row in the flat, thumping about, there's more shouting and in the end it goes quiet but our lot stay awake all night waiting for it to start up again. I had to beg him not to call the police, said we'd deal with it. I still think you should go and talk to Egerton, it's his tenant.'

'We'll do both,' said Neville, 'how about that? We'll work out what to say on the way.' Anton nodded; it sounded like a plan. One thing you could always be sure of was that Neville would have a plan.

They got to Beulah Mansions just after noon.

'We'll get some food after this, yeah?' Neville usually had a plan for the next meal as well.

They parked the car at the end of the road and walked back, getting into the groove. Neville was still hobbling a little although his ankle had mostly recovered.

'Alright, so we've got Paul and Carol,' said Neville, 'it is Paul isn't it? Your rival, he is called Paul, isn't he?'

'He's not my rival,' said Anton, 'yes, it's Paul.'

'We should know his name, if we're saying they're our friends.' They had reached the front door now, 'He probably doesn't know anyway, it'll do.'

Neville opened the door and Anton ran up the stairs, waiting for his brother on each landing. On reaching the top floor they stopped outside the door, listened for a moment, looked at each other and Neville knocked on the door. There was silence, then a faint bump, not much but someone was in. Neville knocked again. After a few seconds he knocked again, he was ready to keep this up for a long time if needed. They heard movement then the door opened, just a little.

He stood there, pale, dyed blonde hair, smaller than they'd expected; *super lightweight* thought Anton, *maybe welterweight.*

'What?'

But Neville was primed, he pushed the door open, knocking the little guy off balance and walked inside, being big and jovial.

'Hey….' the pale guy off guard, Neville looking round, like he was expecting to see someone. 'Oy, what's…what do you think you're…'

'Carol and Paul,' said Neville, now a long way inside the flat, Anton having followed him in. 'Where are they? They're expecting us,' he'd reached the door to the bedroom now, but the little guy was there too and stood in his way. 'Carol?' Neville stared down at him like he was stupid, 'Where's Carol?'

'There's no Carol here. You're in the wrong place, now get the fuck out of here.'

'That's not very nice, we're just here to see our friends,' said Neville managing quite a nice smile along the way. 'How can it be the wrong place? Carol. Carol and Paul Morrison. Live here, right?'

'Morrison? No, downstairs, they're downstairs, next floor.' He looked at the brothers, assuming this would do it, be enough, they'd turn around and go now.

'Carol and Paul?' said Neville, getting close to him now, looking him in the eye, 'Not here? Downstairs you say?'

'Yeah.'

'Who are you, then?' said Neville. 'You're not the noisy twat they talk about, are you? No, I'm sure you're not,' in his face now, keeping him on edge. Anton watched him fidget, look around, try to keep his eyes on both of them. He watched him carefully in case he tried anything, but the guy was trying to play it cool.

'I'm just a peace-loving kind of person.'

'Oh, peace-loving, that's good.' Neville had presence that was for sure, and Anton was happy for him to run the game. Neville was looking past the guy now, taking it all in. 'Nice decoration. Unusual colour scheme, but you know, no accounting for taste.'

'Do you want to leave now? Paul and Carol live down a floor.'

'Yeah, we'll be on our way, nice to meet you…?' but there was no response. Neville pushed past him to walk back to the door, on the way he stooped and picked up an envelope from the floor.

'Hey-'

'-Don't worry, just trying to find out your name, seeing as how you've forgotten.'

'Darren. My name's fucking Darren.'

'Well then, Fucking Darren, it's been good to meet you. Maybe we'll see you again.'

'So, what are your names?' Getting a bit of his confidence back.

'Joe,' said Neville. 'And he's Cassius,' *Cassius?* thought Anton, 'we'll see you next time.' He handed the envelope to him and left with Anton following, looking back over his shoulder on the way.

They sauntered down the stairs, Anton stopped at Flat C and put his arm out to stop his brother going further.

'We'd better…' he rang the bell. They didn't hear the door upstairs close until Carol had opened up and invited them in.

'We've come to pick up some trousers I believe,' said Neville with an innocent smile.

They made sure they stayed a few minutes with Carol, told her they were dealing with the problem and were off to see the landlord now, everything would be alright, sorry for the inconvenience.

When they got back to the road, Anton was still puzzled. 'Cassius?'

'Clay. Cassius Clay. Ali. Dad's always going on about him, there'll never be another Ali…'

Right. And Joe?'

'Calzaghe. First one I could think of. He was on the telly. A while ago I suppose.'

'Cassius though. I thought you were talking about Julius Caesar.'

'What's he got to do with it?'

'Julius Caesar. Didn't they do that when you were at school?

You were at the same school as me…'

'We didn't do history. Or I didn't pay any attention in history.'

'It was drama. Shakespeare. Julius Caesar. Never mind.'

'No. Cassius Clay mate.'

'Joe and Cassius, you silly sod,' a little laugh; release. They reached the car.

'What do you think?' asked Anton.

'You're right, he's a headcase. Cokey I'd say. The place is a mess, bit of a pong too. I don't know what you think but I think we made our point. You can tell your girlfriend he should behave himself now.' Anton drew breath to respond but Neville was quicker, doing a familiar imitation of his brother sounding fey, 'She's not my girlfriend.' *Wanker,* thought Anton.

Egerton was the kind of guy who went out and bought himself a suit, rented an office in a cheap part of town and thought he was somebody; Anton disliked him immediately. He'd gone over there alone, Neville returning to the students' flat to carry on trying to fix their radiators.

Anton had decided to chance it and turn up unannounced. It paid off; Egerton buzzed him in then appeared out of a door leading off the entrance hallway to see who it was. He didn't say anything, just stared at Anton, waiting for him to speak and state his business.

Anton talked him into letting him in to his office. Sitting there a few moments later, Anton saw he was a man who didn't like to spend. The furniture was old, there was almost no ornamentation, just a desk, a few unmatched chairs and a tea-stained mug badly in need of a wash. In the corner, behind the desk was a rubber plant that was doing really quite well although its growth was out of control, *should have been potted up months ago.*

Egerton didn't offer him a drink and didn't seem too interested in him or what he had to say.

'So... your tenant thinks my tenant is a bit noisy? What do you expect me to do?'

'It's more than a bit noisy, he's a lot noisy. He acts strange too, has visitors who he rows with, others who he doesn't answer the door to who make a nuisance...' Anton paused to give him a chance to at least offer a little in the way of help, but he just shrugged. '...thing is, if you could maybe have a quiet word.'

'As far as I'm concerned, he's a good tenant, pays the rent. That's all I care about,' he stared at Anton again. 'Maybe, you go round and speak to him. Maybe you already did, eh?' Anton didn't respond to this, concentrated on keeping his poker face. 'I don't suppose you know a guy calls himself Cassius?' *Shit, that got out quick,* thought Anton.

'Cassius? As in Julius Caesar?'

'I suppose so,' said Egerton. Anton shook his head, tried to look uninterested, 'Anyway, to be honest I don't care.'

'To be honest with *you*, I was hoping for something a bit more, you know, helpful,' said Anton but Egerton had started checking his phone.

'They'll sort it out between them, I'm sure...' Egerton mumbled. This was not going the way Anton had planned but he stayed silent until Egerton looked up again. 'Look, I don't care, you go round, you talk to him, its fine by me. As far as I'm concerned, he's a good tenant and he pays on time, so I don't have any reason to go and bother him.'

'You don't care at all that someone else might be... bothered by this guy's behaviour?'

'Correct. And even if I did, I don't see what I could do about it.'

'You could go and talk to him-'

'-And I'm not going to, I don't have the time, so now we're going round in circles.'

Anton gave a little theatrical shake of his head, wasted because Egerton was back looking at his phone.

'Thanks for your time Mr. Egerton, perhaps we can pick this conversation up again another time.' Egerton just shrugged without looking up, 'I look forward to that.' He let himself out.

Back home, Anton reported his conversation, considered making it sound more positive than it had been but had to admit Egerton was a worm.

'Okay…' said Malcolm, looking like he was thinking it through, 'let's hope your visit to this Darren geezer does the trick,' he waved in Neville's direction, 'your brother told me about it, he sounds like a charmer… interesting that Egerton knew you'd been there.'

'Must have called him up as soon as we left presumably.'

'Yeah. Weird, if you think about it,' Malcolm was putting his coat on, 'see what happens, eh?' He picked up the small black cue case with the snooker cue sections neatly nestled inside on velvet bedding. 'I'll see you later.'

'Let's have a pint,' Neville suggested to his brother, 'it's been a day, let's be honest.'

'I'm not drinking,' said Anton.

'Brilliant, so you can drive.'

The brothers followed Malcolm out of the door and Neville locked it behind them, then called out as he walked toward the Outlander,

'You want a lift Dad?'

Malcolm didn't look round but just waved and said, 'No, you're alright son, walk will do me good.' Neville watched him walk away and made his way to the car. Reaching it, he ran his finger along the bodywork and looked over at Anton who was about to get into the driver's seat.

'You ever clean this car?'

'No, that's your job, you love doing it,' said Anton.

'I'm injured,' Anton looked at him as if to say *so what?* 'So, I haven't been driving it around and getting it dirty… it needs to be looked after.'

'We'll find a car wash Nev,' said Anton and got inside.

They drove for a short while, Neville saying he had an idea where to go. Anton was aware of his brother's stare. He looked over at him and Neville pointed at his glasses. Anton sighed:

'I told you, I need them for driving… I can wear them other times too if I want to. I've had them over a year. Where are we going?'

'Come off second exit at the roundabout, then get over to the right and take the next right turn… that's the one, now just park up on the right, there's a gap,' he pointed ahead, 'it's one way… just here is good.' Anton brought the car to a stop; they were in a quiet suburban street. He looked over at his brother.

'Okay, so what are we doing here?' he asked.

'I'll show you in a moment. First tell me about the glasses,' said Neville.

Anton gave him an exasperated look, 'Nothing more to tell Nev, they're glasses, that's all, I have to be careful… I got a couple of knocks when I was sparring. I have slightly fragile retina apparently, if I'm unlucky they could detach,' Neville made a face and stayed silent, wanting more from his brother. 'That's it, that's all, I'm okay, I just have to be a little careful. Can you tell me why we're here?'

'See the building over there, on the other side, about ten metres down, big oak door?' Anton nodded. 'Just wait and see.'

Anton sat back in the driver's seat and took the glasses off while he waited. 'This is a great night out, Nev, really glad you suggested it.'

'Just wait a little.' A few minutes later, he leant forward and strained to see, then pointed at a figure who had just turned into the road from the other end, 'There, see him? Walking this way…' Anton put the glasses back on and peered through the windscreen.

'Dad?'

'Yep, now watch him go to that door,' Anton watched him walk to the door, stop outside, and wait for it to open. He stepped inside and the door shut behind him.

'So… what, it's a snooker club?' Anton looked at his brother who just raised his eyebrows. 'What then?' Neville didn't answer so he stepped out and walked across the road, along to the dark brown door; he turned to see Neville still sitting in the car, his expression unreadable.

The door was heavy looking, had a small window at head height and was set back inside a shallow porch. There was a CCTV camera on the overhang and Anton looked up at it then pushed the door which stayed put. He tried the handle which didn't turn and looked around for a bell push. A face appeared at the window for a moment and the door opened. A woman stepped back to let him in, she was wearing a pink and dark purple patterned kimono.

Anton stepped inside, into a dimly lit room with a few tables and dark wooden chairs scattered around along with a couple of sofas against the wall and on one side of the room a bar, dark wood again and set in front of a shelf with an array of bottles and glasses. There was a younger girl behind the bar, pouring wine into two glasses, she was also wearing a kimono, white this time and open at the front to display more cleavage than might normally be expected.

'Good evening, sir. I don't believe we've had the pleasure before…' he looked round to see a woman walking toward him, she was older than the other two and dressed a little more conservatively although not in anything that might be worn outdoors. She smoked a cigarette and stopped to have a good look at him. He wondered how she got round the smoking ban but gathered his thoughts and said,

'Is there a, um, snooker table here?'

The woman smiled, 'Snooker? No, do you think you've come to the right place?' Anton smiled and looked round the room, he could see a few others in the gloom now, sitting quietly, waiting, all women.

'No, I think I'm, I've… got the wrong place, I'm sorry.'

'Are you sure?' She was closer to him now, he could smell her perfume mixed in with the smoke. He looked round and saw the woman who had let him in still by the door, waiting.

'Yes, I'm sorry, my mistake,' he said, backing away. He turned and the door was opened for him. He left and ran back up the road, crossing over only when he reached the car. Neville grinned as he climbed back behind the wheel. 'It's, a…'

'It's a knocking shop, yep,' said Neville. Anton put his head on the steering wheel, then in his hands and he looked up,

'So why the snooker cue?'

'He does play snooker. On Fridays. Wednesdays he pretends to, and he comes here. He doesn't think we know. I followed him once and did what you just did. I stayed a bit longer to tell you the truth.'

'So why...?'

'Embarrassment maybe. Doesn't want to upset us. We were just kids once, remember. I think he wanted to protect us, so he didn't date, didn't bring other women home. This is just his way. Nowadays he could just swipe right of course.'

Anton leant back and turned the key,
'Still want that pint?'
'Oh yes,' said Neville.

6

The brothers were relieved when the calls from Beulah Mansions stopped. Anton had other priorities after all, there was a tournament to train for and whatever time was left was time he wanted to spend with Franca.

Since the visit to Darren and his encounter with Egerton, he had felt unsettled, not sure that they hadn't just stirred the pot and made things worse, irritated everyone involved and caused more trouble for Carol and Paul. But there had been no calls and no more complaints.

Neville was convinced it was job done, there was no way that Fucking Darren could have failed to understand their message, he was surely going to keep his head down now and draw less attention to himself.

It took Anton a little while, but he started to believe that too.

His training routine picked up; it was always that way before a big event. The tickets were selling well, members of the public would be there and that made it a big deal in his eyes.

The professional trainers at the gym took on a direct role with the team selected for the tournament and in the run up would be devoting most of their time to them. Old George the father of the gym, was too old now to do much of the hands-on work, but over the years, he had put together a small group of professionals who had raised the standards.

In Anton's weight group, there was Dave Campbell, a flinty, Scottish ex-pro himself who took the lead. Each day Anton came in first thing, stretched and ran on a machine for thirty minutes before lifting weights and loosening up further with some pad work. Dave took it from there and worked with him to put together a programme that would bring him to his optimum level at just the right moment.

Anton was fired up by the idea of working up to something, even if it was just a little tournament, pitching lads from the Army against their team for nothing more than bragging rights and a few moments of glory.

The poster declared the event to be "the Army versus North London" which rather overstated the scale of it but conferred a certain grandiosity that annoyed some of those from rival clubs. Nonetheless, it had become an annual fixture, a social event that people looked forward to. Its core purpose was to raise funds for certain charities and over the years the organisers had created strong local networks to sell tickets. A full house was guaranteed, high spirits and a lively, drink sodden atmosphere was anticipated.

Anton wanted to do well and to impress Franca, let her see what he could do. To that end, he kept her away from the gym even when she asked if she could come and watch him train. He put her off, not wanting the distraction, not wanting her to see him working up to it but rather to wait until he was ready to step out. Part of it, he knew, was that he wanted to keep the gym for himself, it was his place.

Once he was done for the day however, he invariably ran over to see her and they hung out, went to a movie or their wine bar where he stuck with non-alcoholic drinks and watched her sipping white wine and soda. Afterwards, they would do a lot of walking round, going nowhere, huddling together and being close, it didn't matter how cold it was. Sometimes they went back to her place and often at the end of the evening he went home. 'I've got to sleep…' was how most of the days ended, and it felt fine, they were relaxed and secure with each other and neither fussed too much about the future.

Franca had an idea to invite Anton over to dinner and to include her uncle Nico with whom she was trying to bring about some kind of family reconciliation to put right a long forgotten falling out. Her reckoning was that he and Anton would get on, having the boxing club in common, and would have plenty to talk about. The occasion would justify her and Rosa making something special to eat. Anton was never going to say no.

'After the fight then, after this weekend, so I can relax and enjoy the evening, is that okay? We could do it next week or the one after...?' Franca agreed but had also set his mind running. 'You haven't met my dad yet, or my idiot brother… how about something a bit less formal later this week? I'm just eating steak and pasta so as long as that's okay with you then come over and I can introduce you, what do you think? You don't have to-'

'-I'd love to. Let's do it, steak and pasta sounds good, not too much for me though.'

'You sure? I know they want to meet you, they're weird but they're my family, you know how it is…' he realised that he wanted badly to show her off.

'I'm sure they're not that weird; if he's your dad, he can't be all that bad… brothers though, ugh,' they agreed to do it the next day; it would be a Tuesday so no snooker and anyway, *there's no time like the present.*

When he got back, Malcolm and Neville were watching TV: some film, supposed to be a comedy, explained Neville, but written by someone without a sense of humour.

'I want to bring Franca over tomorrow evening, is that OK with-'

'-Yes,' said the other two at exactly the same moment.

'She's cool with steak and pasta.'

'You sure son? I could do… um, salad,' said Malcolm.

'She's cool with steak and pasta, really.'

'Dad,' Neville said, about to be helpful, 'he picked her up in a pizza parlour don't forget.'

'I didn't pick her up… if anything she picked me up.'

'I definitely want to meet her though,' said Neville, a bit too enthusiastically.

'Best behaviour,' said Anton.

'When have I ever let you down?' asked Neville.

'Every single time I've ever introduced you to a girl,' said Anton but then he had to admit, when he gave it some thought, that the answer was, never. Or almost never.

'I'll get the steaks,' said Malcolm, the unfunny film now completely abandoned by all.

'You sure?'

'Definitely, you do your training, I'll sort the food out.'

'What else do we need?' Anton slowly understanding that some organisation was needed.

'Flowers?' said Malcolm, 'never go wrong with flowers.'

'Hang on,' said Neville, 'she's the guest, shouldn't she be the one bringing something?'

'I'll get some flowers,' said Anton, 'I'll do it on the way back… what do I get? Which ones do I get?'

'What did you get last time?' asked Malcolm.

'That was for her mother, I just picked out two of everything.'

'Which ones do you get for your girlfriend in Beulah Mansions?' asked Neville, again unhelpfully.

'She's not…' and he stopped, let it go. 'What flowers do I get Dad?'

'What's her favourite colour?' asked Malcolm.

'How am I supposed to know that?'

'What colour clothes does she wear?'

'I don't know… black mainly.' Neville found this very funny.

'What apart from black?' asked Malcolm patiently.

'I don't know, it's difficult… white I suppose?' Neville now finding the whole thing hilarious threw in,

'Basically, a zebra then.' Anton looked for help from his father.

'She's not exactly a rainbow is she son?' said Malcolm, 'Just go to the stall and get some that you like, if she's serious about you, she'll tell you they're great, she won't mind what ones they are.' Neville hadn't finished though,

'Just don't get any in the shape of a name, or a title, like "Grandma"… or a wreath.'

'Just get what you think looks nice, in time, she'll tell you what her favourites are, make sure you listen and remember,' said Malcolm.

'Did you get Mum flowers?' asked Anton, surprising himself with the question.

Malcolm hesitated for a moment then said, 'Yeah, sometimes. She liked daffodils, that sort of thing… anything yellow, she liked strong bright yellows.' It went quiet for a few moments.

'Okay, can we have a quick tidy tomorrow when I get back please?' said Anton and they nodded agreement. They were going to put on a show.

7

The intensity of his training had been picking up, not so much because Dave was pushing him, but rather that Anton was pushing himself. It was important to him to do well in front of Franca, he wanted to be confident that he was going to give a decent account. She had been slow to decide that she was coming to the fight, it wasn't her thing, she said, but he had been patient, said his father was going to be there and that it was a charity fundraiser, and she had slowly come round to the idea.

For the gym there was a degree of pride at stake. They had come a long way in the past few years and a tournament was a great way to make a point. They knew it wouldn't be easy, the army tended to take these things seriously as well, they wanted to impress as much as anyone else. In Anton's head, the army boys would have a sense of superiority and would not want to lose to mere civilians; that gave it enough of an edge.

Anton's daily routine had been building and he was posting personal bests most days on the bike and occasionally with the weights. His heart rate was exactly where he wanted it, and he was enjoying the build-up. He often didn't shower after his work outs, choosing instead to jog home by way of a warming down routine. The day Franca was due to come over, he stopped at the street florist and put together a collection of roses of different colours mixed up with purple, lilac, and white stems.

'We'll make it into a medley,' said the florist which sounded good to him; there had to be something in there she liked.

When he got home, he was mildly surprised to see the place had actually been tidied. His Dad was tenderising steaks with a lump hammer covered in a tea towel and the table was set with more or less matching cutlery. He went to the fridge to grab a cold drink and peered inside at a mass of red and green, glistening wet and spilling out from a large bowl.

'I did the salad,' said Neville from behind him. It was some salad, predominately made up of radishes, the necessary number of which he had over-estimated by quite a long way but there was green stuff too, mostly chopped up cos lettuce. Anton stared at it then looked round nodding his approval, genuinely impressed.

'Go and clean yourself up, you look like a sweaty oik,' said Neville, 'smell like one too to be honest.'

'Go on son, have a shower and go and get her,' said Malcolm.

Half an hour later, he came back downstairs. Someone had found candles and Neville was busy forcing one into the top of an empty wine bottle.

'Let's just keep it, you know relaxed eh?' said Anton, 'Thank you… both of you for doing all this, but let's just be nice and low key, okay? She might be nervous about meeting you. I'm going to meet her for a drink first, so we'll be an hour at least.'

'That's good,' said Malcolm, 'it's going to take me a while to get the rest of it done and to get these ready,' he threatened the steaks with the lump hammer again as Anton made an exit.

He was first to arrive at the wine bar, got settled and waited. Franca walked in looking like she was taking the whole thing very seriously. She was holding a generous bunch of flowers: chrysanthemums, carnations and some alstroemeria.

'It's just steak and pasta, you know that, right?'

'Its meeting your dad and your brother-'

'-My idiot brother…'

'He's still your brother. So, I don't want to let you down.'

'You wouldn't let me down,' said Anton, 'you look amazing.' They kissed and he went to the bar and came back with a large vodka and coke. He still had most of a glass of fruit juice to finish.

'What are those?' he asked, nodding towards the flowers.

'They're flowers Anton, I know you've seen flowers before because you bought some for my mum.'

'It's just that, I bought *you* flowers; they're back at the house.'

'We're going to have a lot of flowers then. I bought them for your dad, for your house. I bet you lot never buy any for yourselves, do you? The place could probably do with a bit of brightening up. It's okay, Anton, I'm the guest.'

'I know. I know, thank you,' she downed the drink in two and looked set to go. 'Ready?' asked Anton, 'You sure you're okay?'

'Yes,' she said, 'it's all fine, I'm looking forward to it.'

'Let's go then, he said, offering her his arm.

By the time they reached the house, it wasn't clear who was the most on edge. Anton led her in, anxious to get the first part out of the way as quickly as possible. Franca was all confidence from the outside: she handed the flowers to Malcolm and extended a hand to shake; he was polite to the point of formality and looked puzzled at the flowers.

'They're a present for the house, brighten the place up a bit,' said Anton.

'Right, thank you,' said Malcolm, fussing now, trying to find somewhere to put them down, in the end opting to take them into the kitchen where he lay them by the sink and picked up a bunch he had left there earlier: more chrysanthemums, plus irises, freesias, and some foliage.

Meanwhile, Neville had appeared and introduced himself, he half bowed when he shook her hand although he wasn't sure why. Malcolm returned and handed Franca the flowers, while Neville left the room again.

'These are for you. Welcome to our house.'

'Thank you,' she said, 'you really shouldn't have.'

'These are for you as well,' said Neville, now back and brandishing his own bunch of flowers that he had been hiding somewhere. Neville's collection was a riot of colour and was big: pink lilies, orange and pink gerbera and more foliage along with some bright purple tulips. Franca took the flowers and thanked him, laughing nervously. 'Nice to meet you,' Neville filled the silence.

'Ummm…' Anton began and left the room leaving the three of them standing there, Franca not knowing what to do with the flowers but grateful at this point for a hand prop, she buried her face in them, breathed in and sighed.

Malcolm smiled warmly and added: 'Where's he off to now?' Neville just stared at her. Anton returned, holding the roses and stems, all in full bloom.

'Seeing as how you're *my* girlfriend, I thought I would get you some flowers, but it looks like my family have sort of stolen some of my glory,' he offered her the roses, 'it's a medley; of roses, obviously.'

'I haven't got any hands left,' she said, at which point Malcolm lost it and started to laugh which gave everyone else the cue to do the same.

'Come on, come through to the kitchen and we'll put them all in a bucket while you're here... two buckets, that florist probably closed up early today.' Malcolm led them through to the kitchen, found a bucket under the sink, filled it with water and put as many flowers as he could into it, those that were left were put into the washing up bowl. 'Neville, get some wine going…come through into the back…' he led them to the room at the back of the house where the table was set, the candles were lit, one was even in an actual candlestick. 'It's just steak and pasta, Anton told you, right?'

'I love steak and pasta,' Franca said.

'Good, it's for him really, does it when he's got a match coming up, it's what they eat on the Tour de France apparently.'

'I didn't know that, are you sure?'

'Yep,' said Anton. 'Protein,' he added, by way of full explanation.

'Anyway, I've done the pasta, got some nice-looking basil and tomato stuff to go with it and some lovely looking steaks from the butcher on the main road, you probably know it, just over the way here…'

Neville had returned with a bottle of red. 'I did the salad,' he said.

The dinner went well as far as Anton was concerned, helped by generous servings of Rioja. He remained sober which ensured he retained a degree of nervous energy while everyone else slowly relaxed into the evening.

When the dinner was over and after more chat, Anton said he would walk Franca home. Neville offered to do that if Anton was feeling tired and earned a friendly cuff around his head.

'That's assault. If you're a proper boxer and you hit someone who isn't, that's assault, right? It's got to be against the rules,' said Neville. He helped to load them both up with the excess of flora they had bought for her, and Malcolm said more than once how she had to come over again, anytime she wanted to, she was always more than welcome.

'Your family is lovely, I can't believe how nice they were to me,' said Franca as they walked.

'They were on their best behaviour tonight,' said Anton, 'no idea why they all had to buy you flowers though, I'm pretty sure they won't do it every time you come over.'

'Rosa will love them,' she said and huddled closer to him. When they reached her home, they kissed in the street, slowly and gently, before walking up to the door, then passionately and with fervour once they were there. 'Thank you for a really nice evening,' she smiled at him and added, 'Neville made the salad, you know.'

'I have never seen so many radishes in one place before…' they laughed and kissed again.

'You sure you don't want to come in…?' she asked. Anton was tempted but kept his focus.

'Soon…' he brushed her cheek with the back of his hand. 'Soon. After Friday.'

'See you there, Champ.'

'It's just a charity thing, no big deal.'

'I'm teasing…' she opened the door, and he helped her to carry the flowers through to the kitchen. 'Put them in the sink and I'll sort them out in a minute,' he did so, laying the medley of roses beside them on the draining board. 'Thank you for a lovely evening and for introducing me to your family.' She kissed him one more time, held him tight for a few moments and said, 'See you Friday.'

8

Anton slept badly on Thursday night, which was no surprise, but he allowed himself a slow start to the day and took a siesta after lunch to settle his mind. He lay on the sofa at home and drifted easily to a semi-sleep from which he woke in good time to get to the gym for 4pm.

The team was gathering, eight in all, different weights, all keyed up to one degree or another. For any of them thinking of going pro one day it would be valuable experience to get out in front of a crowd. For the rest, the event was an end in itself, there was a thrill; it was a chance to compete on level terms, throw punches meant to hurt, set yourself against another.

George was there and greeted them all as they arrived. He would often say he felt all of his seventy odd years, but he loved nights like this, even more so since the boys had started to have half a chance. He stood by the door and greeted them when they arrived:

'Here we go, eh son?' to the first, 'Alright son, how are you feeling, you ready for it?' to the next, working himself up as much as anyone else. One or two of them were bouncing up and down on their toes while they waited for the others, warming up way too soon but finding it difficult to stay still. Kirby was one of the last to appear, coming through from the back of the building. Anton wondered how long he'd been waiting out there. Once they were all present, George called them together for the team talk.

'Have a great time out there tonight lads. Just go out and express yourselves, enjoy the moment,' they stood round him, knowing pretty much what was coming but needing it anyway: the boss, the old man, someone who's seen it all.

'It's special, fighting in front of a crowd, it feels great, I know. Barney, Dave, Deano, everyone here, they've done their job, up to you now. Do us proud, remember our rules,' he pointed at the club rules, a single sheet of paper, hanging on the wall by the lockers, still in its original frame from years ago.

'They're good rules, they haven't changed since we started this club. Alright, we added the one about mobile phones when you lot started coming in with them and stopped looking where you were going, but the others are the same: same values, same principles. Remember, it's your club, your gym; you go out tonight and you represent it, us, all of us. Like it says,' and he pointed to the piece of paper again, "you should conduct yourself in a sportsmanlike manner", so just do that, show them who we are, be a credit to yourselves. I'll be there and I'll make sure you get a cheer, just do the best you can.' He stopped and looked at them, each one, then reached out and applauded them. In return they clapped him and began to disburse, the restless and the nervous calmer now, everyone counting down the time in their heads, keeping it together, caught up in their own thoughts.

Kirby was one of the first names on the team list, he was one of their best boxers, easily the best at his weight. He was still keeping his distance from Anton although that got a little awkward when they got into the minibus, Kirby being the last to board and the only empty seat being in the row in front of Anton.

'Alright?' said Anton, Kirby grunted, turned and sat. Not the right time for small talk.

The venue was a huge municipal leisure centre, something from the sixties which at one time would have been a manifestation of enormous civic pride. It housed a theatre which doubled as a concert hall, a bowling alley and countless function rooms and studios for hire. The boxing took place in the largest of the flat floor rooms, one that was designed for big events: banquets, parties, trade shows and the like and it made a surprisingly atmospheric boxing arena. There was seating for about 150 surrounding the ring which had been placed in the centre. There was a bar at one end of the room with space around it to stand and already there were queues two or three deep when the boys arrived. Guests had dressed up, there were quite a few bow ties, some sharp suits and evening gowns; the women wore their jewellery, lots of it.

Funds were to be raised for the local hospice and a sick children's charity, it was never really clear who the main organiser was, but the local Rotary Club seemed to take a lead and the Chamber of Commerce had something to do with it. George's club had supplied a team each year for as long as anyone could remember, and the barracks would put their lads up. The guests had paid good money for their tables, and they enjoyed a better than might be expected dinner, lots of wine and a boisterously good-natured night. The friends and supporters of the fighters themselves stayed standing around the bar, keeping themselves topped up with beer and shouting for their boys.

Anton looked around for Franca when he got there but didn't see her, he worried that she might feel a bit intimidated by the beery and largely male vibe around the bar but then figured if anyone could look after herself then it was Franca.

The team were shown into a large room that had been emptied of furniture except for some functional plastic chairs, a couple of seen-better-days massage beds and a row of hired-in lockers. The boys who were up first started to change and the rest sat around, looking at their phones or just trying to relax, one or two even tried to do a bit of yoga.

Anton was programmed in for the fourth match and decided to change early and try to find some space to be quiet. He left the changing room, turned into the corridor outside, walked along and turned again at the end into yet another corridor which was wide and empty and just right for a bit of gentle warming up. There was a full-length mirror on one of the walls and he took a good look at himself and thought he looked suitably mean: a singlet that showed off his biceps and silver and black shorts with a sparkly "A" on the trim that he had treated himself to for the occasion; he took a second look and decided he looked the business. There was music, gentle and flowing, coming from somewhere nearby and he struck a pose or two in front of the mirror before settling in for a bit of shadow boxing and getting his head together.

A couple of minutes later, just as he was one-two-ing into the air he sensed movement and saw two people appear, arm in arm, a well-dressed couple, turning into the corridor from the direction he'd arrived and walking toward him. They hesitated for a moment then carried on, going past him, the woman moving in closer to her companion, holding his arm a little tighter. Anton felt self-conscious and resorted to jogging on the spot, letting them pass by with plenty of room. Then another couple turned in, a little younger this time, well-to-do and looking puzzled when they saw him; then a woman on her own, then more people, a steady trickle now, all headed the same way, down the corridor past Anton and then left at the end before disappearing.

By now Anton had started throwing punches at imaginary shadows and it was obvious even to him that he must have looked strange and unnerving to whoever these people were. A few minutes later and from the other end of the corridor, a man emerged, dressed in black evening wear, wearing a name badge, and looking official. He saw Anton and strode toward him. When he was a few strides away he told Anton in a well-rehearsed and authoritative way that he couldn't stay there, he had to go back to the changing room. He was firm but obviously not about to put up with any nonsense.

'I was just warming up out here, getting some space.'

'Well, I'm sorry but as far as my concert goers are concerned, there's a strange man in his underpants, punching the air and looking threatening.'

'What's the concert?' asked Anton.

'Why does that make any difference?'

'It doesn't I know, I'm just curious.'

'It's Svetlana Karamatkova. She's a world-renowned harpist. In our studio this evening, she's doing a recital. She's world-renowned.'

'I'll look her up when I get home,' Anton trying to make light of it and keep his dignity, 'these aren't underpants.'

'Sir, please…' and he indicated the direction Anton should go in just as a woman pushing a very elderly man in a wheelchair passed by, the man who wore medals on his smartly pressed suit jacket looked up at Anton with a knowing but faintly disapproving expression. '…Please.'

Anton smiled and set off back in the direction from which he had arrived, passing a few more concert goers as he did so and feeling distinctly underdressed. He looked back at the uniform and waved,

'These are boxing shorts.'

'Very nice sir, thank you,' and he was gone, back to manage the more conventionally dressed concertgoers.

Back in the changing room, it was clear that two fights had already completed. Little Dan, the flyweight and the first on the bill had apparently taken a pasting: his face was reddened and swollen all over, he was cut at the edge of his mouth, and it looked like it stung. He was wrapped in a huge towel and sat alone on the bench, swinging his legs and muttering to himself. Just along from him was Franny, the club's best featherweight and one of their top prospects, he sat sweaty and grinning in vivid contrast to poor Little Dan. Some of the others were congratulating him, patting his head as they walked by, Anton gave him the thumbs up,

'Alright Fran'? How was it?'

'Easy, mate. These army boys are pussy cats.'

'We'll see.'

'You'll sort him out, whoever it is.'

'Thanks Fran', we'll see,' he looked around, 'Ronnie on?'

'He just went out there, probably catch it if you go through.' Anton knew the way, this was his third time in the hall, so he knew the short cut to the kitchen, how to skirt round the edge once inside, dodging the chefs and the frenzied waiters as they nipped from oven to table to work surface. At the far end, he found the service door, no-one was using it, the crowd was between courses, and they wouldn't get onto their mains until after his fight. He edged the door open a little and looked out.

Pretty much everyone was focussed on the ring, there was a low hum, not too much noise from the spectators and the fighters were circling each other more than throwing anything, just keeping each other at bay. The room was packed, the tables were all full and the bar was surrounded. Anton looked for Franca but couldn't see her.

The bell sounded and the boxers went to their corners. A young woman in very short shorts and a heavily logo'd tee shirt, a size too small for her, picked up a board with the number 3 written on it and circled the ring with it held out in front of her. She earned a boozy cheer from the direction of the bar. One round to go. He let the door close and returned to the changing room, he was on his toes now: *next up.*

When they called him, he was coiled and ready, he had a head guard on and felt good, a few nerves but he loved these moments. He had no idea who his opponent was, just that he would be a welterweight and presumably a soldier. More importantly, he had no idea whether Franca had made it.

Dave walked through with him, Ronnie passing them going the other way, looking like he'd won but moaning about something with Barney. To be fair Ronnie was always moaning about something. Barney was shouting something in his ear and making complicated hand gestures, a bit of post-match coaching; *let him have a beer and chill,* thought Anton.

He walked in and it was lot noisier than before. With nothing going on in the ring, the crowd were talking to each other, laughing, gesturing, walking back and forth with pitchers of beer and bottles of wine. For a moment he thought about the staff, this lot were going to be a handful to deal with later on. He looked over at the bar and still couldn't see Franca. Little Dan had come through to watch the rest of the fights, looking better now, none the worse for whatever ordeal he'd been through. A couple of the men at the bar were buying him a drink and patting his shoulders, they felt confident in his company, most likely because they were bigger than him. Anton knew that although he was a little guy, he could pack a punch and most likely take any of them if he so decided.

Dave led him to the ring, to the steps which he climbed carefully, it wouldn't do to fall over at this point. Dave lifted the ropes and helped him climb through. Up there, it seemed higher than he was used to, and he could see the room was really full, more so even than he'd realised before. Pretty much no-one was paying him any attention, not interested, at least not yet. And then he saw her, Franca, and his father, not standing at the bar but sitting down at one of the outer tables, *how had they managed that?* They were watching him, clapping him, Franca whistling, Malcolm shouting something, but he couldn't hear much except for the general hubbub.

The MC was a semi-famous somebody from a sports channel, there to do the intros and to encourage the crowd to dip into their pockets later on when the auction took place. He beckoned Anton over to the middle of the ring and did the same with his opponent, he tried to hush the crowd and introduced the army boy first, Charlie something, Anton couldn't hear it properly above the cheers of Charlie's supporters. He took a good look at him: too tall for a welterweight. Then he heard his own name and the cheers from Little Dan and others from the club; he looked over at Franca who was clapping as hard as she could and looked like she was shouting something now. He allowed himself a little wave over at Franca and Malcolm, knocked his gloves together and got ready.

'Focus,' said Dave, back in the corner, looking him straight in the eye, 'don't worry about what's out there,' he pointed to the crowd, 'just keep your head. He's tall but that makes him easier to knock over,' he helped Anton adjust the headguard and handed him a gumshield. 'Go on then...'

Anton nodded at him and jogged on the spot. He watched the young woman in the shorts walk round inside the ring holding up the "1" board, she had a smile that suggested she was having just the best possible time.

The bell rang and he almost ran into the centre, towards the other corner, too eagerly, Dave saw it immediately and shouted above the noise, 'Focus!' That did it and Anton stopped suddenly, letting Charlie come to him for the last step which seemed to confuse him a little, but Anton was just thinking *this guy is really fucking tall.*

They traded soft blows for a while, settling in, Anton disciplined now, holding his balance, looking for a way through, his opponent keeping his guard in place, hiding his face. Anton took a solid left which hurt, then a second to his jaw. Okay, Charlie's reach was superior, that would mean taking a risk to get in closer, Anton was a good dodger though, he'd learnt that from George. He didn't land much onto Charlie but made it through the first round without a real fright.

'He's reaching you too easily, get in close if you can, put a few on him,' said Dave.

'No shit,' said Anton.

Anton caught him by surprise early in the second, using his left to push up onto Charlie's chin, opening him up then throwing a series of rapid punches, only some of which landed but it kept him on his front foot for a while and pushed the army boy back onto the ropes. The ref was in there quickly and separated them. Anton immediately tried the same trick and got back in, but this time Charlie concentrated on parrying him off, knocking him out of the way, waiting for his moment. Anton knew it was coming and watched him carefully, he was sure there was a right coming, that's how it looked, and he was ready for it. What he wasn't ready for was Charlie stopping rigid for a moment, just standing still, getting his breath then suddenly ducking as if avoiding a punch and letting go with a left that caught Anton on his right side, hard to his temple, knocking him off balance. He was in now and Anton struggled to get his balance back, taking two more to his jaw, another close to his eye. The army boys were cheering now, their man was beginning to look the business. Anton stepped back but caught one of his legs on the other and went down hard on his left knee, he saw Charlie approach, about to throw one when the ref put his arm out and stopped him. The crowd jeered him, denied a killer blow. Anton took the moment to get his breath and compose himself. He thought about Willie Pep, they all knew about Willie Pep, George taught them about him, how he could dance his way out of trouble, how he was supposed to have won a round once without actually landing a punch. *Willie Pep,* thought Anton and put his guard up, keeping it solid and getting to the bell.

Dave had a good look at his eye at the break but amazingly seemed to have a different view of what was happening.

'You've got him. He's weaker than you, he has a great reach but he's not strong, just stay close and don't get hit,' Anton looked at him as if to say, *really?* '…and keep calm.'

The girl in the shorts was carrying the "3" board round the ring again and the crowd were showing their appreciation.

One round is all you need, he thought, *give it all for three minutes is all you have to do.* He got to Charlie straight away, making it hard for the tall guy to line anything up, and started a non-stop assault. He connected with Charlie's gloves mostly, he was good at covering himself, but it kept him occupied and Anton found the gaps, enough for a right hook to get through and make him wobble, then a second, same side, on his jaw. He dropped his hands to try and push Anton away but that left him open for a follow through and Anton caught him on his nose which started to bleed immediately. There was a scream from the crowd, Charlie looked at the blood on his arm and Anton landed two body blows, a left and a right. Anton was getting out of breath now, but he'd done the job, his opponent looked unsteady. Anton kept his hands over his face, Charlie landed one on his body which hurt and which he should have moved away from to take the force out of it, but it didn't matter, he stayed up and kept him at bay until the bell.

There were cheers and a few whistles, someone ran over to Charlie and put a towel on his nose. Anton's chest suddenly hurt a lot and he crept back to his corner.

'Reckon you might have won that, son,' said Dave, patting his shoulders and helping with the headguard. Anton spat out the gumshield and gasped for some air, that last punch had really hurt. The MC was walking round, gathering up bits of paper from the judges around the edge of the ring, stopping to ask one of them something, looking at the sheets and doing a quick bit of mental arithmetic before calling them both back to the centre. Anton couldn't hear the first part of what he said but the crowd then went quieter as the MC with a bit of drama said,

'Our welterweight contest winner is…... Anton Matheson.' He raised Anton's arm high in the air, so it ached, but he didn't mind. Charlie went back to attending to his nose. Anton looked up and through the stinging sweat in his eyes could see Franca and Malcolm hugging, then waving their arms, then hugging again, celebrating. Dave put his arm round him, ruffled his hair and led him away.

By the time Anton had managed to pull on a capped sleeve t-shirt and some trousers and head back out, the diners were being served their main courses and Franca and Malcolm were no longer at the table. In their place were a couple in evening dress who looked like they belonged there, tucking in hungrily.

Anton looked around and found Franca near the bar, he hugged her, and they kissed, she was still pumped up from the fight.

'Your Dad's getting a drink,' she gestured in the direction of the bar where the crowd was three deep, 'he's in there somewhere, he's getting you one.'

'What happened to your seats?' asked Anton.

'They weren't really ours, let's be honest. The people who paid for them turned up… couldn't really argue. We had a couple of starters and the best part of a bottle of wine before they arrived. And we had a good view of you,' she looked at his slightly battered but smiling face and leant in and kissed him again. Malcolm appeared through the crowd, carrying two pints and what Anton assumed to be a large vodka and tonic.

'Nice one, son, here you go… reckon you've earnt this.' Malcolm passed the drinks out and raised his glass to Anton.

'Thanks for coming.'

'Wouldn't have missed it,' said Malcolm.

'I probably would have but I'm glad I didn't,' said Franca.

'I have to be honest though,' Malcolm added, 'you do honk a bit…' Anton realised this was true, '…people are eating.' He reached out and grabbed Anton around the shoulders and pulled him into a tight hug, 'Proud of you son.'

Anton downed the pint and left them to it to find a shower. When he came back out, dinner was done and Kirby was in the middle of his middleweight contest, taking a beating. As far as Anton could see, Kirby was unlucky, the army boy could have been a pro.

Anton relaxed into the evening, watching and cheering with Franca and his father, enjoying their company, pressure off now. Overall, the club did well, taking five of the eight contests, although one result was loudly disputed by the army boys who maybe had a point about some questionable scoring, but the decision stood. The night ended drunkenly with an auction of various donated items, mostly sporting memorabilia, the audience showing off by out-bidding each other for stuff they hadn't known they wanted up to this point.

'All in a good cause,' said just about anyone when pressed.

Before they left, Anton went back to the changing room to say some goodbyes, join in on a couple of high fives and a brotherly pat on the shoulder here and there. He considered commiserating with Kirby who was sitting on a bench, looking miserable, *as usual,* but thought better of it.

Malcolm drove them home even though he was a long way over the limit, assuring them he'd be fine, he knew the roads like the back of his hand. They made it back alive and raided the fridge for whatever they could find, mostly leftovers, but no-one was fussy. Having made some coffee, Anton was desperate to be with Franca and took a while to say he thought it would be good to go back to her place, if that was okay.

'Course it is son, course it is, go and have a nice time,' Anton looked at him. It looked like he meant it.

'Thanks for coming Dad. Thanks for looking after Franca.' Franca hardly seemed like she needed any looking after, but she didn't object.

'I loved it, had a great time,' said Malcolm.

'Me too,' said Franca and kissed Malcolm on the cheek.

'It's just that, it's a bit easier at Franca's… she has her own sort of apartment in the house,' Anton was feeling bad about leaving.

'Its fine son, really. Go on, let me get some peace.' They called up a taxi and Malcolm got one more bonus goodnight kiss.

9

Anton would usually give himself a couple of days away from training after a fight. Stay away from the gym and rest up a little. He had another reason to do so now, to make some Franca time. They spent most of it in bed with occasional expeditions to the local burger bar or the wine shop, then back to Franca's room, back to their hideaway. It felt like a holiday, and they relished their freedom, no schedules or obligations.

Franca made a call and somehow didn't need to go into work; it did occur to Anton that she might get into trouble for her sudden absence, but they had checked out from normality for a while, and she didn't seem to think it would be a problem.

On the third day, Anton jogged back home to check in, he looked a bit sheepish when he saw Neville but managed to avoid any awkward questioning.

'I'll be back in the swing tomorrow, promise…' he said, 'training too.'

That night he and Franca went to a movie, found one of the new sofas the cinema had put in to encourage dating couples and snuggled. He even dozed off for a few minutes, warm and carefree despite the on-screen mayhem. They went on to Purely Pizza, joked about the first time they met there, and about Franca's sour friend Sally, went back to bed, tired, full of food and relaxed enough to not have sex. They lay side by side, floating in space, in the moment and with an endless fascination in each other.

'I've got to know,' said Anton, 'what does a dental assistant do?'

'Really?' Franca propped herself on an elbow to look down at him, 'That's been bothering you?'

'Not bothering me, I'm just curious.'

'I assist. I get the surgery ready, sterilise instruments, put everything out, prepare the patients, reassure them, put the draping on them… do the admin, record keeping, stock control, stuff like that.'

Anton thought about this for a while then said, 'Do you wear a uniform?' She nodded, 'White?' she nodded again, 'Okay, that I would like to see.' She lay back on his shoulder and he put his arm around her to keep her there. When he was close to sleep, his mind drifted, at peace, aware of something new, a kind of freedom; whatever it was they had, it rose above the everyday. Although Franca in a dental assistant's uniform would make a great screensaver...

It was still dark when his phone rang. He reached out to find it on the low bedside table. Everywhere beyond the duvet was cold.

'Dad?' He took the phone from his ear to see the time, it was just before six. 'What's happened?'

'It's okay, don't worry,' said Malcolm in a tone that would have worried anyone.

'What's up?'

'Beulah,' there was a pause while Anton rubbed his face, 'Neville's on his way to pick you up.'

'Decided he can drive again has he?'

'Just get ready. He'll be there in a few minutes,' sounding irritated.

On the way to Beulah Mansions, Neville filled Anton in on what he knew.

'So apparently our mate Fucking Darren gets in late last night, usual sort of thing but he's not on his own, person or persons unknown are with him, he puts on some music, nice and loud just to be sure everyone remembers what a cock he is and there's some shouting, after a while his friend or somebody leaves, our tenants hear someone going down the stairs and out through the front door but the music carries on. And on, and on and on…. Our lot go up and knock on the door: nothing, no answer and it's the same later when they try again. It all carries on until six when they finally break and call us. Dad says we have to sort this out now.'

'Why don't they just call the cops?'

'Don't want the trouble. They're afraid, I see that. As far as they're concerned, it's our problem.'

'Brilliant.'

They made good time, Neville enjoying the drive through the quiet streets.

'I love this time of day… just have to watch out for the odd dope head coming home… ' He turned into the street and looked for a place to stop, it was always tight for parking space around Beulah Mansions.

Neville squeezed the Outlander between a hastily parked SUV and the start of a double yellow line, pushing up tight to the SUV as much to make a point as to fit into the gap. He switched the engine off and patted the steering wheel affectionately, a habit which continued to baffle his brother.

'She got us here in one piece, didn't she?' said Neville.

'Nev, let's just get this done,' said Anton, still waking up. 'What happens if he wants to get out?' he asked looking at the thin gap in front of the SUV.

'We'll be gone before the school run,' said Neville. He had a thing about the school run, something to do with pampered kids, overprotective parents… Anton had heard it all before. They walked back along the street to Beulah Mansions and looked up, lights were on all over the top two floors.

'They're expecting us, that's nice,' said Neville. He rang the doorbell; Paul answered and buzzed them in. Even on the ground floor, they could hear the music from above: electronic dance music loud, relentless. When they reached the second floor, Paul was at his door. Neville tried his best to be friendly and positive. 'Okay, we'll go and talk to him.'

Paul followed as they climbed to the next floor. When they reached the door, Neville used the side of his fist to thump it.

'Oy! Oy…anyone here?' He waited a moment then started to pound the door. 'Oy mate, open up.'

'I did that already,' said Paul.

They stood and waited for a moment before Neville started up again, pounding the door with his fist then kicking it and shouting to try to be heard over the music.

'What do we do?' He looked at Anton. 'Break it down?'

'Call the cops,' said Anton, 'we have to, we don't know what's going on in there.'

'We could call Egerton; he could come out with a key…'

'It's half past six in the morning, he probably won't answer the phone,' said Anton.

'Dad could do it,' Neville took his phone out and called. Anton took over knocking on the door duty while Neville covered his ear and walked down a flight of stairs. A minute later he came back. 'Okay, he agrees: we call the cops, he's going to try and get through to Egerton.'

Neville called 999, deciding it qualified as an emergency. Paul agreed with Anton to return to his flat and they would let him know what happened, they would try and keep him out of anything.

'We can't live like this,' he said as he walked down the stairs. Anton sympathised.

'I know. I'm sorry, we'll sort it out. I'm sorry it's come to this.'

Anton followed him down on his way to the front to wait for the police. Neville stayed outside Flat D just in case Darren woke up. He sat on the top stair and tried not to listen to the music, he hated EDM at the best of times and this was not that. Occasionally a DJ interrupted and mumbled something he couldn't understand, then it was back to the beat. After a few minutes he called Anton.

'What's happened? Has he appeared?'

'I'm amazed they didn't come upstairs with an axe and break the door down,' said Neville.

'It's not everyone that keeps an axe in their home you know.'

'Swop.'

'I just got down here. I don't want to swop. And I hate EDM.'

'Fucking music is driving me insane; he's got terrible taste.'

'Come down here then and wait with me… he's not going to suddenly wake up, is he? No-one could sleep through that…'

'… as has been pointed out by the people who pay our wages, not unreasonably in the circumstances. Alright, I'll come down.'

By the time he got there, they could hear sirens in the distance. Two police cars swerved around the tight corner into the narrow, double-parked street and stopped in the middle of the road, blocking it. Two officers from each got out; one from the first car was older and obviously in charge. He asked them who they were, what the story was and to lead the way up the stairs.

'Your tenants left it a long time before they called you…?'

'Yeah, they don't want trouble officer, Sergeant… three stripes, that's sergeant, right?' said Neville.

'If you wish, sir. Officer is fine though.'

They reached the top floor and the Sergeant knocked on the Flat D door, gently first, then with force.

'That's what we did,' said Neville.

'Important that we try everything in the right order sir, don't want to be too aggressive, do we?'

'I'm not aggressive,' said Neville aggressively, the music getting to him.

'You have a number for him?' the sergeant asked.

'Us? No, we don't really know him, met him once,' Anton looked at his brother, wishing he hadn't said that but not sure why.

'Alright,' the sergeant spoke to one of his men, 'break it down.'

Everything changed, suddenly there was energy in the air. The officer ran down the stairs, returning a few moments later carrying a heavy looking glossy black ram which looked like it could deal with any sort of lock you might point it at.

'Nice,' said Neville, the officer carrying it nodding back, one of the others getting hyped up shouted,

'Get back,' the officer with the ram swung it back and looked at the sergeant who nodded and shouted,

'Police. Stand away from the door.'

The next few moments were a blur of noise, splintering wood and frenzied voices as the door gave way and all four police pushed through. Anton followed right behind them and although one of them stopped him going too far, he saw clearly a body on the floor in the kitchen doorway, a man, on his back with his face turned away and a syringe in the crook of his arm. One of them shouted at Anton to stay put and he watched as two of the others went to the figure on the floor, talked to it, checked for signs of life and started CPR. When they moved the body, the face turned towards him: Darren.

The sergeant had found the source of the music and turned it off, in the silence that followed the only sounds were of the attempts to resuscitate the unfortunate body on the floor. The sergeant called for an ambulance and by the time he finished the call his colleagues had abandoned their efforts. Fucking Darren was no more.

'He's been gone for a while, guv',' said one.

'Look around,' said the Sergeant to his men and then turned his attention back to the brothers. 'You know him?'

'We know he's called Darren, that's about it,' said Anton.

'You said you met him.'

'Only once. A week or so ago… is he dead?' trying to buy a little thinking time. The sergeant looked back round at the body on the floor.

'He's certainly not having a good day; yes. So how did you meet?' Anton was still thinking so Neville answered,

'We came over. We own the flat downstairs, below this one. The people there made a complaint about noise, lots of noise coming from this one so we came over to make a polite request to keep it down, be a bit considerate, you know.'

'A polite request?' the sergeant giving him a look.

'It was, yes. A polite request, that was all. All very friendly, although *he* wasn't particularly friendly to be honest, but we were just there to ask him to be more considerate. We thought he was alright with it.'

'So then, it was noisy again last night and into the morning and you and your friend-'

'-brother, he's my brother.'

'-you and your brother came over to have another little word.'

'Yeah, but nothing heavy, you know.'

'Yes, I know,' the sergeant getting a little chummier now, 'drive me crazy to live below him, I hate that music.'

'Me too,' said Neville, Anton watching and listening, wondering where this was going.

'Do you know if he had any friends? Any family maybe?'

'We didn't really know him, we only met him the once and we didn't get very social if you know what I mean. We've tried to contact his landlord, the owner of the flat,' said Neville.

'Good. Do you have his details?'

'No, our dad does, he's trying to get hold of him. Don't know if he got through.'

'Family business then?' the sergeant trying to build a picture.

'Yes, sort of. Basically.'

Anton was trying to work out why he felt guilty while his brother answered the questions, Darren's death was nothing to do with them.

'Shall I… um, shall I see if he got through? Managed to contact him?' Neville took his phone out and waited for some kind of positive response to this idea. Instead, the sergeant shrugged as if to say: *If you like, I'm not going to stop you.* Neville made the call and the sergeant focussed back on Anton.

'What I don't really understand is…the music was going on all night?'

'Yes, that's what we were told.'

'Why didn't the people in the flat below call us up?'

'They don't want to be involved. As far as they're concerned, he's not – he wasn't a particularly nice guy. They were a bit afraid of him, they don't want any trouble.' More sirens could be heard in the street outside, one of the officers was sent to bring the ambulance crew in.

'I see… if we'd got here earlier of course, we might have saved him,' the sergeant looking at Anton like his teachers used to. Neville arrived back and interrupted.

'Okay, so he got through to Egerton, that's the owner of the flat, he said he's sending someone over. He knows we called you, our dad told him.'

'I'll just take your details and contact numbers then please, before you leave,' the sergeant took out a notebook and looked at Neville waiting for him to start.

Before he had a chance to speak, two ambulance crew bustled in behind him, bumping him out of the way as they took the shortest path to the body on the floor. In their wake, a woman followed, mid-thirties, tall and dressed sharply like she was arriving for a day in the office, she looked generally irritated with everything. Behind her was a shorter man, older, suited as well but looking like he'd just been dragged out of bed and forced to dress in the first thing that came to hand, his shirt barely tucked in and one of his shoelaces flapping freely. The woman looked round and spoke first to Anton.

'Who are you?' The abruptness caught him out and he took a moment to gather himself together.

'Who are you?' he asked her back.

'I asked first but as it's clearly a confusing question for you, I'll start. I represent my client, Mr E. A. Egerton who is the owner of this property. I understand who all the people in uniforms are and why they're here, but not you. Unless you can tell me otherwise, I suggest you are trespassing.' The sergeant stepped in.

'Thank you, Miss…?' She produced a business card and handed it to him.

'Atkinson-Pike, Valerie Atkinson-Pike.'

'Very good,' the sergeant smiled at her, she stared back at him, no interest in niceties. 'Good, thank you for coming over.'

'Can we go now?' asked Neville.

'Um, no. Write down your names, addresses and contact numbers please,' he handed the notebook to Neville who took it and quickly scrawled out the details for them both.

Atkinson-Pike walked over to the prone figure on the floor and took a look; the ambulance crew had checked him out and decided there was nothing to be done. *He's been gone for a while;* the PC's words came back into Anton's head.

Neville handed the notebook back, the sergeant checked it and nodded, 'Thank you sir, thank you for your help,' he kept an eye on the woman standing by the body on the floor and still looking bad tempered, 'we've got your details, we'll be in touch I would think.'

'Of course,' said Neville, turning and leaving, 'c'mon Cassius,' he said to his brother and started walking to the door. In his peripheral vision Anton could see the older man who had walked in with Atkinson-Pike watch them as they left, it made him hurry to catch up with Neville as they started down the stairs. Neville stopped at the next floor, about to knock on the door but Anton had his arm on his shoulder, pushing him on.

'Not now, we'll call them,' said Anton. They reached the front and out onto the street where the police cars were still blocking the road at one end and there was a line of traffic awkwardly turning to go back and find other routes.

'What's up?' asked Neville, 'thought you'd want to tell your girlfriend the good news.'

'One of them clocked it when you said Cassius, the guy who walked in with Miss Happiness, he heard you and looked round. Maybe our late chum told him about our visit.'

'Alright, maybe…' said Neville, working it through in his mind. 'They don't know who we are, we're alright, we'll just disappear as far as they're concerned. Tell you truth I don't want to bump into any of them again.'

When they reached home, Anton volunteered to make the call. Paul answered,

'Hello?'

'It's me, Anton. We said we'd let you know what happened. There were people everywhere, that's why we didn't call in on the way out-'

'-Is there going to be trouble?'

'No, it's not that, we just didn't want to draw attention to you.'

'They're still going in and out, up and down the stairs.'

'The police are going to come and get a statement from you, bound to.'

'Carol will be here. I have to go to work.'

'I know. You've got our number if you need anything, right?' No answer. 'Anyway, he's a goner. They found him, dead. Accident I think, I saw a needle… could be suicide I suppose.' Paul stayed silent. 'I'm sorry this has happened-'

'-We're not exactly going to miss him.'

'Fair point. There were people there from the landlord, we'll try and find out what they're going to do. I suppose the police will be there for a while, get Carol to call us if she needs to. They'll find another tenant, hopefully this one will be a human being… you can get some peace.'

'I don't know what we're going to do, Carol's pretty upset.'

'I know. I understand. Wait and see, eh? Let's wait and see who they put in there, perhaps it'll be a normal person,' he paused again, Paul sighed. 'Let me know if there's anything we can do, okay?'

'We still need the sash window fixed.'

'Yes, of course, sorry. We'll get round there next week if that's alright. I'll call and fix a time.' There was a pause, Anton didn't know how to sign off, then Paul spoke,

'So, if the police come and talk to us, what do you want us to say? About you I mean, Carol said you and your brother went round to see him.' It was Anton's turn now to be quiet. 'Carol heard you when you did it, you have to realise, we can't help hearing everything.'

'What did she hear?'

'No detail, we just know that you went to see him.'

'Just the truth then, it's okay to tell them what you know.'

Anton said goodbye and called Franca, told her he was alright, just a problem with one of the flats that had to be dealt with immediately and that he was going to the gym, start to work off those burgers. She reminded him of the calorie count involved in energetic sex and he suggested they return to the subject later. Before they finished, she brought up the subject of dinner with her Uncle Nico again.

'It'll be fun, I promise. So, we'll do it, yes? Next week sometime?'

Anton had to think, he'd lost track of the days, 'Yes, of course. What's the date? It must be the first of the month next week isn't it? Any day apart from that, go for it.'

'I'll sort it, I'll get Rosa to help, you'll love it. You'll like Uncle Nico too; you can talk about boxing…'

'Okay…' he wasn't convinced, 'see you later?'

'Better had, sunshine,' Franca said with just a pinch of menace, then blew him a kiss down the line and hung up.

The gym opened at nine o'clock and Anton was at the door when Barney opened up from inside.

'Ah, there he is,' said Barney with a smirk, 'what have you been up to?' Anton just smiled at him. 'Oh, I get it, shagging; time for a bit of proper work then.' Anton walked in, it felt good to be back. On the far side of the gym, running on a machine and at something more than a warmup pace, was Kirby.

Anton looked over at Barney, 'How did he…?' but Barney just shrugged and walked away to the side office. Anton waited for him to turn back and reveal the secret, but he just carried on and disappeared inside. Anton made a face and crossed over to the lockers, keeping an eye on Kirby as he went. As he changed, he was thinking what he really wanted to do was run; thinking a bit more, he decided he could be the grown up for a change. As he did up the laces on his trainers, he looked up at Kirby again, the guy was working up a sweat, that was for sure. He stood up and started walking over to the treadmills, Kirby watching him as he got closer, his expression blank, his focus apparently on the running.

Anton stepped on to the machine next to Kirby, it seemed absurd to choose a different one. He pushed a button and started a gentle jog.

'Morning… I was sure I was going to be the first one here today. Actually, I assumed I was going to be the only one here…'

Kirby didn't look at him, just kept facing forward, but he did manage, 'Morning,' and that was that.

Anton worked through the morning, mostly alone, just working himself back in to things. His body ached but it felt good to work out and he had to hold himself back from over-doing it. After a break, even a short one, it was easy to rush in and injure yourself, he had done it before.

When he was getting ready to leave at lunchtime, he found a quiet moment to ask Barney: 'Seriously, how did Kirby get in ahead of me?'

'You'll have to ask him yourself, son,' was all Barney was prepared to say.

Anton spent the afternoon in the students' flat. They were annoyingly accident prone and had recently flooded their bathroom leading to water leakage into the room below and a need for a major repair to the ceiling. The new plaster had dried sufficiently to take a coat of paint which Anton applied while doing his best to avoid lengthy conversation with the only one of them who was at home and who not only seemed to resent his presence but didn't offer so much as a cup of tea.

He finished, tidied up and left in time to reach Franca's door by seven. They went straight away to the wine bar where Anton stretched and complained about his aching body. Franca teased him for being old before his time and he held her close, touching her face, her arms, feeling her softness and letting himself be drawn in.

He wasn't surprised that she had sorted out the arrangements for the dinner with Uncle Nico. 'I know you can't do the First which is Thursday, so we'll make it Friday, yes? That's good for Uncle Nico too. You're not vegetarian I know that, or allergic to anything…?'

'Avocado,' she looked at him, 'Avocado. I hate avocado.'

'How can anyone hate avocado?'

'I do. I think I'm allergic.'

'I think you're talking nonsense, but I'll let you off: no avocado. Apart from that, we have a free hand, yes? Uncle Nico likes anything Italian, surprise, surprise, so it'll be something along those lines.'

'It all sounds good to me,' he said, wisely.

That night, they made love slowly and with quiet passion. There was no need for urgency, no desperate rush to the next thing, just pleasure in each other. Afterwards, Anton began to think about what plans they might make.

'I do alright. With the family business. I have freedom; I could do some coaching perhaps.'

'You want to do more work?'

'No, but make more money maybe,' said Anton, 'buy some freedom. I just want to spend time with you.'

'You do already. We're doing alright, aren't we?'

'Definitely, this is everything. I was just thinking… maybe, we could get a place.' Franca didn't answer but lay on her side looking at him, stroking his face. He turned his head to look at her. 'I just want to be with you.'

'It's the same for me,' said Franca.

He put his arm out and hauled her in to lie on his shoulder. 'I just want to be like this forever.'

10

Anton was soon back into a routine at the gym, and he was quick to regain his fitness. If anything, he was keener than ever to be in good shape, Franca providing a little extra motivation.

As always, on the last weekday of the month, there was the regular club meeting. This was usually led by Barney who would provide an update of club news, including any significant personal achievements, notice of any professional opportunities coming up and sometimes news about past members.

Anton arrived in good time for it and saw George standing in front of the club rules, framed to emphasise their importance, and hung next to the notice board. He stopped and stood next to him.

'You alright George?'

'Eh? Oh, Anton, yes, I'm fine thank you.'

'Should know them by now,' he smiled as George turned to look at him.

'We need a new frame,' Anton looked more carefully and saw he was right, the old one was chipped, and the corner joints were beginning to separate. The glass was discoloured when he looked closely.

George continued, 'To be fair its five or six years since we changed them last, even then all I did was print a new one and put it back in the same old frame.'

'What changed?' asked Anton, then, 'Oh I know… mobile phones.' George nodded, 'I used to wonder why there were 11 of them, why not roll it into 10…. The others all there from the start?'

'Yep,' said George, nodding and wiping the glass with his sleeve. Anton looked again.

The Rules

1. You are a member of THIS club, this is your club. Boxers are not to train in any other boxing gym except by permission of their trainers.
2. No valuables to be worn when training, use the lockers provided.
3. No smoking is allowed in the gym.
4. No drinking of alcohol is allowed in the gym nor is training under the influence of alcohol or drugs.
5. Boxers must conduct themselves in a sportsmanlike manner.
6. Boxers must train regularly and in accordance with their plan and must not leave training sessions early except by permission of their trainers.
7. Boxers must report all health problems to their trainers.
8. Bad behaviour, bad language or derogatory remarks are not allowed. Boxers must respect each other.
9. Boxers must exercise discipline in their lives and in the gym. Boxing must not be used against law and order.
10. Being stupid isn't clever.
11. No mobile phones.

'They're good rules Uncle,' he said, George just nodded quietly and stared at the glass, 'did you write them?'

George sighed and said, 'Yes, back then.' He spoke quietly, Anton had to strain to hear him above the rising sound of others arriving for the meeting.

'I've meant to ask before, the one about being stupid… what was that about?' George looked at him,

'Too many of the boys were proud of being dim, they wouldn't bother, buy crap newspapers, just look at the tits, feel good about being stupid. I just wanted them to think they could do better.' Anton listened and nodded. 'Anyway, I'm taking the meeting today, so I'd better start.'

It was unusual for George to take the meeting. On the rare occasions that he did, the others would be sure to pay close attention.

He sat on the edge of the ring, making sure he could be seen.

'Two of our boys are going pro, that makes me very proud. It's not the be-all and end-all and you know that's how I see it but it's a great thing when its right for someone,' George paused, he was thinking about something, how to say it. Anton also wondered who the two pro's-to-be were: he knew about Franny, that was no surprise to anyone.

'So, we have Franny here, taking his broken nose and lippy attitude out into the wide world in the new year,' Franny looked embarrassed but like he was having fun anyway, 'and the other one is Kirby, he got spotted at the charity gig and he's got a chance on the same undercard.'

Kirby? thought Anton, *that explains the early training… sort of.* George wasn't finished.

'There's something else. I haven't told anyone else this yet, not Barney nor anyone, I wanted you all to hear at the same time,' the room was silent, Anton felt uneasy for some reason.

'Thing is… I'm retiring, stepping away. I have to lads, I'm old, I need to slow down a bit. I'm not disappearing, I'll still come along and cheer you lot when you haul your lazy arses into a ring somewhere, but I have to accept that I'm getting on a bit.' No-one else spoke; Anton looked over at Barney standing next to the old man, taking it all in.

'This carries on though, all this… it has to. We have to find a new owner, that's all, find someone who will want to take this on, look after the place, nothing else has to change… that's it, that's all I have to say.' There were a few low murmurs from the floor. George looked down, 'I'll miss it here... need to pass it on though, it's time for a change.'

There was a pause, one of the boys started to clap then thought better of it. Then another one started and a few more. The rest joined in although most of them weren't sure if that was the right thing to do or not. George stood and Barney put his arm round his shoulder and walked him away.

Dave took the initiative and put everything back to normal,

'Back to it then lads.'

George's speech became the sole subject of the general chat amongst them all for the rest of the day, during workouts and in the breaks; no-one really knew what it would all mean. George had been there from the start, he had grown it from not much to what it was now, he *was* the club. There was a lot of speculation about who would take over, differing opinions about the quality of the trainers there, whether any of them were management material. It was going to be a question of wait and see.

Anton had something else on his mind. He found Kirby doing hard sparring with one of the lads in a higher weight range, pushing himself. The extra work he seemed to be doing all made sense now. When he was done, he left the ring and sat, sweating, breathing deep and fast. Anton waited for a moment then said,

'Just want to say congratulations mate, I didn't know you were on that path. You deserve it.' Kirby looked at him, he was breathing fast, sweat running down his face.

'I need to earn something, need to make a living.' It was the most he'd spoken to Anton since the unfortunate incident.

'You'll be brilliant mate,' Kirby nodded acknowledgement. *That'll do, don't push your luck,* thought Anton and walked away.

The next day was the first of the month, early finish at the gym and out on the rent run with Neville. Just before they left the house, Neville asked for the latest on Beulah Mansions.

'All gone quiet, I think,' said Malcolm, 'I called them daily for a while afterwards, there was a bit of coming and going, police mainly, then nothing. Last time I called I got her on the phone, she was saying it was bliss being able to sleep through, but they still jump if they hear a noise. Just see what you can do to keep them in there, do what it takes. We haven't got anywhere else to put them at the moment and they're good tenants. I don't want to lose them.'

'When did you last speak to them?' asked Anton.

'Couple of days ago, three maybe, she reminded me there's a window to fix.' Anton nodded, put his wallet and phone on the kitchen top and pulled his jacket on. Neville had already said he was driving so the glasses stayed put as well.

The weather was grim, cold and damp, winter was settling in. For Neville however, this was a welcome chance to catch up with his little brother,

'Good to talk, we don't see you much these days.' Anton looked at him, it was a fair point.

'I know, I'm training hard… I've been working through the list for Dad as well, did that ceiling at the students', other bits and bobs… I'm at Franca's a lot too.'

'She's nice.'

'She is.'

'Serious, eh?' asked Neville, probing just a bit.

'I don't know. I don't know what serious is, really.'

'We should have her over again, Dad really liked it.'

'Florist would like it as well.'

'Yeah, we might have overdone that,' said Neville, then, 'hold it, look,' he slowed the car and pointed to a sign outside a garage as they passed. 'What do you think?' Anton followed his hand and read: "Hand Car Wash, 15 minutes, £8."

'What, now?'

'Yeah, come on,' Neville turned off the road and drove into the forecourt, 'car's filthy, it needs a bit of a wash,' he stopped and let the engine idle. Out from under a canopy in front of them emerged four men, dressed in boiler suits and holding cloths and buckets, they walked slowly towards the car.

'One problem Nev,' said Anton.

'What?'

'Have you got any money on you?'

'Ah, shit,' said Neville and hit the steering wheel. By now the first of the men had reached them and was about to start sponging the car, Neville opened the door and put his hands up, 'stop, wait, hold it, hold it, hoooold it,' the men looked at him, puzzled, 'sorry, we have no cash,' he pulled his trouser pocket inside out to show them, 'my mistake, sorry.'

He climbed back in the car and called out of the window, 'Sorry, we'll come back.' He drove back out onto the road and away. Anton was quiet for a moment then said:

'So, those guys…' his brother looked over at him, 'how much is the minimum wage?'

'How do I know? Six quid? Seven?'

'So, there's four of them, it takes fifteen minutes… they could just about do four cars an hour except there isn't a queue, so they don't. It doesn't work, the numbers don't work.'

'What's your point?'

'I don't know, the numbers don't add up.'

'I really wouldn't worry about it, don't let it bother you; you pay eight quid, you're happy, right?' Anton sat back and didn't answer, whatever his brother might say, it did bother him. Neville wasn't one to dwell on things however,

'What are you training towards?'

'Nothing particular yet, I just enjoy it… there might be a tournament place in the spring, just the usual, you know.'

'I will try,' said Neville, 'I will try hard next time, to be there, I just got caught up last time.'

'It's not a problem. Dad and Franca were there.'

'What did she think?'

'Not sure she was that into it at first, but she seemed to have a nice time in the end. She and Dad got pissed up while I was doing my thing.'

'She's cool.'

'She is,' said Anton. They stopped outside the girls' flat. Anton beat his brother in the sprint up the stairs to the third floor, Neville protested that he hadn't fully recovered from his paving stone accident, but Anton stood at the door nonetheless and teased Neville who was panting by the time he got there. Anton stood aside at the last moment to let him ring the bell and lead them in.

Once they were back in the car, Neville looked at Anton, 'That Lucy… I think she likes me… do you think so?'

Anton thought for a moment then said, 'No.'

'Not sure you're right about that, sunshine.'

The run went smoothly: the couple with the kid asked if someone could come and check the radiators as some were not very warm and Anton said he'd be back tomorrow, he meant it as well. Neville admired Anton's plasterwork in the students' flat and the irritating couples who shared the large flat actually had the right money ready.

As they drove towards Beulah Mansions, Anton was thoughtful. 'You going to do this forever?'

Why not?' said Neville, 'What are you getting at?' Anton shrugged. 'Yes, why not? Do odd jobs to keep the places going, collect the rents once a month, it's easy. You thinking of something else?'

'It's not that… I don't know. It works for me too, I guess.'

'What's bothering you, little bro'?' Neville clicking into his wise older brother role.

'I don't know, nothing really, everything's alright. It's just, this thing with Franca, it seems really adult-'

'-oh yeah?' said Neville a bit too salaciously.

'No, alright then, mature, she just seems more mature.'

'Girls mate, they are more mature, they're always more mature than we are.'

'Speak for yourself.'

'Scientific fact,' said Neville in his and-that's-the-end-of-it way.

Anton couldn't resist it though. 'Girls are always more mature than boys?'

'Age for age. Girl of sixteen is going to be more mature than a boy of sixteen.'

'And that's scientific, is it?'

'Look it up. Its established fact.'

'You want me to do a Google search on mature sixteen-year-old girls?'

Neville grinned, 'Definitely. Go on, do it when we get back.'

Anton paused then said, 'Which I suppose just goes to prove your point.'

'Exactly.' They drove on in silence for a while.

After a while, Anton said, 'Being with her makes me feel like I'm being serious with someone for the first time. I'm going to dinner with her mother and uncle tomorrow, how much more grown up is there?'

'What about Jenn?'

'Shut up, I'm not proud of myself.'

'Alice?'

'No, this is different, it really is.'

They pulled up outside Beulah Mansions. Neville leant forward and looked up at the block.

'Well, it's not on fire, that's something.'

'Come on,' said Anton, 'it should all be fine now.'

Paul answered the door and let them in to the flat, Neville leading, Anton close behind. Somehow, Carol appeared from a doorway as they passed, almost bumping into Anton who she greeted with a kiss. Neville looked over his shoulder and caught his brother's eye.

'So, how are you guys doing?' said Anton. Paul handed an envelope to Neville who opened it and started counting the money.

'It's been blissfully quiet,' said Paul 'once the police and the rest of them had finished whatever it was they had to do. They came down and asked us about him, what we knew, I don't think they were all that interested to be honest, we hardly knew him after all.' Anton saw that Neville had finished counting and was signing the book and thought a quick exit might be a good idea, but Paul wasn't finished. 'The thing is, we really did hardly know him…' Anton nodded, wondering how to wind this up politely, 'like we told the other guy that came round.'

'Other guy?' said Anton.

'Yesterday,' said Paul, 'shortish bloke, probably my age but looks older, scruffy, a bit balding, kind of sneery face, said he was winding up the tenant's affairs.'

'Right,' said Anton, not sure where this was going, 'what sort of affairs would those be?'

'He said you'd know.'

'I'd know?' said Anton.

'Know what?' asked Neville.

'He said, you knew his boss, Edgington or something-'

'-Egerton,' said Anton.

'That could be it. He described you both pretty well, so I think he definitely meant you. Didn't know your names though, thought one of you was called Cassius, you know, like Clay, otherwise he was bang on. I said it was probably a joke, you know, you being a boxer and all.'

'So… did you tell him our actual names?' asked Anton.

'Yeah, I put him right,' the room was silent for a few moments, then, 'that was okay, wasn't it? I mean, they're just tidying up the guy's affairs, right?'

'Yeah, of course,' said Anton, thinking it wasn't alright, 'its fine, no problem.'

'What was his name?' asked Neville.

'Brown. That's what he said,' Paul crossed over to the mantelpiece and started looking through the items on it. 'There's a card somewhere.'

'Was that all?' said Anton.

'He asked if we'd been given anything to look after by the guy, the upstairs guy, we said no, we hardly knew him, then he said had we been asked to look after anything by you.'

'By us?' said Neville, 'What kind of thing?'

'He wasn't sure I think, he said maybe a bag or something like that. There was something missing from the flat. Don't know why he thought we might have it.'

'That was it?' asked Anton.

Paul nodded. 'Just about. He left a card, said to call if anything occurred to us.' He found the card underneath a framed photograph, 'Here you go,' Anton took the card, looked at it and showed it to Neville. All it said was "J. R. Brown" and there was a mobile number.

'Doesn't tell you too much,' said Anton, 'can we just write that number down?' Paul found an old post-it note and copied the number onto it, Anton put it away in his pocket. 'Just in case.'

Paul started to walk them to the door. 'We're going to wait and see who moves in upstairs. If they're like the last guy then we're gone, we can't live like that anymore.'

'I know,' said Anton, 'fair enough.'

Before they reached the door, Carol stopped them.

'Do you think you could mend that window soon…?'

'Yes,' said Anton, feeling bad, 'definitely, I'm sorry, it's just slipped. I'll do it Tuesday next week if that's okay, in the afternoon? About two?'

'That's a good time,' said Carol.

'It'll take maybe two hours, max. But I'll stay until its done.' Carol smiled at him and said goodbye.

On the way down the stairs, Anton started to worry. 'I don't like the sound of the short guy, pretty sure he was the one that turned up with the scary two- surnames woman, all working for Egerton.'

'What are we even talking about?' said Neville, 'this "working for Egerton", he's a small-time landlord, what's he doing with having staff?'

They reached the street, and the chill air made them tense up and pull their collars in.

'I got a bad vibe off Egerton,' said Anton.

'Maybe we call this Brown geezer, see what he wants, let him know we weren't exactly close friends of dear old Darren but say if he wants anything else to come and talk to us instead of those two.'

Anton thought about that for a moment and said, 'I'm not so sure. I think leave it, ignore him, hope he just goes away.' They reached the car.

'Alright Cassius, hang on to his number though, eh?' Neville was back behind the wheel of the Outlander. 'If he comes back, no doubt we'll hear about it. Probably when you go round and fix that window.'

'Oh right. *I'm* doing that, am I?' said Anton, just making the point.

'She's *your* girlfriend,' said Neville, still enjoying it.

11

The next day, Anton was due for dinner with Franca, Rosa and Uncle Nico. Franca had been making a big thing out of it, so he knew it was important; he was going to be on show.

He arrived at the house at seven sharp. He wore a good shirt, the best he owned, it had cost a lot but was difficult to iron and the collar didn't stay in shape for very long, but he'd managed to set it right. He wore the only trousers he owned that weren't jeans and a textured blue designer jacket he'd bought from a charity shop, but which was tailored and sat well on him. He brought After Eight mints for the guests and flowers for Rosa, a smaller selection this time, mainly freesias of various colours.

Rosa and Franca had spent the afternoon putting together a feast: chickpea and pancetta soup, homemade focaccia which Rosa had flavoured with sun-dried tomatoes and sage, which was a lot of effort to make but tasted like nothing you could buy and topped it off with a Luganica sausage risotto which Rosa had developed over the years and remained a favourite with just about everyone who tried it.

Nico had taken on wine duties and brought hard to source Italian reds which he adored although Franca found them rather heavy. Nico was already there when Anton arrived and he stood to greet him, offering a grizzled hand to shake and a hawkish stare. Anton recognised him of course, although he'd never spoken to him before.

'I bought it years ago,' he told Anton when they started talking about the gym, 'it was a wreck but in the right place, it was George's idea. You know George?'

'Yes, of course.'

'He built it up, did a decent job although it took a while to smarten it up. You won't know this, but it wasn't so long ago that the boys from there were known as George's losers on account of their never winning anything; they'd be put into matches and tournaments by promoters to help others climb the pole, they were fodder. They'd go along to a match, always with a little hope inside them, and I'd watch them get beaten, every time.'

'What changed?' asked Anton.

'Good question, I'm not sure, it was gradual. George built it up. It got better, standards improved. Sometimes now, as you know, there are boys who go on and win things. A few turn professional, then they leave of course, change gyms, feel they have to move on to realise their potential.' Anton listened, gave him time to think.

'I suppose he realised that he needed more and better trainers. It was too much for him on his own. I believed in him and… things changed.'

'I can see that.'

'I saw you there, of course, that day when my Franca came to see me, when you sucker punched the tall guy. That was naughty.'

'I know. Rush of blood, what can I say?'

'Made me laugh inside, I knew Barney would rip you a new one-'

'-Nico,' said Rosa. He waved her objection away and she left to attend the food.

'He let you back, though...?'

'Yeah. I had to grovel. Fair enough, I was in the wrong,' Nico was looking hard at him now.

'Where you from?'

'-Uncle Nico…' Franca, this time.

'What? I can't ask a man where he lives?'

'Its fine,' said Anton and pointed, 'I live that way, about fifteen minutes' jog.'

'Which road? I've lived here for more than forty years.'

'Arthur Road. Its-'

'-I know it, top of the High Street, go right and it's on the right as you go north.'

'That's the one. It's my dad's house, family home.'

'I sold a house once, on that road.'

'My dad does that too, or did, we tend to hold on to them now, rent them out; he's a landlord.'

'You're not in the big house, about halfway down the road on the bend, probably was the builder's house?'

'Yes, if it's the one you're thinking of…'

'I might know him,' said Nico, 'there were a few people buying up when the prices were low, some years ago, a few of us, we knew each other…' he was reaching for something in his memory now, 'your father, is he tall, pale?'

Franca stopped him, 'Uncle Nico why are you so nosey?'

'He's white if that's what you mean,' said Anton, then pointed a thumb at himself, 'white dad, black mother.' Rosa had come back in and wanted them to move to the table in the next room.

'Food. Come, we should eat it while its hot,' said Rosa. Once sat, Nico was back on it.

'I didn't just mean that, I meant pale.'

Anton laughed, 'He doesn't really go for sunlight.'

'Malcolm….?'

'Malcolm, yes, how do you know?' asked Anton, impressed.

'Like I say, there were a few of us at the time, I sold him a house once, in Bridge Street, he was going to make flats out of it.'

'Bridge Street, yes, we still have it, part of it. He did make it into flats sold two and kept two, it's what we do for a business now, look after them.'

'I know your mother too,' said Nico and there was silence. Franca realised she knew nothing about Anton's mother, and she looked over at him. After a few seconds, Anton spoke,

'Ah, no. I don't think so. My mother died. She's been gone for nearly twenty years.' Nico looked surprised.

'Uncle Nico, leave him alone,' said Franca.

'Soup,' said Rosa.

'It's okay,' said Anton, 'It was a long time ago.'

'I'm sorry to hear it…' said Nico, not sure now.

'Small world though eh?' said Anton.

'Small world,' said Rosa, spooning out the soup, 'and a dinner, which we have been working on all day so let's draw a veil over the joys of landlording and eat.'

Anton could see Franca looking at Nico, watching him, wondering about something. Rosa tried again: 'Eat.'

One by one, they let her know that the soup was exceptionally good.

'You're a good fighter though, you could go on,' said Nico after dinner, while they sat and let it digest. Anton smiled back and nodded, not sure what to say. 'Go further I mean. You could go further.'

'Not sure if I want to, you know? I like what I do, I like to be fit, stay strong, enjoy the matches when they come along….' Nico nodded.

'I get it. It's not for everyone. I'm curious though about something. You were better than him, the army boy, you won it fairly… why did you let him in at the end?'

'Did I?'

'You let him hit you, gave him a soft target, to the chest. He could have broken a rib or winded you.'

'I didn't let him, he was just quicker than me.'

'Hmmm,' said Nico, not sounding convinced.

'I was defending my face.'

'Keeping his handsome looks,' said Franca, ruffling his hair.

Anton wondered how much Nico knew about George's retirement plans. 'So, George is retiring, you know, right?' Nico nodded. 'We're going to miss him; the lads went quiet when he told us.'

'End of an era,' said Nico.

'But someone will take over, right? A new manager… keep it all going, keep the whole thing on the road.' Nico wasn't being drawn, 'I mean, it will carry on, the club, the gym, everything, won't it?'

'It's not something we know yet,' said Nico.

'But you're the owner, Uncle Nico,' said Franca, 'you can say what happens, can't you?'

'It's not simple. Everything costs more these days. We have bills to pay, rates, insurances, staff, it's a young man's game, it needs a younger man to take over.'

Franca couldn't resist, 'Or woman.'

'Or woman, of course. But George going, it just means it's harder to carry on.'

'You can't let it go, it means too much to everyone,' said Anton. Nico nodded again, not really wanting to carry on this line of conversation.

'I know,' he said.

Rosa decided they should move to another room and Anton insisted on clearing everything, filling the dishwasher, and tidying up. He'd half expected Nico to join in, figuring this was a man thing that would logically occur to him, but it wasn't to be. It didn't bother him, in fact he was grateful for the time to relax a little, think about the conversation. When he'd finished, he went back to the living room where the rest of them were looking very relaxed themselves, cradling glasses of thick, dark red liquid.

'You didn't have to do all that,' said Franca.

'You haven't seen the state I've left the kitchen in,' said Anton, smiling to make sure even Nico got the joke, 'it's the least I could do, that was an amazing dinner, really. Thank you.'

'Grappa?' said Rosa, lifting the bottle to show him, 'Or there's whisky, I think, a good one.... Or we have port?'

'I'm okay, thanks,' said Anton then thought again, 'go on then, let me try some of that grappa.'

An hour or so later, the grappa was gone. Little Gregory had made a short, sleepy appearance and everyone had wished him a good night before Rosa took him back to his bed. Franca was satisfied with the evening, she had wanted to show off Anton and to bring Uncle Nico back into their lives, and it had gone well. She made fresh coffee which Uncle Nico declined, having decided it was time to leave. Rosa saw him off when the taxi arrived, and they spent time at the front door talking before he was gone. Franca decided Anton was staying over which was fine by him.

When she came back into the room, Rosa was thoughtful. 'Thank you for coming over this evening, for joining in with our family. Nico had a good time too; I know he has a funny way of showing it.'

'I had a great time, thank you,' said Anton, 'it was nice to meet him.'

'Is it true about the gym?' asked Franca.

'I think so, it's a worry... it means a lot to people, it mustn't be lost,' said Anton, looking to Rosa for an opinion, 'do you think he'd let it go?'

'I don't know, it's not my business. He likes it there, but the land is probably worth a lot. None of us are getting any younger, I think he wants to retire.'

'You could talk to him, persuade him to keep it, find another manager,' said Franca.

'Maybe, maybe not. You know your uncle. I'm worn out.'

'We all need to sleep,' said Franca and stood up, she was passing Rosa when she stopped and held her for a moment, looked at her and kissed her gently on her forehead. 'Thank you Mum.'

'Bedtime,' said Rosa, her eyes looking a little tired.

In bed, Anton held Franca close and stroked her hair, their closeness unforced.

'What happened to your father?' asked Anton. There was a long silence. He thought to say more, to say it was okay, he didn't need to know if she didn't want to say but then Franca spoke.

'He died.'

'I'm really sorry. You don't need to say any more, sorry I asked.'

'It's okay. It's not just that. He killed himself,' Anton held her and waited, silently. 'When I was ten. He jumped. It was a holiday, we were on a holiday, the three of us. In a hotel, in France, the south of France, Nice. He went to the roof, he'd done that before, gone to the roof and smoked a cigarette, looking out over the sea. This time, he jumped off. We don't know why. People said he had worries but we don't know what they could have been. We had money, enough anyway, we had a house, this one… Rosa loved him, I'm sure. We just don't know. I don't think Rosa does either, she says she doesn't. She also said she thought of dying too, of doing the same thing after he'd gone, said she wanted to but didn't… because of me, because I needed her. I was ten… so she kept going, because of me.' Anton could feel her tears on his chest, and he held her closer still. 'And that's why I'll never leave her.'

Anton waited a moment then said, 'Dear God.'

12

'I have an idea,' said Egerton, stepping into the corridor outside his office, having buzzed Anton in moments before, 'when you want to come and see me, how about you make an appointment, like a normal person, then I'll work out whether I want to see you?'

'I was passing,' said Anton.

'Nice of you to think of me, I missed you too,' said Egerton, turning and walking back into his office, leaving the door open. Anton followed him inside and closed the door, 'come in, make yourself at home.'

Anton had woken up troubled and had decided to try to fix things, put right whatever was wrong. Just so everything could go back to normal.

He took in more of the room than the first time: there was nothing on the walls, no pictures, no professional qualifications, no insurance certificates, just bare walls, plain, pale and grey, *this guy sits in here all day?* He also noticed how the edges of the carpet, fitted right up snug to the paint caked skirting boards were filthy, the colour changing from a speckled beige textured weave to a dark, grey, oily smudge. Whoever cleaned this place did so in a seriously slapdash way. There was also a smell around Egerton, something like body odour but not something he had noticed before, it lingered in his wake in the doorway.

Egerton went behind the desk and sat. 'So, what can I do for you today?' Anton took the seat opposite and pulled it up to the desk, 'Oh, take a seat, help yourself,' *getting snippy now.* 'So, what is it? Can I take a guess?' Anton looked at him, shrugged and waited. 'You just remembered; you have something for me…?'

'No. What?' said Anton.

'Alright, let's try it another way. You found something, just lying around somewhere, back home maybe and you thought to yourself, I know, that belonged to the guy who died upstairs in Beulah Mansions, I should give it back, and you thought to yourself, maybe there's a reward.'

'I have no idea what you're talking about.'

'So why are you here? Is it just my sunny disposition and the always warm welcome?' *Two jokes from the most humourless person I ever met,* thought Anton.

'I came round to say that we would very much appreciate it if you could avoid sending anyone round to our tenants in Beulah Mansions and asking them questions any more, they've been through a lot lately, it's been very upsetting for them.'

Egerton looked across the desk at him. 'I just wondered if they might know about a missing item, from *my* tenants flat, their being friends of yours,'

'They're our clients, our tenants and we just want to make sure they can continue to live their lives in peace.'

'Why would they not be able to live their lives in peace? I'm sure that any colleague of mine would have been polite and charming, not unpeaceful.'

'All I'm saying is, come to me next time, please.'

'And here you are, but you keep saying that you don't know what I'm talking about so coming to you would seem to be a complete waste of time.'

'They don't know what you're talking about either.' Egerton just stared at him, 'What?'

'I'm trying to work out,' said Egerton, 'whether you're just taking me for a complete fucking idiot.' Anton didn't have a reply to that, just shook his head, this wasn't going to plan. 'We don't seem to be on the same wavelength,' said Egerton, pushing his chair back and standing.

'There is one more thing, do you have another tenant for the flat yet?'

'What business is that of yours?'

'It would be good of you to put maybe… a nicer person in there, someone a bit more normal, our tenants went through a lot with the last one.'

'Why would I care?'

'Why wouldn't you?'

'Its business, someone moves in and pays me the rent, I don't care what they do. Look, it's nice that you want it to be all tickety-boo for your friends, that you care, the thing is, I don't. I don't care and I don't see any reason why I should,'

Anton stood now, aware of his blood pumping a little faster.

Egerton hadn't finished, 'I'll tell you what, why don't you just give me back my property?'

'What makes you think I've got something?' Anton shouting at him now.

'Because he told us you took it-'

'-What?-'

'-When you went round and roughed him up-'

'-we didn't rough anyone up. We didn't touch him.'

'So, you did go round and see him,' Anton sighed, this was getting messier, 'he told us anyway, he told us he gave it to you because he was frightened. That he gave it to you to make you go away.'

'That's a heap of crap Mr Egerton and you know it,' he paused for effect, but Egerton didn't look impressed, 'we don't have anything that belongs to you or to him.'

Egerton had turned away to the window and was checking something on his phone. 'Close the door please on your way out.' Anton hesitated but didn't know what else to say so Egerton had the last word, 'Oh, and if you suddenly do find you have it after all-'

'I don't even know what *it* is.'

'If. Then do please get in touch,' he turned and smiled at Anton. Like a snake.

Anton was irritated when he left Egerton's office and scratchy with Franca when she called him while he was on his way to the gym. She was fussing over Christmas and wanted some pointers for what to get for his father and brother.

'There's ages to go,' said Anton.

'I want to get started, get it done early before the shops get too crowded.' He had been running when she called, and he had stopped to answer. The one thing he wanted now was to be running again, it was a way to push Egerton out of his mind.

'Look, I just don't know Franca, I haven't thought about it,' he said, realising that this was a less than helpful answer, 'sorry, I don't know, we haven't really done it much before... Christmas so I don't know what to suggest. Let me think about it and talk later. Look, I just had to deal with something, I can tell you about it later, I need to just calm down a bit, let me do that and I'll see you later, okay?'

'Okay,' she sounded hurt.

'I'll come over later, everything's fine, sorry, I just had a frustrating morning so far, I'll see you about six if that's okay?'

She muttered something and hung up, he looked at the phone, swore, put it back in his pocket and carried on running, working up a sweat, working off his anger.

He got to the gym around ten-thirty. Barney was there, in the middle of a group of boys, supervising two of the younger ones and showing them how to use the pads, he looked up and said:

'Afternoon.'

'What?' said Anton, then remembered, 'Shit, sorry.'

'Don't put yourself on the rota if you can't do it,' said Barney, irritated.

'I forgot, sorry. I had some business to attend to and I forgot.'

'I've been doing this for half an hour,' said Barney, stopping the boys and telling them to wait a moment. 'it's all yours,' he said, handing the pads to Anton as he passed him.

'Alright then,' said Anton, eyeing up the group. The Boys Group comprised a varying membership, aged between 12 and 16, looking to impress each other with how hard they were. Mostly, they had nowhere else to be, were excluded from schools and often not allowed at home on their own, under any circumstances. He happily volunteered to take sessions and by doing so, would get to know them a little. He enjoyed the work, teaching them basic boxing moves or just keep fit routines, keeping it fun, at least, that was the idea. On this morning, there were eight of them, a decent turn out.

'Okay then, let's see what you know, what did the old boy teach you?'

'I heard that,' said Barney. A couple of the boys laughed at Anton.

'So, this is about working with someone else, teamwork,' he put on the pads. 'Okay, somebody, show me what you can do,' he pointed to one of the boys, a skinny ginger kid who looked like he was there just for the chance to hit someone and get away with it. The kid came over and stood in front of Anton who put the pads up, inviting him to strike. The kid swung and connected with the side of his hand, his face red with the effort. 'Hold it. What's this, karate? Either he didn't teach you anything or you weren't listening. We're going to start with the basics.'

Anton spilt them into pairs, told them to take their gloves off for now; the boys didn't seem too keen on doing that, but went along with it, each placing them in a particular place on the side, where they knew they could find them again later.

'You all got gloves that fit you, yeah?' he asked them.

'Boss man found them for us,' said the ginger kid.

Anton looked at them all, they looked small, younger than the last time he had taken a class. That was before the summer, before Franca. He was usually busy over the summer, getting the properties ready for winter so spent less time at the gym anyway. He'd taken the odd class here and there with a couple of them but that had been about it. He was happy to be back now, doing this, he'd forgotten how much he enjoyed it.

'We're going to start by putting together a few moves; come on back mate,' he beckoned the ginger kid. 'Now remember, you don't have any gloves on so don't try and put any force into it yet or you'll hurt yourself.' The kid stood in front of him, the others watching, paying various degrees of attention.

'What's your name?' asked Anton.

'Turbo,' said the kid.

'If you say so. Now Turbo, look at me, do what I say,' Anton crouched a little and held the pads up. 'Okay, so you've got no gloves on, remember we're just trying a routine, okay? So, Turbo, just try a gentle jab at this one,' he wiggled the pad on his left hand. Turbo tilted his head and lined up a punch, 'gently this time, just working out a sequence, don't try and hurt me with this one… you can have a go at that later.'

'Yeah,' said one of the boys, a bit too quickly.

Turbo let fly with a right that Anton saw coming and caught with the pad, pulling away as contact was made and sending the kid off balance.

'Gently, I said,' said Anton, calmly, 'I said I will show you what to do. You do what I show you and you can box, you want that?' One or two of the boys said yeah or mumbled something affirmative and Turbo grunted. Anton wasn't sure if that was a yes or whether he was clearing his throat but either way he had more to say,

'Come on then, what are we waiting for?'

Anton looked at him and suppressed his immediate inclination to smack him round the head. 'Patience. The way we're going to do it is properly. You throw a punch like that without gloves on and I promise you it'll hurt you more than it hurts me,' some of the others giggled, Anton held his hand up to stop them.

'Okay, watch, all of you,' he held the pad up again and looked at Turbo. 'Jab.' The boy aimed a right jab, straight out from his body, less force this time and Anton didn't move the pad away but left it there, a solid wall. Turbo connected and blinked, it hurt but he wasn't going to show it. 'Good, now slow again, gentle, just to work out a sequence. Jab again, same hand, right hand,' Turbo did so, lighter this time. 'Good, now a left, gently.... Good, now a right again... good, now wait and breathe....' The kid watched him closely, listening at last, 'now same again, right, right, left and right.' Turbo did it; he was good, steady on his feet too.

'That was good,' said Anton, 'thank you. That's how you do it, build it up. Someone else now, how about you?' He pointed at a boy who looked a bit older than the rest, who had been fidgeting the whole time, holding his energy in but wanting to do something. 'Who are you?'

'Gaz,' said the boy.

'Gaz, okay, come over here, stand in the same place, hold your stance. Okay, a little dance if you like, keep your balance. Again, like Turbo and keep it gentle for now: right, right, left then right again.' The kid did it, but he was itching to go another step. 'Okay, do it again and take a breath at the end then repeat, remember, keep it at head height, aim for the pads, ready?' Gaz nodded and did a little jog on the spot, 'let's go: right, right, left, right… and wait, good; breathe… and again, right, right, left then right again,' but Gaz was losing his rhythm and started flailing, Anton held his padded hand up to stop him, 'wo… stop, hold on there, no rush, keep your rhythm steady, you're not a windmill,' a couple of the others laughed and one found it hysterically funny. Gaz looked round and caught the kid's eye, which calmed him down a little. 'We'll try it again.' This time Gaz concentrated a little more and got a rhythm going, building up intensity before Anton stopped him.

One of others said, 'Sir, can we do it with the gloves now?'

'You don't have to call me Sir,' said Anton, 'who are you?' The boy said:

'Kai.'

'Okay, I'm Anton, you can use my name. Did he make you call him Sir?' He gestured in the vague direction that Barney had left in. The boys murmured *yes*. 'Okay, that's because he's old, I'm not, so you can call me by my name.' He beckoned Kai to come over and pointed to one of the others, 'Come and join us, what's your name?' The kid was small with longish black hair, he looked as if he didn't spend a lot of time outside. He didn't answer but someone else did,

'Nipple,' the boys all laughed, the kid with the black hair just stood there.

'Okay, so that's very funny,' said Anton, then to the kid again, 'what's your name?'

'Nipple, his name's Nipple sir,' said one of the others.

'Don't call me sir, okay… really? Nipple?' The boys laughed again, there was no choice but to go with it, 'That okay with you?' he said to Nipple who nodded in a way that said, *may as well, it isn't going to change.* 'Kai, hold the pads,' he showed him how to put his hands in the straps and hold them up, 'Nipple, you come over here, now do the jabs like I showed Gaz.' The boy jabbed and held his balance well: right, right, left, right, like before.

'Now, you all know it doesn't have to be just that sequence, right? So now I want you to punch out, forward, not too much swinging, do it how you like but always aim at the pads, doesn't matter which one, try it.' Nipple looked at him and he nodded encouragement before the kid let fly with alternative punches: left, right, left, right… first on one side then the other, Kai trying hold his balance under the onslaught. Anton put his hand out to stop them.

'Good. Well done. Okay, we're going to go into pairs now and those who are punching, try both ways, try the sequence and repeating it and then try just making up your own, see which one suits you best. So, Turbo, Gaz, Kai and Nipple, you hold the pads, the others get your gloves on.'

There was immediate confusion and everyone apart from Turbo put gloves on, so Anton had to step in and sort them out with much complaining from the boys who were assigned to hold the pads first time round.

'We do this and then we swop round okay? It's about working together, taking it in turns. Although boxing is one individual against another, when we're working together in training, we're a team, we're helping each other, you got that?'

They nodded or mumbled assent, 'Good, you'll all get to punch someone, I promise.'

Anton worked with them, showing the ones holding pads how to absorb the energy from the blows and the others how to keep their jabs straight, how to stand and balance and stay steady on their feet, and how to return their gloved hands to protect their faces after they connected even though, this time round, no one was going to try and hit them back.

'Make it a habit to hold your hands in front of your face, always remember, make it so you do it automatically, so you don't have to think about it. That way, it makes it hard for anyone to hit you. Again…'

After a while, he made them swop roles and the pad holders finally got to throw a punch or two; having waited all that time, they were a little over exuberant so once again Anton cooled them down, showed them how to control their strength, how to keep their shape and balance and how to defend. They worked the drill, and he taught them new ones, swopping between the gloves and the pads, working up in speed and intensity as he gradually let them put a little venom into their shots. The boys started to sweat, and he pushed them on until the time was up. When they stopped, they sat on the nearest bench or leant over and rested their elbows on their knees, all of them were breathing heavily.

'There you go, was that fun?' asked Anton. A few of them said *yeah, it was,* they wanted to do it again next time, Turbo was even smiling. 'So, what have you got next?'

'Cross country running, ten K, so thanks for wearing us the fuck out,' said one of the younger ones with a shaved head, a tattoo of a spider's web on his neck and a bit of attitude; he was all of fourteen.

'Give yourselves a few minutes, breathe good and deep. It's

pretty cold out there, you sure you boys are tough enough for that?' They mostly smiled or muttered some half-formed affectionate insults and high fived him as they gathered track suits and kit bags before leaving to find the minibus that waited out in the street. 'We can do some more tomorrow,' Anton said as they slowly drifted off.

One of them put on what looked at first like a pair of glasses but with a little bit of extra glass on an arm stretching out in front on one side.

'Okay, you've got me, what's that?' asked Anton.

'Google Glass,' said the boy.

'Go on then, tell me... Jason, isn't it?'

'Jason, yeah. It's a computer you can wear, you get information onto the little screen… its wearable tech; have you got a smartwatch?' Anton shrugged his shoulders, 'It's a way to be connected while you go about your day… someday soon everyone's going to be wearing these.'

'No, they won't,' said Anton.

'Yes, they will, it's the future.'

'They won't,' said Anton, wondering why he was trying to win this argument.

'They will, I bet you,' said Jason, looking like he meant it.

'Okay, I bet you a Bitcoin,' said Anton which made Jason laugh.

'I don't think you know what a Bitcoin is…'

'Yes I do, it's ummm… we'll see,' said Anton, getting the last word as Jason left to catch up with the rest.

Anton did his own work out then, pushing himself until he too was covered in sweat. He thought about what he was going to buy Franca for Christmas, it was apparent that she was going to take the whole thing very seriously, so he was going to have to go along with it. He also realised that he was going to have to think of Rosa too and presumably little Gregory, this was going to need some proper planning.

He had no work that needed doing that day so when he finished at the gym he just caught the bus home where he showered, changed, and went back out to see Franca, not completely sure what kind of a mood she was going to be in.

On the way he bought a dozen deep red roses, not particularly original but his dad had taught him, if in doubt get flowers.

He had a touch of nerves when he pressed the doorbell, but when Franca answered, she was smiling and kissed him as she took the flowers, told him he shouldn't have and said wait while she put them in the kitchen. Anton took that to be an instruction to stay put as they were going out and it struck him that he never really felt secure in knowing what the plan was going to be: stay in, go out… whatever, the whole thing seemed to be reliant on Franca's whims. When he saw her coming back, he thought he'd try and suggest something.

'Movie?'

'Movie,' she said, 'let's go and find out what's on.'

On the way there, she asked him about his morning.

'It's this guy, the landlord of the bloke that died-'

'-the druggie?'

'I don't really know that,' said Anton, 'he looked that way, but I don't really know. Anyway, this landlord is a lowlife… he doesn't care about anyone else, how what he does might affect them. He smelt weird today as well, of bodies, not just BO, you know, like the gym I suppose.'

'Perhaps he works out.'

'Trust me, he doesn't work out. He's a slug.'

'He sounds lovely,' said Franca, ready to change the subject now.

'To be fair, I'm pretty sure I'm not on his Christmas list either,' said Anton, equally happy to talk about something else.

Despite their choosing an action movie which was relentlessly unrelaxing, they spent half of it kissing each other and even sat through the entire ten minutes of the end credits doing so until the ushers who were doing between show cleans turfed them out.

'What happened at the end?' asked Anton on the way home.

'He rescued her, the world didn't end but the president wasn't the real one; the real one was hiding. I've no idea why what's-his-name blew up the train, I thought he was one of the good guys.'

'He was, wasn't he? Didn't he blow the train up to protect his cover?' But Anton wasn't really sure.

'Have you thought any more about what I can get your family for Christmas?' asked Franca, catching him unawares.

'No, I'm sorry, I promise to give it more thought. Trouble is, we don't really do it… Christmas, we never have.

'We do and you should. It's fun.' And that was that.

Anton woke the next day, in Franca's bed and thinking about Christmas, no arguing, it was a thing now. Franca rolled over and pushed up close to him, her hair everywhere. He held her close and stroked her hair, straightening it out and away from his face. They lay together, quietly drifting, their breaths gradually synchronising. Away, for now, from reality.

After breakfast, Anton headed off for the gym, trying think about Christmas. It certainly felt like Christmas now, the temperature was close to zero and the freezing air could cut through any coat. He had no other calls to make so he went straight to the gym and arrived just after the doors had opened.

People were already there, Kirby being one of them of course, cycling for all he was worth. Wonder if he's thinking about Christmas thought Anton. Barney saw him and came over.

'Alright? You okay to take the boys again at ten?'

'Course,' said Anton, 'I just got caught up with something yesterday, sorry.'

'I thought you forgot?'

'I did. As well. I'll sort them, don't worry.'

'We lost one. His mum, or someone claiming to be his mum called and said he wouldn't be able to come in anymore, didn't say why. Sandy is it? What kind of a kid's name is Sandy?'

'Okay, seven it is then,' said Anton. 'I'm teaching them how to spar today,' then, anticipating Barney's next words he said quickly, 'I'll be very careful and be sure to keep a close eye on them at all times.'

'Go easy, eh? They're just kids.'

'Oh really? I was going to challenge one of them, three rounds, pound a point…it would be good for them, character building.'

'Don't be a twat Anton,' said Barney. Anton gave him an eyeroll, 'Oh and there's someone to see you,' Anton made a questioning face at him as Barney turned and led him into his office.

He recognised her as he walked through the door even though she was sitting with her back to him, checking her phone. She must have heard them come in, but didn't look up, just carried on until he had moved into her line of sight. Anton was behind the desk before she looked away from the phone. He'd seen her before in Darren's flat.

'Mr Matheson. I hope you don't mind too much… me turning up like this, surprising you,' she looked round at Barney to make sure he understood he was no longer needed.

'I'll um… leave you to it then,' he said, pulling the door closed as he left.

Anton looked at her and tried to remember her name, he knew it was supposed to be memorable, but it had gone.

'Miss…?'

'Atkinson-Pike, Valerie Atkinson-Pike,' *that was it, a mouthful.*

'How did you find me here? Why did you find me here?'

'We know about the holdall, Mr Matheson.'

Anton had no obvious response to this other than, 'What holdall?'

Atkinson-Pike sighed and finally put her phone away. 'Please… Mr Matheson. Anton. Can I call you Anton?' Anton nodded. 'I'm not a half-wit like our Mr Egerton. I know you know the answer to that question and I'm here to help you.'

'That's nice of you, thank you,' said Anton, 'but the truth is, I don't know what you're talking about.' He sat down in Barney's chair, feeling a little bit more confident sitting there but still unsettled by this woman who seemed to know too much about him. She wore expensive looking clothes: tailored jacket over a business-like, intensely white blouse; dark skirt, and shiny black shoes. She didn't look like she was used to hearing the word *no.* Sitting in Barney's chair gave him the idea that he too could maybe, just possibly look a bit business like. He looked her straight in the eye. 'I really don't know.'

She sighed again and held her arms up, about a yard apart. 'There's a holdall bag, like a sports bag so you will know the type and it's about yay big would be my guess,' she paused and stared back at him. 'Beige with some navy-blue trim, piping it's called. It's got something in it and its ours. I think you have taken it… accidentally, could easily happen, I can see that. Anyway, I'm here to help and I very much hope now that you will want to return it.'

She opened her handbag which Anton clocked now for the first time, *was that snakeskin?* She was definitely out to make an impression. She produced a business card, checked it, and handed it to Anton who leaned forward to take it.

'Take it to this address. Monday would be good, that gives you the weekend to find it, in case you've put it somewhere and forgotten; easily done,' she smiled, but not convincingly.

She stood, closed her bag, and smoothed her skirt. Anton got up and moved to the door to open it for her. On their way through the gym to the outside door, Anton tried to think of a way to convince her that he really didn't have a clue about the holdall, but he couldn't think of anything new to say.

At the door, they stopped, and she looked around. 'Big place, good amount of space here, right location… you know, this would make a great night club.'

'It makes a great boxing club,' said Anton.

Atkinson-Pike smiled again, reached out and cupped her hand to his cheek. 'I know, but time moves on. See you Monday,' and left. Anton watched her walk away, trying to think what to do. When he turned back into the gym, Barney was there.

'You alright?'

'Yeah, no problem,' said Anton and walked over to a ring where Franny had just finished sparring with his trainer. As he climbed down, he indicated the door and said to Anton,

'Is that….?' Anton looked at him, puzzled, 'the one you've been talking about,'

'Oh. No. No, that was someone else.'

Franny gave him a look, 'Right, otherwise she's a bit older than I imagined... classy though.'

13

Anton called Neville while he was on his way home to check he was going to be there, telling him they had something to talk about. He told him briefly about Valerie Atkinson-Pike's visit to the gym, about the missing holdall which presumably was what Egerton had been talking about the day before. Neville hadn't seemed too bothered about it, so Anton wanted to make sure he took it more seriously. After all, he'd seen the look in her eyes.

'So, what you're saying,' said Neville, sitting on the edge of the kitchen table, trying to piece the story together, 'is that our mate, Fucking Darren was looking after a bag, a holdall no less, containing…. something, and it wasn't there in the flat after the police had cleared out?'

'Basically,' said Anton.

'So perhaps the police found it and took it away, which is what they would do if there was anything dodgy in it-'

'-if there was something in it which he shouldn't have had… drugs-'

'-for example. But then presumably they'd go after Egerton and his chums. Why does this woman think we've got it?'

'Valerie Atkinson-Pike. She arrived when we there, remember? Perhaps she thinks we were there earlier, or that we saw it and somehow half-inched it,' said Anton.

'And we had paid a little visit to him previously of course,' Neville was drinking his tea, still not convinced this was adding up to anything.

'We genuinely don't know anything about all this, why don't we just ignore her?'

Anton thought about this for a moment then said, 'She just doesn't seem to be the kind of person who is used to being ignored… and Egerton, remember, when I went round to see him yesterday-'

'-Why *did* you go and see him yesterday?'

'He sent someone to see Carol and Paul, I asked him not to,' Neville looked disapproving. 'Maybe in retrospect, that wasn't a good idea.' Neville nodded; at last, something he agreed with.

'Still not our problem,' said Neville.

'What about the Monday deadline? She's expecting us to bring the bag over on Monday.'

'Ignore it, see what happens,' Anton looked uncertain about the suggestion.

'Only other option is to go and look for it ourselves, see if we can find the thing… it's possible that it's still in the flat, Darren might have hidden it away somewhere clever, particularly if its valuable.'

'Egerton's been through the place as well.'

'So, he missed it too,' Anton looked at Neville as if to say this wasn't very likely, then said,

'We'd have to break in, and without Carol and Paul knowing.'

'And it's probably not there anyway and this isn't our problem,' said Neville, finishing his tea, 'and if we got caught then that really would look dodgy. Forget it, leave well alone and hope it goes away.'

Anton thought about that for a moment, 'One thing… if there really had been a holdall, and it's gone missing… then it went missing before we all got there, probably before Darren died, so… someone took it. Does that mean Darren was bumped off?' In the silence, they looked at each other before Neville said,

'No… He was unstable, he did something with it before that night, hid it somewhere or gave it to someone, came back to the flat and overdosed, that's how it looks to me,' said Neville. 'One thing for sure though, we stay as far away from all this as possible.'

'Deal,' said Anton.

By the time Monday came around, Anton and Neville had mostly put Valerie Atkinson-Pike out of their minds. What had seemed menacing a few days ago was now less so. At some point on Monday afternoon while Anton was working with his brother to move some old furniture out of storage and into a van to go for auction he wondered if she was sitting in a chair in her office, waiting for him to walk through the door. No sooner had the thought come along than he was able to push it away again. As for Neville, he didn't have to do a lot of pushing, Anton doubted whether he'd taken it all seriously in the first place.

When he woke on Tuesday morning, Anton reached for his phone, half expecting to see a message from Atkinson-Pike but there was none. He told himself she didn't have his number. Of course, Egerton did, if he'd kept it… or she could just find it out, she was the kind who would be able to just find things out if she wanted to. Again, he tried to push her out of his mind, to calm himself, say to himself that there was no reason to worry, he and his brother were not involved. He saw that Malcolm had texted to remind him he was due over at Beulah Mansions to fix the window. He had remembered, but Malcolm knew very well that it was wise to send a reminder.

He arrived just after lunch and Carol answered the door to the flat, leaning in for a kissed greeting and looking pleased to see him. He went to the living room and took a look at the window to check that he'd remembered the job correctly then laid out a tool roll he had brought with him on the rug in the middle of the floor.

'It's jammed completely now,' said Carol. Anton looked round and saw her leaning against the door frame, watching him. The thought came to him that she was an attractive woman. She was wearing jeans and an oversize white shirt, presumably one of Paul's. He guessed she was in her thirties, she would be a gym regular somewhere, or she did Pilates or some such. She'd changed her hair recently, coloured it lighter than it used to be and had it cut to a stylish, scuffed up bob. He noticed too, that she had make-up on, just a little.

'We'll get it fixed up, don't worry.' She had good legs too, now he thought about it.

'Tea?'

'Uh, yes. Please. No sugar, thanks,' she turned and walked away, Anton watching her as she left, he liked that she was friendly and warm towards him.

The sash on one side of the lower window had broken completely and needed replacement. Someone had tried to force the window and it sat crookedly in the frame. Anton wrestled it free by easing it to a level position and carefully inching it up. To his relief, it wasn't in too bad a condition. He went to the tool roll and took out an old screwdriver which he used to prise away the surrounding beading, gently easing it out without breaking it, pulling out some of the retaining pins as he went along. It occurred to him to check the top window which dropped down normally, and the sash looked in good condition. He pushed it back up into place and was suddenly aware of Carol standing at his side.

'Tea,' she said and placed the mug on the windowsill.

'The room's going to get cold, I'm afraid,' said Anton, 'I have to lift the bottom window out.'

'I'll be in the kitchen if you need anything or need any help. Just let me know,' she smiled at him again and he wondered to himself if she wasn't being just a tiny bit flirtatious, then dismissed the thought.

The window was old and mostly intact, so Anton wanted to keep it in one piece which meant a lot of gentle persuasion was needed to loosen the beading and the covers over the weight pocket which were all nailed into place as well as heavily painted in. Eventually everything came apart without splitting the wood or any other mishap.

'Don't forget your tea, don't let it get cold,' he heard her call from the kitchen. He called out *okay,* thought *good point,* and took a sip. Replacing the sash was fiddly, he had to feed one end over the pulley and down into the weight compartment where he fixed it to the weight itself. With the weight attached he started to reassemble some of the frame. His earlier care paid off, everything slipped back into position without fuss. Anton enjoyed jobs like this, where it needed a bit of concentration, a little patience and where you could fix something.

'Another one?' he looked round at Carol, leaning in the doorway again, *how long had she been standing there?* 'Tea…' she explained. He nodded and said thanks.

When she returned it was with two cups.

'Actually, I could use a little help here if you have a moment,' he said, 'if you could just hold this cord with the weight on the end while I fix the other end to the window, that would be amazing.'

'Of course, I wouldn't want to pass up the chance to be amazing.' She put her tea down next to his on the table and listened carefully while he showed her how to hold the weight up and give him enough slack in the cord to work with while he pushed the other end down into the inner frame and fixed it in place. While she helped, he noticed she was staying close to him, chatting away happily, asking him about his life. He asked her how things were now, how she and Paul were dealing with it all, if it was at least more peaceful now; she said *yes,* and that it was definitely better, but they had been through a lot, they were still nervous, they would quickly find themselves on edge if there was any sudden sound from outside for example.

Having fixed the sash to the window itself, Anton took the end that Carol had been holding and let the weight fall back. He offered the window back up to its frame and let it travel up and down a few times to check the tension.

'There you go, you have a functioning sash window, not that you're going to want to open it that much in this cold,' he stood back and admired his work. He bent down to pick up a length of beading and as he did so the window leant into room a little, it wasn't going to go far but he instinctively put an arm out to catch it and stop it dropping out. Carol did something similar except her hand went to his waist to steady him, even though he hadn't looked much like he was about to fall over.

She left her hand there for just a moment until he said he was okay, he was just stopping the window moving too far. She smiled and took her hand away. For a moment he imagined what it might be like to be with her but let the thought pass by. He put the surrounding beads back, with just a couple of pins on each length to hold it this time. He pushed the window up and eased it back down gently, repeating the movement, letting it settle and travel smoothly a few times to be sure it worked properly.

He finished and tidied the tools away, even vacuuming the area below the window. 'It's going to need a touch of paint, some of the old paint chipped away when I took it apart. I'll pop round and do that in a few days.' She thanked him and he got ready to leave, picking up the tool roll and pulling his thick winter coat around himself in anticipation of the chill outside.

Carol was between him and the door, so he put an arm around her lightly and kissed her goodbye on the mouth. As he did so, he felt her lean into his arm until he was taking her weight and she seemed to melt. He held her, his mouth on hers and she began to kiss him back, this time with more purpose. He pulled her gently towards him and felt her hand on his back. He dropped one arm, letting go of the tool roll then shook his arm out of the coat sleeve and let go with the other arm to let his coat fall to the floor. He put his arms back around her, tighter now, pulling her in, she pushed against him, and her hand reached below his shirt to touch the bare skin of his back. She kissed deeply now, slowly, pressing her body into his as he pushed back. When they stopped to breathe, Anton almost spoke before her mouth was on his again, her hands unbuttoning his shirt and somehow pulling her own top off at the same time.

Anton was bewildered and turned on at the same time, 'Door?' he nodded towards their front door.

'The chain's on, I did it earlier. I often do it when I'm on my own,' she looked him straight in the eye as her hands moved down over his waist to the belt on his jeans, 'I did it an hour ago.'

They fucked, frantically and in a frenzy, there on the sofa, still half dressed. He reached his climax quickly and held her in his arms afterwards, making her come with his fingers, causing her to scream rather alarmingly, and he held on to her as she shook before calming. When it was over, he leant back and she lay on top of him, in his arms.

'I've been so scared. The people upstairs, the man who came to see us… he was horrible, sleazy.'

'It's over now, all over. Back to normal,' said Anton, wondering how normal this was. They lay there for a while, then Carol spoke,

'I know this is wrong, but-'

'-I know. It's just this once though, yes?' said Anton.

'Just this once, yes. But it was wonderful.'

'For me too,' said Anton, wondering if that was wise, given this was a one-off.

Carol sat up, letting her weight transfer to her knees while she knelt on the edge of the sofa. 'All a bit porny though isn't it? I mean fucking the plumber…'

'Who are you calling a plumber?' he said, 'wrong trade; how many plumbers could fix a sash window? And what kind of porn are you watching? Plumber porn?'

'It's that or the pizza delivery boy, isn't it?' she looked at him.

'Umm, I don't know, I don't really watch-'

'-of course you don't,' she said and playfully slapped him,

'Ow!'

'That didn't hurt you, boxer boy,' she grinned and shaped up for a second go, but he stopped her by reaching down and finding she was ticklish on her side. She squirmed and squealed then got off the sofa, laughed one more time and stood there looking at him, dishevelled, half dressed, a few bits of chipped paint in his hair. She straightened her dress. 'We can't talk about this, ever. Are we agreed?'

'We're agreed,' said Anton, relieved.

When he got home, Franca was there, in the kitchen, talking with Malcolm.

'Hi,' said Anton, unsteady.

'Nice to see you too,' said Franca, put out that he wasn't more effusive.

'Sorry, I just didn't know… lovely to see you, of course…'

'We were talking about Christmas,' said Franca, behind her Malcolm caught Anton's eye and raised an eyebrow whilst nodding, 'you're all coming over to ours and we'll do a proper dinner.'

'We don't usually make a big thing of it, Christmas… do we?' he said but Malcolm wasn't going to help him this time.

'So, it's about time you did. Your dad thinks it's a good idea.'

'Uh, yeah,' said Malcolm, not wishing to be drawn into it.

'Settled. Come on Anton, it's fun. Neville as well of course.'

'Neville?' said Anton, not obviously delighted, 'he's a-'

'Oy,' said Malcolm, 'he's your brother.'

'Exactly, he's your brother,' said Franca.

'Son,' said Malcolm, looking to bring this to a close, 'we're going there for dinner, we bring the booze, it's all settled.'

'You can't settle things without me,' said Anton suddenly realising he sounded about twelve. He gave way quickly, not needing the argument and anyway, *who knows? It might be fun.* What he really wanted right now was time to think, he felt worn out.

'You fix up Beulah?' his dad asked. *You bet,* thought Anton and nodded his answer. He said he felt tired, it had been a long day, said to Franca he needed an early night, suggested a quick drink to end the day and ushered her out.

After a short stop at the pub where he drank two pints rapidly and Franca sipped a small glass of white whilst making small talk, he walked her home and kissed her goodnight at the door.

'I'm sorry, I'm knackered, I need to get some sleep, is that okay?'

'Of course,' she said and kissed him again, 'everything's cool.'

Anton woke the next day in his own bed and feeling *more* tired if anything, not sure he was ready for the day to come. His head was full, a mess of ideas, feelings, replays of the previous day, a confused jumble. He washed, dressed, drank coffee, ate cereal and a couple of apples, all without improvement to his foggy state.

Jogging to the gym, he wondered for a moment whether this was a version of maturity. In his teenage years, his moment with Carol would have been a conquest, a proud notch on the bedpost; now he had a proper girlfriend who he loved (as he had to admit), he just felt guilt. Guilt and fear, how easy had it been to stray? Would it be easy for her as well? Realising that feeling guilty and jealous at the same time was a little crazy he tried to talk some reason into himself, in doing so he said it out loud as he jogged along.

'You just have to think straight, think: what do you want, what do you want?' he muttered in rhythm with his strides, 'What do you want, what do you want, what do you want…?' Chanting in time, like a madman, 'What do you value? What do you owe Franca? What do you owe Carol? – Nothing, right? She started this, it was Carol who seduced you not the other way round, it was an impulse, a one-off, we both know it. Our secret, keep it that way.' *Love can drive you mad,* he thought, *listen to me talking to myself.*

In the gym he got stuck in, he needed to work, to clear his head and narrow his focus for a while. Inevitably, Kirby was there when he arrived, just ending his warmup, then going straight into a punishing sequence of star jumps, squats, press ups, planking and burpees all in pre-determined groups, in sequence, counted out by Kenny Dean who had taken on his cause; the cycle then repeated.

Franny was there too, the other budding pro, he was finishing his warmup and looking for a sparring partner, a role that Anton was happy to fill, in truth he much preferred that to solo work and knew that Franny was more than capable of testing him.

Franny's work was carefully planned out. He had a focussed and intense programme to work to, Barney had seen to that. Nowadays at George's any stepping up to professional status was taken very seriously, they were a long way from the days of providing cannon fodder for the undercards. Franny's spars were six rounders and Anton agreed to take the first three, someone else would be asked to step in for the second.

In the ring and with the big gloves on to soften the blows, Anton was able to concentrate on the spar and clear his head. Franny was good, no doubt about it, consistent now in a way Anton found hard to keep up with, solidly defending and looking for the gaps. He was coming on.

'What do you think?' asked Barney when Anton was done and climbing out of the ring to make way for Dave, who had put the detail into Barney's broad training programme, to take over.

'I think he's good, seriously good,' said Anton, 'just needs to stay away from the Christmas pud now.'

'He's alright with taking weight off, seen him do it before, not a big lad but he's fit enough to just work it away.'

'How's Kirby doing?' asked Anton, looking over at him, still working on his own.

'Coming on well too, he won't fail through lack of work. He needs to spar though; I need to sort that. Probably not with you yet, eh?'

Anton nodded, 'Ah, no, maybe not yet.'

'What about you?' asked Barney, unexpectedly.

'I'm fine,' Anton said, 'everything's good actually, girlfriend, Franca, brilliant, it's all good.'

'You ever going to step up?'

'No. I don't think so. Not sure I want all that. You have to really want it, right?'

'Yeah,' said Barney, coughing suddenly, 'you could do it though, if you ever wanted it.'

14

When he'd finished at the gym, Anton checked his phone: Malcolm had called him, but he didn't call back, whatever it was could wait until he got home.

'What happened to you?' his father said when he walked in, 'I called.'

'I was coming home anyway, see what needed doing,' said Anton, 'what's happened?'

'Your brother's gone to the nick is what's happened. Two plain clothes high ups came round, asking about Beulah, the one who died there, Neville agreed to go with them to be interviewed, they want to know whatever he knows-'

'-He doesn't know anything,'

'Alright, don't blame me. They want you there as well, asked for you to go down there when you came in.'

Anton stood still for a moment, thinking. Nothing to panic about, they really didn't know anything, they hadn't done anything wrong, perhaps they might even find a way to sort out this thing with Atkinson-Pike and the bag. Malcolm was looking through the mess of paper that was on the kitchen table until he found a business card which he handed to Anton.

'There you go, ask for this one.'

'Okay,' said Anton.

'Be careful,' said Malcolm.

'We haven't done anything.'

'Even so, just keep your wits about you.' Anton went to the fridge, found half a slice of cold pizza and quickly scoffed it as he found a coat from the back of one of the chairs and put it on. 'Know where you're going?'

'Police Station, said Anton, 'on the High Street.'

'You haven't looked at the card, have you? You don't pay attention either, the one on the High Street closed a couple of years ago.'

'Next to Sainsburys?' Malcolm nodded and pointed at the card in Anton's hands. He looked at it and sighed, 'It's miles away, I'll have to get a bus, you can't park round there.'

'Just be careful what you say son,' said Malcolm.

The Police Station was an unimposing building, easy to spot from the line of marked cars outside. Anton realised he'd never actually been in a Police Station before; he had no idea what to expect unless it was like on the telly. He asked for Detective Inspector Summerscales, gave his name and was shown to a small waiting room which had three bare walls and a fourth covered in public information notices about reporting crimes or noticing suspicious behaviour.

There was little furniture, just a low table with a lot of heat stains and dark smudges on it and a dozen or so blue plastic chairs. The only other person there was an older man, *in his fifties perhaps, maybe sixty* thought Anton, and he looked angry, not happy to be there, knowing nothing good was going to come of it. Anton nodded and smiled at him as he sat down, the man said nothing, didn't move, just stared straight ahead at Anton.

It wasn't a long wait. The door opened and Anton looked up to see an older man, tall, thinning white hair cut short, gaunt faced and tired eyes which made him look like he needed to go back to bed for a couple more hours. He wore a grey suit which looked lived in.

'Anton Matheson? Come with me, please,' he led him out of the room and guided him down a corridor with numbered doors leading off it, presumably Neville was sitting inside one of the rooms. The place was undecorated, bland and depressing; *why not at least have a few pictures up?*

'I'm DI Summerscales, thank you for coming in; we just have a few things we'd like to ask you,' Anton noticed his highly polished black leather shoes as they walked, he was the opposite of the jaded copper that he had imagined. They stopped outside a door which Summerscales opened, and Anton was shown in.

'Just wait in here if you would,' and he was gone. Anton looked round, just four chairs in this one, same blue plastic and one of them was frankly filthy and should have been retired a long time ago. He chose the cleanest looking of the remaining three and sat. The walls were beige and in need of a fresh coat of paint to cover up the dark grey shadows where clothes had rubbed up against them over the years along with splash stains from God-knows-what which added to the air of neglect.

The only other furniture was a formica topped table on which was a dusty grey digital recorder with a microphone sitting on top and a notepad on which the top sheet was bent up, as if the sheet before it had been ripped away in a hurry. Two biros lay next to it, *police issue biros, presumably.*

The door opened again and Summerscales walked back in followed by another man of similar age but a lot less dapper, this one had a worn-out look, an old suit, no tie and scuffed shoes, a lot more how Anton thought detectives looked.

'This is Detective Trewin, he's working with me on this case.' They sat on the other side of the table, Trewin on the festering chair, not bothered by it. 'If I could just check your name and details please…'

Anton gave his name, date of birth and address, Trewin wrote them down. Anton asked if his brother was there.

'He's fine Mr Matheson, he's been helping us too.' Anton regretted not having waited to speak with Neville before coming down, it would have been good to have an idea of what they were going to ask about, he'd been too keen to come in and get it all over with.

'So, Mr Matheson, thank you again for coming here, just to be clear, you are here on a voluntary basis,' Anton nodded, not sure if that was a question or not, 'Detective Trewin and I are investigating the death of Darren Lombard,' he paused.

'The guy from Beulah Mansions?' said Anton.

'Yes sir,' said Summerscales looking straight at him.

'I didn't know his surname was Lombard.'

'We thought he was an acquaintance of yours. That you knew him.'

'Not really,' said Anton, 'we met him once, my brother and me. We spoke with him at his flat, I wouldn't say he was an acquaintance.'

'How many times did you speak with him?'

'Once,' said Anton. Summerscales looked surprised.

'You're sure about that?'

'Of course. We went there once to talk to him,' Anton really wishing now that he'd waited to talk with Neville before coming here, but surely he hadn't said anything different?

'Did you call him up as well?'

'No, I don't have his number.'

'Can you tell us about the time you went to see him?'

Anton nodded. 'Of course… we went to his flat, on the top floor. Our tenants, we're their landlord, are in the flat below,' Summerscales nodded, 'they were worried about him, he made them nervous, he made a lot of noise in the night, kept them awake and he was intimidating them.'

'Intimidating?' said Trewin, speaking for the first time.

'Kind of.'

'Kind of,' said Trewin, writing on the notepad again.

'He didn't answer the door when they went up to ask him to turn the noise down, and he had rows, shouting sessions with his visitors.' The detectives just watched him, saying nothing letting him get it out in his own way.

'So, we, Neville and I went round to see him to ask him, politely, just to be a bit more considerate. We just went round to talk to him, help our tenants out, keep it friendly.' Anton stopped and looked over at them, they said nothing but indicated he should carry on. 'So, we went there, knocked on his door,'

'When was this?' asked Summerscales.

'When? Ummm, not sure, about three weeks ago, four maybe. It was a Wednesday.'

'Go on.'

'We knocked on the door and he answered. We said who we were and asked him if he would perhaps be a little bit quieter, at night… if he'd help us out by doing that.'

'Where did this conversation take place?'

'At his flat.'

'In the flat?'

'No, just at the door, we just spoke with him at the door,' Anton was thinking back, wanting to get this over and done with and guessed that the best way was to make this sound as uninteresting as possible. 'He was fine with it, said *okay,* or words to that effect. As far as we were concerned, that was the end of it.'

There was silence as Summerscales watched him, waiting to see if there was more but Anton had decided that was enough.

The DI leant to his side and conferred in whispers with his colleague.

'Can I go now?' asked Anton. Summerscales looked up at him and smiled.

'You can leave at any time sir. We'd like you to stay just a little longer though, we still have a few more questions, would that be okay?' Anton nodded.

Summerscales leant forward, 'Mr Matheson, we'd like to do this a bit more formally if you don't mind. What we'd like to do is to interview you under caution. What that means is that we record the conversation, so we have an accurate record. We need to make sure that you understand that you're giving us evidence, so it's important that you're very clear about what you're saying, is that alright?'

'Are you arresting me?'

'No, no,' said Summerscales, 'what for? You hardly knew him.' Anton fidgeted in his chair, unsure whether to try and leave or stay and see it through, thinking about it, he couldn't see an easy way out. *Just get up and go?* What if he did that and they decided to make him stay, arrest him… *for what?* Trewin had been fiddling with the recording machine, a well-worn box of buttons and dials that looked a bit like one of his dad's hi-fi separates except for the small screen that sat on top. Eventually he looked pleased with it, opened a drawer in the table, brought out a memory stick and found a port in the front panel.

'Before we start,' said Summerscales, 'you are entitled to have your solicitor here if you wish, do you have one?'

How would I have one of those? Anton thought. 'No.'

'That's no problem, there is a duty solicitor, if you wish. It's up to you, you are here on a voluntary basis, remember, if you don't have a solicitor and you would like one, we can ask the duty solicitor to come down as soon as they're free.'

Anton thought about it, more than anything, he wanted this to be over. He also didn't want to look guilty. He wasn't guilty. If the solicitor came down, he'd be stuck here, this way he could walk at any time.

'No, it's okay, thanks, I don't think it's necessary.'

'Okay, we'll note that for the record, thank you,' Summerscales looked over at Trewin who switched the machine on. Summerscales continued, 'Interview with Mr Anton Matheson…' he gave the time and date, asked Anton to confirm his name and address and identified himself and his colleague, then carried on, 'This interview is in relation to the death of Mr Darren Lombard of Flat D, Beulah Mansions…' Anton had zoned out, he was out of his depth and knew it, none of this was what he had expected, he'd no idea how to behave and he felt like a suspect. Perhaps he was a suspect.

'Mr Matheson?' Anton looked up, Summerscales was waiting for an answer to something. He nodded back. 'Mr Matheson, I just said that you are attending this interview on a voluntary basis and that it has been explained to you that you are entitled to be accompanied by a solicitor, you have been offered the services of the duty solicitor and you have declined this, would you confirm that is the case please?'

'Yes. That is the case,' said Anton.

'Thank you. Just to reiterate that this interview is conducted under caution, you do not have to say anything, but it may harm your defence…' *My defence?* '…if you don't mention something when questioned which you may later rely on in court, anything you do say may be given in evidence, do you fully understand what I have said Mr Matheson?' Anton nodded, then added for the sake of the recording,

'Yes.'

'Thank you. So, if I may start, you say that you and your brother paid a visit to the deceased, Mr Lombard on a Wednesday evening about three weeks ago, would that be Wednesday the 19th of November, do you think?'

Anton mumbled, 'Maybe, yes, around about then.'

'I can confirm that your brother gave that date to the best of his memory.'

'That's what it will be then.'

'Thank you, and you say you spoke with the deceased, that you asked him to be more considerate as a neighbour, to keep the noise down that was coming from his apartment at night because it was disturbing your tenants who live below, is that right?'

'Yes, it was a polite conversation.'

'Did you enter Mr Lombard's flat at this time?'

'No, like I said, we just talked in the doorway, outside his front door.'

'This contradicts your brother's account. He said that Mr Lombard invited you in, that you had this conversation in his living room.' Summerscales looked pleased with himself.

Anton felt sick. 'I don't really remember… I thought we stayed at the door.'

'Have another think Mr Matheson, it was only three weeks ago, do you think you could try to remember it a bit more accurately, so that you're sure of what you remember?'

Anton sat in silence for a few seconds then said, 'I don't remember.'

'Very well. Would you consent to our taking your fingerprints Mr Matheson, it might help us?'

'I don't know… maybe,' said Anton.

'We can come back to that later,' said Summerscales, 'Did you visit Mr Lombard in his flat more than once?'

'No, just that one time.'

'Did you see him in the street, or a café for instance?'

'No, we didn't know him.'

'His solicitor-'

'-Solicitor? He had a solicitor?'

'I don't know about then, but he does now sir. Anyway, his solicitor alleges that her client was subjected to harassment by you and your brother, by, what she terms "unrelenting abuse" that she says led to his death.'

'Who by? Not by us.'

'She says by you sir. And your brother.'

'I don't know what to say to that, it's…'

'You didn't follow him in the street? Didn't constantly ring his doorbell from the entrance lobby? Knock on his door at all hours?'

'Detective, we didn't know him. We spoke to him once and we didn't harass him, he was quite capable of looking after himself.'

'If she's right-' Summerscales continued,

'-She isn't,' said Anton.

'If she is right and Mr Lombard was indeed subject to this unrelenting abuse that she speaks of, then it is possible that we could be looking at a charge of manslaughter, Mr Matheson.' Anton sat back, silently now, trying take it all in. 'Furthermore, she also alleges that a number of items of Mr Lombard's personal property are missing, that he had complained to his landlord before his death that he believed you and your brother were stealing from him.'

'I want that solicitor now please,' said Anton.

'Very well sir,' said Summerscales, again looking pleased with himself, 'we'll make the call. Interview suspended at 15.07, call to be made to the duty solicitor.' Trewin switched the recorder off, popped the memory stick out and put it in a small plastic bag which he sealed and labelled.

'What's going on?' asked Anton.

'I explained it to you Mr Matheson, we'll get the duty solicitor, and they will help you.'

'Am I under arrest?'

'No sir, we explained that as well. Your presence here is voluntary, we're very grateful.'

'Is my brother still here?'

'I'm afraid I don't know sir.'

'How can you not know? You just said you interviewed him,' Anton felt angry but was holding it back. Trewin leant over and whispered in Summerscales' ear. Summerscales looked up,

'I can confirm your brother left here about half an hour ago.'

'Okay, I'm leaving then,' said Anton, only half believing that was even possible now.

'Very well sir. Thank you for your help so far,' Anton stood and felt heady, he had to steady himself for a moment, Summerscales hadn't finished. 'We will want to carry on with this interview please, do you think you could drop in tomorrow? Same sort of time perhaps? We'll ask the duty solicitor to attend. Just ask for me if you would, please make it before 5pm, I go off shift at six.'

'Yeah. Okay,' said Anton and moved to the door. Summerscales gave him a smile again and Trewin led him out, back down the corridor, out into the entrance lobby and in sight of the front door. In the lobby, sitting and checking her phone was Valerie Atkinson-Pike. Anton saw her, went to speak but thought better of it; she looked up, gave him a half smile and a nod and went back to her phone.

Trewin left him there and he walked as slowly as he could manage through the front door and out into the cold air which hit him like a slap. He stood on the pavement, breathed deeply twice, and walked quickly away.

As he walked, he felt his phone ring in his pocket, taking it out he was unsurprised to see it was Neville.

'Where are you?'

'I've just left the nick, what the fuck, Nev?'

'Get home, we'll talk. How did you get there?'

'Bus, I just have to find a bus going back, they talk to you about unrelenting abuse?'

'Yep. Atkinson-Pike bullshit. Just get back here,' said Neville and hung up.

Half an hour later they were sitting opposite each other at their kitchen table, Malcolm had joined and was biting his nails while he listened.

'I assumed they were investigating our mate for, I don't know, drugs or something, he must have been into all sorts, I was just thinking we could look helpful,' said Neville.

'Did they say they were interviewing you under caution?' asked Anton.

'Caution? No.'

'Caution? What do you mean under caution?' said Malcolm, at the same time searching the term on his phone.

'They didn't say it was under caution,' said Neville, 'but they didn't believe a single word I said, they kept asking the same thing over and over. As far as they're concerned, we did something.'

They went over their interviews and compared notes, going over the points and finding similarities and worryingly, differences in their accounts of their encounter with Darren Lombard. Malcolm listened, weighing it all up. Both of them insisted they had done nothing wrong, there could be nothing on them, the whole thing was made up by Valerie Atkinson-Pike or Egerton… someone, presumably to put pressure on them to give back a bag they didn't have in the first place.

'It's a mess,' said Malcolm, 'doesn't help that you had different stories.'

'Yeah, why did you have to say we didn't go into his flat?' asked Neville, 'Now it looks like we have something to hide.'

'I assumed that's what you would have said, I didn't know you were spilling your guts out to them-'

'-spilling my guts? You twat.'

'Oy, stop now,' said Malcolm. 'Tea. Fixes everything. Put the kettle on someone,' he got up and looked in an old bread bin where there were usually biscuits, 'brilliant, who had the last of the biscuits?'

'Probably Neville getting his strength up to tell the policeman where the loot is,' said Anton.

'Don't push me,' said Malcolm, put the kettle on.'

'Why me?' asked Anton.

'Are you twelve?' said his father, 'Why not you?' Anton got up and went to the sink.

'Why don't I tell them about the holdall, about Atkinson-Pike, that we're the ones being harassed?' said Anton, 'It sort of explains everything.'

His brother thought for a moment and said, 'I don't know, they already believe Atkinson-Pike when she says we harassed him, she's a solicitor… it sounds like we're making stuff up to deflect attention… and we don't know how much shit we'd be stirring with Egerton. What's he like Dad? How well do you know him?'

'Not that well. Do you mean, is he dangerous?' Neville nodded, 'Maybe. I've known of him since we bought Beulah about ten or twelve years ago, he's a pain, doesn't pay the maintenance charges, that's about it. We need to stay away from any trouble.' He was quiet for a moment then looked up as the kettle switched off, 'Kettle's boiled.'

Anton turned back and poured boiling water onto the teabags, 'What should we do?' he asked.

Malcolm thought for a few moments. 'Tell the truth. Go back tomorrow, say you were nervous, being in the cop shop and all, say you remember now, you did go into the flat, but you haven't, and you never would have taken anything.'

Anton glugged a shot of milk into each of the mugs and brought them to the table. 'I presume there's no reason why you couldn't stick with the truth?' He looked at them both as Anton put the mugs down. They both shook their heads and mumbled *no*. 'I wouldn't mention the holdall, hopefully this Atkinson-Pike woman will find it somewhere and it'll all be over, she'll forget about you.'

'Hopefully,' said Neville.

'Yep,' said Malcolm and took a sip of tea, 'fuck, that's hot,' he said looking accusingly at Anton.

The next day, after training, Anton went back to the police station. Summerscales was apologetic, saying the duty solicitor was delayed but Anton said he was fine, on reflection, he was happy to carry on without them.

He resumed his interview under caution, tried to use some charm, said he remembered now that Darren Lombard had actually invited them in, but they hadn't stayed long. He explained his lapse of memory as being down to nerves, doesn't everyone who is interviewed by the police get nervous? Just being in this place makes you feel guilty doesn't it?

The detectives asked him again about how many times he'd met Lombard, but he stuck solidly with his story that it was just the once, it was the truth after all.

It slowly dawned on him that they had no evidence, nothing other than Atkinson-Pike's allegations and as far as Anton was concerned, she was just trying to turn the heat up under them, mistakenly thinking that would persuade them to hand the holdall back.

When it was over, Summerscales thanked him again, over-politely and then switched the recorder off. Anton said thank you and goodbye, they said they'd see him again. Anton hoped not. When he got to the street, he checked his phone, there was a text from Carol: *please call, urgent.*

15

She answered immediately, speaking close into the phone, 'I need to see you.'

'Carol, look, we agreed, we're not-'

'-I know we're not, I just need to see you, to talk. Can you come over?'

Anton was silent while he thought of a few good reasons why he shouldn't go but she sounded scared, anxious. She and Paul had both been through a lot, a nightmare… they were traumatised, he understood that much.

'Please. Come over.'

'Carol…'

'I know, I know… I'm not sorry about what happened, and I know we can't carry on, I know. But I really need you to come over just this once, please.' Anton didn't speak, 'Please.'

On the way there, he told himself he could resist, it didn't matter what she might say, he could say no, he was mature, he was able to say no, of course he was. By the time he reached Beulah Mansions, he had it all worked out: if she came on to him, he'd say she was a great person, beautiful too, but this was wrong, he didn't regret a single moment and they would still be friends, the mature thing was to stop though, think about their partners, think about how it might affect them.

The way it turned out was different. She looked nervous when she opened the door and asked him in; as soon as he was in the hall, she put the security chain on. He went to speak but she put a finger over his mouth. Her other hand was busy unbuckling his belt and pulling at the button holding his jeans together. She took the finger away from his mouth and used both hands to ease the jeans down over his hips.

He managed to say, 'Carol…' and she said,

'I know,' before settling on her knees in front of him, her hands busy. He looked down at her, watched her turn into someone he barely knew. She held him in her hand and looked up, 'I'm going to put this in my mouth, if you don't want me to, it's time to say so,' she said.

I'm only human, he thought, and offered no resistance. Being there, being in this situation he should probably just be a part of it, go with it, just do his best, no point in kidding himself, no point in pretending to be a reluctant spectator. *You're doing this, you may as well do it.*

'Just this time, this once,' he said. She even made a sound which sounded to Anton like it meant yes but in truth it could have meant anything. His ecstasy was intense and overwhelming and blanked everything else out. There was no thought of consequences, no obligations, nothing other than pleasure, giving and taking.

Afterwards, they ended up back on the sofa, he still a little shaken, she a different person to the smiling, quiet, gentle woman he thought he knew; she was hunger, vitality and not a little frightening. Once enough clothing had been clumsily removed, he gently kissed her neck, she moaned encouragement, and he went down on her. She cried out and held on to him, pushing his head hard onto her. When she came, she screamed like before, her screams turning to laughter as she slowly regained some degree of composure. He laughed too, it was funny: two adults, out of control, misbehaving and knowing it.

'Fuck me then,' she said and to his mild surprise Anton found he could. This time they did it with a measure of control, savouring the moment, taking a little time, still shutting out the rest of the world, at least for a moment.

Later, sipping white wine that had been sitting already opened in the fridge, they agreed again that this was once and once only, that it was truly amazing, wonderful, hot, and without regrets but not to be repeated.

'I needed something, it's been a hard few months,' she said, 'and you're more than something,' as Anton went to speak the doorbell rang twice, he jumped but she pulled him back down. 'It's nothing, it's not Paul, it'll be someone for upstairs, they still come round, not so much now but there's still the odd one.'

Anton looked at her, intoxicated by her sultry, flustered, half-dressed state. She smiled at him and poured some more wine, then lay back in his arms. 'Hold me some more.' He felt her head rest against him, her hair damp against his shoulder, he stroked it. 'When we did it, the first time-'

'-The other time,'

'The other time, yes… Paul and I made love that night. It was some of the best sex we've ever had.' Anton had no idea what to say so just kept stroking her hair, 'so you shouldn't feel bad about it is what I'm trying to say.' Anton was not sure what to say but thinking back, he realised that it was different for him, he'd gone out of his way to avoid Franca afterwards.

He left the flat an hour or so later. It had become a little strange once they had moved off the sofa. It was Anton who had finally made the first move, needing to pee and from the moment of his return things gradually became more awkward, they were more self-conscious, more aware, and back in the real world.

He had gathered his clothes and dressed without saying much. Carol made it easier by saying she needed to tidy up, she'd see him next rent day, 'I'll see you next year,' she joked. Anton found his coat and took time buttoning it up, finding it difficult to leave. Carol started to busy herself, taking the wine glasses out to the kitchen, puffing up the cushions.

'Okay, I'll see you then,' said Anton, moving to the door. Carol stopped him and kissed him, as before, as usual, a little chaste kiss with no meaning.

'No regrets,' she said.

'No regrets,' he agreed and left. He walked slowly down the stairs, still a little disoriented, elated and confused at the same time, not completely sure if Carol had been serious when she'd said it was a one-off. He reached the ground floor and the entrance lobby and checked his phone before setting off, there was a missed call from Franca. *There would be.*

He braced himself against the cold air outside and unlatched the front door; as it started to open, he felt pressure, there was someone there, pushing it and going for the gap. He stepped back and put an arm out as someone came in and tried to push past him. It was a young woman, small, with spiky straw coloured haired, she looked past him, but he blocked her.

'Hold it.'

'I'm meant to be here, I'm staying here,' she said, still not looking at him. Anton got in front of her and as gently as he could, pushed her back out of the door, 'I need to get in, I've lost my key,' she said.

'No you haven't, you don't live here. I don't know you,' said Anton.

'I'm staying with Darren, top flat,' she tried, now looking at him, reddish-brown eyes flicking across his face, 'please, I have to get in.'

'Darren?' he said, not looking forward to the next bit, 'When did you last see him?' By now he had manoeuvred them both out onto the street and pulled the door shut.

'Earlier, I'm staying here… please.'

'I'm afraid that's not true, I have some news for you…' He explained as tactfully as possible and as gently as he could manage that Darren was gone, as he did so she began to cry, tears at first, then more, she told him he was a liar and he quietly explained that he was not. She sobbed, then choked and cried some more, cries of genuine despair and anguish. Anton put his hand on her shoulder to somehow make her feel better, but her sobs just got louder, and she sounded like she was struggling to breathe. Passers-by looked at them, Anton assumed they would be thinking, what kind of person makes a young girl cry like that? He was also thinking that something didn't ring true: *Darren was a dick, surely nobody could be this upset at his demise?*

After a while, he suggested they go for a coffee, and he guided her round the corner to a café he half remembered. Finding a table as far away from other people as he could manage, he asked what she wanted. She didn't know so he suggested a cappuccino, she didn't answer but just nodded and cried, although quietly now, to Anton's relief.

He went to the counter, bought her a cappuccino and himself a large black Americano and looked round at her. Even without the sobbing she drew attention. She was all colour: a patchwork jacket of blues, purple and red, the kind that the more you looked at it, the more you had to look; a yellow corduroy skirt, dark purple tights, and bright red shoes. It was hard to see her face, she spent most of the time looking down.

'Here you go,' he said, placing the steaming cups down, 'this'll help. I'm sorry I had to be the one to tell you.' He braced himself for more tears, but she had steadied herself and just nodded as he spoke.

'What's your name?'

She sniffed and wiped her nose on her sleeve, 'Sedge.'

'Nice name. I'm Anton,' he put his hand out to shake, she looked at it for a moment then took it in hers and shook it weakly, 'pleased to meet you.' She looked into his eyes, working something out, maybe how much he could be trusted; her eyes were wet, make-up all over the place. Anton took a couple of the tissues from a dispenser on the table and handed them to her, she took them, wiped her face, smudging the make-up, then blew her nose into them and dropped them on the floor. Anton saw one of the counter staff watching and avoided catching his eye.

'Is it true?' she asked.

'About Darren? Yes, I'm sorry,' he took another of the tissues and handed it to her, 'your eye-' she took the tissue and dabbed at her eye which just seemed to make it worse, 'did you know him well?'

'I… sort of… love him, I suppose. Loved him. He could be a… but I do... I did,' she cried again but quietly, Anton kept the supply of tissues going. 'When did he…?'

'Just over a week ago. When did you last see him?'

'Same, I thought it was about a week ago. How-?'

'-I don't know, I wasn't there,' Anton not wanting to go too far into what he did know at this point. Sedge sipped the cappuccino, made a face, and added some sugar, she tried it again and said it was okay after all and took a few bigger gulps. 'Where do you know him from?' asked Anton.

'The Campus Bar, in town,' she paused and looked at him, see if he knew it; he shrugged his shoulders, 'It's really called The Lamb, it's a pub, we call it the Campus because a lot of students go there. It's nice, has a terrace outside looking out over the river, he used to drink there, he had friends there… me for one.'

'People there not know about this?' said Anton, worrying that if word hadn't exactly got out there might still be a string of people calling round for him.

'I haven't been there for a while. Other things going on,' said Sedge by way of an explanation, and finished her drink.

'Another?' said Anton. She nodded and he stood, bending down to pick up the discarded tissues which he bundled into a soggy ball and looked round for a bin. He went to the counter asked for the same again and asked if there was a bin behind the counter. The staff member looked at him as if to say *you must be joking* and pointed at a service point where empty cups and plates were supposed to be left, there was a bin there where he duly deposited the tissues then looked for a toilet to go and wash his hands. The nearest was an accessible toilet with a big wheelchair pictogram on it but he was in no mood to look further so he tried the door and found it was locked.

'You need a key,' said the boy behind the counter. Anton went back and waited for the boy to fetch the key but instead he just looked at him, 'You're not disabled.' *No, but you will be in a moment,* thought Anton.

'I just want to wash my hands.'

'What if someone in a wheelchair needs to go there?'

'I'll be one minute,' said Anton suddenly aware that Sedge was watching him and smiling. The boy behind the counter sighed, found the key, and handed it to him.

'Be quick, please.'

By the time Anton had washed his hands, there was a queue at the counter, and he had to push past the waiting people to get to his drinks which had been left on the top; the boy was serving someone else, and Anton leant over the counter and dropped the key on the shelf behind. The boy looked over and away again, really wanting nothing more to do with him. Anton picked the drinks up and went back to the table.

'So, the good news is, these seem to be on the house because biscuit boy behind the counter was so bothered about me washing my hands in the disabled toilet that he forgot to charge us,' said Anton suddenly slightly ashamed of his small mindedness. Sedge laughed though, which was a definite improvement.

'Serve him right, he's a twat,' she said, surprising Anton with the finality of her judgement.

A thought occurred to him, 'Do you know about a bag? A holdall?' she looked sheepish, caught his eye but looked away quickly.

'What bag?'

'A holdall. It's missing, you know where it is?'

'I didn't take it.'

'I didn't say you did, Sedge, but you know where it is?' He looked at her, trying to look her in the eye but she was hard to hold eye contact with, all nerves and evasion. 'Sedge, come on, help me here.'

'He asked me to look after it,' she said. *Bingo* thought Anton.

'It's all fine. You're not in any trouble or anything but people are asking about it,' he said.

'People?'

'Friends of Darren, people he knew. You know what's in it, right?'

She looked at him before replying, 'Do *you* know what's in it?' Anton thought for a moment then realised that he didn't have a lot of options other than the simple truth, he shook his head.

'No.'

She looked away again, he was losing her. 'Sedge, these people who knew Darren, as far as they're concerned, whatever it is that is in the bag is theirs and they want it back, and we should really try and give it to them. They're not exactly… friendly from what I've seen, we need to get it back to them.'

'We?'

'Yes, I can do it, I can get it back to them if you give it to me.'

'If I don't, will you tell them I've got it?' She looked at him, not trusting. He took a few moments to think then sighed,

'No. I don't even know who you are, apart from your name, but no, I won't tell them. You definitely have it, or you can get it?' She bit her nails and nodded, 'Okay, and it's a holdall, right? Beige…'

'Yeah, a holdall,' she said, looking at him, as if explaining to an idiot.

'What's in it, Sedge?'

She bit off a chunk of thumb nail and ground it between her teeth before answering, 'Money, mostly, and a couple of old jumpers…'

'How much?'

'I don't know, some.'

'Is it safe?' She nodded, thinking about it. 'Would you trust me to get it back to them?'

It was obvious that she wasn't sure that she would but there was another detail she hadn't mentioned yet, 'I had to take some.'

'Some of the money? How much?'

'Two hundred, it was exactly two hundred.'

'Pounds?' he asked, praying.

'Pounds, yes, of course,' the idiot thing again.

'Okay, we've got to try and put that back then, make it back up to the full amount so Sedge, don't take any more, right? These people are really going to want it all back.'

'Mr Brown?' she asked.

'Mr Brown, yes, I think he's one of them. You know Mr Brown?' She looked straight at him now and nodded yes. 'How about someone called Valerie?' She shook her head, 'Okay, but yes, Mr Brown certainly has something to do with it.'

'Darren was afraid,' she said, 'he thought other people were going to come for it and take it from him, he was scared of what would happen if he didn't get it to Mr Brown.'

'And it's just money, right?'

'Jumpers, cardigans…'

'Right, so we put two hundred pounds in and it's just as it was when Darren asked you to look after it?' She nodded again but looked down at the ground. Anton reached over and gently lifted her chin. 'We can do that and give it to Mr Brown, I've got his number.'

'I don't have two hundred pounds,' she said.

'I do. I'll do it if you bring me the bag. I just want this over and done with and so should you.'

'Why do you care?' she asked him.

'I'm just trying to put things right,' he said. 'How will you get the bag?' she was silent, 'Sedge, help me here, how will you get it?'

'I'll get it, I know where it is.'

'Safe?'

'Yes, it's with someone I know.'

'And they definitely won't take any more of the money?'

'No, I trust them, they wouldn't want to get me into trouble.'

'Good,' said Anton, 'we need to try and move fast, can we go and get it now?'

'Now? No, you can't come with me, he doesn't know you, won't trust you. I don't even know if *I* trust you, not sure why I should.'

'I'm just like you, I don't want any trouble either.'

Sedge sat back, looked at him and her eyes seemed to say, *just like me is not how I would describe you.* She told him she could probably get the bag back tomorrow or maybe the next day, end of the week at the latest, what day was it today? The weekend then, she could do it by the weekend. Anton asked for her number, but she said she didn't have a phone right now, so he gave her his number, wrote it on the back of a shop receipt he found in his pocket and made her promise to keep it safe. He also made her promise to call him as soon as she had the bag, by the weekend at the latest. When she got up to leave, he said it to her again, just to be sure.

'Please don't let me down Sedge,' he looked at her, hoping he could trust her, 'It's been nice to talk. I'm sorry I had to break the bad news…'

'Thanks for the coffee,' she said.

'Don't lose the number and don't forget to call,' he said as she left.

Anton stood to go, he was almost out of the door when he changed his mind and went back to the counter, he waited there until the boy he'd spoken to earlier was free.

'I owe you. You didn't charge me for a second cappuccino and an Americano,' he looked at the tariff on the wall, saw it came to £4.70, took out a fiver from his wallet and put it on the counter. 'Have a nice day now.'

He waited for Neville to come home that evening and told him about the day, missing out the having-sex-with-the-tenant-again bit. They agreed that it seemed like the police had nothing on them, so they just needed to sit tight and see what happened; Atkinson-Pike and co. were surely not going to bother them as long as the police were investigating. As for the mysterious

Sedge, if she really could turn up the holdall then in theory their troubles were over.

'Wait and see, yeah?' said Neville, 'Fingers crossed then. You going back out?' Anton looked at him, 'You know, see your girlfriend? Your *actual* girlfriend?'

'Um, I need to call her,' said Anton, wondering what he was going to say. He went up to his room to make the call.

'I've got a bit of a cold, that's all, it's nothing much, I just need to go to bed, get an early night, is that okay?' trying to sound slightly pathetic.

'Of course it is, dopey. Anyway, I don't want to catch it,' she said, 'call you tomorrow?'

'Yes, definitely, I'm sure I'll feel better tomorrow.'

'Goodnight babe,' she said, making him feel bad.

''Night,' he blew a kiss and hung up. He stood there for a moment then put his coat on and walked to the pub on the corner, it was never his first choice for a night out, but it was just right for moments like this. He bought a pint and sat at a table in the corner, thinking quietly to himself.

16

The business of the gym slowed down as Christmas drew near. The regulars kept coming in, working out as normal, but the other activities eased off.

The Boys Group took a break until the new year, something which bothered George who worried what the boys might get up to without the structure the club brought.

The more casual users of the gym fell away, many simply accepting the inevitable festive gorging before they would return in the new year to work it all off again.

Franny and Kirby, working to their tailored programmes, were allowed to slow a little. They had diets to follow which were not too difficult and allowed for a bit of fun, but not so much that they would have to waste a lot of valuable time getting going again in the new year.

In contrast, Anton picked up the intensity of his training, using it to clear his head and try and get some perspective. For a couple of days after he'd met Sedge, he hoped she would call him but then decided or maybe just kidded himself that she would take all the time she'd given herself, and call him over the weekend, as far as Anton was concerned, that would be fine.

It was the last Friday before Christmas and Anton was getting ready to leave for home when he saw two strangers walk in. They stood out: flashy suits and ties done up so tight they must have been choking on them. It would have been an understatement to say they looked out of place.

Dave went over, spoke with them, then led them to the office and left them there. They came out a couple minutes later with Barney and started making notes on a tablet, looking around and talking to each other.

Anton looked for his coat, forgetting for a moment where he'd left it, then as he put it on and was about to leave he saw a bright red dot of light on his leg. He froze and looked over to the source: one of the suits was using a laser measure and he mouthed *excuse me,* to Anton and politely gestured for him to move out of the way to let the beam hit the wall. Anton put his bag over his shoulder and caught Barney's eye as he turned to leave.

It bothered Anton that he had neglected his relationship with Franca, and he knew he needed to put some work in to try and make it up to her. He couldn't escape his guilt even though he kept telling himself that what had happened with Carol was just a momentary thing, it wasn't going to happen anymore. He needed to build things up again.

One way to start was to embrace Christmas, or at least Franca's vision of a family Christmas and it was becoming abundantly clear that only total commitment to it was going to be enough. It had been surprisingly easy to persuade Neville and his father to go along with it, they were even keen. Whether it was a memory of a time when the brothers had been children and their mother had been around or whether it was just a welcome chance to try something different and get a decent dinner, they had thrown themselves into the planning and buying with what looked like genuine enthusiasm.

Anton wasn't sure what to buy Franca for a present so he opted to go for two things on the basis that at least one would hit the mark. She wore a lot of scarves, wraps, cloaks, and apparently shapeless coloured swathes of cloth over her top half and would often be seen with many layers comprising many design ideas all at once. His conclusion was that a moderately expensive silk scarf would be a decent bet. He picked one he liked and tried to imagine her wearing it, which worked in his head and was therefore good enough.

When they watched TV together they joked about the proliferation of perfume ads that appeared in the run up to Christmas. The ads were alluring but Anton decided it would be more impressive to step outside the heavily promoted brands and took a trip to a department store where a lavishly made-up sales assistant all but seduced him whilst describing some of the possibilities she had to offer, spraying samples freely enough to make him sneeze a couple of times. In the end he opted for one that the assistant assured him was subtle but had a tasteful hint of luxury and, essentially, although not in so many words, would get *her* into bed if she were the recipient. Besides, it came in a velvet purple box with raised gold lettering which you had to be impressed by.

When he was with Franca, he became more attentive. He helped with preparations, listened to her plans, helped to put decorations up, and went to a local garden centre and bought a tree. He also made sure that Malcolm and Neville bought the right sort of wine and dug out some crackers they had in a cupboard which had been bought for the previous year but remained unused due to an excess of beer and a general indifference that had been the order of the day back then.

There was a general present gifting truce declared on the basis that most of the people who would be there didn't yet really know each other so it wasn't felt necessary to risk the potential awkwardness that may have otherwise resulted, although everyone agreed that little Gregory should get presents, a decision that pleased Neville in particular and allowed him to spend a joyful half day in a large toy department, trying out and choosing things that he thought looked like fun. Anton was grateful for this level of commitment from his brother but feared that the real motive, probably even unknown to Neville was that he was buying toys and games that Gregory would be compelled to share with him on the day and therefore there was an element of buying things for himself. *It's the thought that counts,* he reasoned.

With so much to think about, Anton had almost put Sedge out of this mind but by Sunday night she was back in his thoughts, and he started to come to terms with her likely disappearance.

'What do we do? Dob her in with Atkinson-Pike and co…?' asked Neville, 'if they still keep coming after us?'

'I don't know who she is, or where she lives, just her first name,' said Anton.

'They could probably find her, it's an unusual name,' Neville said, worrying Anton that he now sounded like he was ready to give her up.

'We can't do that to her, they could do anything, we don't know what they're capable of… I think ignorance is bliss, we just stick with: we know nothing, which *was* true, after all.'

'Yeah, was.'

'She might still call,' Anton said, unconvincingly.

On Christmas morning, Anton, Neville, and a suddenly nervous Malcolm stood at the front door to Franca's home.

'Are we going to have to sing carols or something?' asked Malcolm. The brothers looked at him then Anton said simply,

'No. Why would we?'

Anton rang the bell and Franca answered the door, she was dressed as an elf.

The brothers looked at each other again. Malcolm had been holding a large bunch of flowers which he not so much handed to her as inadvertently attacked her with them, thrusting them proudly forward and saying, 'Merry Christmas.'

'Were we meant to be, like elves or something?' asked Anton.

'No,' said Franca, struggling with the flowers and turning to go back into the warmth of the house, 'you can be whatever you like. I like dressing up, come on… its Christmas,' she said, leading them in.

'Ho, ho, ho,' said Neville, for no obvious reason.

The house was welcomingly warm, full of cooking smells and music from a radio station working through a Christmas playlist. Rosa came through from the kitchen wearing a bright red Santa hat and a huge smile as Franca made the introductions.

From out of nowhere, Gregory appeared, dressed as Spiderman. Neville stopped shaking Rosa's hand and looked down at the diminutive superhero; Gregory stared back, not sure what to make of him, then Neville extended his arm toward him and sang,

'Spiderman, Spiderman, does whatever a spider can,' Little Gregory was mildly impressed that this stranger knew the song and straightened his arm out toward Neville, palm upward. Neville just about had time to spot the tube running down Gregory's arm and out to his wrist and say,

'No way…' when a string of web flew out from Gregory's wrist, hitting Neville full on in the face and causing him to theatrically wave his arms in the air in defence. 'No way, you've actually got Spidey-web maker… you are the man, dude,' and high-fived Gregory, almost knocking him over in the process.

'Well, you've made my brother very happy today, thank you,' said Anton.

Neville had been carrying the bag of presents but was now fairly well covered in fake spider's web, so Anton helped by taking the bag from him and putting it in the corner of the living room, Gregory eyeing it up greedily as he did so.

'I'm feeling kind of under-dressed,' said Anton.

'We have hats,' said Franca.

'That's what I was afraid of,' he said. Franca frowned so he followed up, 'I'm kidding, bring on the hats!'

Neville had wrestled himself free of most of the web stuff and was still holding on to a bag with bottles in it. He followed Rosa out to the kitchen and took out two bottles of Prosecco which he said needed chilling. She took them from him and put them in the freezer while he put the other bottles of wine on the worktop, at the same time scanning the food that was laid out on every available surface.

'Something smells good,' he said, 'everything smells good.'

It wasn't long before Uncle Nico turned up, using a walking stick but somehow carrying yet more presents and a bottle of wine,

'Decent stuff, for the dinner,' he said, making the point that, whoever the guests were, it was he who knew the most about wine. Anton took the presents from him and added them to the pile in the corner before pouring himself more wine and making introductions.

It was clear that Rosa and Franca were not just expert hosts but were relishing the whole occasion. The dinner was admired, declared delicious by everyone, and devoured with no leftovers, Neville playing a major role in that. Even the turkey which was the centrepiece was stripped down to the bone, Franca having wisely removed the legs for later in the week before serving it. Hats were worn without the need for undue persuasion and the conversation was amiable and non-stop. There was a general feeling of relief that Franca's vision had been realised.

After the dinner and the clearing up which was supervised and undertaken by the men, most of them sat and slowly finished the wine whilst presents were opened and discarded wrapping paper coated the floor. Franca told Anton she loved her presents and put the scarf on there and then, keeping it in place for the rest of the day. Her present to him was a 1952 edition of Boxing News ("the World's Premier Fight Weekly") which had somehow survived more than sixty years and was presented in a plastic folder to preserve it. Anton took it out carefully and slowly turned the discoloured pages full of pictures of eager young men in various action shots and reviews of battles long forgotten, he kissed her and put it safely out of harm's way ready to go back with him when they came to leave.

Gregory and Neville took over the corner of the room with the TV and played Titanfall, one of Gregory's presents but one which Neville was keen to help him enjoy.

Anton noticed his dad in close conversation with Nico, so close it looked like they were even whispering. He took his glass over to where they were sitting and pulled up a stool to join in. They seemed to be remembering old times, people they had both known, comings and goings in the world of real estate. It was a surprise to Anton that it seemed to be such a small world. Inevitably, Egerton's name came up, Nico shaking his head disapprovingly at the mention of it.

'I stayed clear of the gentleman, I still would,' he said.

'He's been around for a while then?' asked Anton.

Nico nodded, 'He would have been a slum landlord in the sixties if he'd been in business then. His father *was* a slum landlord. Egerton copied the model, bought up cheap properties in the eighties and nineties, filled them with whoever was needy enough, students and the like.'

'Someone died,' said Malcolm, remembering, 'that's right, isn't it? One of the student houses, there was a death…'

Nico nodded, 'Monoxide poisoning, faulty boiler, nobody had bothered to service it, the thing pumped out toxic gas and one of the students died. Egerton got away with it, there was a court case I remember, but he got off somehow, I've no idea how. I hear he's got hotels now.'

'Hotels?'

'I'm not talking about trouser presses and in-room tea making facilities, I'm talking about cheap blocks made from big houses that are too big for normal families and can be divided up. He crams them full of whoever he can find, foreign workers, illegals, that sort of thing.'

'Illegals?'

'It's what I hear, I don't really know but it fits the pattern, find the desperate people of the day and put a roof over them, they become yours to live off.'

'Is he dangerous?' asked Anton.

'Dangerous? I don't know. My advice would be to keep your distance. He didn't used to have what you and I might understand to be a moral compass if you know what I mean.' Anton nodded.

At that moment there was a break in the music, and everyone became aware of the increasing volume coming from the TV where a now highly competitive game of Titanfall was at a frantic and violent stage, the screen was blood soaked as bodies were blown away by the unseen gunmen controlled by Gregory and Neville, the whole scene washed in fog and set in a futuristic dystopia with enemies around every corner.

'What exactly is your brother playing there?' asked Rosa, slightly hypnotised by the chaotic spectacle on the screen. Franca picked up the game box and read the cover.

'It's a 16 or over, he's bit young for it isn't he?' she said.

'You're right,' said Anton, 'Neville, stop now, you're too young for it,' Neville didn't look away from the screen but tried to apply some part of his brain to finding acceptable language to reply with, settling on,

'Naff off,' through gritted teeth.

'I think they'll be alright,' said Anton, looking at Franca who didn't look quite so relaxed about it,

'Five more minutes Gregory, then you take a break.' Gregory was silent, concentrating on the screen and still blowing away the bad guys. 'I mean it,' she said but no-one really thought she did.

'So, you two know each other a bit, from before?' asked Anton, returning to his father and Nico.

'Yes, we were remembering things just now,' said Malcolm, smiling and nodding but refusing to be drawn any further.

'Nico was saying he knew Mum… back in the day,' Anton said to Malcolm who had turned to look at Nico.

Nico said, 'No, I got it wrong. I was thinking of someone else… old man's memory.'

'Right,' said Anton.

'Any more of those mince pies son?' asked Malcolm.

When it came time to leave, Uncle Nico led the way. He decided it was late enough and he needed his sleep, Malcolm and Neville took this as their cue to do the same, taxis were called for and there were extended goodbyes. Most of all, lavish praise was once again heaped on the dinner and Rosa and Franca's expert organisation of the whole thing, everyone saying what a great day it had been, how they must all make sure they get together again and sooner rather than later.

The cabs arrived and Uncle Nico was waved off first. Anton had decided to stay with Franca, and he helped Malcolm out to the car.

'It's okay, isn't it? If I stay here? You're cool with that?' he said.

'Son, of course I am, I'm so knackered, I don't want to talk to anyone anymore tonight, I just want to go to sleep.' He put an arm round Anton's shoulder. 'She's a lovely girl, Son. You're very lucky.'

'I know, thanks Dad.' Neville appeared behind them, Anton added, 'Thanks for doing this, it meant a lot to Franca, her mum too, I think.'

'It was brilliant,' said Neville, 'we've got to buy that game, I need to practice… we could come back perhaps, and I could have a chance of beating the kid,' he said, only half joking.

Back in the house, Gregory, still dressed as Spiderman, had fallen asleep on the sofa and Rosa was on her way up the stairs when Anton came back in. She looked back and wished him a goodnight; he thanked her again and locked the front door. Franca was in the living room staring at Gregory.

'What do we do?' asked Anton, 'Can we leave him here?'

'No, you have to carry him up to his room.'

Anton woke Gregory who refused to engage any further than to blearily open an eye then close it again. Anton put his arms under him and lifted him up, he was lighter than Anton had thought he would be, and he easily carried him upstairs to his room where Franca took his slippers and socks off and put the covers over him. She switched the light off and went back downstairs with Anton where they sat together on the sofa, close together, contentedly going over the day.

'Just so you know…' said Franca, 'I love you - don't speak, I mean it, don't say anything.'

Anton pulled her in even closer and kissed her head. As instructed, he said nothing.

17

It was another three days before the call came. Anton was making a reasonably good job of looking like he was enjoying ice skating on a temporary public rink that had been set up for the season in the centre of town. Franca had decided that a double date with her lately neglected friend Sally and her new boyfriend would be a lot of fun. When Sally proudly introduced the new boyfriend, Anton had found him to be much like Sally: abrasive, irritating and a little dim.

'There's someone for everyone,' said Anton when Franca asked him what he thought and when they were out of earshot. The four of them joined the unsteady swirl of nervous skaters who were doing their best to stay on their feet and travel more or less anti-clockwise around the ice and Anton did his best to look as if he was having fun.

It was a relief when he felt the phone vibrate in his pocket and he made his way carefully to the edge of the rink where he found a railing he could cling on to. By the time he had extricated the phone from an inside pocket the ringing had stopped. He checked the number but didn't recognise it. As he was putting it back it rang again, same number,

'It's me, Sedge,' he didn't recognise her voice, she sounded far away, 'I've got it.'

'The bag?' said Anton, pressing the phone hard up to his ear. There was silence. 'Sedge?'

'I'm scared… two men came to the Campus, they were asking if there were any friends of Darren there, they had some news…'

'You didn't-'

'-No, I kept quiet, they didn't look friendly. I'm afraid, Anton.'

'You remembered my name.'

'You wrote it on the bit of paper with your number.'

'Okay, let's get the bag back and they'll go away, that's all they want, I'm sure. You trust me to do it?'

'I don't know,' she said, 'I don't know you.'

'Sedge, you met me, you talked with me. I don't know you either, but we seem to have the same problem, at least now we have the answer to it.' She stayed silent. 'You could give it back to them yourself, of course,' he said, assuming that was probably just about the last thing she wanted to do.

'You'll do it? You'll promise to give it back to them?'

'You know I will Sedge, I want this all to stop,' waiting for her to come to the decision in her own time. 'Where are you now? Do you have it with you?'

'No, don't come to me, I'll come to the coffee shop that we went to, around the corner from Darren… from where Darren used to…'

'I know. When?'

'An hour?'

'See you there Sedge. We're doing the right thing.' She hung up. Anton looked up at the slowly carouselling throng and tried to spot Franca. He could see Sally and her new boyfriend who was in the process of losing his balance and toppling forward, whirling his arms to try and get back up straight and somehow succeeding, making Anton smile and catch his breath; he hadn't breathed in for a while, having been straining to hear what

Sedge had been saying. Over to his left and just coming into sight, he saw Franca, she had peeled off and was moving out to the edge, heading towards him at speed and all of a sudden she was there, a gentle bounce off the side barrier and she came to a juddering halt hard up against his left shoulder.

'Well, hello,' she said, eyeing him, 'who was that?'

'One of the tenants, there's a leak, I have to go and fix it, it's an emergency,' she looked disappointed, 'I have to Franca, sorry, its water. I'll meet you all somewhere. Pizza?'

'How long will you be?' she asked.

'Couple of hours, not too long, I hope. I'll do it as quick as I can,' wishing he didn't feel the need to lie. 'I'll call as soon as I'm on my way.'

Franca said *okay,* looked a little gloomy, kissed him and went back to her friend who, by contrast, looked like she was having a whole heap of fun.

'Sorry,' said Anton as she skated away, and he left the rink to collect his shoes.

An hour later, he was in the café drinking a pot of tea. He checked his watch and double checked his phone to make sure the volume was turned up. After half an hour more, he was still alone, he had ordered a second pot of tea, checked out his social media, found a compilation of funny dog videos and was slowly coming to the belief that something bad had happened. It was another twenty minutes before the phone rang. It was her; he knew from the number, but she was just crying, trying to speak but only sobbing. He listened for a few moments then said,

'Sedge? What's happened? Hey, come on, everything's okay, I'm here. Sedge?'

She continued to sob then said, 'I'm sorry.... I'm sorry.'

'Okay... where are you now?'

She didn't answer but said, 'I haven't been able to put the money back...'

Anton breathed deeply and tried to sound calm and reassuring. 'That's okay, we can deal with that. I'll put the money in, I'll make it up. I need the bag though.'

'I haven't got it, I'm sorry….'

'Its fine, I promise. Just get to the café, with the bag, can you still do that?' Silence again, he hated these silences, 'Sedge, speak to me, how far away are you?'

'You promise?'

'Yes, of course I do, I promise. Everything's going to be alright. Bring me the bag and I'll make everything alright. Sedge?' She had hung up.

Anton sat back in the creaking wooden chair, checked his phone, and called the number back. As it connected, he heard a ringtone and looked up to the door where she stood, holding her phone in one hand, and in the other, a beige holdall with navy trim. For a moment he felt like crying himself. He went to her and helped her find her way to his table where he pulled a chair out and waited while she sat, then went to the counter to order a cappuccino and yet more tea, keeping an eye on her, and on the bag.

He looked around as he brought the drinks over. No-one was paying them any attention, they were anonymous. He coaxed her into giving him the holdall and looked inside: there were some thin bundles of £20 notes, counted into £100's and two or three dark coloured jumpers.

'This is it?'

'That's it,' she said, 'what were you expecting? I took two hundred, that's all, I had no choice.'

'I know, its fine,' he quickly counted the bundles without removing them then whispered to her, 'two and half thousand, is that it? All this fuss for two and a half grand?' She looked at him and shrugged.

'You promise you'll give it to them?' anxious now.

'Yes. I promise. I'll tell you when I've done it if you like, I've got your number now,' he showed her the phone. 'I'll call you, okay? Thank you for coming here. I'll sort this.'

She wasn't crying any more, but something was still wrong, he couldn't work it out as he watched her drink the cappuccino. She took a little while to compose herself and he waited before asking if she was going to be okay, if she had a way to get home. She said she was fine, could look after herself, then abruptly stood, said goodbye, and left, not looking back, just pulling her coat around her as she walked back out into the bitter air.

Anton finished his tea and left the café. He was conscious of the holdall, nervous of losing it now he'd managed to finally get hold of it. He hurried home, the burden of the bag and the biting wind driving him on. Once inside, he checked the contents of the holdall again, pulled out the money and counted it. Exactly £2,300 tied up in hundreds.

He found Valerie Atkinson-Pike's number in his wallet and called her, there was no answer, and he decided not to leave a message. He called Franca and found out she was still with Sally and the new boyfriend; they had finished at the rink and were heading for Purely Pizza. After hiding the holdall under his bed, he headed back out.

It was still early but had turned dark outside in the winter gloom. By the time he reached the restaurant, the others had ordered. Franca had made a guess and ordered him one with pineapple on the top to somehow complement the ham which was the featured ingredient. Anton was no fan of pineapple on pizzas and said so, Sally suggested he get a side plate and just put the pineapple pieces on that, which he did, smiling, trying to be friendly, trying to be sociable but finding it tiring to do so. Franca picked up on it, *of course,* and once the food was finished, said she felt tired, and it was time to go home.

'Good fun though, wasn't it?' said Sally, 'The skating… we should do it again.'

'Yeah, we should,' said the boyfriend, Anton had forgotten his name. Everyone looked at Anton, apparently it was his turn to say how they should do it all again sometime, but he couldn't bring himself to say it and just sat there with a fixed grin that said, *no fucking way.*

On the way home, Franca held his arm and pulled herself into him to get some of his warmth.

'Keith seems a bit…'

'He's a moron,' said Anton.

'…not the fizziest firework in the box was what I was thinking, but nice that Sally has someone.'

'She's a moron too,' he said.

'She's my friend,' said Franca, squeezing his arm to hurt him a little, 'what's the matter with you?'

He thought for a moment then said, 'Sorry, it's been a bit of a day,' he put his arm round her shoulder and pulled her back in, 'but she is.'

The next day, on his way into the gym, he called Neville and told him about the holdall. Neville was surprised that the mysterious Sedge turned out to be real and had actually shown up but also that the money or most of it was still there.

'You sure she only took a couple of hundred?' he asked, 'how would we know if she took more? We don't know what was in there in the first place, *I* wouldn't stop at two hundred quid.'

'You're not scared like she is,' said Anton. 'Look, I don't know for sure but that's what she said. I believe her, I believe her because she's scared of them, I had to promise her that I would put the money back in before I handed it over.'

'You're not going to, are you?'

'I flipping well am Nev, if it means peace of mind. If it costs two hundred quid to make sure we don't get any more visits from the Atkinson-Pike woman or Mr Brown, then yes, I'm happy to pay that price.'

'Let me call Summerscales first,' said Neville.

'Why?'

'See what the state of play is, see if they're still after us for anything. I think we should find that out before you hand it over.'

'Don't mention the bag though,' said Anton.

'Duh,' said his brother and hung up.

When he reached the gym, he worked out alone, using the time to think. He knew he needed to make things up to Franca and finish the business with the holdall. It seemed simple but he worried that things wouldn't easily return to normal, too much had changed. After working out for a couple of hours he started back home and saw he had a missed call from Neville. He called him back.

'They've put the investigation on ice, apparently, there's no real evidence against us, *as yet* as he put it. He's not ruling out something in the future, but they haven't got anything now. Tell you the truth, it sounded to me like they can't be bothered.'

'I'll call Atkinson-Pike again then. She didn't answer before, it's the holidays I suppose,' said Anton.

'What about Egerton if she's not there?'

'How do we know he's a part of this?'

'They all work for him, don't they? Only if you can't get hold of her,' said Neville. 'Just be careful, I really worry there was more money in there. I'll come with you, if you like, when you drop it off.' Anton said he'd think about that and thanked him for the offer. He rang off and tried Atkinson-Pike's number again, it rang for a while and this time went to voicemail, with a message saying she was away for the holidays. Anton hung up.

Over the next few days, Anton made a point of spending more time with Franca. He was careful to be kind, generous and considerate, as if he was still making a first impression. He was in love; he understood that much. This was unlike anything he had ever known before. She was mysterious, intuitive, and smart, always one step ahead. And she was all that mattered. He still went to the gym each day but for short, intense workouts, the rest of the time he spent with her.

As for the holdall, he checked it was there under the bed each day and decided to let the holidays end before he would call Atkinson-Pike again. He didn't fancy contacting Mr Brown and he was convinced that talking with Egerton was bad for his peace of mind so he persuaded himself that everything could wait for Atkinson-Pike's return, presumably in the New Year.

The day before New Year's Eve, Anton lay in Franca's bed letting the day start slowly. His phone rang. When he checked it, he saw it was his dad, he almost let it go to voicemail but answered at the last moment.

'Your brother's in hospital, there's been an accident.'

He was at the hospital within an hour, Franca with him. They found the ward and Neville's bed quickly; Malcolm was there, sitting and facing his son. He looked up at them as they walked in, his eyes red, looking tired. Anton suddenly thought to himself that he'd never seen his father cry.

Neville was lying half upright, the sheet covering his bottom half was lifted away from him, above his legs, on some kind of frame. There was a tube in one arm, bandages all over the other and one side of his face was bloody and partly patched with dressings, his eyes were closed.

'He's alright,' said Malcolm, 'he's alright. He's gonna be alright…' then quietly, 'he's alright.'

'He doesn't look alright, Dad,' said Anton.

'I'm here, you know,' Neville croaked and opened his eyes slowly like it hurt to do so. He saw his brother, 'Am I still beautiful?'

'You never were, so don't worry,' said Anton. 'What the fuck Nev? What…' he moved closer, to the side of the bed to get a clearer look.

'Hurts. To speak,' said Neville. Anton looked over at Malcolm who just shook his head to indicate he didn't really understand how it happened,

'He was walking along earlier, coming back from the shop, near to home. A car mounted the pavement behind him, he heard it and went to look round then wham, he thinks someone opened the door as it went past him, he was over, on the deck and that's it. Someone called an ambulance.' Neville grunted to indicate this was an accurate account. Anton looked at his brother who had closed his eyes again, he looked a mess.

'I'll stay with him,' said Anton, 'why don't you go and get a cup of tea?'

'No, that's alright son, I'm fine,' said Malcolm, missing the point.

'Go on dad, I've got stuff to tell him, I can sit and talk to him, he doesn't have to speak. You go and get a break.' For a moment, Malcom looked at him and looked as if he were about to ask something, but he decided it could wait and he just stood up to go.

'I could do with a cuppa, you want to come, Franca?' She said yes and followed him out. Anton pulled the chair closer to the bed and spoke quietly.

'Deliberate?' Neville grunted *yes.* 'Atkinson-Pike's lot?'

'Did you tell her yet?' asked Neville.

'She's away, I think. I left a message. Fuck it, Nev, I'm so sorry.'

'Not your…'

'I'll go and see them, find them, find somebody... put an end to it. Maybe she didn't get the message yet. I'll sort it…' He leaned forward and brushed some hair away from his brother's forehead, making him flinch, 'sorry…' he took his hand away but still felt the need to touch him so reached out and gently squeezed the shoulder of the arm without the bandages.

The day wore on. A uniformed PC came and took a statement which used up what little energy Neville had, and he fell asleep as soon as she was gone. Franca left them there and went home, Anton saying he'd call later. Neville looked like he was out for a while and the nurse suggested they go home and come back the next day.

'Why would this happen?' asked Malcolm when they were back home.

'I don't know Dad, it could just be bad luck, some little git playing silly buggers, there are some nutters out there.'

'You think it's got anything to do with this Egerton business?'

'Is it the kind of thing he'd do?' asked Anton. Malcolm shook his head.

'I don't know, I'd be surprised. I don't know. What did you talk about when I went for tea?'

'Just boxing stuff mainly, I'm helping a couple of the lads who are going pro soon.' Malcolm nodded to show he understood but he didn't look like he believed him.

Anton said he needed to go for a run, clear his head, Malcolm said he'd make some food and not to be gone long. Anton jogged away from the house, turned the corner at the end of the road and stopped to lean against a high wall that he often used to stretch his legs out at the start of a run. He'd found the scrap of paper with Mr Brown's number, but he called Atkinson-Pike first. Again, it went to voicemail but this time he left a message.

'It's Anton Matheson. I've recovered the holdall, we didn't have it before, but I tracked it down. I've put it somewhere safe. I'll bring it to you when you call me and say where.' He also rang the number for Mr Brown, but it just rang. *Atkinson-Pike should be enough* he reasoned.

The next day Neville was pretty much the same and not really all that interested in talking so they stayed an hour or so and left him to rest.

That night their New Year's Eve celebrations were subdued. Franca said she was fine with just going along with Anton and his dad to their local where they usually spent New Year's. Rosa stayed at home saying it wasn't her thing and she'd be fine, Franca said they'd have a glass of something later when they got back.

It was the rent run the next evening. Malcolm offered to go out with Anton and take Neville's place, but Anton said he'd be fine and not to worry, he could do it on his own this once. In all the years they had been doing this, there had never been any trouble and besides, January was always the quietest one, everyone was subdued, still on holiday from whatever it was they did.

'You never have any trouble but that might be because there are always two of you,' said Malcolm.

'I'll be okay Dad, really, I won't go looking for trouble.'

'Just don't,' said Malcolm, 'I'm a little on edge right now, as you might expect.'

Anton told him not to worry, he knew what he was doing and what about cooking up some dinner while he was out? It would be good to come back to something hot on a night like this; his dad said *Okay, that's a deal.* Franca had come back with them from the hospital, and she offered to hang around and help and they could have dinner together, the three of them when Anton returned.

He found his glasses case and put a thick coat on, Franca watched as he put his wallet and phone on the kitchen table, looked in the fruit bowl that sat on the table and was full of useful stuff, found the keys to the Outlander and said *see you later* to them. Franca asked him about the glasses case and made him take the glasses out and put them on, it was the first time she had seen them, the first time she even knew he needed them.

'Just for driving, to be safe…' said Anton, kissed her and left.

On the drive, he felt apprehensive. It wasn't good when things started to fall apart, when routines were broken, and it didn't feel right to be doing the rent run on his own.

The first stop was Neville's favourite: the student nurses or whatever they were. It was Neville's fantasy that they were student nurses, neither of them had the faintest idea what they actually did. Only one of the women was there when he arrived; politely, he asked after the others. They were away with family or partying still and she was enjoying the quiet. He wished her and her flatmates a Happy New Year from himself and his brother at which point she remembered,

'Oh yes, not with you today?'

'He had an accident; he'll be alright though.'

'Okay,' she said and immediately went back to watching the TV, not interested in any more detail. Anton thought to himself that he'd dress that up a bit for Neville, make out that she'd sounded concerned.

He got through the round quickly. Even the two couples who never quite seemed to understand the concept of paying in full and in cash had the money ready, everyone was just worn out from the festive season.

Arriving at Beulah Mansions, he wondered how tricky that might turn out to be, he hoped Carol would play it cool, no way would she have told Paul what happened. Hopefully.

Carol opened the door and let him in, looking past him, expecting to see Neville.

'I'm on my own, Neville had an accident-'

'-Oh, what? Is he okay?' she asked, genuinely interested.

'Yeah, he'll be okay, he'll live. No doubt he'll tell you all about it next time.' Anton moved away but she grabbed his arm and pulled him back and put her mouth to his ear,

'Did you get my text?' she whispered.

'No,' said Anton, 'everything alright?'

'Yes,' she said, 'just…' she put a finger to her lips.

'Of course,' said Anton. He reached the living room where Paul was gazing at a laptop and muttered a greeting without looking up; Carol went to the coffee table, picked up an envelope and handed it to Anton who quickly counted the money inside, signed the rent book and made a hurried exit. Back in the car he vaguely wondered what the text said but put it out of his mind, it could wait until later.

The rest of the round passed without incident, he told all of them about Neville's accident and wished them a Happy New Year.

As he parked the Outlander outside his home, he felt relieved that it was done, he could get inside and get warm. He took the box out from the back, locked the car and went into the house. He could smell cooking.

'Something smells good,'

'Shepherd's pie,' said Malcolm from the kitchen. Anton walked through and saw him at the stove, tipping something green into a saucepan, 'Everything alright?'

'Yes, no problems, here you go,' he put the box on the table. 'Where's Franca?'

18

'What do you mean she's gone? Where?' asked Anton.

'No idea. She just got up and walked out, didn't say anything.'

'Well, what was going on at the time, what happened?'

'Son, nothing,' said Malcolm, still busying himself with stirring vegetables into the saucepan, 'I don't know.'

'Tell me what happened, exactly,' said Anton.

'We were talking. Just chit chat, I can't even remember most of it or what it was about. She asked about your mother, what happened… she was playing with your phone,' Anton saw the phone on the table, more or less where he'd left it, 'it beeped, you had a message I think, she was looking at the screen for a few moments…' Anton picked up the phone and switched it on, the first line of a text message came up, it read:

Carol Morrison - Please don't say anything to Paul…

'What else?' Anton asked.

'She asked some weird questions, do you have a lucky number, when is your birthday…'

'You tell her?'

'Of course I told her,' said Malcolm, 'fourth of March, why wouldn't I tell her? She's probably planning to get you something.'

Anton felt queasy, swiped the screen and pressed in 0403. The phone came to life. He checked the texts and saw the most recent:

Please don't say anything to Paul about us I don't think you would but for my sake please let it stay our secret.

'She was looking at my phone?'

'Yes, she was playing around with it. I couldn't stop her, could I?'

Anton called Franca's number; it went straight to voicemail. He rang off, took two long deep breaths, and called again; this time he left a message,

'Hi, it's me. Franca, please call me,' and he hung up. He sat down at the table, feeling queasy, his stomach churning, and put his head in his hands.

'What's happened?' asked Malcolm. Anton looked up, angry with him but knowing it was unfair, she'd only asked what his birthday was.

'She saw something she wasn't meant to see.' Malcolm stopped what he was doing, came over to the table and stood across from Anton.

'What have you been up to?'

'Nothing. I haven't been up to anything,' said Anton, at the same time realising he wasn't going to get away with that, 'everybody has secrets, right?' He looked at his father hoping for an indulgent nod of the head or a word of encouragement but instead he turned away and returned to the cooker. Malcolm stood there for a moment, switched the heat off, lifted the saucepan and took it to the sink to drain water off then put it down, leaving the lid on.

'I just hope for your sake your secret is a small one, she-'

'-she what?'

'She doesn't seem like the kind of girl you want to mess around.'

Anton put his hands back over his face and said, 'Sorry. Sorry… it's not your fault.' Malcolm looked at him, tried to make it alright by giving him a grim smile then went to the fridge and pulled out two bottles of beer, took the tops off and put one in front of Anton. He stood back and took a sizeable swig from the other while Anton searched through numbers on his phone, picking one out and pressing it. 'I'm calling the house,' it rang twice, and Rosa answered.

'Rosa? Hi, its-'

'-Anton, she's not going to talk to you,' she said.

'Can't you just-'

'-Anton, you know what's happened between you, I don't. Do you think talking on the phone is going to sort it out?'

'Yes, I think it might,' said Anton.

'She won't talk to you. I think you should try again tomorrow.' She hung up.

'Shepherd's pie?' Malcolm opened the oven door and was inviting Anton to look inside and be impressed. Anton gave a short, pained laugh and said,

'I don't think I'm hungry.'

'Of course you are,' said Malcolm lifting the casserole dish out of the oven, 'shouldn't let this go to waste, it's not like I can rely on Neville to walk in pissed and hoover it up. Could take him in a dish tomorrow I suppose…'

'I'm sorry Dad, you have it.'

'I made a lot of effort here, when I started I was cooking for three…' Anton looked at him and felt bad.

'Alright,' he said, 'go on then, dish me some up.'

'I done some veg as well, keep you healthy,' he put the casserole on the table, put the greens into a bowl and brought it over. 'Grab a couple of plates, help yourself and then you can tell me just how much of a dickhead you've been.'

While they ate, Anton relayed the basics of the story, missing out the fact that the other woman was Carol Morrison but realising that leaving out that important detail made him sound even more feckless.

'Blimey, you actually are a dickhead,' his dad said.

'Thanks,'

'Well, explain to me why that's not the case,' Anton kept silent but also kept eating, 'she's beautiful, intelligent, as you say yourself, basically out of your league…'

'Dad, if this is meant to be helping me, it's not really and it's not as effective as this shepherd's pie which, I have to say now, is bloody lovely, thank you.'

'Thank you,' said Malcolm, not finished, 'I'm just asking, what did this other one give you that she doesn't? If I'm not prying…'

'You are prying, and I'd rather not go into detail if that's okay with you.' They carried on eating without further conversation other than Anton saying how good the food was. When they were done and two more bottles despatched, Malcolm was worn out.

'Maybe get an early night eh? It might all be better tomorrow; you can go and see your brother and tell him all about it.' As he was clearing away, he leaned across the table and ruffled Anton's hair, 'Of course, if you do, he'll probably just ask if it's okay if he asks her out now.' Anton looked at him and managed a smile. 'Come on, it'll all look different tomorrow.'

Anton slept badly, waking suddenly every few hours, the same thoughts, regrets, anxiety, sense of loss and terrible knowledge that there was no going back to how things had been before. At seven-thirty, he got up and called Franca again, it went to voicemail.

'Franca, please. Please just speak to me,' was all he could think of to say.

He went running to clear his thoughts but all it did was to give him a headache, so he returned home and called again.

'Go round there,' said Malcolm, 'not sure you have much to lose.'

'Think so?'

'I think it's your best bet at the moment, see if you can turn on some charm. Or something. I'll go and see your brother; you can come along afterwards. I'll tell him to be gentle with you.'

Anton walked to Franca's home. He used the time to think, he had to have a plausible explanation for Carol's text; that or come clean, tell her the truth. One thing he was fairly sure of was that Franca would sense if he were lying. Rosa answered the door.

'I'm sorry Anton, she doesn't want-'

'-It's okay, let him in,' said Franca, from somewhere behind her. Anton looked around Rosa and saw her at the top of the stairs. Rosa moved aside to let him in, he said *thank you* and started up the stairs. Franca turned away and went back into her room. Anton climbed slowly, he was halfway up when he looked back, Rosa had closed the door and disappeared. He was on his own.

Franca sat in an armchair, her legs crossed, elbow resting on the arm of the chair, her palm under her chin. She stared hard at him.

'I know what you saw. The text,' said Anton.

'And the explanation is…?'

'I made a mistake. I'm deeply sorry, I made a mistake. I let someone…'

'Carol,' she said slowly and with emphasis.

'She's called Carol, yes. She was in trouble, upset, she turned to me and… I didn't invite anything, she wanted to be comforted…'

'You didn't invite anything?' she paused, 'You were forced?'

Anton closed his eyes and rubbed his hand over them, 'No.'

'But you fucked her?'

Anton thought a long time before nodding his answer. 'But it didn't mean anything.'

'Oh, that's okay then.'

'Franca, don't make it more difficult than it already is. I didn't want to do it, I was in a situation, I didn't know how to get out of it.'

'Who is she?' she asked, not letting go.

'You don't know her,' said Anton, 'she was in trouble, she was in need.'

'She was very lucky you were passing by.'

'Franca,' he said, stepping forward and reaching out to touch her shoulder, trying to make some physical contact, 'I-'

'-Don't. Don't touch me, don't even try to touch me.'

'Come on, Franca,' he stood back and held his arms open, 'it's not carrying on.'

Franca stood now and took a step away from the chair, and from him, 'This happened once?' She turned and was staring deep into him. Anton drew breath,

'Twice,' he said almost immediately regretting it, but he'd become a little boy being made to confess and he was going for full disclosure.

'Twice?' she laughed, dismissively. 'Twice. You made a mistake, but then you made the same mistake again.'

'The mistake I made was doing it at all.' Franca started to pace around the room; Anton tried again to reach out and hold her, but she flinched violently away from him, hissing, her movement so abrupt his training kicked in and he switched his legs to a defensive position.

'Don't touch me. Ever. Ever... again,' she said in a tone he was hearing for the first time. She walked past him and into the bathroom, closed the door and he heard her throw the bolt. A moment later he heard a scream, a scream that came from deep inside her, a scream of rage, of frustration and of unfettered anger. He heard her stamp her feet and scream again, this time louder still. He backed away from the bathroom door and out onto the landing. He looked down the stairs and saw Rosa, he gestured to her, mouthed *sorry* as Franca let rip again. He stood there for a moment then slowly walked down the stairs, Rosa watching him, Franca still wailing terrifyingly behind him. As he reached the bottom of the stairs and looked at Rosa, she turned and opened the front door. He looked around and saw little Gregory further away, by the kitchen door, holding onto a soft toy, gripping it close to him.

Anton looked back at Rosa and said, 'Sorry,' she nodded and stood by the door.

'Goodbye,' she sounded final, absolute. He didn't want to answer, to confirm its finality, so just walked away with no plan, no destination in mind. He heard the door close and walked.

Eventually, he came to a bench outside an old pub that had closed a few months earlier, its windows boarded up, graffiti covering the brickwork and sat and watched the traffic go by, his mind blank, punch drunk and without any idea what to do.

After a while the cold began to penetrate his clothing, the wind had picked up and was getting into his bones. He stood and walked again, aimlessly, feeling numb. He tried to think but found himself just wishing he could turn the clock back, wishing he hadn't left his phone on the kitchen table. He wasn't far from the gym, so he set off toward it with some sense of purpose at last, heading for a refuge.

It was busy inside, buzzing, and welcoming. He tried small talk with some of the lads, hung out for a while and talked about who knows what, just passing the time in friendly human company. He checked his locker and found an old pair of running shoes in the back, they were worn but still useable. He grabbed the shorts that were always there and a T shirt that needed a wash but would do and changed into them, the shoes a bit dusty but surprisingly snug.

He climbed onto one of the static bikes and started to pedal, warming up for a short while then increasing speed and upping the resistance level. Soon he was cruising along at a supposed 40km/h and holding steady at close to his maximum resistance. He dropped the level a notch and picked up speed, his legs now in a rapid rhythm and starting to ache. He kept at the same level and pushed harder, not easing, not bothering with one of the programmed routes with its simulated hills and valleys, just keeping on at a constant speed. The ache in his legs began to turn to pain, his breaths were deeper and more rapid, his chest filling and emptying with a regular beat. He closed his eyes and focussed on the speed, imagining himself on a vast, smooth stretch of road, somewhere hot and sunny, no cars, just desert on either side, a few mountains in the distance, a cactus or two every now and again. He pushed harder still, eating up the road, the sun beating down on him and sweat now beginning to pour down his face; some went into his eye and it stung but he carried on. He was thirsty but he didn't want to stop or disrupt the rhythm. Soon his breathing was so loud that Barney came over.

'Son? You alright?' he asked, but he was far away, 'Anton…'

Anton left his dream and came back, opening his eyes to see Barney's concerned face. He couldn't speak so just nodded and gasped for air.

'Why don't you take a break, eh?' said Barney, 'Think you've gone off on one…'

He stopped and slumped forward on the machine, unhooked his feet from the pedals and just hung there for a moment, his legs dangling, pulling down, his weight all on the saddle which dug in painfully now, but he was too tired to move. Barney offered an arm, which he took and climbed off, hobbling over to a plastic chair where he sat clumsily. Barney pulled another chair up beside him and sat.

'You alright?' Anton nodded. 'Sure?'

'Yeah, sorry, I was miles away. I'm fine,' said Anton. Barney pulled his chair closer.

'I wanted to talk with you… we've got Franny and Kirby's fights coming up, could you help them? Spend a bit of time with them? You're here most days so it makes a lot of sense. I've put together a programme for them, well Dave's done Franny's but it's the same idea and they need to pick up the pace, get some regular sparring in, focus on areas that need work. Try not to knock them out, of course,' he smiled at Anton.

'Yeah, of course,' said Anton.

'Nice one. I know you've done a bit with Franny already. He needs to calm down and strengthen up, you're bigger than him obviously but it's all about stamina so you just need to keep him going and building up, we can schedule some regular times.' Anton nodded again thinking it was a good idea from his perspective too: it was a job, a project with a purpose and there was an end point. Time would pass and he would see how everything looked at the end of it.

Anton took a quick shower before putting his clothes back on, as he did so he checked his phone and saw there was a missed call from Valerie Atkinson-Pike. He rang her back and she was to the point. The holdall was to be delivered to her office; she would text the address. When he suggested he could call by tomorrow she replied that today would be fine. He was hungry and didn't exactly look forward to meeting her and definitely not on an empty stomach, so he made up a story about needing to go somewhere to pick the bag up and said he'd be there in three hours.

'Alright but try and hurry, I'd like to leave the office sometime this evening,' she said, as if it was him who was being unreasonable.

On the way home, he stopped off at a bank and asked for some twenties and a couple of paper ties to bundle them together, the clerk looked at him a little strangely as he was only withdrawing £200, Anton explained that he liked to keep things neat, and the clerk just looked pleased when he left.

He found Atkinson-Pike's office easily enough, it was in the City, on a street that exuded history, a history of law making and litigation, places where disputes were settled or perhaps fomented for gain.

Her office was behind a well-kept frontage which comprised a heavy oak door with a polished brass plaque displaying her name followed by "& Partners." He pressed the buzzer and the door unlocked. Inside, the receptionist, still immaculately made up and smartly dressed even at the tail end of the day, looked up and asked if he was Mr Matheson as he was expected. Anton confirmed his identity and stood while she made a call and let someone know he was there. He didn't wait long.

Atkinson-Pike appeared at the door and gestured for him to follow her. She led him to an office which was as slick and clean as the rest of the building, it smelt a little of wood polish.

'Thank you, Mr Matheson, I'll take that,' she said, holding out her hand to take the holdall. Anton handed it to her, and she took it behind the enormous desk and put it down behind her chair.

'Don't you want to check it?' he asked, disappointed.

'What for?' she looked at him, 'It's not mine and I have no idea what's supposed to be in it.'

'I assumed you'd check it, that's all.'

'You assumed wrong,' she said, already starting to get her things together in readiness to leave. Anton hadn't moved so she added, 'Thank you. Goodbye.'

'Don't I get a receipt or something?' he said.

Atkinson-Pike sighed, then laughed and said, 'A receipt? Hmmm, let me see now: we have a suspicious death, which you may or may not have something to do with; someone else's property which has been in your possession for some reason or another and that you've been withholding… and now you want a receipt?'

'I didn't withhold anything, I went out and found this for you, you think I should have taken it to the police?'

'I don't think anything Mr Matheson, except that you have returned some property belonging to a client of mine and I will ensure he gets it safely, thank you, that's it.'

Anton took out his phone and prepared to take a picture of the bag, sitting on the floor in her office, his proof that he had delivered as promised. Atkinson-Pike came out from behind the desk and put her hand over the front of the phone,

'You try and do that, and I will break your nose and destroy your phone… and remember please that I'm a qualified solicitor so one of the nicer ones involved in all this. Seriously, don't piss me off,' staring him out. He put the phone away, holding her stare but not feeling good about it.

'I want to know something,' he said, 'did you have anything to do with my brother's accident?'

'Did he have an accident?' she asked. He couldn't tell whether she was bluffing or not. 'Have a think Mr Matheson, do you really imagine I would be involved in something like that?' She turned away now and went to the corner of the room where there was a coat stand, took the solitary coat off and started to put it on.

'Are we agreed that's it, now?' he asked. 'This is the end of it? I don't want any more to do with this.'

'Go,' she said, 'you've done what you needed to do.'

Anton left but was irritated; it felt like he hadn't finished the job somehow, hadn't closed the whole thing down, it still felt like an open wound.

The receptionist also had her coat on and smiled weakly as he passed her and walked out of the door. He felt some small amount of satisfaction that he had kept them all at the office waiting for him.

He made his way to the hospital, guessing that his dad would have been there earlier. He bought some chocolate on the way thinking that would cheer Neville up a bit, food in general cheered Neville up, and one of them needed to be cheerful, it wasn't as if the new year had got off to a great start.

Neville was not just awake but apparently full of beans and although he looked, if anything, worse than the previous day, he said he felt a whole lot better. Anton commented that although the bruises on his face had come out properly now, he was no uglier than before. Neville let that go but chiefly because he wanted to talk about Franca.

'I can't believe you let her go, you are a proper dickhead you know.'

'Thanks, that helps. Dad agrees with you as well, exact words. It's good to know you can turn to family for help when things go a bit wrong.'

'Mate, the way I heard it, you managed to do this all by yourself, she just found you out,' said Neville, 'who was it anyway?' Before Anton could say anything, the answer came to Neville, 'No, no…. not…? You are joking, not your other girlfriend. Carol? I thought that was just a lot of kissy kissy… you didn't…'

Anton looked at him, he was looking way too pleased with this possibility, so pleased that Anton considered lying to him just to wipe the smirk off his face.

'Much as it pains me to say and much as it might amuse you to know it, yes. Carol. It wasn't my decision, she jumped me, seriously.'

'Oh, you poor lambkin,'

'Nev, I'm upset here, I'm suffering.'

'But you're getting a fair bit of action by the sound of it… well, aren't you?' Anton looked at him, 'Sorry, sorry. But, blimey, what was she like? Was it worth it?'

'I never meant it to be a thing, I never meant for Franca to find out, when she did. I just couldn't lie to her.'

'I'll be honest mate, you should have,' said Neville, doing the older brother bit.

'Well, thank you for that. A bit after-the-event, to say the least but thanks anyway,' he sat back, deflated then remembered, 'I bought you some chocolate,' he said, offering it to his brother.

'You are a star. I'm desperate for this, thank you, seriously, this is much appreciated. The food here is slop, really vile.'

'And you'll eat anything,' said Anton, cheered a little. Neville sat up and broke some of the chocolate off to eat, closing his eyes and savouring it. 'I'll say this much Nev, you are one appreciative dude.'

'It's bliss mate, thank you for this.' He ate in silence leaving a little for later then said, 'It's not really going to plan yet, is it? This year I mean.'

'Except there is a silver lining,' said Anton, 'the Atkinson-Pike woman got in touch, and I took the bag over to her this afternoon, just before I came here. I put the missing money back in it. It's over.'

'Hopefully,' said Neville.

'Yeah. Hopefully,' said his brother.

19

The gym was always busy at the start of a new year as lapsed members returned along with a handful of newcomers, all fired up by new year resolutions.

This time, there were clear priorities and Anton was happily drawn in to the effort to get Franny and Kirby to their professional debuts; for him, it was a more than welcome distraction. Furthermore, there was kudos for the gym; members going pro would always be a talking point and it gave everyone a boost.

He had his own fitness to consider as well. However painful things were regarding Franca, he resolved at least to stay in good physical shape, try to be positive. He was supported in this view by his father and brother who at various times would remind him that: life is long, is full of surprises, that there is always something or someone around the corner… what doesn't kill you makes you stronger… plenty more fish in the sea; clichés that were intended to be motivational, to help him carry on, even though they also felt compelled to tell him he was a dickhead at frequent intervals as well.

Despite his troubles, Anton was ready to work, and he arrived at the gym in a mood that, if not exactly positive, was at least willing. He had jogged there through the first snow of winter, not much more than a light dusting but it was enough to settle and whitewash the streets.

Barney wanted Anton's immediate focus to be on Franny

and the first step was to get him back into shape after the holidays. Franny didn't have a weight problem, but he did like a drink at Christmas, and it was going to take a few days to get him ready for the serious part of his run in. As lead trainer, Dave was grateful for Anton's help, grateful in particular for the consistency that he would be able to offer, he could get close to him, get inside his head and work with him on the crucial technical aspects of Franny's game. Anton would also help with taking his blood pressure and heart rate and tracking them, something he would need to do before and after his sessions.

That first day back and after warming up, Dave ordered a sparring session of six rounds to start the day off.

'No-one's trying to hurt anyone, right? It's about tippy tappy punches right now, keep it all moving…' he said, stepping out of the ring to watch.

Anton was bigger all round than Franny, so it was up to him to keep things calm, but he knew enough to be able to move him around so they both worked up a sweat. Dave took a lot of notes and Anton made a few mental ones of his own.

At the end he helped with checking Franny's heart rate and blood pressure and entered the results on a chart that Dave had created which mapped everything out, all the necessary elements leading up to the big day: stamina tests, technical training, diet, weight, lung and heart functions, recovery times and more, all recorded on a GANTT chart, the whole thing planned out to the end which, at this point, still seemed a long way off.

Kirby too was on a path to his professional debut and Anton knew that Barney would have worked everything out for him, right down to every last detail of a carefully controlled programme. Having let himself be talked into helping Kirby as well, Anton wondered how that first sparring session was going to go. He wasn't exactly dreading it, but he wasn't looking forward to it either, his hope was that Barney would think of something to make it less awkward than it might otherwise be, for both their sakes.

Once his shift with Franny was done, Anton took over on the first Boys Group of the year. Numbers were good given it was the first week back, they always grew as the terms went on, but it was noticeable how many new faces there were. Anton wondered what happened to the ones who didn't reappear, knowing there were all sorts of reasons for it, from families breaking up and moving to being accepted finally at a school or being sent to an institution. Some would just have lost interest, found it required too much effort to come out in the cold. He knew that the numbers would likely grow over the coming weeks, to include one or two slow returners who found themselves missing the camaraderie and realising they needed to get out and away from wherever they were.

Barney had been in charge of the Boys Groups from the start and had been the one who persuaded George that they were a good idea. He had gradually expanded the range of activities on offer over the years, even adding an art class recently which he had gambled would be sufficiently different to draw in the curious. It didn't hurt that the tutor was a thirty-something woman who dressed to be noticed and swore freely; she was a practising artist whose guiding principle was that the whole thing should be fun, and she positively encouraged them all to believe they were inherently creative and could make something, even if wasn't necessarily Art.

It was well into the afternoon before Anton finished up at the gym and despite all the distraction his mind wandered back, unavoidably to Franca. He thought vaguely about calling her but knew there was no point. Instead, he went to the hospital where Neville was celebrating the news that he was likely to be discharged the next morning, albeit on crutches, but it meant freedom and above all, decent food. Anton agreed he would come over with the car the next day and pick him up, Neville extracting a promise that they would stop off at a greasy spoon on the way home.

He decided to walk home from the hospital, it was a long way, but he wanted time to think. There had been no more snow and the fall from the night before had melted away, but the wind gave the cold air some bite, so he pulled his coat tight, put the hood up and all but disappeared into it, letting thoughts of Franca just drift in and out. He decided to walk past Purely Pizza just in case she was there although he had no plan ready if she was. In the event, Franca was nowhere to be seen but Sally and her dimwit boyfriend were there. Anton went inside when he saw them then didn't know what to say, so just said,

'Alright?' Sally nodded, her mouth full of pizza, her boyfriend looked to her for a cue then looked back at Anton and did the same. Anton stood at their table with his hands in his pockets. It was a Wednesday and no chance of food at home so he ordered a pizza to go and wondered what to do next, the choices being: stand at the counter awkwardly and look at his phone pretending there was something important to deal with or go and talk to Sally, which was the more normal thing to do and, he reasoned, when Sally reported back to Franca, he would sound like he was holding it together.

'She doesn't want to talk to you,' said Sally as soon as he arrived back at the table. *She was a bit too pleased with that.*

'That's okay, I know, thank you. How are you both?' he asked, now wishing he had opted to read that interesting thing on his phone.

'We're fine thanks, Franca's fine too,' said Sally smiling, showing scraps of tomato on her teeth.

'Good,' said Anton, 'send her… say I said hi, will you?'

'She won't care, she's got a new boyfriend anyway,' said Sally. Anton looked at her.

'We only broke up a couple of days ago…'

'She's very popular when she wants to be, boys will always chase after her.'

'Umm, yes, good,' he said, thinking to himself she was almost certainly lying, presumably in her mind she was getting revenge on her friend's behalf. He looked at her boyfriend who had a mouthful of pizza and clearly didn't want to engage, so he looked back at Sally. 'Well, enjoy your pizza. It's been a pleasure,' he said as he walked back to the counter.

'I'll tell her we saw you,' said Sally. *I bet you will,* he thought.

The next day, he was at the gym when it opened. Inside, Kirby was somehow already there, well into a session on a rowing machine. His apparently supernatural ability to pass through locked doors no longer bothered Anton who just accepted that it happened and no longer really questioned how.

Neville had called earlier from the hospital to confirm his imminent release, so Anton wanted to get on with things and get over there for lunchtime. He was quickly into a testing warm up routine, push ups, burpees, press ups and squats all in groups of ten followed by some high-speed skipping so that within thirty minutes he was beginning to sweat and was well and truly in the groove.

His plan was to spar with Franny then go and liberate his brother. Dave came over to brief him on the day's objectives. They had worked on some new ideas the previous afternoon, Franny needed to try them out; it meant repetitive work, trying the same moves over and over. That was all fine with Anton, he was more than happy to work to some fixed routines, it didn't require too much thought, just a willingness to knuckle down and get on with it. As a result, the morning flew by, and he was soon on his way to rescue his long-suffering brother.

By the look of him, Neville had been waiting for some time. Anton got to the hospital around noon and found his brother sitting outside the ward, in the corridor, his bed already taken by the next patient. He was dressed and ready to go, a state he'd been in since breakfast. He'd been formally discharged; a nurse had run through his medication, and another had instructed him in the safe use of his crutches. When he saw Anton, he looked up and said pathetically,

'Lunch. I'm begging you…'

Anton helped him to his feet and into the coat he'd brought with him. Neville put his arm around his brother's shoulder and got to his feet.

'You alright?'

'Apart from chronic hunger, yes,' said Neville. He was still unsteady on his feet, his left leg had suffered some muscle damage and even though no bones were broken, some flesh had been scraped away and there was a bruise that he promised to show off later at home; it was one of those bruises that needed to be photographed for posterity.

At the front, the automatic doors swished open to let in a wave of freezing air.

'Wait here, I'll bring the car closer,' said Anton, 'car park's miles away.'

'Did you bring…?'

'Certainly did,' said Anton, knowing he loved that Outlander.

Neville huddled inside and waited until Anton returned a few minutes later, leaving the engine running while he came inside and helped his brother out.

'Ask me how much it costs to park here,' said Anton.

'How much does it cost to park here, young bro' of mine?' said Neville.

'Five pounds flipping fifty, I've been here about ten minutes.'

'Well, if it's any help, its much appreciated,' said Neville, wondering what point his brother was trying to make.

'It's not a problem mate, but that's ridiculous, they always want more money.'

'I'll tell you one thing for sure and that is they don't spend it on the food.' Neville had made it to the Outlander, and immediately, he felt better there, even in the passenger seat; it was home, and it was his ride to freedom. He remembered a place nearby that cooked excellent all-day breakfasts and navigated their way.

They ordered two full Englishes with fried eggs, brown toast and tea, the toast being brown making it a nod to healthy eating. Neville was nothing if not a grateful eater and he made it clear this was in the premier league of breakfasts. Once his little moans and cries of ecstasy had calmed a little, Anton asked,

'Did the cops ever come back to see you?'

'Nah. They haven't got a clue. No-one witnessed it and I was too shocked to get the number of the car, they have nothing to go on. They'll just put it down to a random hit and run.'

'What do you think? Do you think it was just a random hit and run?' asked Anton. Neville was still relishing the food but replied with a shake of his head.

'I'm just pleased you got the bag back to them, thanks for doing that. Do you want that black pudding?' He didn't wait for an answer but just hooked the dark and speckled circle off Anton's plate, knowing his brother hated the stuff. The café offered free refills of tea and it was during their second refill that Anton's phone went. He took it out and they both saw the name on the screen: *Carol Morrison.* Neville started to say something, but Anton swiped the screen.

'Hello?'

'I need you to come over,' she sounded different, detached, strange.

'Carol, we talked about this. I can't. It has to be over,' said Anton.

'It's not about that, it's something else,' she spoke slowly, and he got the idea that she was checking out what she was saying with someone else, 'there's someone who wants to talk with you.'

'Is he there? Put him on,' said Anton.

'He needs to see you in person,' she said.

'Is it Paul?'

'-No,' she said quickly, 'nothing like that. Its…' he imagined her looking at whoever it was, asking permission, 'it's Mr Brown, the man I told you about, the friend of the man upstairs… who used to be upstairs,' she paused. Anton put her on hands-free, 'he says you need to come over or there… he says you need to be here within an hour or… I'm just telling you what he's told me to say. You can't tell anyone, you mustn't tell anyone. Anton, please come,' she sounded frightened now.

'I'll be there, just tell him to wait,' said Anton and rang off. They sat back and looked at each other before Neville said,

'You're not going?'

'I have to, he's threatening her. He's not going to go away; I have to go and see what he wants. Maybe he doesn't know I took the bag back.'

'I'll come with you.'

'I don't want to be rude or seem ungrateful Nev but you're not really in a fit state.'

'I'll wait for you in the car. Call you every five minutes, check you're okay.' Anton nodded, that made some sort of sense. They drove to Beulah Mansions, at first in silence.

'It's got to be the money, right?' said Anton, his brother nodded, 'must have been more in there than Sedge let on.'

'How much more though?' asked his brother, Anton just shrugged.

He parked a few doors away from the house, they looked up at it, everything looked normal. Anton unbuckled and started to get out.

'Be careful,' said Neville, 'I'll call every five minutes, you don't answer, I call the police, yeah?' Anton nodded in agreement, checked the volume on his phone was up and left, crossing the road before walking up to Beulah *flipping* Mansions. The way it looked, if the missing money were more than a grand or so, they were not going to be able to make it up and they'd have to go to the police. *Then what? What were the consequences of that?*

He let himself in the front door and climbed slowly to Flat C. Everything was still, there was no sign of anyone. He knocked on the door. Carol answered, opened the door just a little, she looked scared. Behind her in the hallway was a man: thirties, good suit, not very tall but bulked up, *middleweight,* thought Anton. The man stayed looking at the back of Carol's head. She didn't speak but gestured, pointing upwards to the floor above. Anton looked up but saw nothing. She pointed again, with her thumb. He stepped back and looked up the stairs, the door to Flat D was open. From inside, he heard a man's voice,

'Come on Anton, up you come.'

Anton started up the stairs again, slowly now. He looked down and Carol was looking out of her door, watching him. He heard the voice again,

'Come on, hurry up, haven't got all day…'

He reached the door to Flat D and pushed it open further, he could see someone standing halfway down the corridor, he was short, balding, round face, probably older than the one downstairs and this one was overweight, he was wearing a beige overcoat, and his hands were in the pockets.

'Here he is, the funny man, come on come on in… funny man. Funny, funny man,' Anton was inside now and walking towards him. From the living room another man came out into the corridor, just ahead of Anton who stopped when he saw him. This one was bigger, heavy set again, shaved head, same style of well-cut grey suit as the middleweight downstairs, *a heavyweight for sure.* He walked toward Anton who braced himself and took up a defensive stance, but he just walked past him and stood by the entrance door, blocking it.

'You Mr Brown?' asked Anton, trying to sound like he wasn't scared of him. Brown nodded and rubbed his chin with his hand.

'Where is it, Anton?' asked Brown.

Anton's phone rang, he took it out of his jacket, Brown stepped forward and held the palm of his hand up to signal he shouldn't answer.

'If I don't answer, the police come here,' said Anton. Brown stood watching him, saying nothing while Anton swiped the screen, 'Hello? Yes, it's alright. Tell you what, make it every three minutes, okay?' He hung up.

'I said not to tell anyone about this,' said Brown.

'It's just a friend, my insurance, making sure everything stays cool.'

'Don't be silly Anton, you've done the funny guy bit, played the trick, now tell me where it is,' said Brown.

'I don't know what you want, and I don't know what *it* is,' said Anton, looking round, aware now that the heavyweight was making his way back from the door, along the corridor towards him, 'I found the bag and I've handed it over, even though I didn't take it in the first place. I just went out and found it for you, for Egerton, for whoever it is that it belongs to. I don't want anything more to do with it. The person I got it from said there had been two and a half grand in it, nothing more, that's what I was told.' Brown just stared at him, listening. 'How much should be in there?'

Brown raised his chin and gave a little nod and Anton caught a glimpse of the heavyweight behind him before his right arm was pulled round his back and a fat arm folded around his neck, holding him firmly in a headlock. Anton tried to work out what damage he could do with his legs which were still free, he could almost certainly manage to land a painful kick on Brown but that wasn't going to release him from the heavyweight's grip.

Brown came right up close and said to him, 'One more time, where is it?'

'Tell me how much is missing, and I'll sort it,' said Anton, trying his best to sound in control. Brown sighed and walked away, disappeared into the kitchen for a moment before coming back out holding a large set of bolt cutters: three feet long handles and polished steel jaws. Brown looked at him, Anton lost control of his bladder and it emptied down his leg, quickly soaking through his trousers which Brown could hardly have missed.

'Oh Anton. Not so funny now eh? You're right to be scared though,' Brown walked up to him and went through his jacket pockets until he found Anton's phone, 'I'll help you when he calls, you can tell him you're fine.' With his free hand Brown found his own phone and made a call, 'Get up here, make sure she knows not to do anything silly,' he rang off and put it back in his pocket and stood waiting.

Anton's phone rang. Brown looked at the screen, 'Neville, ah, how nice. How's he doing after his accident?' Brown swiped the screen and held the phone to Anton's mouth.

'Everything's fine, Nev,' he said.

'What's happening there?'

'Just talking with Mr Brown.'

'Everything's cool?'

'Everything's cool,' said Anton as the door behind him opened and he was aware of the middleweight from downstairs walking in.

'Ah, fuck it,' said Brown and took the phone away from Anton and spoke into it, 'listen to me, your brother's okay at the moment, you do anything stupid like call the police or anything like that and he won't be, we'll start snipping bits off him, you understand?'

There was silence then Neville said, 'Yes.'

'Good… he'll call you shortly, don't be dumb,' he switched the phone off, threw it over his shoulder and spoke to the middleweight,

'Shoes, socks… in fact, take his trousers off,' Anton was easily overpowered by the two of them and was soon standing, still in a headlock, in his underpants and with bare feet.

'He's pissed himself,' said the middleweight.

'He's not stupid, he knows to be scared,' said Brown, 'toes first.' The middleweight picked up the bolt cutters and tried clumsily to place the jaws around Anton's foot, but he thrashed about enough to make it impossible. The middleweight stood up and punched Anton in the face which stopped him.

'Not too much,' said Brown, 'don't want to mess him up for his girlfriend downstairs.'

'She's not my girlfriend,' said Anton.

'What?' said Brown, 'so when you come over here, when the old man's out and she does all that, "oh, oh, oh, oh God, yes"... you know what I'm talking about, that isn't because you're slipping her one? What are you two doing then, dubbing a porno?' Brown stood on Anton's left foot and lifted his right leg into the air, immediately stopping all resistance, the heavyweight leaning back to take the weight, effectively disabling him. The middleweight tried again with the bolt cutters. 'Little toe first,' said Brown, 'amazing how much you need it, but you don't realise it until it's not there,' the jaws were now around Anton's little toe, and he felt the steel cutting edge against his skin. 'Last chance...' Anton tried to struggle but couldn't move, the middleweight looked up at him and gave him a big smile as he got ready to squeeze.

Anton was close to hysterical and shouted, 'I don't know... I don't know... I don't know, tell me how much and I'll get it.'

Brown came up close to him and spoke quietly. 'You are dumb. Or brave, but I don't think you're that brave so, it has to be dumb.' Brown paused, waiting to see if he got a response, 'It's not how much, it's what.'

'What?' asked Anton.

'Precisely. What. What's missing is a laptop. An especially important laptop computer.'

'I don't know anything about a laptop,' Anton shouted, his throat now hurting from a combination of his shouting and being in a headlock for so long. Brown brought his face up, right up close to Anton's and looked into his eyes, breathing slowly in and out a couple of times while Anton gasped and gulped air painfully down his throat.

'You know what?' said Brown, 'I actually believe you. Might take a toe anyway, just while we're here-'

'-No,' screamed Anton. The middleweight left the bolt cutters there for just a few seconds more then took them away, chuckling.

They let him go and he fell to the floor.

'Now you see, you're not the only one who likes a laugh,' said Brown. Anton knelt on the floor, holding his left foot which was bleeding from the weight of Brown's boot. Where did you get the bag from?'

'I got lucky,' said Anton.

'Get lucky again. I'll give you three days,' said Brown. He reached inside his coat and found an envelope which he opened and took out a folded sheet of paper.

'It might be a long way away, I might need longer,' said Anton, thinking he had no idea how to do this, 'I'll get it…' he wiped his nose and saw blood on his hand. 'How was I supposed to know there was a laptop in the bag?'

Brown looked down at him, 'It was wrapped in a couple of jumpers, probably had a proper case once but there you go,' he wrote a number on the back of the paper and handed it to Anton. 'Call me when you have it,' Anton started to fold the paper, but Brown stopped him, 'go on, have a look,' he said, allowing himself a little chuckle.

Anton turned the paper over and saw a picture of his father, underneath was their address, below that, a picture of Franca and little Gregory and their address, then the address of George's Gym, there was even a picture of the pub where his father played snooker.

'Seriously, don't be stupid. I really am very happy to start snipping bits off.' Brown stepped back and spoke to the others, 'Let's go.'

'How did you know about Carol… and me?' said Anton.

'We bought the flat below, and the one on the ground floor, one of our people heard you, you weren't exactly discreet. Three days,'

'I may need a week,' said Anton.

'And I said three days. Pull the door to when you go, will you?' They left with Anton still kneeling on the floor, trouserless and holding the piece of paper. He stayed there for a while, listening, fearing their return.

His phone rang, he could see it on the floor and crawled toward it. It stopped before he got there but rang again immediately and this time he answered.

'You alright?'

'Just about.'

'Three of them just left. I'm guessing the one in the beige raincoat who doesn't actually look like a wanted poster is Mr Brown.'

'Good guess. I'm coming down,' said Anton sounding and feeling fragile.

He looked around for his trousers which had been flung along the corridor and crawled toward them. He realised he was close to tears, more than that, he wanted to cry. There was no-one else there, so he let it happen: a release, a mixture of fear, anger and despair. Half an hour ago, everything was all sorted, now people he cared about were in danger. He let the tears come, shocking himself with how good it felt. Eventually, he was done, and he sat on the floor, pulled his trousers back on and stood. Although his foot still hurt, the damage wasn't so bad that he couldn't walk on it. He found his socks and shoes and gradually composed himself, ready to join the world outside again.

As he left, he closed the door behind him and started down the stairs, tentatively at first then with a little more confidence.

He had feared there were broken bones in his left foot but that didn't seem to be the case. When he reached the landing outside Flat C, the door opened and Carol looked out, still wary.

'It's okay, they're gone,' said Anton.

'You alright? Should I call someone?'

'Yeah, I'm fine, No, don't call; everything's fine,' he said, trying to sound chipper.

'We might move out. Sorry,' said Carol. Anton just nodded and carried on down the stairs. When he reached the street, Neville was standing by the front door, leaning on his crutches.

'I tried to come up,' he said.

'I'm glad you didn't, it would have been worse. Anyway, you can't do stairs, you're basically a dalek.'

They turned and walked slowly back toward the car.

'The state of you, mate,' said Neville, 'you alright to drive?'

'Yeah, I'm just a bit shaky tell you the truth. I'll be alright in a minute.'

When they were back in the warmth of the car, Anton went through what had happened, trying to piece it together in his own head at the same time, everything seemed unreal.

'Whatever you do,' said Anton, 'don't tell Dad, he'll say we should go to the cops.'

'Shouldn't we?' his brother asked. They sat in silence thinking, Anton aware that he'd started biting his nails, something he hadn't done for years.

'Not if we can actually find the laptop,' said Anton, 'that has to be the best way,' he found the folded piece of paper in his pocket and handed it to Neville. 'If we go to the police, they'll come for us, or Dad, or Franca…'

Neville unfolded the paper and stared at it with horror. 'Okay. Ideas?'

'Sedge. It has to be her,' he took his phone out and looked

back through his call history. 'She called me, when she came over to give me the holdall… here we go,' he pressed the number, put his phone on speaker, turned the volume up and sat back.

A voice said: *The number you have dialled has not been recognised, please check, and dial again.* They looked at each other, Anton leant forward, started the engine up and drove away.

'We'll think of something,' he said.

20

Malcolm was at home when they got there but getting ready to go out. Anton's bruised face was explained away as the result of a particularly tough sparring session.

Once their father had left, Neville opened the computer and started to search for the Campus Bar. Anton remembered the real name of the pub was The Lamb and that Sedge had said something about sitting out the back looking across the river. It was enough to return a couple of possibilities.

'We'll start with those then,' said Anton.

'Hold on, she said it was known as the Campus yes?' Anton looked at him and nodded. 'None of these are anywhere near the colleges.'

'How about student residencies? Or maybe one of them does really cheap beer, students would walk a long way for cheap beer.' But Neville was back on the computer and searching.

'What about these? There's The Lamb Inn…. The Lamb Riverside, no, forget that one, it's out of town.'

'We could start at the colleges, work outwards,' said Anton.

'Ah, look…' said Neville.

'What?' Neville turned the screen to face him.

'If you search *The Lamb* in *Images* you get all these,' a row of pictures of innocent looking and undeniably cute lambs looked out at them, 'I think I might go veggie.'

'Mint sauce,' said Anton. Neville went back and continued to click and search. His brother said again, 'I say we go to the colleges and work outwards.'

'How about The Lamb and Flag? She's a druggie, right? She might not remember the whole name, this one is on the river, look,' Anton looked over his brother's shoulder, 'and, more importantly, right next to a college with all those lovely fresh-faced student-types...'

'You're a perv Nev but I think you may have done it. I don't think she's a druggie...'

'No but, if she is just a little bit then The Lamb and Flag becomes The Lamb, and anyway she calls it the Campus Bar, so precision isn't the point here,' Neville scrolled through the pictures and stopped at a particularly alluring image of beautiful young people sitting on a terrace, looking out over the river.

'We could go there now,' said Anton, suddenly hopeful.

Anton almost sprinted to the Outlander although his foot was still sore, so his running had a hint of hobbling about it; Neville just did his best to keep up and joked that they looked like a relay team put out by a sports injuries clinic.

Anton drove, fired up with the prospect of finding Sedge and putting an end to their problems. Once they were moving, Anton was aware his brother was nervous, he was looking around and seemed distracted.

'You alright? What's up?'

'Nothing, its fine,' said Neville and sat back but kept looking over his shoulder as they made their slow way into town. 'Which way are you going?'

'Down here, all the way to the end, do a right and stay on the road with all the roundabouts... takes us nearly all the way.'

'Do me a small favour, when you turn right, come off at the first of the roundabouts, go into the KFC car park.'

'You're hungry? Of course you're hungry,' said Anton. He carried on and turned into the car park as requested, it was nearly empty.

'Don't do the drive-through, go to the far end where the shop is.'

Neville bent forward and angled himself to see out of the wing mirror as his brother drove past the pumps and the row of gleaming new charging points, then, with a sweeping turn brought the car to a stop alongside the path outside the shop, not bothering to slot into one of the many empty bays. Neville had straightened up and was looking over to his right,

'We're being followed, don't look over. Go into the shop, get some stuff, and check out the black Merc that just pulled up by the pumps. It was outside the house when we left, I noticed because it was flash and the bloke at the wheel looked a lot like one of your mates from earlier.'

Anton shivered and looked over at his brother for a moment before getting out and walking into the shop, doing his best not to look around. From inside, he could just about see the Mercedes through the window. He bought some gum and walked back out to the Outlander, looking over to his left in the direction of the Mercedes. It was hard to make out the driver or indeed his passenger from this distance, but he could see they were just waiting, not filling up. He got back in, started up and drove out, passing a little closer but not too close to the Mercedes, trying to get a look at the driver but he couldn't be sure. Neville looked round as they drove on.

'Yep, he's started up again.'

'We'll go north, find a pub. We can't lead them to Sedge, we don't know what they might do.'

'I'd say we have a pretty good idea,' said Neville and settled back.

They stopped at a pub set back from the road and with space at the front to park, not too far for Neville to walk. The black Mercedes parked a little way up the road behind them and someone got out of the passenger side.

Once inside the pub, Anton went to the bar and Neville stood by the door for a few moments, watching the passenger from the Mercedes trot across the road and head their way. After sitting at a table near the door, Neville watched him come in and go to the bar where he found a stool.

Anton returned with drinks and Neville gestured toward the bar, Anton checked the guy out: he was short, a bit scrawny and had a cheaper suit than Mr Brown's crew. From a distance it looked to them like he'd ordered a Coke.

Anton slowly drank his pint and Neville put away two in under ten minutes.

'Freedom,' said Neville, waving the first of his empty glasses for emphasis. 'What now?'

'Get a good look at this guy,' said Anton, 'remember him, in case we see him again.'

'If we're right, he'll leave when we do so he's going to walk right past the car as long as we don't make a quick getaway. We go home I suppose, come up with a plan. We could both do with some rest.'

Anton looked at him, 'Yeah. It's been a day.'

They finished their drinks and left, walked slowly to the car, and sat inside for a few moments until they saw the scrawny man leave the pub and walk back toward them. They watched him walk past, getting a good look.

'Something's bothering me, can we go back via Franca's?' asked Anton, starting up.

'You want to lead them there?'

'They already know it, it's on the list.'

'You're the boss.'

As they drove away, Anton could see the scrawny man in the mirror running back toward the Mercedes and he saw it start up, stop to let him in, then move away to follow them.

'These guys are pretty crap at being discreet,' said Anton.

'Perhaps they want us to know they're there.'

Twenty minutes later they stopped outside Franca's home. The lights were on.

'What are we hoping to get here?' asked Neville.

'It's not that, it's something Sally said.'

'Who's Sally?'

'She's an idiot friend of Franca's, I bumped into her.'

'Right, so we're here because you were talking to an idiot.'

'She told me Franca has a new boyfriend.' Neville sighed and looked over at his brother.

'I doubt that's true, even if it were what is to you now?'

Anton was silent for a long time before he said, 'I think I loved her. Still do.'

Neville reached over, put an arm round his neck, pulled him in and ruffled his hair.

'Plenty more fish, little bro', I promise you.' Anton smiled at him but sat back up and stared at the house until eventually Neville said, 'Can we go now?'

When they arrived home, Malcolm was there, looking grumpy.

'Where was you?'

'We just went out, for a drive around and a drink, you went out to see friends, right?'

'Right, but as you can see, I came home nice and early to celebrate my eldest getting out of the death trap that is our much-loved local hospital.' Anton gestured at Neville to indicate their trip had been for his benefit. 'He's supposed to be recovering, he just got out.'

'It's okay, Dad, it was good to be out, good to be normal. It was my idea,' said Neville but Malcolm wasn't finished.

'What do you either of you two know about Beulah Mansions?'

There was silence then Anton managed an 'ummm…'

'They're moving out. There was a message on the phone. They're moving out this week, going to a hotel, they don't even have anywhere to move *to* yet and they're moving out.'

'They called and we went round, earlier,' said Anton.

'We? What, you took your brother there? The Lone Ranger and Tonto? You didn't say anything earlier.'

'We didn't want to bother you,' said Anton.

'Didn't want to bother me? It's our business, what are you fucking talking about? What's going on?'

'Egerton's bought the two flats below, his people were there today, seemed keen to let us know.'

'Sod it, that's the value gone from the place now,' said Malcolm, 'he'll just fill the block with dope heads and fucking idiots like the last one and our place becomes impossible to let, probably thinks it will force us to sell it to him for less than it's worth.'

'We must be able to do something,' said Neville.

'What though? I've been chasing him and his solicitors for more than two years to get them to pay their share of the maintenance, he just ignores it. Leaseholder disputes: they're expensive and you never get anywhere, he can just behave how he likes, especially now he owns nearly the whole thing.'

'He's looking at the gym as well,' said Anton, 'I think it's him or his crew; the solicitor woman was there and some people came round to measure up. George wants to sell because he wants to retire. Does that sound like him?'

'It's like the eighties,' said Malcolm, 'grabbing what he can. I'd love to know where he gets his money from, hard to imagine him doing any actual work for it.' He was rattled but keen to change the subject and make the most of having Neville back, 'Forget him. It's good to have you home, son.'

'Good to be here,' said Neville, 'I'll say one thing, if I get old and infirm and they try to put me in that hospital, just kill me, okay?' They looked at him.

'Noted,' said Anton.

21

Anton woke early with an idea in his head, a way to find Sedge without having to be there in person. He didn't say anything about it to Neville, not yet, but turned the idea over in his mind as he left the house and jogged all the way to the gym. He wasn't aware of being followed but when he got there he saw the black Mercedes parked a few doors down, no driver but someone who looked a lot like the scrawny one was in the front passenger seat, possibly asleep and leaning against the window.

It was still early when he walked into the gym. A handful of the keener ones were there, Kirby, of course, among them. Unusually for the time of day, George was there as well. Equally unusually, he was sweeping the floor around the edges of one of the practice rings.

'George…'

He looked up, 'Morning lad.'

'Everything alright?'

'Doing the cleaners' job for them,' he said, using the broom to get into the corners, 'they don't see the dirt… this is like the old days,' he bent down to pick up a scrap of paper, it looked like a till receipt, and held it out as he straightened up, 'look, invisible litter, apparently.' He walked over to a bin and dropped it in. Anton watched him walk back, a bit of a limp, bandy legged perhaps but he still had presence, a bit of what he must have once had about him. He was probably a tough guy back then, he thought. 'Other people can't see it, I must have special powers, I can see things ordinary mortals are denied.' He had built up a little pile of dirt next to one of the corners.

'I'll get a dustpan,' said Anton and hurried over to the cleaners' cupboard, grabbing a well-worn dustpan and brush before returning. 'Here you go, I'll do this bit,' he swept up the pile and brushed around the corner for good measure.

'Do you know what's happening with the sale?' Anton trying to sound casual about it. George stopped and leant on the broom.

'I have to get out while I can.'

'I know,' said Anton, 'I understand.'

'I want it to go on, but I can't do it anymore, I need my money to live. I'm old Anton, my wife is old, she can't do much anymore, we need to stop and buy ourselves some care for whatever time we have left.' Anton nodded to show he understood. 'We don't have anything else; our house isn't ours, it's just rented, everything I ever had went into this.'

'It's owned by you and Nico, right?'

'Nico... yes, the bigger share is his, but he wants out too. My share is enough. Enough for my wife and me, make sure we have a safe place to be.'

'Makes a lot of sense. Is there anyone offering to buy?'

'Yes… I don't know, hard to tell if they're serious but yes, there's a buyer.' He turned and carried on; it was clear he didn't want to take this particular conversation any further. Anton took the dustpan back and was stopped by Barney on the way.

'Everything okay with the old boy?'

'Yeah, I think so. He wants to retire.'

'So I gather. You okay to work with Franny again this morning?

'Of course, just need to warm up a little.'

'He does too, there's no rush, as and when, thanks.'

Barney walked away and Anton hauled himself onto one of the bikes and started a gentle pedal to get his muscles moving, facing the door, watching people come in. When it was close to ten, the younger lads who were there for the Boys Club started to arrive. One of them was Jason.

Anton saw him and climbed off the bike to catch him before he got too far. 'Jason, alright? Listen, you got a minute?' The boy looked at him, assuming something was wrong. 'Everything's fine, I have something you might be able to help me with….'

Five minutes later, Jason was hooked. Anton had gambled, correctly, that dressing up his problem as a covert mission that required secrecy and some technical genius would be enough to excite him. The problem he had was that Jason didn't look old enough to be walking round a pub on his own so Anton said he would find someone else who could go if he'd help with the set up. Jason suggested his sister for the job,

'She needs some work at the moment, she knows how the Glass works too.'

'Can you get her to come down here this afternoon?'

'I don't see why not, leave it with me. We're finished at two, I'll get her to meet me.'

Anton watched him go to join the group and saw him send a text on the way. He called Neville to talk the plan through, see what thought. He assumed he would point out what was wrong with the idea but to Anton's surprise, he was reasonably positive. More than that, he was impressed, or so he said, but sceptical: they still had to get lucky, they couldn't be sure Sedge was a regular in the bar, nor for that matter that she would be there tonight.

'Worth a try, though,' agreed Neville, 'if it doesn't work, we go to the police, right?'

'Right,' said Anton, not really willing to contemplate failure yet.

There wasn't much else Anton could do before Jason's sister got there so he looked for Franny to start working with him. He was sitting on the edge of a practice ring, legs dangling, chatting to Barney, looking like he might have been waiting for a while.

'Ah, your Lordship, you grace us with your presence?' said Barney, bowing as he approached.

'You said no rush,' said Anton.

'I didn't mean it, though, obviously. There's work to do.'

Barney's idea was for Franny to try things and it was Anton's job to keep everything rolling along and to give him some time, let him try out the moves he'd been working on. They sparred in two-minute bursts, that way Franny had to get on with it, there was no dancing around, he had to get a move on before they paused. Anton did his best, but his mind wasn't fully in the ring. However, he did register how fast Franny was getting and that he had a deadly little jab action now which got through Anton's defences every time he tried it. By the end, Barney looked pleased.

'We'll push him harder next time, let you try and hit him,' he said as Anton stepped out of the ring.

'I did try and hit him, he's quick at getting out of the way.'

Yeah, he is,' Barney grinned, 'it's not all on you so don't worry, I've got Dave on it too, between you, you'll have him nice and ready.'

At the rear of the gym was a room, big enough to accommodate a light blue formica-topped table around which about six of the dozen or so plastic chairs that were lying around could fit. There was a well-worn brown suede sofa and a few other mismatched chairs, an old bedside table and other bits and bobs that people had donated over the years. In addition, there was a sink, a fridge, and some shelving, along with a kettle and a microwave which sat on the single worktop all of which allowed George to call the room the Canteen.

It was into the Canteen that Anton invited Jason and his sister Jacqui just after she arrived at two o'clock. To Anton's eyes, Jacqui was an unsettling double of her brother, even though she was two or three years older; they had the same look about them. He indicated they should all sit round the table, and he had to make a conscious effort to stop staring at her, the likeness was uncomfortably close. They watched as Jacqui placed the carrier bag she had brought with her carefully on the table, reached in and eased a small bundle out of it and placed it gently on the plastic top. With a sense of occasion, she slowly unwrapped a strip of dark blue velvet cloth to reveal a shiny white box with the word "GLASS" embossed on the lid. Anton couldn't stop himself from stroking the lid before Jason lifted it off with a degree of ceremony and took out what looked like a small pair of steel rimmed glasses.

'Let me see,' said Anton. Jason carefully handed it to him, and he put it on his face, 'no lenses…'

'Just the one little one here,' said Jason adjusting the small square of glass which sat just above Anton's eyeline on the right-hand side of the frame, 'everything you want to see is on there.'

Jason took them back and pressed a small button on the inside of the right arm, a small light came on beside it. He put the unit on himself and took out his phone, pressed the screen and waited a moment while it paired. He looked at Anton and said: 'Okay Glass, take a picture.' Anton looked down at Jason's phone and saw a picture of his surprised face looking back at him. Jason stood and looked round, said: 'Okay Glass, take a video,' and panned around the room taking in all the detail, the images appearing on his phone almost simultaneously.

'Alright, that is amazing. But it's not exactly discreet if you have to tell it what to do,' said Anton. Jason held his hand up, then with his index finger pressed the outside of the right arm, yet another picture of a slightly startled Anton appeared on the phone.

'There's a button to start and stop video as well, it's just that the voice command is more fun,' said Jason, looking rather proud of it all.

'So, you could scan the room every now and then,' Jason nodded and looked at his sister who shrugged and nodded too, 'and send the pictures to a phone?'

'It needs to be tethered to something, a phone or a tablet, so it needs to be close by,' said Jacqui.

'I can't be there though; I can't be close by and I'm the one who knows who we're looking for.'

'What if we linked it to him over the net?' said Jacqui, looking at her brother, 'do it via social media. It would be close to real time…' Jason bit his lip but nodded.

'So I could be at home?' said Anton.

'As long as we've got an internet connection… if the place has wi-fi, yes,' said Jason, 'you'll need to be online too, obviously. Give me your phone,' Anton took out his phone, switched it on and handed it to Jason who sat back and started to work on it. 'I'll put an app on it for you.' Anton smiled, aware he was out of his depth at this point.

'Who are we looking for?' said Jacqui.

'She's about twenty to maybe twenty-three, small to medium height, gingery-straw hair, kinda punky, probably not too much make-up. She wears colourful clothes, like an art student, lots of colour…'

'Why can't you just go and find her?'

'She may be in danger; I need to warn her. There are people who know me who might be there and if they see me speak with her that might put her in danger.'

'So, people who speak with you might be in danger?' Jacqui looked at him and Jason looked up from what he was doing.

'Not in here, it's all friends in here,' said Anton. 'I need to make contact with this girl and to try and get her to come here.'

'Is this illegal? Any of it?' said Jacqui.

'No. I'm just trying to put some things right. I promise you, there's nothing illegal.'

'Sounds like I might be in danger though,' said Jacqui.

'How does £100 cash sound?' Jacqui didn't respond but checked out the fingernails on her left hand, 'And let's say another twenty for a couple of drinks while you're in there so you can relax and blend in.'

She looked up at him, 'I took this little baby out,' she lifted the Glass up to show him, 'when Jason first bought it. He loved wearing it around town but then he's a boy and therefore unaware that he looked like a knobhead,' Jason was caught out so too slow to protest, 'anyway, when *I* took it out, I felt a little self-conscious shall we say. I found out that when you wear this, you attract attention, you get into conversations. Like pixels and megabytes type conversations. I'm going to need to go with someone, take a friend with me to talk to.'

'Why don't I buy them a drink or two as well… add another twenty?'

'Why don't we just round it up to £150?' Anton sighed and nodded agreement. 'How will I know when it's her?'

'You'll have your phone with you, right? I'll call you when I see her.' Jason was just about to hand Anton his phone back but took it away again and said,

'I'll put her number in for you… under Jacqui, okay?'

'I'll get there for eight o'clock,' said Jacqui. 'We're gone by ten, sound okay?'

'Okay,' said Anton.

'For you,' said Jason, handing the phone back, 'I've put an app on your homescreen, you just press it. Leave it on and anything she snaps will come through.'

'You're a genius,' said Anton.

'I know, and I believe you said something about £50 for the hire of the kit and for my trouble… even though this *is* fun.' Anton took out his wallet and gave £50 each to Jason and his sister.

'Down payment,' he said to Jacqui, 'cover expenses… If you do find her and if we can persuade her to come here to meet me, ideally tomorrow sometime during the day, there's another £50 on top of what we've agreed.' Jacqui smiled and put the money in her pocket.

That evening, Anton was ready in good time, just before eight. He sat on his bed, leaning against the wall at the head of it, fully charged phone in his hand and a scrap of paper and a pen ready just in case. Neville walked in and swept a pile of clothes from a chair onto the floor, drawing a cry of protest from Anton,

'Oi, watch my stuff,'

'I'm on crutches, you know, I need to sit, or I can't concentrate.'

They waited until just after eight then couldn't wait any longer, Anton pressed the app and watched as a little patch of light came up on his screen, he gave Neville the thumbs-up, and used his brother's phone to call Jacqui.

'Hello?'

'Jacqui, hi, we're here, its Anton,'

'What number is this?'

It's my brother's, he's helping, it means I can watch the pictures and talk to you.'

'You got the app switched on?'

'Yep,'

'Standby then,' moments later a picture of another young woman appeared on his screen, she was smiling and holding up a glass with a bright orange cocktail. Meet Shaz… how's the picture?'

'It's brilliant, hey Shaz…'

'She can't hear you. Let's try a walk through,' they watched the screen as Jacqui got down from her stool and started to walk around the room. She paused when she reached groups of people and tried to scan as many tables and standing groups as she could. Anton tried to speak with her, but she didn't answer, they assumed she had put her phone away. After a minute or so she completed the circuit and sat back down opposite her friend Shaz, they heard her take her phone out again. 'How was that? Any of these lovely people your lost lady love?'

'Not this time but it works, you need to move slowly, if you go too fast it blurs up easily.'

'Okay, we'll try again in fifteen minutes,' she said, 'I have got some good news, however. We are in the right place, I walked past one of the kids who was calling someone, said she was in the Campus.'

'Okay, that is good news, thanks Jacqui. I'll wait for you to send something new in fifteen minutes or so.'

'Roger, roger,' she said, getting into it now.

They settled into a routine. Anton would make sure the app was live, and his screen would suddenly light up and a new sequence would come through. Jacqui varied the route a little, scanning different areas, trying to include new arrivals. Anton watched carefully, searching in the shadows, looking for some small detail he recognised, even asking her to go back and find someone who had been obscured by people walking in front of them, just in case, but there was no sign of Sedge. After seven attempts she was flagging.

'You okay if I come home now?'

'Yes, of course, thanks for trying.'

'Sorry.'

'Not your fault,' said Anton, 'you did a great job.' He paused before saying, 'What have you got planned for tomorrow night?' Neville looked up with a start and waved at his brother, trying to stop him. 'You want to try again?' There was a pause when he could hear her talking to her friend without catching the detail, then,

'Same deal?'

'Same deal, but could you try it a bit later? Start at nine, say?'

'It's your money boyo. Okay, we'll be here, you call me when you're ready, see you.' She rang off, Neville looked at his brother and shook his head, a little dramatically.

'Good money after bad,' he said, and Anton wondered if he didn't have a point, but it was about the only idea he had.

'What's this?' asked Neville, holding up a greetings card with an elaborate flowery pattern design which he had picked up from the top of a pile of magazines on the bedside table.

'I was going to try and write something to Franca.'

'Mate, you are going to have to just let her go. Seriously. If she wants to come back to you, she'll let you know.'

'I know,' said Anton, deflated from the fruitless search for Sedge. 'I'm still going to send it.'

22

The next night at nine o'clock, Anton called Jacqui.

'We're here, lover boy, just getting me and Shaz a nice drink on your expense account. Jason passed on the money, thank you.'

'Glad to hear it, hope it was all still there.'

'You calling my brother dodgy? All accounted for, don't worry. Wouldn't be here if it wasn't. Okay, open up the app and I'll have a look around.'

They settled into the same routine as the previous evening, Jacqui using the Glass and taking a walk round the bar every quarter of an hour or so, only this time Neville got bored after the first attempt and left his brother to it, leaving his phone behind for him to use.

Around ten thirty, just when Jacqui was starting to get a little bored herself, Anton saw the place was getting busier and concentrated a little harder. There were more faces to scan now and it was hard to see detail. Jacqui came back to the table she and Shaz had seized just after they had arrived; by now she was texting and just sent a simple *?*. Anton called her,

'There's a group, wasn't there before, over to your left I think, eight or nine of them, they look arty…' She looked over, stood, and took a few steps toward them. 'That's them, yes.' The screen went blank and there was a pause then she started up again, the picture came through and he strained to look.

'Yes. Jacqui, yes, maybe. Yellow top, kind of a waistcoat thing, can you get closer?'

'Anton, I'm walking around looking like a dick and I'm holding a phone to my ear, just how unobtrusive do you think I can be?' She moved a little closer, Anton watched carefully. The screen went blank. He heard her say, 'fucking thing, the battery life on this is shit,' he tried to stop her ringing off, but she was gone. He sat and pressed the app a few times but there was nothing. He suddenly had cramp and needed to stretch so stood, cursing his phone which remained blank. He used the redial on his brother's phone to call her up but got the engaged tone. As he hung up, his own phone rang,

'You're in luck boyo, I just tried my luck and asked her if her name was Sedge and bingo. I believe a finder's fee is in order.'

'I believe it is,' he said, 'can you put her on?' There was a lot of noise, muffled voices, bumping and shuffling then, faintly, he heard her.

'Hello?'

'Sedge, it's me, Anton, from the house where Darren used to live, the one you gave the holdall to. Everything's cool, I put the money back in the bag, all of it, I gave it all back,' she stayed silent, 'but there's something else Sedge, I need to see you. There's still danger, for you and me, for us. I need to meet you and talk with you. Can you come over tomorrow? It's not far. The girl you're talking to, she knows how to get here, she can bring you safely… you mustn't tell anyone okay? It's really important that you don't say anything to anyone.'

'Okay,' she said, quietly, not making him feel at all sure.

'Can you give the phone back now?' There was more noise, and he waited for it to settle.

'Mission accomplished,' said Jacqui.

'Nearly, you've done really well… can you bring her to the

gym tomorrow? You need to go in the back door, Jason should know it, it's in Forest Road, by the junction with Briar Lane. Please try and bring her there, it's really important, I need to speak with her, then there really will be a finder's fee.'

'She gonna be safe?'

'I promise, but you have to use the door at the back.'

'Let me try.' Anton drew breath but she hung up. He thought about calling back but decided his best chance was to leave her to it. And cross his fingers.

Neville had dropped back in, having heard Anton talking and he looked questioningly at him. His brother nodded and said simply,

'We have contact.'

Neville raised his eyebrows and nodded to show he was impressed that his brother's crackpot idea had actually worked. He looked around and saw the greetings card was now in its envelope, sealed down and with Franca's address on it.

'Got to give it a try,' said Anton.

Half an hour later, Jacqui called him.

'Okay, I'm going home now, she's agreed to come with me tomorrow, I'll pick her up and we'll get to the gym about midday, hope that works for you,'

'Back door.'

'I know, I know.'

'Thanks Jacqui. Really thank you. I'll go to the bank on the way there.' He heard her yawn and say,

'G'night,' before she hung up.

It was cold again the next morning, but Anton's heart was racing when he woke up. He saw snow through the window, but no more than a light coating. He opened the bedroom window and breathed in the sharp morning air, it stung his throat, but he was keen to jog to the gym, get the air in his lungs.

He had woken up feeling invigorated, pleased with himself that his plan had worked and reasonably sure that Sedge would turn up. With luck he was within touching distance of the missing laptop.

He picked up the envelope, looked around and found some second-class stamps in a drawer in the kitchen and fixed two to it. When he'd written the card the night before he was unsure, apprehensive even, he didn't know how Franca was going to take it. Now in the sober light of the morning he reasoned simply that it might work, and it might not but if he didn't send it, didn't try something then Franca was likely to be gone for good.

He posted it on the way to the gym and checked the time of the collection which was at the end of the day. Presumably, that meant she would get it the day after tomorrow, so be it, patience was called for, at least he was taking some kind of action. As soon as he'd let go of the card and it dropped into the depths of the post box he had doubts, and worried about what he'd written, suddenly not trusting himself to have got it right, going back over what he'd said, wondering if he'd picked the right words. He was no poet, but he'd been sincere: he missed her, she was the best thing that ever happened to him, he was truly sorry for what had happened. It had all come from the heart, it was the truth, simple and straight, she could take it or leave it but at least he had got to say it.

Barney was on him as soon as he arrived,

'Six rounds this morning, go for it though, headguards all that but have a go, push him a bit, Dave's gonna do six more later on.'

Anton looked at Franny who was stretching his arms and shoulders out. 'You ready for this?'

'Definitely,' he said. Anton grabbed some kit and brought it back to the ringside.

'How's it going?'

'I'm good, feeling really good,' said Franny, 'still got another seven weeks or so to go but I'm fitter now than I've ever been, got rid of the Christmas belly nice and fast,' he patted himself, pushing what was left of his belly out.

'We're all rooting for you. And Kirby of course,' he looked over at Kirby who was sitting in the corner of the room looking generally unhappy with life, blowing his nose, and pulling his track suit top tighter around himself. 'What's up with him?'

'He's got the cold, the one that's going round, I'm keeping away, I definitely don't want it, I'm eating oranges, taking Vitamin D… the last thing I need is to get a cold.'

'Why's he even here?'

'Where else is he going to go?' said Franny, confusingly.

Anton stretched his hamstrings, still working off the cold from the run in. 'You heard any more about the sale?'

'No, Barney doesn't talk about anything that isn't the fight, wants me to be single minded. It doesn't bother me, I trust him. I need to give this my best shot.'

Anton was ready now and climbed into the ring with him, 'Okay, let's see what you've got.'

Six rounds later, Anton was out of breath and stood leaning forward holding on to his knees. Franny was sweating but breathing normally. Anton put a friendly arm round his shoulder and patted him, 'Nice one,' he said then headed for the shower.

'You done for the day?' Barney called out to him.

'Probably, I'm meeting someone in a minute,' said Anton.

'I need to talk to you about Kirby, get you started with him. There's no rush, he's got to start feeling better first anyway.' Anton smiled and nodded, that was all fine by him.

The showers at the gym never really worked properly, they were either too hot or too cold, trying find the sweet spot was close to impossible. Given the weather outside, Anton opted for too hot so was only able to stay under just enough to get cleaned up and to turn a ruddy pink. As he stepped out and grabbed a towel, he heard his phone ring. He had to dig it out from his jeans which were at the bottom of the pile of clothes he'd dropped onto one of the old chairs. He pulled the towel around himself as he answered,

'Hello?'

'We're here.' Jacqui.

'You're early… aren't you?' he quickly looked at the screen to check the time, they were about ten minutes early.

'Yeah, or prompt, depends how you look at it.'

'Let me get some clothes on…'

'What do you lot get up to in there?'

'Never mind, give me a couple of minutes, and come to the door. Can you see it? It's got a little wooden plaque next to it.'

'You're going to have to come to us, boyo.'

'Jacqui, I just got out the shower, don't make me come outside. Just come to the door and I'll let you in.' There was silence then she said,

'She doesn't want to come in there, you're gonna have to come out to the car if you want to talk to her. We're in the lane, like you said, dark blue Focus, we'll wait for you. You're gonna need clothes though, it's as cold as an Inuit's tits out here.' Anton sighed and hung up, vaguely irritated that he had to go outside but thinking about it, Sedge was probably nervous about walking into a boxing club which was fair enough. He finished getting dressed, let Barney know he was just popping out.

As he opened the back door, the chill hit him, painfully contrasting with the scalding shower he'd just left. He stepped out.

The road at the back of the gym was generally quiet, there were some old lock-up garages that had seen better days and a few houses further along the road, some more neglected than others. He took a few steps, looking around in case anyone was watching the place, but there was nothing. He jumped as a car door opened suddenly just in front of him and had a second shock when he saw Kirby get out, bundled up in many layers of clothing and with a scarf wrapped around his face. Kirby nodded when he saw him but said nothing, Anton smiled and said, 'Alright?' as they passed each other, Kirby hurrying to the back door of the gym. Anton turned and watched him disappear inside. He looked down at the car he had emerged from, an old Vauxhall estate of some sort, dark grey and in need of a wash. The bodywork was covered in dust and dirt and the windows were smeary and hard to see through. One of the tyres was flat, the other on the same side only half inflated.

Anton didn't stop, deciding he could think about it all later, back in the warm. He turned to look up Briar Lane which branched off to his left and saw headlights flash twice, about halfway up the lane on the right. Putting his collar up against the weather, he started walking toward them, checking around him again in case he'd missed something, but the place was deserted. As he got near, he could see Jacqui sitting alone in the front. He hurried the last few steps and gave her a little wave as he reached the car. She returned the wave and indicated he should get in the back. Anton opened the door and saw Sedge sitting on the far side, waiting for him. She was holding a laptop.

'Hey boyo, get in,' said Jacqui.

'Hi, thanks for doing this. Hello Sedge.'

She looked at him and said, 'Hi.'

Anton climbed into the back seat beside her. 'You brought it, the laptop,' said Anton, 'thank you. I suppose you guessed I was going to ask about it.' He leant over and made a move to take it from her, but she pulled it away.

'No, you don't.'

'Sedge, we have to give it back. We're all in danger if we don't.'

'This isn't it,' she said, 'this one's mine.'

'Yours? Okay, but have you got the one that was in the bag?'

'Not here but yes.'

'We need to give it back to them. I need you to give it to me so I can take it back to them.'

'You need to listen to her,' said Jacqui. He looked up, caught sight of her in the mirror and stopped. He looked back at Sedge and made a gesture with his hand to show he was listening.

'I know you want the laptop. You're not the only one. You remember I said there were men in the Campus asking about Darren's friends? They came back asking about a missing laptop, asking if anyone had seen one around the place, asking if anyone had one to sell. These people are not nice, we're agreed on that, right?' Anton nodded, 'So I wondered, why were they so desperate to get it back? Why did Darren have it anyway? It's a piece of shit laptop, you can get one for a couple of hundred pounds so it's not like it's a posh model. So, I held on to it, see if I could work out what might be on it that was so important,' Anton looked up at the mirror, Jacqui was watching him. 'So, I switched it on.'

'You guessed the password?'

'I went round the password and hacked it,' he looked at her, now a little incredulous. 'I've got a master's in computer science; I've been messing with these babies for a long time.'

'Think you may have underestimated your friend here, boyo,' said Jacqui, smiling at him in the mirror.

'Anyway, that doesn't matter,' Sedge continued, 'I looked around, there wasn't much on it, boring stuff: accounts, emails, nothing interesting… some porn,' Anton looked up, 'again, not interesting, nothing illegal, just sleazy shit. The owner is fundamentally boring, but…. then I looked a bit more. There are some traces of webcam activity, chat rooms. Most chat rooms leave no trace or lasting record on the hard drive, not even a shadow, you use them and its gone. Most of them. There is one though that leaves a copy on the hard drive if you know where to look.'

'And you know where to look.'

'I wasn't thinking of it at first, but there it was. Chances are our friend, Egerton or whoever, didn't know until somebody told him, probably the other party, so he decided he had to get it wiped properly, erased or even the whole thing destroyed.'

'That's why Darren had it?'

'Darren knew about this sort of stuff too, it's how I met him, on the computer science course, so yes. He was supposed to clean it up, he told me, he didn't know which bit though, asked me to help him. Want to know what they talked about?' She opened up her laptop, switched it on and turned the screen towards him. 'I copied it.'

The screen was a mess of lines at first, then horizontal zig zags, slowly settling to show a man's face that Anton didn't recognise and another, smaller one in a box in the top right-hand corner of the image, that one was Egerton. The main face was talking but there was no sound at first, Sedge told him to be patient, then it started to come through.

'… Alex. Whatever you like, construction, car wash, workers for your plant farms eh? I know you have those… it's up to you, they'll do whatever you say…two lorries a day on fifth, sixth, seventh and eighth September, same port, no checks going to be made, they go to the laybys like before. Sixty men in each, is that too many?' Anton could see Egerton in the corner of the screen shake his head and he heard a faint,

'No'.

'Good. You have places to put them? Same price. Tomorrow I send you accounts to pay into, equal sums. The men know they owe you; they give you their wages, same as before…' Sedge paused the recording.

'You want more?' Anton shook his head but didn't know what to say. 'There is more, a lot more. He gets on to the women later, putting his order in, sounded like the lucky ones get to work in Nail Bars.'

'What the fuck?' said Anton and closed his eyes. After a while, he sat up and said, 'What do you want to do?'

'See him stopped,' she said, 'I know you have a problem too.'

'*We* have a problem.'

'But I can disappear,' said Sedge, 'I've been doing that for years.' Jacqui watched him in the mirror.

'How well do you know Egerton?' said Anton.

'Not well, he's a grubby bottom feeder, a small part of this really, a chancer. Small time but looking to be bigger. He's greedy I'd say, he's got properties, along with certain friends who do this sort of thing, it all fits together for him. He's all about real estate, it's what he understands. He puts them up, they give him their money, the people smuggling thing is a bigger network, he's just a cog.'

'He's threatening me, us, my family, friends… anyone I know,' said Anton.

'I know and I know that's why you want to just give him back the laptop. I don't want to see you hurt but I would like to bring him down, take him out of the picture.' She looked at Anton, 'If you really need me to, I'll give you the laptop.'

Anton said he needed to think. Sedge asked him for his phone which he gave her, and she put her number in it, saying this time it was the real one, she'd put it under "Sandra", and he could call anytime. He said he'd call later, maybe in the morning, when he'd had a chance to think. He gave Jacqui the money he owed her and left the car, still a little dumbstruck.

He watched as Jacqui manoeuvred the car out of its parking spot and drove away, disappearing up the hill, then shivered as he became aware of the cold again.

On the short walk back to the gym, he took another look at the car he'd seen Kirby stepping out of, it definitely looked like it hadn't moved in a long time, months at least.

Back in the gym, the air was thick with the smell of physical work, of leather and sweat, it was familiar and usually comforting but this time it felt oppressive, redolent of something far more troubling, it was too much of a contrast with the cold clean air outside. Without taking his coat off, he walked through the gym to the front and stepped outside. He looked up and down the street for signs of anyone watching the building but didn't see anything. There was a low brick wall, around waist height that ran from the door down to the pavement, edging the short pathway. He leant over it and gasped for air, it felt like he'd been holding his breath for ages. The door opened and Barney came out.

'You alright son?'

Anton nodded, tried to look like he was in control, everything was fine, but he couldn't bring it off. 'Sorry,' he said, 'just feeling a bit…'

'There's something going round.'

'Yeah, perhaps that's it,' said Anton. He straightened up and looked at Barney, 'What's the deal with Kirby? I just saw him, out the back. Is he living in that car?'

Barney looked weary, 'It's his business really, for him to tell you.' He thought for a moment, 'You could ask him. As far as I know, him and his dad live in it, got nowhere else. Something must have happened, I don't know, I don't ask. We let him use the gym to wash, keep himself going. As far as he's concerned, he's stepping up to pro level and that's all that matters, it might enable him to make a living.' Anton asked about Kirby's father, asked how come he never saw him if he lived there as well?

'You have seen him. You know him, its Keith.'

'The cleaner?'

'Janitor, yeah. I think the plan is, they get to save up some dosh and get back on their feet.' Barney was getting that weary look again, 'My advice is, you don't know any of this. Kirby's going to be sensitive about it, he don't say a lot in the first place. You've seen him in the car, you can ask him, perhaps… I don't know, see how you feel about it. Can we go in now? I'm freezing my bollocks off.' Anton smiled and followed him back inside.

Franny was nearing the end of his workout with Dave and a few of the others had gathered to watch. It was still high tempo, even at the end of the six rounds, punches were flying in, not to hurt, just to land something, get through defences, test each other. They stopped, touched gloves, and stood, bent over, getting their breath back, one or two of the watching group made comments about Franny's movement, the way he seemed to roll with the punches, how much he was looking the business now. No-one paid much attention when he stayed hunched over, panting, long after Dave had straightened up and stepped out of the ring.

Dave took off his headguard and gloves and saw him still there. He stepped back in and put an arm round his shoulder and asked him if he was okay. Franny didn't speak but tried to take his headguard off and found it difficult. Dave calmed him and helped to ease it off, as he took it from him, sweat dripped from it and he saw Franny's hair was soaked. 'You okay, mate?' he asked as he guided him to the side and helped him step out of the ring, but Franny looked anything but okay.

'Come and sit down, get your breath back,' he said, arm still round his shoulder as he tried to steer him to a chair. Franny stopped walking and put his hands to his head, he looked up, his face tensed then his legs gave way. Dave was too slow to catch him, and he hit the floor, a couple of the onlookers were close by and went to help him, but he cried out, a scream which made them jump back in shock. They watched as he stretched one of his hands out to them, the other still holding his head, he started rolling back and forth on the ground, Dave got down and tried to stop him moving, trying to calm him. He looked over his shoulder and cried out to anyone,

'Ambulance… ambulance,' everyone had their phones out, fumbling away until someone called out,

'Got it,' and they heard him giving his name, address, address of the gym, while he tried to say 'hurry, we just need an ambulance.'

'Cushion,' shouted Dave. Someone pulled one out from a chair and handed it to him, he did his best to place it under Franny's head and held him, trying to keep him still and lying on his side in the recovery position. Franny looked like he was losing consciousness; he had gone quiet and just lay now.

Someone said the ambulance was on its way, it was close by so not long to wait, it was going to be okay, and they stared, all of them in shock. Anton had seen Barney from the other side of the room look over then run toward them through the crowd, stopping when he got there, looking at Franny then at Dave who was looking up and back at him, fear in his eyes.

It felt like a long time before they heard the siren, someone went to the door and waved the crew in, everyone stepped back to let them get down with Franny, everyone except Dave who stayed kneeling beside him, holding him, not letting him go.

'You'll have to move back sir,' said one of the crew, gently taking hold of him and easing him away while his colleague got to work on the now unresponsive figure lying on the floor.

'He's gonna be okay, yeah? Is he gonna be okay?' Dave just talking now, asking, talking, scared.

They took Franny away, stretchered him out and into the ambulance, Dave staying with him, it happened fast, the doors shut, and they were gone. The rest were left behind, silent, still, not knowing what to do.

'Should we call someone?'

'What's going to happen?'

'Dave will call it in, he'll let us know,' said Barney. 'Who do *we* call?'

Someone said, 'He's got a wife.'

'I'll check his file,' said Barney and disappeared into the office.

'What are we supposed to do now?' said someone to the air.

'Nothing,' said Anton, 'wait and see.'

No-one had any appetite to work anymore. The bags, weights, running, rowing, and cycling machines stayed silent, unused. Quiet conversations started up around the place, small pockets of chat, speculation about what had happened to Franny, what would happen next, how it had come about.

The Boys Club broke up, the art teacher who had been trying to inspire them to be creative declared the day over. One or two of the boys left and went home, a few others followed them out slowly, holding back just a little in case there was some news. Four of them had nowhere to go, being variously untrusted to be home alone or outside and unsupervised. Kenny Dean and one of the other trainers who Anton knew only as Sid although that apparently wasn't his real name, encouraged them to do some exercise, to get on the running machines and run some energy off although none of them looked particularly energetic. They were encouraged to use the time to work on their fitness. No-one wanted to punch anyone though, it was strictly solo training, the rings lay abandoned.

After an hour or so Barney came out of the office, he looked around, surprised to see so many still there. Everyone stopped what they were doing and walked over to him, hoping for news.

'They're at the hospital, they're operating on him, Dave's staying there.'

'Is he going to be alright?'

'We don't know, I can't tell you, I don't know.' He looked out at them; they weren't going anywhere without more information. 'They're working on him, Dave says they got him straight in there, into the operating theatre straight away, so that's a miracle in itself these days. We have to hope.'

'And pray, I'm going to pray for him,' said Tyrone. A lot of them were aware he was a Catholic or some such, but this was the first time he'd really declared it.

'Yeah, hope and pray,' said Barney. 'I'm going down there, his wife's on her way. Where's Kirby?' He looked round to try and find him, there was a voice from the back,

'I'm here.' Anton looked round and saw him; he looked pale and scared.

'Lock up, will you son? When everyone's gone?' said Barney and left.

23

Back home, Anton told the story of Franny's collapse, playing down the drama of it, not wanting to cause alarm. Although his father had never tried to stop him boxing or to curb his enthusiasm for the gym, Anton didn't want to start a conversation around safety and risk.

He was, however, desperate to have a private chat with Neville and suggested he take his brother out for a drink as part of his rehabilitation programme.

'Alcohol is good for his recovery, is it?' asked Malcolm, with a tinge of disappointment that his plans for a family dinner were about to be taken apart again, but Anton promised to be back in a couple of hours. 'Okay, but so I don't forget to tell you later, you have to get round to Beulah Mansions tomorrow.'

'What now?'

'They're off; they obviously meant it when they said they were leaving. I need you to go over there in the afternoon, do the condition check, get the keys back…' there was a pause while Anton thought about this but knew in his heart there was no-one else who was going to go and do it. '…Okay?'

'Yes, of course,' he said, slowly guiding Neville to the door and out to the car, 'see you in a bit.'

Neville sat sipping his pint and for once, listened quietly while his brother told him about the meeting with Sedge and the video. When Anton was finished, he sat and nodded wisely, as if what he had just heard had somehow confirmed what he already knew.

'I don't really know Egerton, but I never liked the sound of him,' he said, 'we do, however, seem to be getting into some deep and murky shit here.'

'Yep,' Anton took a swig of his beer, 'he's a bad guy and bad guys have bad guy friends, and I definitely don't want his bad guy friends doing bad guy stuff to us or anywhere near us.'

'Succinctly put, so what's the plan?' Anton shrugged, 'Go to the police, tell them what we know? We could go and see Summerscales maybe.'

'I think that's what Sedge wants to do,' said Anton, 'she's after Egerton, but what if they just keep the laptop, decide it's not enough to arrest him? We're still in the shit and he's still out there, being a bad guy.' They sat and thought about that for a few moments then Neville said,

'You gonna tell Dad?'

'I wasn't.'

'We might have to soon.'

'Yeah, I know.'

Anton slept badly that night and got up early before the heating in the house switched on. It was icy and dark outside but calm, there was no wind and next to no traffic. Time was suspended, the day still hidden, not ready to wake.

He tried some stretches to get warm, then twenty press ups to start to feel more up for the day. After cereal, coffee and a shower he wrapped himself in layers of clothing and left the house thinking he'd get to the gym before it opened and take another look around the back of the building when he got there. Usually, a run in the cold air would clear his head, help with decision making but it didn't work that day, he couldn't think straight or concentrate properly, nothing would fall neatly into place.

As he turned the corner and the gym came into view, he saw a group outside, at least twenty people, regulars but more than usual for the start of the day. It was still a good fifteen minutes before the doors were due to open, but they were gathering, others arriving and joining even as he got there. The general chat was all about Franny, did anyone know anything? What exactly happened yesterday? Is there any news? Anton forgot about his plan to check out the back and joined in the conversation which turned to speculation about Franny's chances along with rumours around the sale of the building.

At five to nine, the door opened, and Kirby looked out, presumably he had been aware of the noise out front and opened up to find out what was going on. He looked vaguely startled to see them and stood back to let them in to the warmth of the gym, ducking questions about Franny as he did so, saying he didn't know anything either.

Anton noticed Barney walking into the office as they came in so assumed Kirby would at least know more than they did but wasn't letting on. Once inside, nobody got changed. A few took off some top layers, but most stayed in coats and jackets, not trusting the temperature yet or maybe just not sure if they were staying.

Anton looked into the office where Barney had disappeared and saw George sitting at a table, looking old in a way he hadn't before, a steaming mug of something in front of him. Barney came back out into the main room, patiently fending off enquiries as he made his way to one of the practice rings; he was going to say what he had to say just once, to everyone.

He sat on the edge of the ring, looking isolated, using his hands to bat away anyone who came up to him, saying he was going to tell them everything in a minute. Just after nine he stood up, climbed through the ropes, and faced them. He raised his hands, and everyone stopped talking.

'Okay, morning everyone, what a turnout… I know you all want to know about Franny, so… I'll tell you what I know. I'm not a doctor, obviously, so…' Anton watched him stumbling, picking his words carefully, this was not the usual Barney, the Barney that would bluster and shout, act on instinct and say whatever was on his mind. This was a man doing his duty, meeting an obligation and not enjoying a moment of it.

'Somehow, he has blood on his brain, he's been bleeding in his skull. That put pressure on his brain and moved it. They operated when he got to the hospital and tried to stop it. When they went to bring him round, it started up again, so they had to operate a second time. This time, they have… put him…' Barney hesitated, 'they've put him in a coma, deliberately, in a coma to stabilise him…' he looked out at the faces all staring at him, 'something like that. He's okay. Well, he's obviously not okay but he's being cared for, they're monitoring him and keeping him stable.' He stopped. He had nothing else to say, nothing else to offer.

No-one spoke. He wanted to end it there, to walk off but having got their collective attention, he now had to find a way to disperse them.

'We'll put notices up on the board, every time there's an update, okay? Up there, next to the Rules, so you can check out the latest whenever you're in here.'

Something was bothering Anton, he said, 'Why did it happen? Do we know?'

Barney shook his head and drew breath to answer but it was George who had left the office and was standing at the noticeboard who spoke,

'No. We don't. Sometimes something like this happens. It's rare, it's nothing to do with Dave or with anyone else who worked with him,' Anton shivered at the use of the past tense, 'I saw something like it before, long time ago. Bad luck is the answer. Boxing has risks, we all know this, you all know this. Life has risks. We do what we can to stay safe, we have rules, that's the best we can do. One of them says,' he pointed at the Rules as he read, '"Boxers must report all health problems to their trainers..." that's the best we can do. Franny didn't report anything, he was feeling fine, it's one of those things.'

'What do we do?' asked one of them.

'Carry on, just be sensible,' said George. Barney had taken the chance to step down from the ring while George had been talking, it meant there was no focal point any longer once George had finished and had turned away. The small crowd started to break up, to get on with their days. Anton stopped Barney as he walked past him.

'Presumably, we can't visit?'

'No, not yet, no point, he's in a coma.'

'I know, I just… feel bad. I sparred with him that morning.'

'Yeah, and I asked you to do it. You heard George, no-one is to blame, seriously son, this has nothing to do with you.'

'Thanks,' said Anton, quietly.

The rings stayed empty through the morning although there was a lot of solo activity going on everywhere else and it wasn't long before the place just looked like any other gym, albeit a busy one for a weekday morning. The Boys Club was due to start at ten and Anton could see the numbers were down on the previous day; word was out and presumably some of the boys actually had parents who cared enough to keep them at home.

His own work out that morning was half hearted and unsatisfying. By noon he was finished, having failed to find enjoyment in anything he'd tried, and he still had no firm view on what to do about the laptop but thought he should call Sedge anyway, make sure all the options were still open. Sitting in the canteen at the back, he tried the number she had put into his phone, half expecting to be told the number he had dialled had not been recognised, but she surprised him again by answering.

'How's it going?' she asked.

'How did you know it was me?'

'I put my number in your phone then sent myself a message. You have to stop thinking of me as a useless girl.'

'I really don't Sedge. Anyway, I said I'd call. Thing is, I really don't know what I want to do.'

'You're afraid?'

'Yep,' he said. *That sums it up.*

'You should be. Probably all of us should be but I can disappear. I get it Anton, I really do. I mean it when I say I'll give you the laptop if you really need me to. I made a copy of the recording, maybe there's something I can do with that.'

'Sedge, I'm sorry, there's just too much going on right now. Let me try to buy some more time with Egerton, I think I know a way to do that. I'll call you tomorrow if that's okay, are you going to be there?'

'Yeah, yeah. We're in this together now,' she said as she hung up.

24

'You don't believe in appointments, do you Mr Matheson?' Valerie Atkinson-Pike stood in the doorway of the waiting room. She looked away from him at the receptionist who just raised her eyes in response.

'Come,' she beckoned him and walked away. He stood up and followed her down the corridor and into her office. She went behind the desk, stayed standing and looked at him. 'Shut the door,' he obeyed and came into the room, she was doing a good job of looking annoyed, not in the mood for a long conversation.

'I met with your Mr Brown,' said Anton.

'Let me stop you there, I have no idea who Mr Brown is.'

'Oh yeah, of course. Anyway, he seems to think I know where the missing laptop is, I don't.'

'So?'

'So, I need someone to help me to convince him; you know me a little bit and know I don't want any trouble, I'm not trying to rip anyone off.'

'Maybe this Mr Brown thinks you do know where it is,' she fixed him with that stare again. 'You do, don't you?' Anton shook his head and tried to speak but she cut him off, 'Maybe your girlfriend knows where it is…?'

'What girlfriend?' said Anton.

'Oh, Mr Matheson… How many are there?'

'Not funny,' said Anton.

'I'm not laughing,' said Atkinson-Pike, 'anyway, I was thinking of the Italian one.'

'She has nothing to do with this, or anything,' said Anton.

'That's fortunate. Otherwise, I am sure she would be of enormous interest to Mr Brown,' she smiled at him and started to look through some papers on her desk. 'I suppose what you're saying is, if I knew Mr Brown, you would like me to persuade him to give you a few days to find the laptop,' she carried on looking through the papers while Anton thought about it, then looked up at him and raised her eyebrows, 'hmmm?'

'Yes. Yes, I suppose that's right. I'm looking.'

'Hmmm. Goodbye Mr Matheson.'

Once again, he was left with the walk from her office back the way he came, the receptionist paying little attention to him. He stopped before he reached the door and leant against the wall while he made a call. Carol Morrison answered.

'It's Anton. I'm coming over, is half an hour good for you?'

'Yes. We're ready, thank you,' he sensed she wasn't finished and waited until she added, 'Anton, it's not you… the reason we're going,'

'I know. I get it, I really do understand. It's probably for the best.'

'We don't have a choice, you'll see when you get here,'

'What do you mean?' He wondered if it was him or whether everyone around him really was being obscure these days.

'You'll see… what I wanted to say was, with us, you and me… I don't regret anything. It was… special. Thank you for keeping it as our secret.'

'I know, me too,' *except of course, I lost my girlfriend who I might well have gone and proposed to otherwise.* 'I'll be there in thirty minutes.'

It was obvious there was something going on at Beulah Mansions as he drew close. Two once-white Transit vans were outside; men were taking boxes and furniture from them into the building, others stood outside, smoking and talking, watching Anton arrive but saying nothing. Once he was inside, he could see into the ground floor flat where the door was wedged open. There were people everywhere, men that is, no women.

They were moving furniture in, a few more were busying themselves at the back, Anton could see through and see them going in and out of the garden. But most were sitting around, some on chairs some on the floor; either this was the most over-staffed removal company ever or there was some kind of weird men-only party going on.

He climbed the stairs to the first floor where the door to that flat was also open, looking inside he could see more men, fewer than downstairs but making more noise: talking, laughing, arguing, there was also at least one television on loud, cutting through the rest of the hubbub; cigarette smoke was all around.

He reached the second floor and rang the bell. Carol answered.

'Told you.'

'What are..?' he gestured in the direction of the floors below.

'Come in,' she said and kissed him lightly on the cheek.

Paul was in the kitchen, washing up a couple of coffee mugs, he looked round when Anton walked in and nodded an acknowledgement then carried on drying the mugs, wrapping them in a tea towel and placing them gently in the top of a removal box.

'Sorry we had to rush this,' said Carol.

'Its fine, I get it,' said Anton, wondering if there was any more to Paul's frostiness than just weariness with the neighbours. 'What's going on downstairs?'

'You tell us,' said Paul as he pushed the cardboard flaps down on the box and stuck a strip of parcel tape over them.

Carol filled the silence, 'It's been going on for a couple of days, people coming and going, a lot of them, more and more. They're not particularly noisy or causing trouble it's just impossible for that many men to be at all quiet.' Paul had finished sealing the box and he stood now leaning against the sink staring Anton out. *She's told him.*

'Let's do a walk round,' said Anton, 'the kitchen looks fine… ' He was in no mood to drag this out.

'It is,' said Paul, 'I'm assuming you're going to give some serious thought to refunding our last month's rent… at least.' *You're pushing your luck mate*, Anton thought to himself, *I'm about to give you your deposit back without any fuss and that doesn't usually happen,* but instead he said,

'Not my decision ultimately but I'll ask on your behalf.'

'Yes, you do that please,' Paul still with a look about him that Anton didn't feel was altogether friendly.

'I'll make the request. Have we got your new address?' Paul handed him a folded sheet of paper that he had ready, Anton opened it and saw the address written out in capital letters for extra clarity; he nodded to show he understood. 'My dad uses cheques still… old school. He'll work it out and whatever we owe will get sent to you.'

'You sure?'

'I'm sure, and you've got my number if you haven't heard anything by the end of the week,' he looked up at Paul who was still staring at him, unsmiling, making a point. Anton even felt a little sorry for him, *can't really blame him for a bit of reasserting.* It was hard to know if Carol had told him anything, but he might just have made a guess or two. That was in addition to the undeniable fact that their home had become an unhomely place to be. 'I need to look round though.'

He turned and left the kitchen, Carol behind him as he walked through each room, looking over each of them but not too closely, he really didn't want to find anything that was going to cost money to put right. He finished up in the living room, moving the table out to check the carpet beneath and the same with the sofa which he patted as he put it back without realising he was doing it until it was too late. He replayed a little memory of the last time he had been there but kept it to himself.

He still had the folded paper in his hand, and he used it as a prop to wave before placing it in his jacket pocket as he said, 'You'll get the deposit back in full.'

'Thank you,' said Carol.

'We'll write, I promise,' Paul had come into the living room, holding two sets of keys which he handed to him, 'thanks,' said Anton.

'Good luck with finding the next tenant,' said Paul and turned away. Anton just nodded and smiled grimly.

Carol walked with him to the front door, opened it to let him out and asked if they should just pull it closed when they came to leave.

'Yes, please,' he said, taking a last look at her. 'I really hope things work out for you both.' She looked tired but there was something in her eyes that made him wonder what she was thinking. She stood aside to let him out and as he passed her, she leant in and kissed him briefly on the lips.

'Bon chance. You're going to need it,' she said, pointing downstairs.

'I really do hope things work out for you,' he looked over her shoulder to be sure Paul had gone then reached out to gently cup her cheek in his palm. She smiled at him, waited for a moment then turned, saying,

'See you.'

Anton pulled the door closed and walked slowly back down the stairs, past the flats full of comings and goings and anonymous men, and out to the street.

He started walking nowhere in particular, it was getting dark, but it was dry, and it felt good to be out in the clear crisp air.

He let his mind wander to think about Carol, about their time together, what she had been wearing, what she'd said, the noise they'd made together. It was a memory out of time, part of another life. History. He thought about Franca, whether she was now history too. He wondered whether she had seen the card yet, whether it would be a good idea to call her, even got as far as taking his phone out and bringing her name up but held back from making the call, what else was there to say?

He took a bus and got off a couple of stops away from his home just so he could walk past Purely Pizza. She wasn't there, neither was her annoying friend Sally; he thought to himself that he would have been pleased to see even her.

The gym was busy again the next day from the moment it opened. Along with everybody else, Anton made the noticeboard his first port of call. On it was pinned a note which read: "Franny Richardson, update. Stable condition. No change." A couple of them complained to each other at the terseness of the message but the way he saw it was that it was good to get to the point.

By the time the Boys Club was due to start there were just two of them. Anton assumed these were two about whom nobody cared at all, a thought that made him shiver. With Franny out of the picture and Barney working one to one with Kirby, he had some time spare so offered to help, give them some boxing coaching. The boys were keen, and it would bring one of the rings back into use, they'd become no-go areas since the incident and that didn't do anyone any good.

The boys changed and Anton showed them a few simple moves, got them working so they had a sense of how it could be competitive. One was a foot taller than the other, so he worked something out where the shorter one got three shots in to the other's two. It was a hopelessly complicated system that both boys quickly forgot or possibly ignored but Anton let them get on with it, it wasn't so bad anyway because the shorter one was a bit of a natural who had to be coached to hold back a little, so keen was he to belt someone.

'It's a sport, remember, a match. You use your skill to win points, to out manoeuvre your opponent… most of all you respect your opponent. Remember that, read the Rules sometime if you haven't already, there's one that says we respect each other. That's important, remember that.'

He stopped them for a moment and brought them together, looking from one to the other, looking them in the eye for emphasis. 'It's not just about trying to batter someone. Do that and you'll find you lose when you come up against someone who knows what they're doing, okay?'

An hour or so later and they were boxing, real boxing of a kind. George had appeared and was sitting at a table with Nico and watching them. Anton hadn't seen Nico arrive, he was just there all of a sudden and he wondered if he should maybe try and talk to him, find a way that didn't feel awkward. The boys continued boxing for one or two minutes at a time, Anton stopping it every now and again and showing them some moves to try, sometimes over and over to get a point across, trying to get them to learn something. After another hour they were done, exhausted but exhilarated too.

'Tomorrow? Can we do this again tomorrow?' said the taller one. Anton looked at him then over to Barney who had joined the watching crowd, he nodded back. Anton said,

'Okay, same time tomorrow, ten o'clock, see if you can remember some of this.' The boys climbed out of the ring, sat on a bench for a while to get their breath back, talked about jabs and feints then pulled some of their clothes back on to stay warm.

'Nice work,' said George.

'Thanks,' said Anton, pulling up a chair across from Nico, 'they're good lads.'

'Lost a few eh?' said George.

'Perhaps they'll be back,' said Anton, 'it was a freak accident, right?'

George nodded, 'But they remember you for it. It's a one-in-a-million chance but one thing goes wrong, suddenly it's dangerous to come here.'

'Do you know what the doctors are saying?' said Anton, to George but loud enough for Barney to hear, just in case he felt inclined to answer. George just shook his head, but Nico spoke,

'It's a sad thing.'

'Yeah,' said Anton, 'it is, very.'

'How are you doing?' said Nico.

'Oh, um, yeah, I'm fine, thanks. You?' Nico nodded, 'I don't know if you know but Franca and me, we…'

'I heard something. Not my business.' Nico looked down at the table. Anton felt awkward now and was grateful to be rescued by Barney.

'Can we have a word?' Anton got up and followed him out to the office.

'George is hurt by all this, you have to give him some time, it's all going fairly tits-up at the moment.'

'He's still selling up?'

'I think so, yes. I don't know. He's embarrassed by it, doesn't want to talk about it, he doesn't realise that just makes it worse for the rest of us.' He sat behind the desk and indicated that Anton should sit on the chair opposite. 'This thing with Franny just makes it more likely… people stop coming, and we can't go on. His heart's gone out of it,'

'You can't persuade him?' said Anton.

'Yeah, if I won the lottery.'

'What do you know about Nico?'

'Nico? I think it's mostly his money. They're good friends. I never really knew the full set up but I'm fairly sure it's Nico who is the main man when it comes to real estate.'

'Yes,' Anton's mind wandering now, thinking back to the dinner they'd shared at Franca's home.

'Sorry Anton.'

'Eh?'

'I think we're going to close,' Barney looked at him, trying to bring him into it, 'I know they've been talking about it; people have been round to check it out. There's an offer. If they take it then I'm fairly certain the club will close.'

'Is this the nightclub plan?'

'Maybe. It's not George and Nico's idea so who knows, but yes, I've heard that. I don't even know what one of those is these days.' Anton sat quietly, not knowing what to say. 'Sorry.'

Anton felt down for the rest of the day, if anything, his gloom grew more profound as the day wore on and he almost forgot he was meant to call Sedge. He got round to it late in the afternoon, there was no answer, but it went to voicemail which at least was promising, it was even her voice on the message.

He thought for a moment then decided he needed to say something.

'It's Anton, hi. I've thought about the laptop… like I said I would, and I think… I think we have to give it back. I'm sorry Sedge and I hope you're okay with this, but I want to talk it through with you whatever so please call me, or I'll call you tomorrow… let's talk.'

He walked home from the gym, changed, picked up the Outlander and drove towards Franca's home. He had no plan but hoped one would occur to him on the way. Maybe he could park up somewhere close by and see her, try to say *hi,* keep it light… try to make it look like he wasn't just spying on her. As he drew near, he thought about turning round but carried on until he turned into her street then drove up and parked on the opposite side of the road about seven or eight houses down. He sat for a few moments looking at the house then said out loud to himself,

'Okay, so I am in fact going to spy on her.' He slumped down in the seat and watched the house. The lights were on, but no-one arrived or left. Half an hour went by before he turned the radio on, found a station playing some mellow music and let it play even though the more he listened, the more melancholic his mood became. A few people passed by, but no-one seemed to pay him any attention. He watched the house, but nothing changed, he carried on watching and waiting.

He went over in his head what he would say if she appeared. If she were alone, he'd just say *hello* and see what happened, if she was with someone else, he'd need to make a snap decision. If she was with another man… *what if she was with someone else? Like a new boyfriend, for example? No, that wasn't like Franca.* He watched some more.

He came to with a start. Someone had tapped on the driver's side window. He looked up and saw one of Brown's men from the flat, the middleweight.

'Hey sucker, what you doing? Playing hard to get? Or she kick you out?' Anton looked at him, trying to work out why he was there. 'Anyway, you stay there, I'll go and sort her out for you,' he straightened up and took a couple of steps back from the car.

Anton fell for it and opened the door. The middleweight took a couple more steps away from him and said, 'That's a good idea, actually, I think I'll go and fuck your girlfriend.' Anton got out of the car and stood facing him, he took a step forward and was about to speak when he felt blinding pain on the back of his head, he saw a flash of light, then just blackness; his legs gave way and he fell forward. He was out before he hit the ground.

25

When he came to, he was back in the driver's seat, his head on the steering wheel. Everything was wet and sticky. There was blood on his face and on the wheel as he lifted his head away; as he tried to straighten up, he saw more blood, over his shirt, his jacket, everywhere.

It hurt to move, everything hurt. The back of his head was the source of intense and angry pain, when he touched it he flinched and felt more stickiness there. One of his eyes wouldn't open, the other had so much viscous gunk in it, he had to wipe it away with his sleeve. He was in the same place, across the road and along a little from Franca's home, only now there were flashing lights outside the house, two police cars and a third just pulling up, an ambulance too, uniforms moving around, talking to each other, walking back and forth into the house, into Franca's home.

He opened the door of the car and stepped out, trying to stand but his legs wouldn't work, and he landed on his knees. His head hurt even more when he tried to move but he needed to get up, so he used the door to steady himself and slowly stood. His legs were unsteady but could bear his weight if he concentrated. He tried to focus but couldn't see enough to understand what was going on. He tried to walk but could only stumble, wincing with pain at the jolts that ran through his body, but he kept on, slowly, carefully across the road toward the house.

As he got closer the flashing lights grew brighter and began to hurt, he put an arm up to shield his eyes, trying see through it all. The front door was open and sitting on the front step was Franca, she was wrapped in a blanket although she was clothed, Anton could see the legs of her jeans below the line of it. She held a towel over her face. He got closer and she looked up,

'What the fuck? Have you got something to do with this?'

One of the police nearby turned and started to walk over to him. Anton tried to speak but found that he couldn't, so he shook his head which hurt too much to do twice.

'What happened to you anyway?' she asked.

The young cop reached them and spoke to her, 'Do you know this man, miss?'

'Yes, he's an arsehole,' she said.

'What do you know about this sir?' asked the cop, Anton looking at him but not yet able to make words, 'do you know who did this, sir?' *You bet,* thought Anton, *I know who it was, not their names of course but I know what they look like.* 'Sir?'

Anton shook his head very gently and managed to say, 'No,' he looked at Franca again and said slowly, 'Did… they...?'

'No,' she said, 'I'm still a virgin...'

'We really need you to tell us what you know about this, sir…' the cop trying to get through, but Anton had stopped listening and so had Franca,

'… but my mum is in that ambulance, and I don't know if she's going to die tonight.'

Anton stumbled again, 'Little… Gregory?'

'He hid, somehow, somewhere… he's in there.' Anton swayed and began to lose his balance, vomited suddenly, and collapsed, the cop reaching out and catching his head as he fell, cushioning him as he folded down onto the pavement and sweet, black, nothingness: oblivion.

He woke up in a hospital bed, there was a tube coming out of his nose and another attached to a needle in his arm. He had something on his head, something wrapped round it, and it still hurt. In a chair at the side of the bed, a young cop was asleep, his feet stretched out, he was snoring. Anton tried to move and found it hurt. When he groaned, the cop opened his eyes.

'Ah, morning.'

'Morning?' said Anton.

'Yes, technically; it's gone midnight. How are we doing?'

Anton thought for a moment then summed it up, 'Everything, everything fucking hurts.'

'Yes, it looks like it might. You're Anton Matheson, is that right?' Anton nodded very carefully and grunted affirmation.

'I'm PC Keyes,' he looked at Anton who didn't react, 'Andrew… Andy if you like; the lads call me Alan…' he waited for a reaction, but Anton was still trying to concentrate on staying as still as possible. '… Keyes.' Anton gave a sign of recognition and nodded slowly, he hadn't found a way to move yet that didn't hurt, and this guy was making jokes about his own name or something… 'you want to tell me what you were doing there?'

'She's… my girlfriend,' Anton tried, hoping that would do.

'I hope this isn't a shock for you sir, but I think you may have broken up now.'

'Ha ha,' said Anton, without laughing.

'What happened? To you?'

'I got jumped, I was out of my car… I don't really remember.'

'Do you know who they were?' Anton was slowly remembering, thinking he sort of did know who they were, but he wasn't sure at this stage that he wanted to share. He shook his head slowly.

'What happened to the people in the house? To Franca and Rosa?'

'It's not that clear but it looks like there were two men, they knocked on the door, the old lady answered…'

'Old lady?'

'Fair enough, she's not that old, older of the two then. She answered and one of the men goes batshit crazy and hits her, more than once we think. She goes down and the girl comes out from the back somewhere and they give it to her too but not so bad.'

'What happened to the old lady?'

'She's in here somewhere. You're in a hospital in case you hadn't worked that out yet.'

'She okay?'

'Not sure, she didn't look it when she came in. So, do you know anything? It would help. The two men, we didn't get a useful description, they had hoods up, so the girl didn't see their faces. Apparently, one of them said *go easy, we're not meant to kill anyone,* so it sounds like it was planned, we don't know why. Think it might have been the same two jumped you?'

'I suppose so,' Anton lifted the tube that was lying on his chest, the one that was coming out of his nose, 'what's this about?'

'They started to pump your stomach; thought you'd taken something. I didn't think so if that helps at all, but they insisted. They stopped when they got your blood tests back and found there was nothing amiss… you don't remember?'

He did, sort of. He remembered what seemed to be a dream: he was kneeling on the bed, being held and someone pushing the tube up his nose, then into his throat, he remembered retching, trying to vomit some more, one of them saying *swallow the tube, try and swallow, come on, swallow, there you go…. well done.*

'Hey,' it was Keyes again, 'I'm going to go and see if we can get this tube taken out at least. If you think of anything, anything you think might be useful then we would really like to know. Who do you want us to call?'

'My brother, Neville. On my phone, he's the only Neville,' Keyes already had his phone; at least he hadn't lost that. He told Keyes his PIN and let him make the call. Keyes left him to go and find a nurse. Anton lay there, as still as he could. All he could think was, *shit, everything changes now. Life is different from here on in.*

It was past three am before Anton was discharged. One of the doctors was concerned enough to try and get him admitted but Neville had made it his mission to spring his brother and save him from the horrors of a night in the hospital, his own recent experience colouring his view of the matter.

'You stay overnight in one of these places, your chances of survival, I'm talking actual survival, reduce; I'm serious.'

The police had their statement, minimal as it was and had left. The blow to Anton's head didn't seem to have resulted in any lasting concussion and Neville had given the staff his assurance that his brother would be nurtured and looked after properly back home, he would personally make sure he was cared for.

'How much have you told Dad?' asked Anton as they sat in the back of a minicab, Neville still not able to drive and besides, the Outlander needed a bit of valeting to say the least.

'Nothing. We don't even really know who it was, do we?'

'Yeah we do, I recognised one of them from the flat.'

'What do you want to do?'

'I left a message for Sedge, yesterday. I want to get the laptop back to Egerton. I don't know if she'll agree to that yet, she's on a mission but I'm going to try and persuade her. If we can do that…'

'I thought you squared all this with Atkinson-Pike?'

'So did I, they must be desperate. Or she doesn't have quite pull with them as we thought.'

Malcolm was awake and had the kettle on when they got back, the first thing he did was hug Anton, hold him tight, Anton realised he had been genuinely scared. They drank tea and Anton managed to duck any really difficult questions. For now, Malcolm was grateful to see his son alive; next thing was to get some sleep.

Anton set an alarm for eight. When it went off, he groaned out loud and when he tried to move, he failed to find a way to do so without inducing pain. He bent his legs to relieve the muscle tension but that took an effort of will to overcome the pain that had set in. It hurt more when he rolled over onto his side and tried to sit up on the edge of the bed. Slowly he got there and sat upright, now his head hurt too. He staggered clumsily out to the bathroom to empty his bladder, then nervously made his way down the stairs to the kitchen. He thought about making some coffee, but the idea made him feel sick, so he drank water in little sips. After a while he ordered a minicab.

When he walked into the gym, people stopped to look at him and stared, he had underestimated just what mess his face was in.

'What the fuck happened to you?' was asked of him more than once.

'You should see the other guy,' he joked back, which worked on everyone except Barney who stayed stony-faced and demanded more information. Anton invented a mugging: *one of those things, just bad luck,* but Barney wasn't having any of it, his gut told him something else was up.

'You can always talk to me, you know, ask for help if you need it.'

'I know,' said Anton, 'appreciated. Really.'

'What are you even doing here? You look like you should be at home.'

'Boys Club. I promised them. There's only two left, we can't lose them.'

When the boys walked in they were impressed with his injuries and they too were not going to be given the brush off with a vague story, so Anton embellished the tale of the mugging, adding layers of detail that he tried to store in his memory in case he had to return to the story sometime later on.

Barney waited until the boys went to change and he put an arm round Anton's shoulder and said to him, 'You know what they say?' Anton looked at him and raised an eyebrow, 'The truth will set you free.' Anton smiled at him but wasn't ready to be any more forthcoming. 'Son, you can't work out with these lads, you're walking about like an arthritic old man and your face looks like a pizza.'

'Thanks. No-one else free to do it, we can't let them down.'

'I'll do it,' a voice came from behind them. Anton looked round to see Kirby.

'You've got your programme to follow,' Anton said, then to Barney, 'hasn't he?'

'I can take a morning off, be good to think about something else, besides, your face *does* look like a pizza.'

'Okay, I got the pizza thing.'

'It's a good idea,' said Barney, which meant it would happen.

'Okay, thanks then,' said Anton, relieved. He really did need to go and lie down. The boys arrived back, 'Okay, this man's going to work with you. He's turning pro soon so you're getting some top coaching here. I'll come back soon, alright?'

Kirby was lifting the ropes to invite them to step into the ring, 'Okay, let's see what he taught you,' he said as he climbed in behind them.

Anton went out back to the canteen to sit down and call Sedge. He was pleasantly surprised when she answered. He was ready for resistance, but she gave none, saying she quite understood his position. He couldn't be sure he wasn't still being followed, indeed recent experience suggested he was, so he asked her to come to the gym, to the back door. She said she would be there shortly. He felt the need to lie down so took a couple of cushions off the chairs and put them on the floor then groaned out loud when he tried to straighten his legs out before settling and pulling his coat up around him, cocooned.

His phone woke him.

'It's me, I'm at the back door.' It took him a minute or two to get on his feet, then lumber out to the door during which time she rang again but he ignored it and concentrated on moving forward. As he reached the door he could hear her on the other side, 'I'm freezing out here.' A wisp of frozen air stole in as he opened the door, she looked startled, 'What the billy-flip happened to you?'

She stood, hunched in a coat that made him think of a furry Battenberg cake, it was made up of pink and yellow squares; she had one hand in the coat pocket, the other holding a supermarket carrier bag.

'Sorry, didn't mean to frighten you.'

'This boxing lark looks kinda dangerous.'

'Nothing to do with boxing,' he closed the door behind her and led her to the canteen, 'I bumped into a couple of your friends,' he picked the cushions up from the floor and put them back in the chairs. 'Is that it?' he reached out to take the bag from her, but she pulled it away.

'Careful cowboy, before you do anything, you need to know this: I've cleaned it, thoroughly, so there are no fingerprints of mine on it, and I strongly recommend you keep yours off it too. We don't know what might happen to this little baby after we hand it over. Keep it in this bag or use gloves, don't touch it, okay?'

'Okay,' he said, unsure why fingerprints could be a thing. She handed the bag to him, and he opened it to look inside, 'What all the fuss is about, eh?' Sedge was looking at him carefully.

'What happened?'

'I got jumped, I didn't see it coming. They must really want this back. Thank you, Sedge, I know you want to get him.'

'Who says I can't? I still have the copy of the webcam conversation.'

'Is it enough? I don't even know what law he's broken.'

'There's going to be one,' he looked at her quizzically, 'a law, I read about it, I'm interested in the subject. They're going to bring one in.'

'Good.'

'Right now, though, I don't know.'

'Stay out of it would be my advice,' said Anton, thinking that was the end of it.

'Too late for that. Where do you think I come from?' Anton didn't answer but gestured that she should say more, 'He brought me over,'

'Egerton?'

She nodded, 'Arranged it all anyway. There were a few of us, all girls that time, I was thirteen. I wasn't being recruited for a nail bar, that's for sure.' She stopped, not sure about carrying on. Anton filled the space.

'Where from?'

'Albania, a village near the capital. He's done well for himself out there. I'd say from the webcam that he's still doing well for himself.'

'I'm sorry,' said Anton, 'I don't know what to say.'

'Wasn't you,' her eyes were watery as she looked back at him.

'Sedge, it's okay, you don't need to-'

'-I don't see why you shouldn't hear it. I'm not going to cry, don't worry, I did all that.'

'What… happened to you?'

'I don't need to fill in the details, do I?' Anton shook his head. 'The truth is, I got lucky. There was a man, a client, he was new to it all. I think he had a notion that he wanted something then found out when he got it that he didn't have the stomach for it… to his credit, you might even say. He had money though. He told me I could run; I said I couldn't, they would kill me, they'd always told us that.

'He said he'd help, and he did as well. He took me in his car, paid my keeper money to let him take me back to his place; she said, make sure you come back, or else… he drove me to London, found a hotel. Oh God, that hotel, it was luxury… paid for two weeks' stay on his credit card. I told him I could make it; I could get by somewhere where I wasn't known. He said he'd come back in a week, and he did, he gave me three thousand pounds cash, just like that, said it was what he could afford. I got a flat share, a job, I studied, and I started again: new name, new friends, real, ordinary people. I made up a story about who I was… and I got free. I'm the only one I know of who ever did. So, for the sake of everyone else who didn't get lucky, I would like to see if I can find a way to stop him, or slow him down, get him put away or…' Anton waited for her to finish the sentence, but she just let it hang in the air.

'How?'

She just nodded gently and said, 'Just make sure you don't touch that laptop, keep it in the bag,' she got up to leave, 'see you around Anton, I hope you get some peace now.'

'Thanks Sedge, I… see you again perhaps?'

She didn't answer but he walked with her to the door, followed her out into the grey winter and watched her go, walk slowly across the road, turn up Briar Lane and carry on up the hill pulling the coat tightly around herself, *definitely looks like a Battenberg* he thought. She didn't look back and the wind was picking up, so Anton went back inside and called Egerton. After a couple of rings, he answered, sounded interested too, not his usual distracted, only half listening drone.

'Anton, I trust you're well?' *And they call me the funny man.*

'I've been better to tell you the truth, but I have something that you are interested in.' Despite his very strong urge to get rid of the laptop once and for all and as quickly as possible, he also had an overwhelming need to lie down and an encounter right now with Egerton was less than appealing. 'I'm going to pick it up tomorrow morning-'

'-I need it back today.'

'I can't, the person who has it is travelling into town tomorrow morning and bringing it, I'll come over to you after that.' He waited while Egerton thought that one over.

'I'm not in the office tomorrow, I have some urgent business to deal with.'

'Okay, I'll hang on to it and come over when you're ready.'

'I'll send someone to pick it up.'

'No way. I'm handing it to you, only you, this thing has been enough trouble, I want to see you take it.' Egerton thought about that for a moment then gave Anton an address that sounded like it wasn't too far away and told him to just turn up and ask for him.

'About twelve okay with you?'

'Twelve is good,' said Egerton. 'Don't forget now.'

Anton got off the phone and saw both his father and brother had been calling, there was a voicemail too from Neville, nagging but *in a brotherly way,* as he put it.

He took a minicab home, sent a message to say he was doing so and asked the driver to go slowly, as the nausea had started to come back. He wanted to call Franca, check out how she was. He wanted to hold her, say he was sorry for bringing down this shit storm but knew he couldn't do that even if she somehow came round to the idea of speaking to him. He almost called from the cab but the chances of the signal cutting out while they were travelling made him wait. He also had no idea what to say apart from asking how she was; knowing Franca, she might just tell him.

Once home, he managed to avoid too much fussing from his father who looked genuinely concerned. Anton tried to reassure him that he was doing okay but needed to lie down now. He retreated to his room with a mug of hot tea and still holding the bag that Sedge had given him, which he placed under the bed.

He sat on the bed, took a deep breath, and dialled. She answered.

'Hey. I know you're pissed off. I just wanted to know how you're doing, and how's Rosa?'

'Pissed off doesn't altogether cover it Anton. I'm really fucking angry,' he kept quiet, she'd picked up after all, it was possibly just so she could shout at him, but it was a start. 'I'm okay I suppose, considering. I got sent home last night but Rosa's still there, apart from shock she has a broken jaw so she's going to need an operation.'

'Shit.'

'That's what it is.' She was quiet for a few moments then said, 'You?'

'Yeah, I'm okay, better than last night. It looks worse than it is. Sorry I freaked you out.'

'Who were they?'

'I don't know, Franca, I'm really sorry, I…'

'And what were you doing there?'

'I came to see you; I wanted to try and talk.'

'It's a heck of a way to get a conversation going.'

'Did they take anything?'

'I don't think that was the idea,' she said. *They were making a point,* thought Anton, 'I still don't get what you were doing there.'

'Just bad timing. I told the police everything I know which is nothing really.' He tried to piece together how Franca would see all this, from her angle it might look like more than just bad luck.

'Were you spying on me?'

'No,' he said. *Yes,* he thought.

'So, you came along, and these two creeps picked on you first before they called on us?' He didn't answer, the less said now the better. 'So, were you planning on calling round?'

'I don't know… yes, maybe. To say that I'm sorry, profoundly sorry. I suppose also I wanted to know how you were.'

'You hurt me, Anton.'

He waited a while before speaking, 'Yes, I know.'

'So, I don't trust you, I will never trust you.'

'I just… I miss you, Franca. That's it, that's all really.'

'How am I supposed to trust you ever again?' He could hear she was crying; he was wise enough to know there was no answer to that yet.

'Can I go and see Rosa? Visit her?'

'I suppose so, she liked you. I didn't tell her what you did, she just thinks we had a falling out.'

'I'll go tomorrow.'

'No flowers, they don't allow them, I know you're all big on fucking flowers.'

'Okay, Franca…'

'Don't say you're sorry again, I'll scream, I can't cope with it. I've got to go; I've got clearing up to do.'

'Okay, thanks for taking the call.'

She said *bye* and was gone. He was weary, aware that he needed to lie down again, needed to drift away.

26

He woke early the next morning. Someone had come in and put a duvet over him, his shoes had been removed too although he wasn't sure he hadn't done that himself before calling Franca.

He remembered the call, it hadn't been all bad, she was still upset but she was talking to him again. Half a mug of cold tea was on the bedside table, and he was desperate to pee. It was dark outside and cold in the room; the heating hadn't clicked on yet. When he got back to bed, he checked his phone which told him it was just after five. He sent a text to Barney to say he needed to rest for the day if that was okay and could someone perhaps just find something productive for the boys to do that morning. He took some of his clothes off and got into bed.

The next time he was awake it was nearly eleven. His body ached and his legs were stiff and slow to move but he felt better for the sleep. While he drank coffee, he sent a text to Egerton to say he'd be there for one, a terse *OK* came back.

The address Egerton had given him was in town, one of the wealthier sounding areas, somewhere he didn't know, there had been no reason for him to go there up to this point. Getting off the bus and clutching the carrier bag, which he'd been smart enough to place inside a second bag to allow him to hand the thing over without any risk of touching it, he took a look around.

He checked the address against the map on his phone, it was a four-minute walk away. He was early, so took his time about it, taking in the sights and sounds. It felt to him like a town within a town. He was a stranger, but no-one seemed to pay him any attention, they were too busy going from place to place, in and out of the shops, weaving along the streets, crossing the roads and forcing any vehicles to move at a crawl.

There was a lot of talk, languages unknown to him, words he could make no sense of that clashed in the air in a constant babble. He walked past cafes and coffee bars, restaurants that were doing good business, grocers and mini markets with exotic looking fruit and vegetables displayed on the street even though it was still winter. Not so much a town within a town, rather a little planet all of its own.

It took him a while to find the address, but he was in no hurry. It was a huge building, looked like it might have been an Embassy or some such previously: six windows wide and it rose four storeys; at ground level there was a door in the middle which was open. He walked in and again, as at Beulah Mansions there were men everywhere: young to middle aged, no old ones and no women. Most were sat or slumped on benches set along the walls or sitting and leaning on tables talking to each other; there was smoke in the air.

One or two of the men who were better dressed were walking about, giving orders, organising things, in charge of some part of whatever this was. One of them, a younger man in a shiny black and flashy looking puffer jacket, fashionably torn jeans and what looked like snakeskin boots, saw him and walked over.

'Yes boss, what can I do for you?'

'I'm looking for Egerton,' said Anton.

'What you want from him?' He tilted his head back while keeping eye contact, 'He expects you?' Anton nodded his reply, 'Out the back, all the way through,' stepping back to let Anton pass by. He thanked him and walked down the corridor, past more open doors, and through to the other side of the building and a set of French windows which opened out onto a patch of grass that was overgrown but edged by a shrub or two and a few patches of vegetation that looked like they might come to life in the summer.

At the end of the short garden was a large shed built up against the boundary wall, it would have been big enough for a couple of cars if there had been a way to get a vehicle anywhere near it. He heard voices from inside so walked to the door and looked in. There were bunk beds, stacked three high against the far wall and along one of sides. Against the other side wall was a rudimentary stove, an unsteady looking table with a kettle on it and three large glass jugs of water. Egerton stood by the bunks at the end holding a clipboard and writing, he looked up and smiled.

'Welcome Anton.'

'What is this place?'

'You've never seen a hotel before?' Egerton guided him out to the garden where Anton handed him the laptop, encased snugly in the carrier bag. 'Did you have it all along?'

'No. I had to go and find it for you, you didn't make that any easier either, your boys following me everywhere…'

'They're not my boys Anton, they work for one of my more nervous colleagues.' He had been staring at Anton's face, 'What happened to you?' *Nice,* thought Anton.

'I think I met some friends of one of your more nervous colleagues.'

'Sorry to hear that,' said Egerton, actually sounding like he might have meant it. 'You take a look at this?' He held up the carrier bag.

Anton shook his head, 'There's no charger,' he looked at him for a moment, 'there wasn't one, was there?' Egerton laughed and shook his head. 'Plus, I would imagine that you have a password and lastly, I have no interest whatsoever in what might be on it.'

'None at all? Not even curious?'

'Not even a smidgen.'

'It's all just business, but it would have been inconvenient to lose it.'

'Business, as in the cut price hotel business? No offence intended.'

'None taken, I'm just fulfilling a need, meeting a demand. They've got nowhere else they can afford to go; I keep the rain off their heads.'

'Nice of you.'

'One way to look at it.' Egerton was more relaxed now and even managed a smile, 'Cassius eh? Since when did a boxer know about Shakespeare?'

'I went to school,'

'So did I,'

'I paid attention.'

'And here we are,' said Egerton, looking pleased with himself.

'Anyway, lovely as it is to chat, you've got the laptop back now; can I assume that you will make sure nothing else happens to me or anyone I know, that you can calm the nerves of your colleagues once and for all?'

Egerton nodded, 'I'm sure your troubles are all over Anton. You know, if you ever felt like you wanted a new job, maybe make a bit more money than you do at the moment, let me know, I could use you.' Anton had started to leave but stopped and looked round at him, Egerton stood there holding the carrier bag, he looked confident, content, happy with his lot.

'Not my cup of tea,' said Anton.

'Don't judge,' said Egerton, 'not unless you have another idea for who's going to do all those jobs you don't want to do,' he paused, smiled again. 'You'd be surprised.' It dawned on Anton that this was now definitely the very last place on Earth that he wanted to be. He turned to go.

'Still not my thing,' he said, not looking back, 'see you.'

He walked out into the streets of this newly discovered mini planet, content in his anonymity. There was little motor traffic, just pedestrians, everywhere. He drew a long deep breath of the keen air into his lungs, feeling deep inside a cold burn that cleansed and purified. He had a notion to talk to Sedge and called her number, she didn't answer but it went to voicemail which gave him hope to think she'd see he had called; he had no idea what message to leave so hung up.

He was relieved, no doubt about it, to no longer have the laptop and believed that Egerton would ensure that he was left alone now but he was unsettled by whatever it was that Egerton was up to.

Sedge's story had been upsetting but he had assumed it was an exaggeration or at least a little played up for his benefit, but maybe not. And why would she anyway? It wasn't as if she wanted or needed to impress him, she wasn't trying to hook him in some way and she didn't seem to want anything except some kind of undefined vengeance. How did she even know it was Egerton who had brought her here?

As he walked, he realised he liked Sedge, he wanted to please her, and he felt he'd let her down in some way by asking her to give up the laptop. The blankness in Egerton's eyes and their short conversation made her story seem only too plausible. Perhaps they would meet again, he would get a chance to talk to her some more.

He was looking out for a coffee shop or something like it to just sit for a moment and let his thoughts calm down; instead, he saw a sign that read "Cioccolatini" above a window display of chocolate that would have broken any dieter's spirit. He remembered that he had intended to go and see Rosa, and this was surely the shop in which to find something to take to her.

After a few minutes walking round inside and admiring the displays, he selected two dozen different dark chocolates, each with its own flavour and each topped with a brightly coloured swirl of icing. He approached the till then doubled back and put together a small box of six for himself, for later.

The woman at the till was around his age but somehow imperious, she had class and was immaculately and expensively dressed. He almost blushed when she took the boxes he'd put together and wrapped them delicately in branded tissue paper. He did a double take when he saw the price rung up on the till but took out his credit card and handed it over as if it were of no concern to him. He nodded, smiled at her, conscious not to smile too creepily, and left the shop, slightly heady and not sure if it was due to her fashion model looks or the seductive sweet aroma from the display of chocolates.

He didn't feel up to spending more time on buses, so he stopped a cab and took it to the hospital. It wasn't hard to find which ward Rosa was in and as he took the lift to the fourth floor, he began to have second thoughts. *What if she was angry about the breakup with her daughter, what story had she even been told?* But he felt bad about the way she had been caught up in things, about what had happened to her. He knew he couldn't come clean about it all so the least he could do was drop by, say *hi* and bring her some posh chocolates.

She was in an open ward, there were two rows of beds, all occupied and most with visitors fussing round them. He spotted Franca sitting next to Rosa's bed, apparently in a moment of reflection, during some kind of pause in their conversation. Franca looked round, saw him approaching and stood up. He said he was sorry to have come at the wrong time, but she insisted he stay, saying she could do with a walk anyway; she'd leave them to it. Next moment she was gone.

Anton was up close now and could see the state of Rosa's battered face: she had dressings around her mouth and jaw, a lot of bruising to one of her cheeks and two black eyes. A patch of her hair had been shaved away to reveal a three-inch wound which had been stitched but still looked raw and angry. He leaned in and kissed her gently on the forehead.

'Dear God Rosa, this is awful, what did they do?' She shifted in the bed and managed a half smile, she looked genuinely pleased to see him.

'Look who's talking,' she smiled at him, and he returned it. 'They didn't hold back, as you can see, couple of punches, one of them kicked me when I was on the floor, that was what happened to my jaw. There was the shock of it all as well.'

He sat on the chair, taking it all in, 'What kind of person kicks someone in the head?'

'Not your Queensbury rules, that's for sure,' she took a closer look at him, 'and you? You're not looking a hundred percent yourself.' Anton wondered how much she knew or even *if* she knew about his having been at the house.

'Not as bad as it looks, I'll be okay. Things got a little out of hand at the gym, it was stupid. I'll live,' he looked at her, waiting for a follow up question but she seemed satisfied with his explanation.

He handed her the chocolates, 'I bought these for you, can you eat?' She took them and peeled back the delicate tissue paper to see inside and smiled.

'I can definitely eat these. They look absolutely wonderful, thank you. They're feeding me through a tube mostly, I'm eating a little but they say I'll be eating normally in a few days so these will be something to look forward to, thank you Anton,' she put her hand out to take his and squeezed it. Anton helped her put the tissue back and placed the chocolates carefully in the bedside cabinet.

He sat back and they talked for a while about how grim hospitals are and how she couldn't wait to get back home, about how the police had been helpful but not exactly confident they would find the attackers. He asked her if she needed anything and she said *no,* Franca was looking after her well.

After a while Franca returned and Anton took that as his cue to leave. He said he needed to go, he had other places he needed to be and wished them both a speedy recovery. Rosa thanked him again for taking the trouble to visit, how kind it was of him to do so, how he was obviously a generous and thoughtful person. He said he'd visit again if she stayed in for much longer.

'I'll walk you out,' said Franca and they walked toward the lift together.

'You okay?' he asked as they left the ward.

'Just about… not really. When you grow up you sort of know deep down that your parents are going to go before you, but you don't dwell on it. It's a shock to see how vulnerable they are, just fragile human beings like the rest of us.' Anton nodded. He thought about his father who was strong, dependable, the pillar of their small family, it was unthinkable that he could one day be no more. They had stopped at the lift. 'What about *your* mother? Is it true what you said?'

Anton was surprised, 'Yeah. That she died? Yes, why do you ask?'

'I asked Uncle Nico about her, after the dinner, he seemed to be so sure he knew her. He knows everyone around the area, he never gets it wrong.'

'What did he say?'

'Not much.'

'Mixing her up with someone else I suppose,' he smiled at her. 'I'd better go, good to see you.'

'Good of you to visit. I didn't tell her you were there; did she ask about your face?'

'Yes, I just said I had a rough day at the gym.'

'Good answer.' Anton stood waiting for the lift to arrive, feeling awkward now, unable to make an exit.

'I'll see you around,' he said.

'Yes, I expect so,' she said, 'thanks for coming.' The lift arrived and he stepped in, turned, and smiled again.

'Happy to do it,' the doors shut, and she was gone. On the way down he saw a message from Malcolm: *what time u home? doing dinner.* He sent one back to say he was on his way to which a reply came back asking him to bring Champagne.

He arrived home half an hour later carrying two bottles of Champagne, the label was one he didn't recognise but the two-for-one offer at the off-licence had been enough to convince him.

'T-bone steak,' said Malcolm as he walked in, 'potato wedges, old style in beef fat, tomatoes, onions and roasted Romanesco, because you said you liked it last time we had it; this all okay with you?' Anton looked past him at his brother who just shrugged and mouthed *no idea.* 'Are they cold?' said Malcolm pointing to the bottles.

'-ish,' said Anton, crossing to the freezer where he carefully placed them, 'give it ten minutes. What's the occasion?'

'Do me a favour, bring three beers while you're there,' said Malcolm. Anton opened the fridge, found three bottles, and brought them to the table along with an opener. He sat, looked over at his brother again and waited for Malcolm to speak.

'Okay, so, we're here, we're alive, still here, still breathing… I only have you two and I probably don't say it enough, how much you mean to me,' Neville tried to interrupt but Malcolm put his hand up, 'shut up Neville, I love you, but now is not the time to be a knob.'

He flipped the tops off the bottles and handed them round. 'You've both managed somehow to get yourselves beaten up, I don't really know how or why or even if there is a how or a why but one thing I do know is I have worried myself to death about you both and I wanted to make this special dinner just to show you how I appreciate you and for us to be a family together tonight.'

He looked at them both, they looked at each other.

'Don't embarrass me or nothing by agreeing with anything I just said,' Anton drew breath and started to speak but Malcolm stopped him, 'no, I mean it, don't embarrass me alright? Let's just enjoy this.'

Neville remained uncharacteristically quiet while he and Anton helped to set the table and find some glasses for the Champagne. The mood relaxed as the food appeared and the beer did its job.

The dinner was enormous: an individual T-bone each, cooked the way they liked it. Neville's was well done, Anton's medium rare and Malcolm's the same. They sipped

Champagne, mocking themselves for behaving like toffs; Anton even considered bringing out the posh chocolates he'd bought for himself but thinking about it, reached a conclusion that it was his dad's occasion, no need to try and out-do him. Malcolm's best brandy was brought out at the end, a cognac he loved and kept for special occasions.

'This is one of those,' he said and poured generous shots into his best wide-bodied brandy glasses. They sat back, full, perhaps slightly too full.

Anton decided this was a good time to ask about his mother.

'What actually happened to her?' He saw his brother look up and across the room at his father, 'She died, right? How did it happen?' There was a long wait before Malcolm spoke.

'Let's not have that conversation tonight eh? Another time.'

'I'm just curious, that's all. I want to know more about her,' he looked across at Neville, 'she's our mother, I just want to know what happened to her.' Neville looked down at his glass. Malcolm looked down at the table, at his hands which he flexed and brought together, then up at Anton, hoping perhaps that he'd give it a rest. He drew breath to speak then changed his mind and looked down again at his fidgeting hands.

'What?'

'Okay,' said Malcolm, 'she didn't die.'

'She didn't *die*… so what did happen?'

'You were too young… we thought about how to tell you, in the end… I don't really know why we did it.'

'Did what?' said Anton.

'We?' said Neville, looking up.

'Yes, we. You went along with it, we agreed,' said Malcolm.

'I was seven. I was fucking seven,' said Neville.

Anton said, 'Wait, would somebody-' but Neville had started,

'Hasn't it ever occurred to you that we don't look much alike?' He looked at Anton.

'Son-' said Malcolm.

'-No. You have to tell him, why not now, how old does he have to be?'

'Tell me what?' said Anton, 'We're not brothers?' He had tears starting in his eyes, something he didn't want.

'No, we're brothers, of course we are. Half-brothers in truth, but we've always been brothers as in… you and me against the rest of the world.' Anton sat, trying to make sense of it all, Malcolm just listened, no choice now but to let it all play out. '*My* mother died, about two years before you were born, I hardly knew her, can't really remember her now.'

Anton stood, his breathing was more rapid, and he was trying to hold back his emotions but several glasses of Champagne not to mention the Brandy was making that harder. He closed his eyes tightly, trying to concentrate.

'What else? What else don't I know?' he said. Malcolm waited to answer and said gently,

'Sit down son.'

'I don't want to,' said Anton.

'Sit down and I'll tell you.'

'I don't want to sit down. What happened to our, to *my* mother?'

'She left,' said Malcolm, 'she left us, went off for a better life. I let her go. I pushed her out is the truth. You were two.'

'You told me she was dead.' Anton looked at him, then at his brother, '*You* told me she was dead.'

Malcolm spoke first. 'No, we didn't. Neither of us did. You had a notion, you said it first, I don't know why you did but that's what happened, you said it first, we just let you go on believing it.'

'How would I have come up with that idea?' said Anton, then to Neville, 'How come you let me believe it?'

'We talked about it,' said Neville, 'Dad and I talked about it, he said we should leave it that way, it was for the best, better for you. So, I let her die too. At school, we were just brothers whose mother had died tragically.' Anton was still standing, and he felt himself close to tears again.

'She's not dead?'

'I don't know,' said Malcolm, 'I don't know what happened to her.'

'When were you going to tell me?'

'It was never the right moment,' said Malcolm, 'I'm sorry.'

Neville tried to calm things, 'Come on Ant… we've had a nice evening-'

'-Leave me alone,' Anton heard himself and wished he hadn't said it, 'just… fuck the fuck off.' He left the room and climbed the stairs to the bathroom where he emptied his bladder noisily and stared at his face in the mirror.

In the quiet of his bedroom, he felt alone, like a child, like he had no control over events around him, even the ones that directly affected him. The world out there was moving along, turning without him, without even a need for him.

They left him alone for the rest of the night. He assumed they'd carried on talking and had decided to leave him in peace, but he couldn't think straight, and he couldn't find any peace. He was confused, slightly drunk and emotional and in the security of his room, he finally allowed himself the luxury of tears and he wept while no-one looked on.

He woke early, the memories of the night before still raw. Rather than risk an encounter with his family, he dressed quickly and left the house. Outside the freezing rain had made the pavements slippery, he moved slowly, still shaky from recent events let alone the hangover. He pulled the hood over his head and hunched his shoulders against the weather. It was early still so he found a café where he ordered coffee and a full English which he found he couldn't finish. The background chatter of the customers, idle small talk about trivial nothings helped though; he felt he was back in the world, a part of something again.

He arrived at the gym just after nine, having decided to ask Nico about his mother, if he happened to be there. Remembering Franny, he checked out the board where there was a new notice: "Doctors say they will attempt to operate again tomorrow or the day after".

'What does that mean? Is that good?' he asked Barney.

'I don't know son, I'd have thought good, they must be trying to bring him out of the coma I suppose. I don't really know, to be honest.'

Despite his troubled sleep and the lingering hangover, he had some energy to expend so he jumped on a static bike and got going. After a while Barney came back to him and asked if he'd start working with Kirby like he'd promised. Anton said of course he would, but what about the Boys Club?

'Deano will do that, he's happy to. Good news as well, there's three of them today.' Anton looked over to the far side of the room and saw Kenny Dean talking to one of them, explaining something that required a lot of hand gestures. The other two were larking about behind him, making each other laugh about something or other, something that doesn't matter one little bit, thought Anton, God bless them for that.

He'd given some thought before as to how he would handle getting into a ring with Kirby again, what he might say to him. In the event, Barney was ahead of both of them and made it easy.

'Speed today, that's all. Six rounds but make it snappy, it's about stamina and reaction time,' he put a hand on Kirby's shoulder, 'don't hit him too hard, he looks like he's had his fair share for the week.'

'Yeah, pizza face,' said Kirby, laughing. *Ha ha* thought Anton although when he thought a bit more, he found it strangely uplifting that Kirby had a sense of humour after all.

After three rounds, the excesses of the night before began to tell, and Anton begged for a break.

'Okay, take five then, lover boy's out of breath,' said Barney.

'We broke up,' said Anton, bent over, holding on to his knees and trying catch his breath.

Truth was, Kirby was fast now, he could duck and weave ahead of anything Anton could manage. They'd played it straight, done what was asked of them, going for pace, and setting a rhythm, give and take, keeping the focus on Kirby, letting him in, Anton parrying his shots then poking a few back through his guard, no great power behind them but testing his defences, nonetheless.

'He's doing alright, yes?' said Barney, looking at Kirby with a degree of pride.

'Definitely, he's gonna wop that kid when the time comes,' said Anton, conscious of keeping up the positive reinforcement at all times. It was to be all about Kirby and right now, that suited him just fine.

That afternoon, Anton went to the hospital to see Franny who was still out. He spoke with one of the nurses who said she thought his operation would most likely be tomorrow, but she wouldn't be drawn on his chances.

He wasn't keen to go home but knew he had to. It was a Wednesday "snooker night", so Malcolm was on his way out.

Anton stayed moody, said very little and nothing at all about anything that mattered, knew he was acting like an annoying teenager but couldn't stop himself. His brother tried to talk to him, but he resisted, said he was tired and just wanted to go to his room, watch TV and fall asleep.

He slept better that night, having decided that an early night was in fact a good idea in itself as well as being a way to avoid awkward conversation. He woke up feeling rested for once and thinking about someone else's problems, specifically Franny.

When he went downstairs, Malcolm was in the kitchen scrolling on his phone and drinking tea, he had started eating a bowl of cereal. Anton grunted a greeting and refilled the kettle.

'Morning,' said Malcolm.

Anton fidgeted around the kitchen while he waited for the kettle to boil, finding things to tidy, small jobs that needed doing, then made a mug of coffee and started to leave. Malcolm tried to stop him. 'Anton, wait.'

'I don't want to,' said Anton, irritating himself with how he sounded like a petulant twelve-year-old again.

'Sit the fuck down, I want to talk.' Anton hovered for a moment, decided flouncing was beneath him and sat on the side of the table. 'I'm sorry I kept all that from you. I didn't know how to tell you, is the truth. It was easier when you were two, three… after that there was never an obvious time to do it. I done my best.'

'You know, you always say that when something goes wrong? *I done my best* – that's going to be on your tombstone. What about me? Why wasn't I entitled to know? Maybe not at two or three but what about nine or ten or when I was a teenager or something,' Malcolm just nodded, he wasn't looking for an argument. 'Where were you last night?'

'You know where I was, it was snooker night.'

'I know where you were and you weren't playing snooker, although a number of jokes about sinking the pink spring to mind.' Malcolm stayed silent, just watched him. 'Why can't I trust what you tell me?' He sipped his coffee, he was getting tired of being stroppy, besides, his father wasn't rising to it.

'Is she still alive?'

'I don't know. That's the truth, I'm sorry, I just don't. She went off with someone else. More than one, I think. I may have driven her to it to a degree, I don't know. We didn't stay in touch. I was embarrassed by it all, I was hurt. I pushed her out in the end, I couldn't stand it anymore. She wanted to take you, but I had a lawyer, a good one who managed to show she was… not suitable as a mother.'

Anton sat listening and sipping his coffee. 'So, you haven't seen her or spoken to her in over twenty years?'

'Correct.' Anton thought about it and finished his coffee. Malcolm had said all he had to say. He finished his tea and carried on eating his bowl of cereal. Anton stood and picked up Malcolm's empty mug.

'Another one?'

'Cheers, tea please,' said Malcolm as Anton switched the kettle back on.

'What do we do about Beulah?' asked Anton.

'I went there the other day, it's a mess, Egerton's put people in the top flat now. I suppose we'll sell it to him. I can't put a normal person in there and no-one else will want to buy it in the state the block is in, the common parts need work, the windows on the stairway are cracked. He's never paid his share of the maintenance which was just about okay when he owned just one of the four apartments but now he's three quarters of it, we'd just end up paying for the lot.'

'Can't we sue him?'

'No point, I've tried before. Even if you can do it, you then have to enforce it, in the end you spend more than you get back in and it's a lot of hassle. We'll end up letting him buy it.' Anton looked annoyed, 'I know but we don't have a lot of options.'

Anton finished making the tea and put it down on the table in front of his father. 'Here you go.'

'You not having another?'

'No, I'm heading to the gym, work to do. I'll see you later,' he stopped at the door and looked back. 'Dad, look… I know. I know you always did your best, okay?'

'Thanks son,' he said, looking at his tea.

27

On Saturday morning, there was a new notice on the board. When Anton arrived, Tyrone was standing in front of it and reading aloud to a couple of the others:

"Franny has been brought out of the coma and operated on again, this has been successful, and he is conscious and recovering but needs to stay very still so no visitors, but he is recovering." Anton found Barney to ask what else he knew.

'That's it really, he's out of the coma, that's the big one. They weren't sure he could do it. They were ready to freeze his brain or something but he made it through so they say its good news but he was in a bad way in the first place so they don't know how well he can recover, probably won't know for a while.'

'When can we visit?'

'Not yet, he has to be kept still, he's wired up and everything, they'll let us know. I'll tell you.'

On Wednesday morning of the following week, Anton had finished leading a Boys Club session when he saw Barney walking across the gym towards him.

'They're coming back I see.'

'Six now, it takes time,' said Anton, 'I don't blame them for being cautious, it's the ones with parents who give a toss who are asking about safety so that's a good thing, I'm happy to talk to them. The point is, this lot are enjoying it and that's the key, they'll tell others.'

Barney nodded approvingly. 'You can go and see Franny if you like.'

'Yeah? When?'

'Tomorrow if you're up for it. Don't say anything to the others yet, he can't have a lot of excitement, but you got on and I think he'd appreciate the visit. He's doing okay... considering.'

Next morning Anton walked into the hospital again, he smiled and said hello to the woman on Reception who seemed to recognise him. *I'm spending too much time in here.*

He took the lift to the third floor, turned left, and walked down a seemingly endless corridor with a clutter of signs pointing to all kinds of units, clinics, departments and eventually wards, then finally the one he was seeking.

He saw him from the side at first, sitting in a wheelchair, which was the first shock, he'd assumed he was still confined to bed. There was a doctor sitting on the edge of the bed, facing him, moving his hand in front of Franny's face,

'Look over here… now here…' the doctor lifted his hand up, 'now up here… and down, good. Follow my finger,' he moved his extended finger across Franny's line of vision, then up and down again, then held it square on to him and slowly moved it toward him, toward his nose, 'try to keep watching my finger, keep focussing on it, good. You're doing really well.' Anton watched him without interrupting. 'Now I want you just to put your arms out in front of you, keep your elbows bent, that's it, now turn your palms up… now over and facing down.' Anton saw him struggle to control his hands but also saw the effort he was making trying to get it right, 'Okay, now stretch those arms out again and… all the way, just straight, try and put them out straight in front of you.' Franny extended his arms out from his shoulders, the left staying more or less straight if not particularly steady, the right flying around as if he was spraying graffiti. 'Okay, relax, good try, don't worry that you can't do it all yet, you will.'

Anton moved forward but stopped as Franny said, 'Wait.' He stretched his arms out again with the same result and held them there, his breathing getting heavier as he concentrated. Anton watched him, saw his body tense, and tighten with the effort, but he couldn't bring them under control, his right arm if anything getting wilder.

'Okay, relax now… stop trying, let yourself rest, you'll get there,' the doctor said, leaning forward and patting his arm, 'good work. Its step-by-step Francis. We'll just take it day by day, okay?' He stood and glanced up. 'Looks like you have a visitor.' Franny turned his head and Anton saw him now, full on, his face drawn and pale, he looked ten years older and a stone lighter.

'Looking good champ,' said Anton moving round to face him and sitting on the bed, 'what's happening, practising a few moves?'

'Mate…' said Franny slowly, he sounded tired as anything. '… good to see you,'

'Its bloody amazing to see you, you had us worried,' he put a hand on Franny's shoulder, 'what happened to you?' The doctor left them to it and Anton leant forward trying to make it easy.

'Good to be back, I don't remember anything. I was in a coma they're saying, Barney knows, he seems to know everything. He told me what happened, that I collapsed after training… I don't remember, they keep asking me what's the last thing I remember, and the truth is, I haven't got a clue.'

'You never had a clue,' said Anton, which prompted a smile from Franny, he didn't look like he had the energy to laugh. 'You're with us though and you're awake, that's all that matters.'

'Yeah but look at this,' he straightened his arms out again, in front of him, once more the left swayed around and the right danced away to a tune all of its own.

'That's me keeping my arms still,' he looked at Anton who didn't know what to say so just gave him an encouraging smile. A nurse came in and went over to Franny, busying herself around him, saying it was time to get him back into the bed. She helped him move carefully from the chair, lifting him to his feet, letting him shuffle over to the bed, bent double and apparently in pain. When he got there, he lay back and she hooked him up, checking everything was in its place before telling Anton not to be too long and tire him out, he needed his rest. He wondered how it was that he was getting a telling off but took the cue anyway and left soon after, saying he'd be back the next day.

'See you mate,' said Franny and closed his eyes.

Anton was keen to talk to Barney, tell him he'd seen Franny, share the news that he was awake and alive, damaged but still here, on Earth, by some miracle.

Barney wasn't in sight when he reached the gym, so he went to the lockers and changed, ready to work out. Tyrone was there, changing back and getting ready to leave.

'Seen this?' he said, handing Anton a tablet. Anton looked at the open page, saw it was something to do with the council,

'What is it?' Anton asked, Tyrone helped him by scrolling the page down.

'Here it is, look: *approved, consent granted, application number blah blah blah,* there you go,' he turned the tablet round to let Anton see properly.

'Okay, that's us, that's this address. What have they consented to?' He looked up at Tyrone who gave him a tight-lipped smile.

'It's the Planning Committee, two nights ago. They gave their consent to this site being used for a licensed premises,' Anton looked more carefully and scrolled back to read more. 'Including use as a nightclub. Anyone bother to tell us? No... the last to know.'

'Doesn't say when,' said Anton.

'They have five years. Its only planning permission, doesn't mean it's going to happen, but it means it could. The point is, they've agreed to the change of use.'

Anton finished changing and found Barney who was deep in conversation with Kirby. When he saw him approaching, he broke off to say,

'How's Franny?'

This made Kirby look over as well, 'You see him?' he said.

'Yes, he's better I think,' said Anton, 'awake which is a start, think he was pleased to see me.'

'Nice one,' said Kirby.

'Definitely. Barney, you hear about the planning permission?' Barney looked back at Anton, clearly irritated with him.

'It's nothing, it just says certain things can happen over the next five years, forget it.'

'What do you mean forget it? I know there are people out there who think this would be a great nightclub which would be goodbye and goodnight for us and I know that George is looking to sell-'

'-Anton, I'm busy. We're busy. I'm working with Kirby, alright? You come and see me later if you want to talk about anything else.'

'I will,' said Anton, nodding for emphasis. Barney gave him a look so he left it there and walked back to the lockers to see if he could find Tyrone again, but he had gone. He retrieved his phone and went to sit in the canteen and search through the council website to find further information, a task that proved to be far more difficult than he felt it should.

He knew from Barney's tone that he wouldn't get his attention until he'd finished up with Kirby. That took more than two more hours during which time Anton tried and failed to clear his head by doing circuits broken up with deep breathing rests. Just as that was becoming unbearably tedious, he saw Barney go into his office. Anton followed him but before he could speak Barney started up,

'Shut the door. Listen: nothing, nothing at all should distract Kirby from his training, understood? So, if you want to whine or moan about anything, anything at all, just be sure to do it somewhere else, got it?'

'I'm not whining Barney; I know these people. I know what they plan on doing with this place. And now it looks like they can.' Barney sat in the chair behind his desk and looked tired.

'George needs out, he needs the money. This building is worth a couple of million, they're going to sell it and there's nothing we can do to stop them. The one thing we can do is keep Kirby out of it, he needs to stay focussed and concentrate on one thing only.'

'There must be a way to stop them. What would it take?'

'You could give George and Nico two million quid; do you have that spare? Thought not. Win the lottery then.' Anton muttered under his breath, turned away and left the office, making a last moment decision not to slam the door but just to leave it open which would no doubt irritate Barney. Again, he felt powerless, frustrated, and that frustration was turning him back into a stroppy teenager.

Walking home he felt adrift, his thoughts were a jumble, he was lost. He wanted Franca back, to talk to her, to tell her what was going on with Franny and the gym, at least she'd make him laugh, put some perspective on things, she was good at that.

He dropped into the house only to pick up the keys to the Outlander which he started up and drove over to her home, he knew it was almost certainly pointless but there was a tiny chance he'd see her. He stopped for a few minutes in the road outside then remembered what had happened last time and thought better of it.

He decided to give Purely Pizza a try, there was always a chance she would be there and even seeing the loathsome Sally would be okay. He parked close by and walked there with low expectations but feeling a little bit hungry so at least he could satisfy that particular basic need.

He was caught off guard when he saw her in there before he'd even reached the door. She was sitting at a table in the window, eating, talking, and laughing with someone, someone he could now see was male. He considered walking past but forced himself to take the initiative and go in. He took a breath and opened the door.

'Hi,' he said at the same time as he walked through the doorway, which didn't feel at all natural and was anything but relaxed. She looked up at him,

'Hello, Anton…' she looked almost pleased to see him. Pleased enough.

'How *are* you? This is a friend of mine, from school… Freddie, meet Anton.' Freddie looked up at him, not particularly impressed. They shook hands, Freddie offering the grip of a man holding on to the top rung of a ladder, making some kind of point presumably. 'How have you been?'

'Not bad, you know,' thinking, *maybe we could go and sit over here, away from your old school chum,* 'busy, you know how it is, got some things happening…' He began to wish he hadn't started this, that he had walked by when he had the chance, *should have done that,* he could have caught her eye and just waved.

'We should catch up,' she said. He looked at her. She meant it.

'Yeah, that would be good,' he said, 'enjoy your pizzas. Nice to meet you Freddie,' but Freddie wasn't listening.

Franca was though and smiled as Anton left them and went to the counter. He didn't want to sit alone and eat with Franca still sitting there so he bought two large pizzas to take home and share, a gesture which never went unappreciated.

Unsurprisingly, the smell of the best that Purely Pizzas had to offer drew his father and brother to the kitchen. Having acknowledged Anton's generosity and taken a slice each, they stood contentedly around the table. Between mouthfuls, Anton asked,

'What's happening about Beulah?'

'He's offering about 70% of what it's worth. I think we'll take it,' said Malcolm, 'it's that or sit on it and hope to sell somewhere down the line but he's going let the block go to ruin, trash it by neglect so that's not a great plan.'

'I agree. He's a worm,' said Anton, trying to be positive and more importantly, helpful. There was a pause while the two of them looked at Neville who looked up from his enthusiastic feasting.

'Me too,' he said.

Anton took another slice. 'Help yourselves… Egerton's trying to buy the gym as well, looks like he might be serious. How do we find two million quid to stop him?'

'Lottery,' said Neville, they looked at him and he shrugged, 'only thing I can think of.'

'You talking about a mortgage?' said Malcolm. 'Trying to buy it yourself?'

'I suppose so,' said Anton, 'truth is, if I did win the lottery then I would buy it.'

'What would you do with it?' asked Malcolm.

'Nothing, just leave it as it is. Let it be.'

'That's your problem then. I assume the owners are selling it because it doesn't make enough. Egerton thinks he has a way to make it pay by turning it into something else-'

'-a nightclub.'

'I'm not even sure what one of those is these days.'

'Somewhere for his boys to sell his drugs,' said Anton.

'Which is the point: you've just described a business plan. You have to come up with one of your own, a legal one ideally, then maybe you could borrow the money to buy it yourself,' he took a bite of pizza while Anton thought about it. 'It's not easy though, or straightforward, if it was then a lot more people would do it.'

Anton nodded, he was thinking now, 'They could do a lot more there though, loads more if I think about it, they've got other stuff going on apart from boxing but there's empty time and it's a big place, you could do much more.'

'Write it down then,' said Malcolm, 'If it all makes sense and if you want, I could come with you to the bank, we could go and talk to them… they've done alright out of us over the years.'

Neville looked up, 'You're kidding, right?'

'No, I'm not kidding,' said Anton, 'it means something to people, we should try and save it if we can.'

'You're going to run a boxing club? As in, own it and run it as a business?' Neville was still doing his incredulous act.

'Eat your pizza,' said Malcolm.

Neville rolled his eyes upward and tore off a couple of squares of kitchen roll and another slice of pizza. 'Okay if I have another one?' he said, Anton nodded, 'I want to finish off the episode I was on next door if that's okay with you two property moguls.'

'Yeah, fuck off Neville,' said Malcolm pretending to slap him round the head as he walked past. When he'd gone, Malcolm went to the fridge,

'Another beer?' He took two bottles out, capped them and brought them to the table to sit with Anton. 'How are you doing?'

'Alright… kind of,' said Anton, 'I saw Franny today, the one who collapsed. He's up out of bed now, for short periods, which is amazing seeing as how he was in a coma. It's tough for him though, he's not back to normal and that's driving him mad,' Malcolm nodded as he listened. 'Makes you think.'

'Yeah, it does. You know I always worried a bit about it.'

'I know you did. Do. I'm careful.

'Wasn't he?' Anton looked away and didn't answer. 'I've got something to tell you…' Anton looked back at him, realising he was struggling to find the words, 'I've found her. I found your mother. You were right, I should have talked to you about it, let you have a chance to know her ages ago.'

'She's alive?' said Anton, 'Where?'

'She moved away, back then, out of town a little, not far. Then she went and lived up north for a while but she's back now, has been for a few years apparently. We have a couple of mutual friends still.'

'Can I speak to her?'

Malcolm nodded, 'I need to do it first. Let me call her. It'll be a shock. I'll ask her if she's okay with it, I'm sure she will be, but I should ask,' he looked at Anton, unsure about it all. 'I haven't seen her or spoken to her in over twenty years.'

28

Anton made a point of dropping in on Franny every day, asking him what was new and getting updates to take back to the gym. He could see how tough it was for him: he was able to move about, but his co-ordination was all over the place. Often his speech would be slurred, Anton was unsure whether that was due to the drugs or a lasting effect of the injury.

Franny would get tired quickly and he was definitely slower in the afternoons, but it was possible to see he was very gradually coming back, getting back to being himself. Each day he remembered something new, Anton would ask him to think, get him to stretch his brain, try and think back, to recall anything he could.

His doctors encouraged Anton, let him know that it was good that he was pushing him; they would be there to make sure he didn't do anything too crazy. When Franny was done in and needed to rest, he would sit back in the bed, and they would talk. The talk gradually turned to planning for the future and this seemed to lift his spirits. He wanted to get back to fighting, to maybe still having a go at turning professional; neither of them knew if that would ever be possible but it was a useful dream and seemed to help him.

Anton shared with him what he knew about George's plans to sell up and take his money, how he wanted to talk him out of it and save the gym but didn't know how. Franny asked after

Kirby, and Anton kept him up to date with his progress, it turned out that Franny knew all along that Kirby was living in his dad's car at the back of the gym.

'I assumed everyone knew,' he said.

One Friday Anton arrived at the gym in the early afternoon having spent the morning at the hospital and he knew as soon as he walked in that something was up. No-one was working out for start, the machines were unoccupied, the rings empty. People stood around talking quietly or whispering. He saw George standing in front of the Rules, looking weary, worn out, beaten; his eyes were small and sore.

'Uncle, what's up?'

'You weren't here, sorry, you missed me telling everyone. I just told them: we exchanged contracts the deal is done,' he looked at Anton, hard to know what he was looking for. 'You knew, right? You knew we were doing this.'

'Uncle, I… no, I was hoping… you know, that we could put a plan together, help to save it, keep it all going.'

George looked at him again. 'Don't make this harder, I'm sorry… I need the money. My wife has been ill, she may not live much longer, I want to have time with her, go some places she wants to visit… be able to have enough money to care for her.'

'Yeah, of course, of course, George… I'm sorry, I know.'

George turned back to look at the Rules. 'Someone needs to make sure these are saved; they should go up in the new gym.'

'What new gym?' said Anton, suddenly hopeful.

'The one you're going to start-'

'-Me?' said Anton.

'Or somebody. Nico and I might be able to contribute, make sure there's a little money to get it going. You lot need to do it though, find a building, do what I did all those years ago.' Anton looked into his bloodshot eyes and wanted to ask how that could ever happen but thought that could wait for another day so just laid a friendly hand on his shoulder and left him there.

Barney saw him coming and knew there would be no peace until he'd spoken with him,

'I know, I know, sorry you had to find out like that. Truth is, none of us knew until just now when George made his little speech. He and Nico have obviously been working up this deal for a while and didn't tell anyone. I honestly didn't know until today. I knew it was in the air I suppose…'

Anton nodded. 'So, what's the plan?'

'We've got a couple of weeks, three almost.'

'Before what?' asked Anton.

'Before we go, leave… walk out the door for the last time. The game's up Anton.'

'We'll get a new place though, yeah?' he asked, 'Take the stuff out of here, set it up somewhere new, somewhere nearby hopefully, find a building.'

'Who's *we*? Where's the money for all this coming from?'

'*We* is you,' Anton staring at him now, looking for the answer, 'of course it's you, you're the boss, you run this place.'

'I just got told I am going to be made redundant,' said Barney. Anton stopped and felt uncomfortable. *Of course,* that was the reality for Barney, he was about to be kicked out.

'Sorry.'

'Not your fault. In answer to your question, I don't know what we can do, I need some time to work it out. They've given us some money, enough to move the gear out and put it into safe storage for up to a year if necessary, so we have some time to find a new home.'

'Everything you've built here…' Anton let it trail off.

'But the real point is this. Five weeks from tomorrow, young Kirby out there steps into a ring and tries his best, at least he better had try his best, to make his mark and we can help him to do that, work with him to get him there. That can be George's legacy, this gym's legacy, make it worth something.' Anton thought about that for a moment, he was right of course, they had to try and rescue something from this, and Kirby deserved his chance like anyone else.

'So where does he train for the last couple of weeks?'

'Now we get to the slightly better news,' said Barney, his mind now focussing on a plan, back into trainer mode, 'Tyrone has somehow managed to talk to his vicar-'

'-his vicar?'

'Yeah, his vicar, bear with me, we're getting some help from the very top with this one; he's persuaded him to let us move into the function room at the church. It's at the back of the church and its big enough apparently, for us to set the ring up with a bit of space around it… hopefully. We can move in when we want and stay there for about three months, there aren't any other bookings until after Easter. It's not too far from here, we can walk there, ten minutes tops. Kirby doesn't even need to move his car.'

'What about his dad?'

Barney paused then said, 'He's redundant too Anton, it's the way it is. We can help Kirby though, get him to his moment.'

'What if he loses?'

'Unthinkable. Out there,' he pointed to the door, 'that's unthinkable, okay? Nothing like that gets said in front of him, okay?'

'Okay…' Anton put his hand up to show he got the point.

'But in here, right now, I'll say this, if… *if* he loses and puts up a good show, if he looks the business, he'll get another chance. He can find another gym, one that's got a structure for him, that can take him on and push him further. We can help him to do his best, that's all,' Anton nodded, 'okay?'

'Okay.'

'Now go out there and run with him, tell him everything's fine, we're all working on a plan, everything's going to be alright.'

Anton talked it over with Franny when he visited him over the weekend, tried to play up the positives: the availability of the church hall, their shared mission to get Kirby to his fight, not forgetting they now had somewhere to put the equipment.

'What about us? What are we supposed to do, find another gym that'll take us in?' said Franny.

'I suppose so. If we want to carry on,' Anton wasn't at all sure it was a good idea for Franny to let himself get hit again.

'Don't you… want to carry on?'

'Yeah, course,' said Anton.

'Same for me, it's what keeps me going, I want to go back.'

'You want to go back into a ring?' asked Anton.

'Of course, I love it like you do.' Anton gave him a smile, thinking, *yeah, I can just see your missus agreeing to that.*

29

A week later, Franca called him.

'Want to get that drink?' guard up but making a move, nonetheless. Anton said *yes,* a drink was a great idea.

They met in the wine bar on a Tuesday evening, assuming it would be easy to find a table that early in the week. She surprised him by getting there first, particularly so because he arrived five minutes early himself. She had found a table she liked the look of and had bought a large glass of white and a bottle of Italian lager which she knew he liked.

'Unless you prefer something else,' she said tipping the bottle towards him as he sat.

'No, that's great, thank you,' he said, sitting opposite her. 'Look at us, getting here all early.' He took a swig from the bottle and smiled at her, 'You're looking well…'

'…considering...?' she teased him.

'No, well yeah. I mean you *are* looking well and you're healing; your face, you can hardly see where… you know.'

'And you got yourself a scar, you old dog,' she said reaching out to touch his face. He flinched, 'Sorry.'

'It's okay, it was sore for a while, better now, it's okay to touch it, that was just a reflex.'

'You want me to touch your scar?'

'Optional,' he smiled again, she was joking with him, that was good.

'I'll leave it for now… You boxing again?'

'Not really, I'm doing quite a bit of working out though. I kind of lost my appetite for getting punched in the face. It'll come back… possibly.'

'How's it going?' She sat back and took a long sip of the wine, looking like she was enjoying it.

'Good. We're working with one of lads, Kirby, he's trying to turn pro. You know him, he was the one I knocked down when I saw you for the first time. I'm working a lot with him, helping him.'

She laughed, 'You're his friend now?'

'I was never *not* his friend; I just got a bit carried away. I'm helping to train him. Making amends perhaps.'

She reached out again, this time putting her hand on his, 'I've missed you.' He looked at her, she wasn't giving too much but she was making the move.

'I missed you too.'

'It was nice to see you the other day, in Marcello's.'

'Yeah, you were with…'

'Freddie.'

'Freddie, yeah,' he paused then said, 'Freddie?'

'Something to do with Arsenal, there was a man of the match one year, cup final I think… when he was born, his dad's a fan,' Anton shrugged, 'Freddie something.'

'Lundberg.'

'Could be, no idea. Don't care, he can't help his name,' Anton did his best to look uninterested. 'We could get back together. Rosa likes you.'

'Malcolm likes *you*.'

'Written in the stars,' she said, taking another sip.

'And you… what, you drop Freddie?' He was finding this harder than he had expected even though he'd hoped the conversation might go in this direction. She nodded to indicate that, yes, she would drop him. He took a swig of the lager, looked at her, not sure how to get this straight in his head. 'Quick out of the traps, though, eh…? When we spilt up.'

'What do you mean?'

'Freddie.'

She thought for a moment before saying, 'To be fair, you were the first one to go and sleep with that woman, whatever her name was…'

'I didn't sleep with her, by which I mean I didn't go out with her, she wasn't a girlfriend as such, it wasn't a romantic thing, she seduced me.'

Franca sat back and nodded, 'Oh, that's right, I remember now, she forced herself on you.'

'That's pretty much it, I told you about it, I was honest with you. I said then that I was sorry, and I meant it and I mean it now.'

She let it hang for a moment then said, 'I didn't come here to fight, I wanted to see you.'

Anton calmed himself, he didn't want to start getting defensive, it was old ground, if they were to have a future, it was going to have to heal over.

'I know, and it's good to see you, it really is,' he took another swig, 'and I know it's not the same as just going out with someone for a pizza but it's over, like I said before, completely. She and her husband have moved away, I don't even know where they've gone.' He finished the bottle, watching her as she sipped her wine and looked down at the table. 'That was all it was, right? Pizza…' She looked up from the table and a voice in his head said *stop there, let it go,* but he couldn't. 'Just pizza, right?'

'I will just point out, if it's okay with you, that we actually had split up,' there was a moment of silence before she finished the point, 'you fucked someone else while we were still together.'

'So, it was more than just pizza?'

Franca made him jump by slapping her own face with her palm and rubbing her eyes, 'Will you stop saying *pizza*? Its driving me mad, yes, I slept with Freddie... *after* you and I spilt up.' Anton was the one now to rub his eyes with his palms. 'What about, what's good for the goose being good for the gander? At least I was officially single, we weren't going out together at the time.'

Anton slammed the empty bottle on the table, 'Fuck it, Franca.'

Franca put her glass down and shook her head in disbelief, 'Oh come on, Anton, when are you going to grow up? Huh? Life doesn't always work out how you want it to, or like you think it should.' Anton stood and grabbed his coat from the back of the chair.

'No, you're right, it doesn't, it really doesn't,' he turned his back and strode away. He was fairly sure he heard her mutter something as he left, it sounded a lot like *wanker*.

'And...?' said Neville expectantly as his brother walked into the kitchen.

'And nothing, she's sleeping with someone else.'

'So why did she want to see you?'

Anton stopped and shook his head; he didn't want this conversation. 'She wanted to get back together.'

'Even though she's seeing someone else?'

'No, she would have dropped him, but that's not the point.'

'Oh mate, come on-'

'-it's not the fucking point,' he said, irritated, 'sorry... sorry. Long day, I need to rest. I'm going upstairs.'

In the familiar comfort of his room, he relaxed a little, sat in the old leather chair he'd rescued from a skip years ago, took out his phone and called Sedge. She surprised him by answering.

'What's up?'

'Just wondered how you're doing?'

'I'm okay, everything alright with you?'

'Not really… just stuff, you know. Sorry, I don't want to burden you with it.'

'Anything to do with Egerton and his mates?'

'No, why?' She didn't answer. 'You fancy a drink sometime? Or a coffee or something?'

'Let's get it straight, I'm not looking for a boyfriend.'

'No, I know, that's not what I meant, I just want to talk. We have something in common after all.'

'Okay. Funnily enough I was going to call you, we *should* talk. I live in Brighton now; can you get down here?'

He said it would be no problem, it wasn't far. They agreed to meet in two days' time, she said she'd meet him at the station.

She was dressed as distinctively as ever. This time it was a full length, rust coloured coat which matched her hair, and a multi-coloured scarf that looked like it might be a whole series of other scarves all sewn together. She kept her hands in her pockets as he walked up to her, then turned to lead him away from the station and down the hill.

'How have you been?' she asked.

'Oh, you know, life gets complicated,' he said. She smiled and kept walking. He looked up at the sky, there were patches of blue, even a little bit of sun creeping through. 'You live here now?'

'Yep. With friends. For now. I'm not one for roots so we'll see. You wanted to talk?'

'I wouldn't mind,' he said, 'there's only you that knows what went on… with Egerton and all. Do you know somewhere we could go? I'll buy you lunch.'

'I want you to meet someone first, they're waiting for us; okay with you?'

'Yeah, I suppose so. Who?'

'You'll see.'

They walked for another ten minutes or so, staying in the town, away from the seafront before reaching a long sweeping terrace of enormous town houses which Anton guessed must be divided up into apartments now, then turned up a side road which was altogether less glamorous. Halfway along was a commercial garage advertising tyre changes and MOT tests, she led him into the courtyard and for a moment he thought that was their destination, but she carried on and stopped at an iron gate set into the boundary wall and pressed a buzzer next to it.

The gate opened and she walked through, inviting him to follow her. Inside was a small garden, basically a scrappy plot of grass, one or two shrubs and a few young trees that were no taller than her. They walked down a noisily crunchy pebbled path to the back door of a not-too-well looked after two storey semi-detached house in need of significant amounts of remedial exterior repairs. Anton couldn't stop himself from calculating that it looked like a good six weeks of work, and that was assuming the weather held. Sedge rang a bell and pushed the door which was open.

'Come in,' she held her hand out and took his, leading him inside into the kitchen, calling out, 'Patsy?' A male voice, not sounding at all like a Patsy replied from one of the rooms nearby and she led him toward it, through a door and into a living room.

Anton stopped just inside the doorway when he saw a man mountain, the definition of super-heavyweight: six and a half feet at least and just huge. Adrenalin kicked in and he tensed, thought about backing out, trying to work out if he could get to the back door and outside before the giant could get to him but Sedge put her arm out and pulled him to her,

'It's okay, he's a friend.'

Anton took it all in, somehow the guy had found a dark green bomber jacket big enough to fit him along with black jeans and what looked like brown cowboy boots, he was taller and wider than anyone he'd ever seen before.

'It's cool,' said the big guy and held out a hand. Anton stepped forward and took it expecting a bone crusher but getting a firm but friendly grip back.

'This is Patsy,' said Sedge, still holding onto Anton's jacket, 'at least as far as you're concerned, this is Patsy,' then to the big guy, 'this is Anton.' Anton looked at him and nodded, Patsy smiled then broke out into a laugh which Anton cautiously echoed.

Sedge relaxed her grip on him and said, 'Okay, here's the deal. Patsy, could you write down the address please?' The big man reached over and found a notebook on the nearby coffee table, tore out a sheet and started writing on it.

'I'm going to bring Egerton down and I'm going to use the laptop to do it. It's possible, not likely but possible that he will link it back to the time when the laptop wasn't in his possession, so he may come to you.'

'Me?' said Anton, heady, beginning to feel real fear.

'Don't panic. You don't know anything, and you didn't even switch it on, did you?' Anton shook his head in agreement, 'Good, so there you go. But he may want to find out from you where you got it from, how you managed to track it down, so we've put a story together for you. If anyone comes asking, you just say you got it from someone called Patsy; can you do that?'

Anton looked at Patsy, 'Tell him it was you?' just wanting to be sure. Patsy nodded and handed him the note, he'd written an address on it.

'That's this address, this house,' said Patsy, 'if he wants to come and find me, he can come here.'

'What if he does?' said Anton.

'Not your concern. Give me your phone,' he put his hand out. Anton looked at Sedge who indicated he should do it. He unlocked the phone and handed it to Patsy who took it, pressed it a few times and handed it back. 'All done, I'm in your contacts under "Patsy", think you can remember that?' Anton nodded, 'And Patsy is a woman as far as anyone else is concerned, obviously.'

'Obviously,' said Anton.

'So that's the story,' said Sedge, going over it slowly to be sure he understood. 'All you know is, you asked around, found a girl called Patsy who drinks at the Campus when she's up from Brighton visiting her college friends and you bought the computer back from her for £100. If they ask for her address, you give it to them, if they ask for her number, you give it to them. You're clean and you're out of it other than that.'

'What does Pasty look like?'

'You tell me, buster.'

'Okay… shortish, slim, in her twenties, blonde hair.'

'There you go, that sounds like Patsy; sounds like you fancy Patsy actually,' Sedge laughed, Patsy joined in.

'If you can call me to say they're on their way, that would help,' said Patsy,' if not, it's no big deal.'

'And this is definitely cool with you?' said Anton. Patsy nodded.

'Let's go and get some lunch,' said Sedge.

'Go in peace,' said Patsy, smiling like he meant it.

Anton didn't say much until they were sitting in a small café, some way from the house and looking out at the sea.

'I don't understand.'

Sedge smiled, 'We help each other. Patsy's on his own mission, sometimes I can do something for him, sometimes he does a little something for me. He's not afraid of scum like Egerton.'

'Egerton has some scary friends.'

'So does Patsy.'

'What if they come and ask and take my phone so I can't call him?'

'You could always write the number down somewhere else… on a piece of paper,' she said as if explaining to a particularly slow child, 'it doesn't really matter, the house is well protected. You can't get in the front and there are cameras and alarm trips all over the back. Patsy knew we were there from the moment we turned into the garage forecourt.' Anton ate his spaghetti and Sedge carried on toying with her vegetarian all-day breakfast, most of which she looked like she was leaving. 'Don't feel sorry for Egerton.'

'I won't,' said Anton. 'So… how are you going to, you know, get him?' Sedge gave up on her food and slid her plate forward, arranging the knife and fork neatly in parallel.

'I wouldn't worry too much about the detail but suffice to say I left a couple of extra little somethings on the laptop for him.' Anton didn't reply but waited for more. 'Remember I said there was some porn on the drive but nothing illegal? That's not quite true now… and there's a little trail of crumbs for a clever policeman to find it. Put it this way, he won't have an easy time of it in jail,' Anton looked concerned, 'like I say, don't feel sorry for him.'

'I don't,' he said, but quieter than before.

'I left something for his chat room chum too, don't know if it'll work but it might cause a bit of tension, sow a little mistrust maybe. It would be nice to damage that network if we could.' Anton thought about this as he finished his spaghetti and placed his plate on top of her's. He called out to the waitress who was passing, asking for more tea and Sedge ordered another cappuccino, joking with him that it was his doing that she had a taste for it now.

She changed the subject. 'How's it going with… what's her name again?'

'Franca. Not so good, still broken up. I thought we might get back together but she's been seeing someone else, did that in a bit of a hurry after we split… I had a drink with her, but… I miss her, but it's not going to work.'

'You don't trust her?' Anton nodded, 'I get that, trust is a big thing for me.'

'And me… I loved her though.'

Sedge sighed and said, 'What do you want me to say? More fish in the sea? Because there are… you will definitely meet more people.' The waitress arrived with their drinks and got them mixed up. When she turned away, Anton swopped the cups over.

'I know what you say is true.' He stirred his tea, feeling a little embarrassed that he was feeling sorry for himself. 'Anyway, forget it, it's just life right? And I know it's nothing compared to what you've had to deal with.' Sedge looked over at him and smiled kindly,

'Love… from what I can see, it just fucks you up,' she was serious but when she looked at him she couldn't help herself and laughed; he laughed with her, and they looked out of the window and talked about the view for a while.

When they got up to leave, Anton asked her why she had taken the money from the bag; she didn't look like she needed it.

'I was testing you. I wasn't sure which side you were on. If you were one of Egerton's little helpers, you'd have squeezed me for the two hundred. You didn't though, you decided to help me out instead. That made me think I could trust you.'

They said goodbye outside the café, Anton knew his way back to the station. Sedge gave him a peck on the cheek and said to remember what to say if things started to get out of hand.

'I know, thanks. See you again perhaps?'

Sedge had started to walk away, she turned and said, 'Who knows? That'd be nice. I know your number.'

30

The next day at the gym, Anton witnessed the miracle. He'd been sitting out in the back in the early afternoon, downing fresh orange juice, calling it one of his five-a-day when he gradually became aware that something sounded different in the main part of the building: the chatter was growing into a slowly building hubbub until there was clapping and a noise like a Sunday league football crowd celebrating a goal.

He walked through to see everyone gathered near the door where, just inside, stood Franny, leaning on crutches, but definitely Franny, upright and alive. He stood like a wounded messiah, surrounded by his disciples, laughing, smiling, and enjoying the surprise he'd sprung on them. Anton could see his wife as well, holding on to him, daring anyone to come too close. Anton made his way to the front of the small crowd.

'You're kidding me,' said Anton.

'That's what the doctor said,' said Franny, 'I heard this place was going to rack and ruin, you stopped coming to see me-'

'-It was one day,' said Anton, Franny reached out and grabbed him around the shoulders and ruffled his hair.

'I thought I needed to get back and save you all from yourselves.'

'Might be too late for that,' said Anton, 'but it's really good to see you.' He couldn't help himself and rather than pull himself free from Franny's enthusiastic embrace, he hugged him back.

Franny's wife looked disapproving, 'No jostling him, be careful,' she said, 'and listen to me, all of you: if I find out he's gone back inside a ring, I'll come back here and skin every one of you alive, every single fucking one of you, do you hear me?' There was a general rumble of *yes* and *uh-huh* letting her know that yes, they heard her, loud and clear.

Sitting later in Barney's office, with Barney, Anton, Tyrone and Kenny Dean, Franny boasted that the doctors had said to him that his was the fastest recovery they'd ever seen, how he beat every challenge they put to him,

'The way I see it is, I'm way too good looking and definitely too young to die.'

Anton looked up, 'well, too young I'll give you,'

'What are you allowed to do?' asked Barney.

'Not a lot, gentle exercise, as much as I feel like as long as it doesn't start to hurt. It's just good to be back here, I'm happy to potter about for now, try and be useful maybe.'

'Not getting in a ring though?'

'No… better not, not just yet, the missus was serious. I've got the exercises, I can do them here, I can do them at home, just got to keep at it. I can get back here and find something useful to do.'

'You know we're packing up and leaving next week?' said Barney, Franny nodded.

'Perhaps I can help find a new place.'

'Why not?' said Anton, 'We need somewhere.'

'How's Kirby coming along?' asked Franny.

'Good,' said Barney, 'good, I think, we just need to keep going with him now. In fact, Anton…?' Anton looked over at him, 'Do you think you could spar with him again tomorrow?'

Anton nodded, 'of course, why not?'

'He needs to get some ring time in him now, try out a few of the things we've worked on, some of the things I've taught him.'

'Hold on,' said Anton, 'what things have you taught him?'

'Ah, nothing you can't handle,' Barney said, grinning just a little, 'Franny, you could watch them, get a bit of an objective eye on how he's doing,' Franny nodded, happy to have a job to do. 'I want to surprise him though, I don't want him to prepare too much so don't say anything, just be here at ten and I'll make out like I just had the idea, okay?'

'Okay,' said Anton, looking at Franny. They both knew Barney was up to something.

Just before ten the next day, Anton was getting to the end of his warmup routine, he'd got himself close to the ring where Kirby was getting ready, bouncing around, expecting Dave or Barney to step in and carry on with his build-up work.

Anton was a little apprehensive, it was clear to all that Kirby's training had taken on a new level of seriousness. To work with him now meant taking responsibility, whoever did so would have a lot on their shoulders all of a sudden. Franny was there and Anton had been chatting and joking with him to keep his mind off it.

'Hey, listen, you want to spar with Kirby this morning?' said Barney, appearing from behind him, like he just had the idea and not waiting for an answer, 'Great, thank you,' he handed Anton a head guard, Kirby was already wearing his. 'Let's do six rounds,' then, to Kirby, 'I want you to try out some of the stuff we've been working on, okay?'

Kirby nodded and grunted back, eyeing Anton as he climbed in. It was still a little awkward for them both but the sooner it started, the better. They fist bumped and stepped back. Kirby put his hands up and waited, staring straight ahead at Anton, concentrating. This wasn't the Kirby Anton remembered, there was menace now.

Barney called out, 'Kirby sets the level, go.'

They came together, a few little taps, nothing much, just saying *hi*. Then Kirby came for him, a one-two, fast; faster than he'd been before, Anton ducked away but was caught by a follow up right hander which stung and made him blink.

Okay, this is for real thought Anton, *except he's setting the pace; nice.* They carried on, going through some standard moves, no real venom but there was an intensity, a sharpness about Kirby that was new.

'Okay, hold it, thirty seconds,' said Barney. They dropped their hands and listened to him. 'Try something different,' he said to Kirby, then, 'Anton, keep your hands up, stop him hitting you.'

They started up again, Kirby got in close, probing, threatening, again keeping the intensity up. Anton's defence was good, but he was being pulled all over the place, he kept his hands up over his face while Kirby let fly with a flurry of blows, making him stay like it, hold his stance. When Kirby stepped back, he dropped his left hand to leave a gap he could look through. Up to this point Anton had been kept in defence, now the gap was there he hesitated, caught Barney's eye, and stepped back, staying on his toes.

'Okay ladies, not sure what you think you're doing now. That was a chance he gave you Anton, next time put one in there.' Anton looked at him, but Barney's face was serious, he wanted him to have a proper pop.

Kirby came forward again, punching up close, forcing Anton into defensive dodges. He caught Anton on the chin which hurt, but mostly he was blocked. Once again, Kirby stepped back, apparently to take a breath, once again he dropped his left hand; this time Anton took the invitation and threw a right jab at Kirby's face. Before he could think, Kirby had blocked it with both arms, deflected the jab with his left and let loose a right uppercut which took Anton off his feet and he fell onto his backside, looking up at Kirby who showed no anger, nor glee but just kept his stare up, checking he'd put his man down.

'Good,' said Barney.

'Yeah, thanks,' said Anton, getting back up.

'Go and get him then,' said Barney. Anton advanced on Kirby, looking for a way in but keeping his following leg well back to allow a retreat. He sent a series of hooks and jabs at him, but Kirby was blocking everything, his arms were always just there. He was going to be hard to hit.

'Hold it, thirty seconds,' said Barney, crossing over to Anton. 'Try and hit him.'

'I am trying to hit him,' said Anton.

'Just really try, okay? Just for this round he won't try and hit you so you can forget defence, okay? He won't come at you,' Barney looked over at Kirby, 'Okay? Hold back, give him a chance,' Kirby nodded and started jogging on the spot again, keeping Anton on edge. 'Just this round, go.'

Anton looked wary and unsure how to approach him, it didn't feel right to have no need to defend. Barney put his hand up to pause them and called Anton down to whisper in his ear: 'It's okay, just try and hit him as hard as you can, any shot you like.'

Anton stood and faced Kirby who faced him back, bouncing gently up and down, waiting for him, hands up. He came forward and led with his left, following up with a powerful right hook, Kirby parrying both easily. Anton repeated the action, assuming Kirby wouldn't expect that, but the result was the same. He came back at him, jabbing with his right, keeping Kirby's arms moving, weaving patterns in the air, looking for space while Kirby kept him at bay. He dropped in a few body shots, but Kirby read them and dodged out of the way. He was getting frustrated now and moved in close, picking up the pace and peppering Kirby with hooks, more body shots and uppercuts, he tried as much variation as he could think of, looking for the gap, trying in vain to find space and a way through.

'Good, stop,' said Barney. Anton was out of breath and leant forward, holding on to his knees, gulping the air, 'Good, don't forget he was only defending, he could concentrate on you, he didn't have to work out any attack.'

'Yeah and I didn't have to work out any defence, but I still couldn't hit him.'

'Good point,' said Barney, smiling. Anton felt tired. He knew this was all about positive reinforcement, all about building Kirby's self-belief but it was hard work.

Now Barney was over with Kirby whispering in his ear and gesturing, showing him some move presumably, Anton watched and tried to work it out, but it was impossible and anyway he was worn out. 'Fourth round, go: Kirby, set the level.'

Which was all very well but the level he seemed to want was pretty high in Anton's view. But they were there for Kirby so he drew the deepest breath he could manage and got back in. For three minutes they traded shots, nothing too serious, but it was fast, there was no let up with Kirby now, he was fired up and he looked like he could go on forever.

'Getting there on your fitness,' said Barney after he stopped them for the fourth time. Anton was puffing hard, and Kirby looked like he was just getting into it. Barney was back talking with Kirby while Anton leant on the ropes getting his breath back, taking in long deep lungfuls of the gymnasium air. Just before they started again Barney spoke to Anton,

'Alright, he's going to stay away from you, stand off a bit, he'll throw some punches at you, but you'll see them coming. Or you will if you pay attention.'

Anton managed to say 'Wait, what?' before Barney called out for them to start again. Kirby came toward Anton and stood a couple of steps away; he leant in and tried a one-two which Anton parried and was able to follow up with a jab of his own. Kirby kept the shots coming but Anton was handling them well and even finding time to force him back into defence. Anton's reach was good, so he felt better like this and felt like they were a little more even.

Kirby seemed to slow the pace a little, Anton wasn't sure if that was to conserve his energy or if he was thinking, because he certainly looked like he was thinking and that was worrying. After a minute or so of back-and-forth Kirby stepped back as if Anton had pushed him off balance, Anton instinctively stepped forward, lining up a shot but he was drawn in and Kirby produced a left-right combination that came from nowhere, both of which connected and the second of which put Anton down again. Barney gave a cheer and cried out,

'That's it, that's the one,' Anton looked over at him and mouthed *what the...?* and stayed down. Barney gave them a two-minute break after which they went for a final three minutes, Barney promising no more fancy stuff for now, just a good honest tidy round which he got although Anton was content just to avoid further injury and Kirby carried on riding his own personal wave of confidence.

Franny sat with Anton afterwards. 'He's got a good chance I'd say, he looks good. Good work letting him grow his confidence.'

'I didn't,' said Anton, 'he was just better out there.'

'I know, I was being nice to you,' Franny playfully batted Anton round his head. 'The work's paying off, he's improving still.'

Anton nodded, 'I know. We just have to keep it up when we're in the church hall.' He wondered how that was going to be possible.

The last week in the gym had a strange feel to it, there were two worlds at work there: most of the activity was focussed on filling boxes and organising the vast amount of stuff, junk that had gradually gathered there over many years and that no-one had the heart to throw out. At the same time a small team kept a sense of business as usual around Kirby and kept him focussed on his training plan, the burden of which fell mainly on Barney, Dave, and Anton.

Franny took it on himself to keep a list of everyone's contact details for when they found a new building so he could make sure they would all be told. It was his intention to put it all on a computer sometime, make a proper database but most people who knew him thought he wouldn't ever get round to it. Instead, and in the meantime, he used an old-style alphabetical address book where he carefully collected email addresses and phone numbers.

With only a few days to go, Barney suggested they should go and sort out the space in the church. No-one knew how much of their stuff they were going to be able to get in there. No-one had even measured it properly to make sure there was enough room for the ring and some other bits and bobs, everyone had relied on Tyrone's rather general comment when the idea first came up,

'Yeah, it'll all fit in there.'

Tyrone was fired up and highly motivated by having the answer to a crisis and only too happy to sort things at the church. It was a chance to show off to his church friends that he had a set of hard man friends outside and for his friends from the gym to see something of his other life, the thing that meant the most to him and to see how cool the vicar could be.

'There's a chance one or two of my parishioners may be a little sniffy about this but the way I see it is we are reaching out to our community,' said the man in the dog collar to Tyrone who was holding one end of a tape measure while Anton called out the measurement from the other, gathering the necessary information they needed to draw up a basic layout plan. Franny sat with a sketch pad and wrote the measurements down, at the same time drawing a rough layout for the ring and the kit they had put aside to take there.

'There's a toilet and a sort of cloakroom out through that door which you can use, perhaps it could even be a changing room,' the vicar continued. Franny got up and went out to look.

'I don't suppose there's a shower anywhere Father….' said Anton, not hopefully.

'Michael, and you don't need to say the father bit, Michael is fine. Or Mike, they call me Mike a lot of them. Ah, no, I'm afraid not. The baptismal fount is about your lot, and I don't think you lads are going fit in there,'

'Kirby can come and use ours, at home… I live about five minutes away,' said Tyrone, 'it's only for a week or two after all.'

'That said,' the vicar continued, 'I'm a bit of a fan of the sport. I was a pugilist myself when I was younger. I watch the big fights on TV when they're on a channel I've actually got… I've been to the O2 a couple of times…' *This guy's going to be in here all the time,* thought Anton. 'We haven't got any room bookings until Easter so I'm quite happy for you to be here until then if it helps.'

'To be honest,' said Anton, 'it really would. Thank you.' Tyrone looked pleased and proprietorial.

With two days to go before they were due to leave the gym, most of the stuff was put away in boxes or skips and there was a general air of practicality, if not quite acceptance. A few of the members had found other gyms to take them in but the rest were working together to keep Kirby on track, the prospect of the upcoming fight enough to keep them happily distracted.

Barney was organising things: 'Skips are all full, we have a couple of spare boxes still which can go to the church. Any pads we're using now, the bags and the travelling kits should all go in. Everything else into the big one in the corner, that one's going to the store.' He scanned the room, 'How many lockers can we get in the church?'

Anton had anticipated the question and worked out the answer in advance with the help of Franny's sketches, 'Just one full set for now, it can fit along the short wall and that leaves enough room around the ring.'

'Okay, the rest goes in the store,' said Barney with a hint of frustration in his voice. 'Just hope the flipping store's big enough,' he said under his breath.

Tyrone had somehow managed to borrow a transit van from one of his church friends who had also been volunteered to drive it, and the two of them made a dozen or so trips over the final week, carefully packing everything away in a shipping container Barney had hired, bit by bit, starting from one end.

'It's all in there but you're not going to get it back in if you ever try and take it out,' said Tyrone.

'Let's hope we're putting it all into a new gym soon,' said Anton, looking at Barney who looked away but made a noise like an *uh-huh* as he did so.

By the last day, the gym was empty apart from a lone cardboard box into which anything left had been dropped; there was still space in the top. Keith had kept a broom back and was sweeping dust from the floor into a small pile at one end of the room; nobody could say for sure why he was bothering. George, Barney, and Anton sat with takeaway coffees on one of the fixed benches which no-one had thought worth saving and were looking round.

'It's a big old room, now you see it,' said Barney.

'How it looked when I first walked in,' said George, 'except it was filthy, litter everywhere, rat droppings… there was a dead pigeon over there in the corner.' He thought for a moment, 'Actually as I remember it, there was a live one in here as well, it took ages to chase it out, crapped everywhere.' Anton laughed then sat silently with the others, even Keith had stopped sweeping and leant against the wall. George still had the floor though, 'What happened to the Rules?'

'I've got them,' said Barney. 'Went in the basics box, labelled, ready for the next place.'

Anton looked at him and said, 'We should go I suppose… Kirby.'

'It's okay, Dave's looking after him,' said Barney, 'Franny too. Wouldn't be surprised if he isn't in the ring and sparring by now.'

'You can tell his missus,' said Anton, standing up. 'Anyone for another tea?'

31

Anton arrived back at the gym holding a cardboard tray with four cups in it and met Nico at the front door.

'Nico… sorry, I didn't get you one, didn't know you were coming over. You can have one of these if you want and I'll nip back and get another.' Nico shook his head and hunched up into his collar as he turned the handle on the door and stepped back to let Anton in.

'Don't worry, I'm not staying.'

George looked up as they walked in. 'Nico,' he said, quietly. No-one was in much of a mood for making noise. The room was the quietest any of them had ever known it.

'Small problem,' said Nico, sitting on the bench next to George, 'they didn't complete.'

'What does that mean?' said George, 'There's still time, isn't there? It's still early afternoon.'

'I talked to the solicitor, there's a hold up. Her client's talking to the police or something, not sure what it's all about but the money's not come through.' Anton was listening carefully.

'Will they have it tomorrow?' said George.

'It's Saturday, they don't work Saturdays.'

'Monday then?'

Nico shook his head, 'I don't know, neither do they, it's a mess but they say they just need a few days to get the funds released. Our solicitor has sent something called a notice to complete, it gives them ten days.'

'So, we're still gone?' said Anton.

Nico nodded, 'We're still gone. They say it's not a problem, its corporate funds and they're secure, it'll all be fine.'

Barney said, 'So we…?'

'We lock up, keep it secure, keep hold of the keys for now,' said Nico.

'Gives us time to find a pigeon,' said Anton although Nico had no idea what he was going on about.

Anton had no plans for the weekend, nowhere to go either. He'd seen it coming but not really taken it in, too much else to think about with the gym needing to be cleared. Suddenly his mind wasn't fully occupied: Kirby had been given an easy weekend before he went full tilt for the run-in and the church hall wasn't really big enough to hang out in. He had time to think although he wasn't sure that was something he necessarily wanted to do. Nothing seemed clear, and he felt a vague sense of loss which he didn't care to dwell on but which he couldn't shake and as a result, he became a generally miserable presence around the house. His brother attempted to cheer him up and get him to go out, but it didn't work, instead he just moped about.

Malcolm spent most of Saturday out, no-one seemed to know where and he was secretive about it too, saying little when he left. That evening, when he returned however, he had news.

'I've got a number,' he said to Anton, 'for your mum, for Angie. I spoke to her as well, she's around tomorrow afternoon if you want to call her.' He handed Anton a bright orange post-it note with a number written on it. Anton took it and stared at the number as if looking for a hidden message in there.

'Tomorrow?'

Malcolm nodded, 'Tomorrow. She'll be at home, and she'll

be waiting for your call.' Anton didn't know what to say but was aware of Neville watching him from the corner of the room. He wanted to be alone.

'Thank you,' he said, put the post-it note in his pocket and left the kitchen.

In his room, he sat and stared again at the number and tried to straighten things out in his head. It was hard enough finding out that the mother you thought you shared with your brother wasn't in fact *his* mother at all and furthermore was alive when you'd taken it for granted she was dead, but somehow being able to talk to her now felt impossible in some way. What was he supposed to say? What was *she* supposed to say? He hit the remote for the TV, found distraction in the form of a darts tournament and fell asleep in front of it.

The next morning, he woke up still not sure what he could expect from the call but fairly sure he needed privacy for it. While he made himself breakfast he dropped some none-to-subtle hints that he would go and sit in the car to make the call, Malcolm picked up on it and offered to buy Neville a couple of pints and maybe get lunch at the same time.

'It's been a while since we did that: Sunday afternoon in the pub, big lunch, sit around and talk bollocks afterwards.' He looked over at Anton, 'When you've finished your call you could join us.'

'Yeah you should,' said Neville, 'you're really good at talking bollocks.'

By one o'clock Anton was on his own in the house; he paced around for a while, still thinking, trying to work out what to say. Deciding he had to get a grip, he made a cup of tea and sat at the kitchen table. For a while he just stared at the post-it note, then rather than wait until he had a cup of *cold* tea to help him through it, he pressed the numbers. Moments later a voice said simply,

'Hello?'

Anton went to speak but choked and couldn't for a moment, he had to compose himself before he could answer, 'Hello? Mum?'

'Anton…. Anton, my baby,' she spoke quietly but her voice was clear and slow.

'I'm a little older now… Mum.'

'You can call me Angie if you like, I know it isn't easy. It's so good to hear you, good to know you're out there.' He was aware that tears were running down his face, but he felt no sadness or pain, he was happy but in a way he didn't understand. He was grateful to be alone in the house.

'Angie… Mum… I don't know, I'll try both okay? See how it works out, is that okay?' She laughed which helped and asked him,

'Is Malcolm there?'

'No, he's gone out and left me some privacy, taken Neville too.'

'Oh God, Neville, how is he?'

'He's alright but *oh God, Neville* is about right.' Keeping it light definitely made it easier.

'What do you do with yourself my baby? I'm sorry, I shouldn't say that, I know, I'm sorry, Anton.'

'It's okay, it's cool Mum, Angie, it's cool. I work with Dad, working on the houses, fixing things, doing them up, collecting the rents. And I do a lot of boxing-'

'-boxing? Why boxing?'

'Why not? I enjoy it, I'm good at it, I'm careful though, my eyes are a bit… fragile. I do it for fun.'

'It's dangerous.'

'Not really, it's a way of keeping fit that's all.'

'You have a girl?' Anton thought for a while before answering.

'No. Not at the moment. Footloose and fancy free.'

'So, you go boxing and you don't have a girlfriend?'

'Yeah Mum, it's okay.'

'What is he doing letting you go boxing all the time?'

'It's okay really, he's okay, we all get along. What about you? Where do you live?'

'I'm not far, in town, not too far from you. I went away for a while, but I came back, its where I know.'

'What happened? Back then.'

'He hasn't told you?' she sighed, and Anton imagined her sitting back in a large armchair while she told him, 'I made a mistake, a few mistakes. A couple of big ones, not you though, you were the best of everything for me,' Anton closed his eyes and listened, he didn't want to interrupt, just listen to her voice. 'I was young, not so wise maybe, I liked to go out, enjoy parties… Malcolm… Malcolm was always a good father, a really good father but something came between us. We both loved you dearly, so much but I… just made a mistake. I met someone else. I'm not making excuses; I know I was in the wrong.'

'Can we meet?'

'Yes. Anton, I don't know what you want from me. I don't want to let you down.'

'You won't. I don't want anything, it's just… I think it would be good to at least know what you look like,' she was silent, 'and I'm a bit taller now.' That did it and she chuckled on the other end.

She said she needed a few days to get ready, to prepare herself but yes, she would meet him. He said that was fine, he'd waited twenty years after all, then immediately regretted putting it quite like that. They arranged to meet in a café near the gym, he knew it well and knew that mid-afternoon in mid-week would be quiet enough to be sure of a table.

Nico paid a visit to the church one morning to watch Kirby. Anton was doing pad work with him, relentlessly working Barney's set routines, keeping him up to it. Anton saw Nico watching and at the end of the session while they took a break, he came and sat next to him on the bench.

'He's looking good, you're doing a good job.'

'I'm just helping,' said Anton, 'Barney's the brains.'

Nico gave a little laugh, 'That's what he says about you,' Anton looked a little surprised, 'not brains exactly… work ethic maybe, he says you're putting the hours in.'

'It's a worthy cause.' Nico nodded and sat quietly, knowing what was coming. 'Is it tomorrow? The cut-off date?' Nico nodded. 'After that, what happens?'

Nico sighed, 'We may have to put it back on the market,' Anton went to speak but Nico got in first, 'or maybe not, they came back with an offer. Your friend Egerton's lawyer.'

'Not my friend,' said Anton emphatically.

'Wise of you, I'd say, it seems he's in some kind of pickle, got arrested apparently, but his company still has money, maybe not so much as it once had… she's tried to drop the price, offered us about half of what it's worth.'

'You're not going to take it?'

'Its cash. And it's still enough for George, he's happy with his share.' Anton tutted and shook his head but knew he didn't really have a say in it.

'What if you kept it? Didn't sell?' said Anton.

'George-'

'-But, I'm sorry and this is rude I know so you can tell me to shut up and mind my own business but… what if Franny and I took it on? Run it for you. We could make it pay; we've been talking about how to do that.'

'What about George?'

'You could loan us the money to pay him his share.'

'Oh, I'm a bank now?' There was an edgy silence while Anton decided not to speak but just to let the idea sit there for a moment. 'What will you both do to make it pay?'

'We have ideas. Still a boxing club obviously, but more. Expand the Boys Club, start a second one, start a weekend one, start a Girls Club, why not? We've never tried, we have one girl but she's always saying there are others out there… we could do more classes for the younger ones, fitness, physical skills, art: the kids that do the art class love it; we could do more things like that, some training, engineering, hairdressing, I don't know, anything anyone can think of… white collar boxing in the evenings so the city boys can knock each other about without the aid of alcohol, the list goes on.'

'Can I say shut up and mind your own business *now*?' said Nico. Anton kept eye contact but didn't respond. 'You have a business plan?'

'No, we don't have a written down business plan.'

'So, you want me to give George his share of the building and let you, what, have a go?'

'It's more than that. You know we could do more, and *we* could do it, Franny and me, he needs something to do… you know we could if we had the chance.'

'What about Barney? Dave? The rest of them?'

'They'd stay,' said Anton, aware he hadn't thought any of this through let alone agreed it with Franny.

'They're redundant, they're all redundant.'

'So now they'll be happy, its good news, we save their jobs,' Anton was working hard on not raising his voice.

Nico shook his head, 'So now you want to start a payroll, register with the tax people, pay business rates, do accounting,' he looked Anton in the eye and said emphatically, 'you want to do accounting?' There was no answer, '… get insurances, have a health and safety plan.'

'Can't we just take over what's already there?'

Nico sat back, 'No, Anton. It doesn't work like that. You know I can't, even though Egerton is… let's say unpleasant, and I personally can't stand his solicitor, there's a deal-'

'-half a deal, you said so,'

'And even if they're ripping us off, its cash and it's enough. We don't need to be greedy.'

Dave had stepped into the ring and was sparring with Kirby. Nico made a thing of crossing his arms and making himself comfortable to sit back and watch. Anton fidgeted for a few moments and said quietly,

'I'm sorry.'

'It's okay,' said Nico, 'I don't want to see it go either. I understand.' Anton stayed there, watching with him, thinking about it, then deciding it was worth one more try.

'You're a wealthy man,' as he said it, he realised he had no solid reason to believe it, 'you don't need to rush. You could give George his share, tell Atkinson-Pike to sling her hook, give us a little bit of time to make it work. We could pay you some rent and you could still sell up in the future but wait until you get the full price for it.' Nico kept staring at the ring and waited until Anton stopped.

'Have you finished?' Can I just sit here and watch this fucking work-out please?' Anton leant back, put his hands up, palms out.

‘Sorry, yes.’ He stood and walked away, it was a point made, he couldn’t do any more, at least he had tried.

Franny was watching Kirby too, from the other end of the room; Anton walked up to him.

‘Alright? How’s the old man?’ said Franny.

‘Oh, you know, ready to close us down,’ he looked at Franny who raised his eyebrows as a gesture of resignation. ‘Listen, its nearly lunchtime, you hungry?’

Franny looked at him, ‘Not really.’

‘Yes, you are, come on, I’ll buy you lunch.’

32

'What were you talking to Nico about yesterday?' Barney had a look about him when Anton arrived at the church the next day, 'It looked to me like he was trying get away from you.'

'I was trying to talk him out of the sale.'

Barney nodded to himself and said, 'You don't listen, do you? All a bit late for that. But…' he took his phone out and started pressing the screen, '…he sent me this, for you.' He handed it to Anton who read the text aloud: *Tell Anton been thinking please ask him to meet me at solicitors 4pm today…* he read on to see the address, it was Valerie Atkinson-Pike's office. 'Hope you know what you're doing.'

'Not really. You okay if I leave about three?'

'Me and Dave are around, we'll carry on with Kirby.' Barney was still giving him that look.

He didn't need directions to find Atkinson-Pike's office again and arrived ten minutes early. The receptionist didn't seem to recognise him or didn't care and when he told her he was there to meet others she waved him vaguely into a chair to wait.

Anton smiled and nodded to the only other person there, an older man, well dressed, classic cut grey suit with a just visible pinstripe, an expensive looking dark maroon tie and a matching handkerchief folded tidily into his top pocket. A dark brown leather briefcase rested on his knees and the man tapped his fingers on it as he waited.

A few minutes later Nico arrived and was treated with a good deal less indifference by the receptionist when he announced himself.

He greeted Anton and the man in the grey suit who he introduced as Mr Harrington, his solicitor. The receptionist had made a call and now stood in front of them asking if they would please follow her. Anton tried to ask Nico what this was all about, but he was evasive,

'Let's just wait and see,' was all he would say.

They were shown into a meeting room, all chrome, steel, and glass. Orders for coffee and tea were taken and they were invited to sit. Harrington had started to pour water from one of the bottles set out on the table when Victoria Atkinson-Pike entered. *She has a way of making an entrance,* thought Anton. She was pin-striped too, but bolder and on a dark navy cloth, her suit cut to size with precision and class. Anton felt under-dressed. He was under-dressed.

'Gentlemen, good afternoon.' She looked at Anton, 'Mr Matheson, goodness me,' Nico looked up at Anton, 'a pleasant surprise.'

'You know each other?' Nico asked him. Atkinson-Pike answered,

'In a way, Mr Matheson is one of the reasons we started to take an interest in your property,' she said.

'Right,' said Nico, a little off balance.

'You have the contracts?' said Atkinson-Pike and Harrington opened his case and brought out a bundle of papers, many of the pages had little yellow post-it notes sticking out. 'Good, my client-'

'-Before we carry on,' said Nico, 'if you don't mind, may I just ask a couple of questions?'

'Fire away,' said Atkinson-Pike. *Smug as ever.*

'Your client, as I understand it, is in custody?'

'Not material, the purchase will be made by a corporate body, the funds are available and cleared, your solicitor's account will be credited immediately on signature.'

Nico nodded. 'Thank you, but I think I would like to understand more about his detention,' Anton watched Atkinson-Pike fidget and look at him, *niggled.*

'It's really not relevant to-'

'-My client really does require full disclosure Ms Atkinson-Pike,' said Harrington, 'although we accept the purchaser is a corporate body, Mr Egerton is a director of that body, as we understand it.'

The receptionist returned with a tray of teacups which she placed carefully on the table, Atkinson-Pike watched her for a moment then said,

'It's immaterial, Mr Harrington.'

'It's a condition for us, Ms Atkinson-Pike,' said Harrington. She picked up one of the glasses of water and sipped it, no-one spoke but Harrington smiled broadly in a way he possibly thought was warm and friendly but maybe didn't come across that way.

'It's no secret,' she said. 'Mr Egerton is being held and is helping the police with their enquiries… over an allegation of possession of indecent images, an allegation which is entirely unfounded and that he will defend.'

'Oh dear. That's not good Ms Atkinson-Pike,' said Harrington.

'He's been wrongly accused, Mr Harrington.'

'Even so…'

'I say again, it's immaterial Mr Harrington,' she was still standing and tried to stare Harrington down, but he didn't seem bothered. It was Nico who broke the silence,

'There's one more thing, do you think your client… your corporate client, would consider maintaining the property in its current use? As a boxing gym?'

'I'm afraid not, we have planning consent which allows for a night club, it's a far better commercial proposition.'

'We have an alternative offer which would see the premises remain in use as a boxing gym,' said Nico.

'You also have a contract with my client-'

'-unsigned, as yet,' said Nico.

'Which is why we are all here of course.' She paused and finally sat down before continuing, 'In what way does the use we make of the building matter? You have our offer, it's a good one in the circumstances; as I understand it you're keen to sell and release some of the equity,' she looked away from Nico now to Harrington, 'and we are ready to go ahead, today. Of course, we require full vacant possession.' She sat back and indicated the tray of hot drinks in front of her, 'Please help yourselves.'

Anton could see she was irritated. Nico looked away from her and down to his hand resting on the table in front of him, nodding slightly to himself then leant over to whisper in Harrington's ear. Harrington whispered something back and Anton watched, fascinated. Atkinson-Pike was clearly losing her patience. Nico sat back, folded his arms and looked across the table.

'Ms Atkinson-Pike. With all due respect. It's a no from us.'

'What?' She was shaking, just a little.

'No, thank you,' said Nico, 'we're not going to sign.'

'I'm afraid you have no choice; Mr Harrington will explain. You see you sent a notice to complete which gave us ten days to do just that and we are now in a position to do so.'

Harrington allowed himself a short dramatic pause, then said, 'It was a notice to complete at £1.95 million Ms Atkinson-Pike, your current offer is almost a million pounds short of that sum.' Anton listened but didn't dare move, 'It also expires at five o'clock which is in… thirty-five minutes. I am happy to wait here if you wish to complete as per the terms of the original offer we accepted and exchanged on, that is, at £1.95 million; otherwise, I'm afraid my client wishes to withdraw.'

Atkinson-Pike looked from Harrington to Nico and back again.

'You're serious?' she asked.

'Oh yes, completely serious,' said Nico, taking the papers from Harrington and dramatically tearing them in half. Atkinson-Pike's face had turned red, Anton wondered if she was about to scream.

'Get out of my office,' she said.

'Is it all off, then?' said Nico.

'Get out,' was all she could manage, she was really shaking now. Anton wondered just who she was going to have to explain all this to. Nico and Harrington took their time to gather up the torn papers, stand and adjust their jackets, straighten the chairs, and take a final sip of water. *They don't want to go, they're enjoying this,* thought Anton.

He was at the door first and they followed him out into the corridor where they sauntered to the front office, past the receptionist who looked up and Nico said a hearty, 'Goodbye,' as they filed past to leave.

Once outside Nico asked Harrington if that was it now, was it over?

'I think so, she still has some time, but I don't think she's coming back to us before five, do you?'

'Let's get a taxi,' said Nico. Anton tried to ask him what would happen now, but Nico kept him at bay and insisted they go and look at the gym, it was only a few miles away.

When they got there, Nico had the keys and opened up. They stood just inside the door; the air was cold and still.

'When you leave somewhere like this, it dies, it just switches off with the last person out of the door, wouldn't you say?' Nico waited while Anton and Harrington both thought about that and agreed with him.

'What now?' asked Anton.

'Come and sit,' said Nico, leading them over to the bench set against the wall. They sat, Harrington in the middle. 'Show him,' said Nico to Harrington who opened his case and took out another set of papers and handed a stapled-together bundle to Anton.

'What is it?' he said and started to read, 'My name...'

'Very good, yes, your name. It's an agreement with you. Between you and me,' said Nico, 'I thought about your offer.'

'Offer? It wasn't really an offer.'

'No, it wasn't, it had no substance. So, this does that, gives it some substance.' Anton read on as Nico spoke, 'It's up to you now. You think you can do it, make it work, you and Franny: okay, you show us.' Anton looked at him, still struggling to understand what was happening to him, Nico carried on as if talking to a particularly slow child, 'It's a lease. I'm buying George out, giving him his cash and keeping my share for now. You pay a rent: I've kept it low for the first couple of years, let you get started properly. There are a couple of special conditions,' Anton looked up again, 'you try and get rid of Barney-'

'-I would never do that-'

'-You try and get rid of Barney, I repossess. You try and get rid of Dave or Keith, I repossess; you look at me a bit funny one day, I repossess... are you getting the gist? You'd better read it.' Anton's heart was thumping, he felt sure it could be heard by the others. He turned the pages to the end.

'It's not signed.'

Nico held his hand out to take the lease back, 'Two things first.' Anton passed it back across Harrington, Nico took a pen out from his jacket and theatrically clicked it open, 'What happens to the Rules?'

'The Rules? They were kept, they're in a box, they're safe,' he looked at Nico who stared back, *wrong answer.* He thought more, 'They go back up, they're good rules.'

'Good answer.' Nico looked at Harrington, 'You heard that,' Harrington nodded. 'Second thing, what time is it?' Harrington checked his phone,

'Ten after five,' he said, then checked his phone, scrolling through his messages and emails, 'no emails.'

'Missed their chance then,' said Nico and with a little flourish signed the lease and handed it back to Anton. 'Just there, where you see your name.' Anton took it and stared at the final page, he hesitated before saying,

'Can I read it first? Take it home tonight?'

Nico laughed, 'Good, very good, we might make some kind of businessman out of you yet... of course, of course, but let's try and sign it tomorrow, yes?' Anton nodded agreement. 'How are you getting on with that business plan?' Anton put his hand up to stop him, reached into his jeans pocket and took out two folded sheets of paper which he held up proudly.

Nico smiled, 'Is that it?'

'So far... we only started yesterday. We've listed our ideas, filled two sides of A4 doing it, we just have to add some more...'

'Substance.'

'Substance, yes, that's it, we have a reason to now.'

He arrived home an hour later, excited, eager to share the news. Malcom listened, made tea and got him to calm down a bit.

'It's great news son, you must have done a great job convincing him. You just need to be really sure you want to do this.'

'I am sure. It was my idea in the first place. I won't be on my own, it makes sense for Franny too, he needs something that isn't fighting. And you, I need your help too.'

'Okay, you know I'll support you, no matter what.'

They talked about it, gradually coming round to understanding some of the implications: Anton would need to spend more time at the gym, there would be new responsibilities and obligations. He knew too that his dad would be thinking that this would draw him away from the business, his business; it would leave just Neville and who knew what he might do one day?

'Can we go through the lease tonight?'

'Definitely,' Malcolm nodded again and said they could sit and check the lease out after dinner, it was only a few pages after all, obvious that Nico had tried to keep it simple.

'Lawyers always add a few pages just to justify their fees, this one looks nice and straightforward,' he said, then, 'listen, I've got to tell you this... Franca called.' Anton looked at him, 'She rang the house, nothing wrong, she just wanted to know if I thought you were going to get back together.'

'What did you say?'

'Said it wasn't my business… but I also said I hoped you would, that me and Neville like her. For what it was worth.'

Anton was irritated, 'She slept with someone else, someone who was named after some bloke who scored a goal in a cup final.'

'What do you care about football?'

'I don't care about football; I'm just making the point that he's a trivial person.'

'Anton, why do you care in the slightest about him? She wants to be with you, it's what you wanted I thought, it's what you were going on about after she broke up with you. Make your flipping mind up.'

Anton shook his head in frustration, 'I can't get past that fact… what she did.'

'Seriously son, for my sake, just think about it. Don't push her away. Take it from me, if you push her away, she might stay pushed.' Anton thought about that, really didn't want to discuss it anymore.

'Come on, I'll make some dinner and we'll have a look at this.'

'Can we have chips? I really want chips,' said Anton.

Next morning Anton arrived at the church just as Barney was opening up.

'Morning boss,' said Barney.

Anton smiled, 'You're the boss Barney, you have to be.'

'Good answer. I accept. Nice one, Anton.'

'So, how come you have the keys now?'

'Turns out we have ourselves a lazy vicar; he has a problem getting here in the mornings, so I offered to do the opening up, at least we're in control of it then.' He led the way inside and pointed at the large envelope Anton was carrying, 'That it?'

'Yep, I read it so many times last night I pretty much know it off by heart.'

'Excited?' Anton nodded. 'Good, you have every right to be. Can we agree one thing? We forget it for a week and just get Kirby to his fight. After that, we'll go back and open up the gym again. Deal?'

'Deal,' said Anton, knowing that actually forgetting it for a week was not even remotely likely.

33

They had been running for two hours, Kirby hardly breaking a sweat, but Anton was feeling it and needed a break. It was Sunday, so the church was unavailable to them.

Barney had the idea to get Kirby outside and doing something closer to a fun run than a real training session. Anton had volunteered and had worked out a route that kept them away from the busy roads. The weather made it a pleasure, it was dry with moments of late winter sunlight which prompted the odd comment to the effect that spring was on its way. Mostly, they ran in silence, Anton checking out that Kirby was happy with the pace every now and then.

Eventually it was Anton who was out of breath and called a stop.

'How are you feeling now?' said Anton.

'Good, you look fucked though.'

'Lucky it's you and not me stepping into the ring on Saturday,' he leant forward on his knees and drew deep breaths in, 'how are you feeling about that?'

'Yeah, ready. Sharp. Ready, I think.'

'You've done well, everyone's saying so.'

'We're gonna find, out right?'

'Given yourself every chance, you can't do any more,' Anton stood back up and squinted as he looked at the sun, 'everyone's looking forward to it, they're all out there selling tickets.'

'I just want to get on with it now.'

Anton nodded, 'We don't know who it is yet do we?' Kirby shook his head and stretched his legs, warming down. 'Yeah, I think we've done for the day, Barney said a couple of hours… you need some rest time,' he looked up at Kirby who laughed. 'Okay, I need some rest time.' He drew a deep breath, 'Where now?'

'Tyrone's making dinner, I'm going back to his.'

'Nice one, I'll walk back with you. He did well to get the church, I even think the vicar has been selling tickets.' Kirby laughed again. Anton carried on as they walked, 'You hear about the gym?'

'I hear you're the new boss.'

'Barney's the boss, has to be. Can you imagine him taking orders from me?' Kirby shook his head and smiled, 'It was Franny and me who put the idea together though, gives him something useful to do now he can't fight. We're going to grow it, do more. You're going to stay, right?' He looked at Kirby who nodded his head in a matter-of-fact way, like he hadn't really thought about it, 'I mean, now you're a pro and all,'

'Where else would I go?' They walked on in silence for a while, enjoying the quiet Sunday streets.

'You might be in demand, get offers from other trainers… get tempted.'

'I'll stay at George's… is it gonna still be called George's?'

Anton hadn't really thought about that but now he did it seemed obvious, 'Yes, definitely. He's retiring but we'll keep the name.' He made a mental note to check that one with Franny later.

'Listen, I'm okay from here, I'm just going to jog along to Tyrone's place, use his shower. I'll see you in the morning,' said Kirby, already moving off.

'Sure? Okay, I'll shoot off then. Take it easy, have a rest this afternoon, yeah?' Kirby muttered something in reply and was gone.

The sun was back out, and the edge was off the chill. Anton walked a little way further and found a bench by a bus stop where he sat and looked up, closed his eyes and let the sun wash over his face.

After a while, he checked his phone. There was a message from an unknown number, it read: *your mate Egerton charged with possession of indecent images, blimey, S.* As he finished it another came through, this one with a picture attachment which took a while to fully open. When it did, he saw it was a photographed page from a local newspaper, the headline read: "3 FOUND DEAD IN PARKED CAR".

He read the story in parts, having to magnify each section to see clearly. The three had been shot, the reporter said it appeared to be a gang related incident, one body remained unidentified but the other two had mugshots which he enlarged enough to see unflattering shots of Mr Brown and the heavyweight from that time at Beulah Mansions. Anton couldn't say he was in any way upset to think the world was now free of Mr Brown and two of his associates, but it rattled him, nonetheless.

He tried to work out how it had come about, presumably the enigmatic Patsy had something to do with it. He closed the picture and read the message that had come with it: *thought Brighton was meant to be peaceful, take care, Sedge X.* He sat back, closed his eyes again and thought about that X.

The week of Kirby's fight was carefully scheduled: Tyrone's home became headquarters, the dining and shower facilities were put to good use and strategy meetings were held around his kitchen table. His parents were tolerant of the invasion, knowing it was just for another week and that the boy they were helping was technically homeless unless you called a Vauxhall estate car a home. Despite the offer of a bed in the spare room, Kirby stuck with his sleeping arrangements and made the short journey to the car, still parked at the back of the gym, at the end of each day.

Everyone around Kirby narrowed their focus. Anton stopped talking about the future of the gym except in private moments with Franny where they added new ideas to their expanding list. The others from the gym rallied round to work with Kirby or were out trying to sell tickets to friends, neighbours, local shopkeepers and anybody who they happened to meet.

Father Mike had taken it on himself to act as an agent and was persuading a fair number of his flock to buy tickets, this despite the simple fact that none of them had the foggiest idea who Kirby was, although Father Mike had decided he was a parishioner so should be considered one of them and they should really think about supporting him in his hour of need.

It was equally obvious to everyone that Father Mike also fancied an evening out at the boxing, and he was eager to bring as many friends with him as possible. He managed to work "fight the good fight" into his sermon on the Sunday and had developed the theme sufficiently well for most of the churchgoers to believe that going to the fight at the weekend would be an act of devotion.

Anton had essentially become Barney's deputy and was given responsibilities such as supervision of Kirby's diet as well as sparring duties and keeping the schedule tight. The run- in was his priority and apart from anything else, he was sure that a win for Kirby would be good news for the gym. The only real distractions he had were the upcoming meeting with his mother on the Wednesday and the usual first-of-the-month rent run the night before.

The rent run was a chance to sell more tickets. Neville had recovered enough to take on driving duties which meant they could expect to get round quickly; now he was back at the wheel of his beloved Outlander, he could once again drive around like a madman.

Neville even took on the ticket selling duties at the first stop, his favourite, the girl share. Anton listened while he spun out his role as an agent for his clever kid brother who was opening up a gym soon and already had their first professional fighter on the books, he even suggested they could enjoy a nurses' discount on the ticket price.

'We're not all nurses though, only Alice,' said Lucy who, as often was the case had been assigned to deal with the rent.

'I thought you all were,' said Neville, 'never mind, who's to know?' Anton kept it to himself that there wasn't a nurses' concession. It wasn't an issue because it turned out they all had other plans for Saturday evening.

'The old charm didn't quite do it, then,' said Anton when they were back in the car.

'Saturday night,' said Neville, excusing himself of any responsibility, 'they'll have things going on. I think that Lucy fancies me, though.'

Anton didn't try to sell tickets to the couple in the house who, he was sure, were struggling to get by. The students in the next flat declared themselves to be ideologically opposed to boxing so they weren't interested and the next flat still contained their least favourite and most argumentative tenants who neither of the brothers could be bothered with.

He got luckier at the immaculately maintained flat with the two sharing men who said, *why not?* It would be something different and they would never have thought of it themselves. Anton didn't try with the solicitor in the flat above as she was not one for engaging in conversation beyond paying the money and requesting the odd repair.

In the car again, Neville said, 'You could knock me down with a feather, I would have sworn they were gay, those two.'

'Who says they're not?' said Anton. Neville thought for a moment.

'Gays don't go to boxing matches.'

'You're sure about that?' asked Anton. Again, Neville took a few moments to think it over before saying,

'Fairly sure.'

With Beulah Mansions no longer part of their run, that left just one stop, the house with the couple and two friends, one of whom bought two tickets for himself and a date. Anton and Neville looked at each other,

'You know what it is, right?' said Neville, 'An evening of boxing matches.'

'Cool, looking forward to it, it's a great idea. See if she enjoys it too.'

'A sale's a sale,' said Anton as they headed home. Neville was enjoying driving, but he had picked up on his brother's quieter-than-usual demeanour.

'You okay bro? Seem a bit far away this evening. Nervous for Saturday?'

'A bit,' said Anton, 'before that though I'm meeting my mother tomorrow.'

'Wo, hang on, you didn't tell me that,' said Neville, trying to look at his brother and the road at the same time.

'Just did.'

'Where?'

'A café. Do you remember her?'

'No, not really, I was young too, don't forget. I can just about picture her, but I don't remember what she was like.... That's big. Does Dad know?'

Anton shook his head. 'Not yet. Maybe afterwards.'

He walked into the café bang on three. Apart from a young woman who was busy behind the counter, there were just three people there: two men in high visibility jackets, tucking into all-day breakfasts and in the corner a woman sitting alone, wearing a dark brown suede coat and watching the door. She saw him as he walked in and smiled, she looked too young, but it had to be her.

'Angie?'

'Anton, oh my G-' she stood to greet him and as he reached her she put her arms out to welcome him. A button on her coat caught the cup of tea she had just bought and turned it on its side, spilling it over the table. She didn't notice but just pulled Anton in close, hugging him, holding on as he put his hand out to try and hold the edge of her coat away from the table where it threatened to upend the milk jug as well.

'Mind your coat... in the tea,' said Anton. The young woman had come out from behind the counter, holding a roll of blue tissue paper and tearing a few squares off as she moved. Angie relaxed her grip and stood back, Anton still trying to guide the errant coat away from further mischief. The young woman threw tissue onto the table and dabbed it down to absorb the spillage.

'I'll get you another, do you want to move to another table?' she said, but Angie was in the moment and couldn't stop staring at Anton.

'Look at you, oh my, Anton, look at you…' he smiled at her and guided her gently away from the table and across to another, the coat still loose and in danger of catching on any random salt or pepper pots, ketchup bottles or carefully balanced menus.

'Let's sit here, let the lady clear the mess up, eh?' He smiled at the young woman who was cleaning the table, she seemed to be very patient with them, probably because of the lack of other customers but he was grateful she hadn't made a thing of it.

He helped Angie off with her coat and put it safely on a spare chair then stepped back to take a good look. He would never have recognised her; she was a stranger but one who was absurdly happy to see him. 'I have a lot of questions,' he said.

'I know,' she sat and straightened her collar, 'I know. It's so good to see you Anton… this is good, I didn't know if it would be, but it is, it really is. I can't believe it.'

'I wouldn't have recognised you. It's crazy,' he said.

'What do you know..?'

'Nothing really… there isn't a photo of you, not that I've seen.' She had calmed a little, but she couldn't stop staring at him and smiling. 'Tea?' She nodded. 'Two teas please,' he called over to the woman who had finished cleaning up and was back behind the counter, 'sorry about the mess.'

'These things happen,' she smiled at them, Anton returned the smile, wondering if she had guessed what was going on or whether she had come up with another story, Angie looked so young after all, forty or so, he guessed.

'I can't believe it, you've become a man,' said Angie.

'And you're too young, you're too young to be my mum,' he smiled at her, keen to let her know everything was alright, whatever her story was, he was just happy to know her.

'I'm not that young but it's very sweet of you to say so. How old are you now?'

'Twenty-two.'

'I was… I was your age, your age now, last time I saw you.'

'I was told… that you were dead.'

'Don't,' she looked down at the table and started to cry, quietly, 'please don't. I'm sorry, I can't help it,' she took out a small packet of tissues from her bag and dabbed at her eyes. 'It's my fault. I went along with it, agreed with it, it seemed like the right thing to do at the time.'

Their teas arrived and the woman who brought them looked with concern at the crying woman, then at Anton as if to ask if everything was okay.

'It's okay, thanks,' he said. When she had gone Angie continued,

'I'm not proud… of what we did then. I didn't behave well. Your father is a good man. I thought he was wonderful, you know? I liked being with him, I didn't set out… I don't think we were really old enough to know what we were doing, what the consequences of our choices would be. We loved you, we both loved you, we really did. I even loved Neville, best I could… it's not the same as your own baby. You were special,' she reached out across the table and touched his face, 'you *are* special.'

'You don't have to tell me this,' said Anton, unsure what exactly he wanted her to say or how much he really wanted to know.

'I want to, I want to be able to tell you. We got some things wrong, we were human, its only right to admit to it, to the truth.'

'You spilt up? Even though you had a baby?' he couldn't help himself.

'I don't want to lose you again,' she looked up, her eyes still wet.

'I'm not going anywhere… I understand. What's past is in the past,' he sat back, drank some tea, and gave her time.

'He threw me out. That's the truth. He had reason, I had other friends, other male friends, I saw other people. The responsibility was too much, I was young, I didn't know what I wanted except not to be tied down. Malcolm found out, it wasn't difficult; he was angry, I can see why, I don't bear any grudges. But there was you, we didn't know how to deal with you.'

Anton reached over and took one of her hands in his. He wanted to spare her, but she wanted to get it all out now.

'I can't make excuses, there aren't any… I was young and scared. I wanted to dance, to party, to be free… I brought it all on myself. I forced him into shutting me out. It was too late in the end, by the time I understood what I'd done he was looking after you and Neville on his own, doing a good job. He couldn't cope with me coming and going… we talked. We agreed I would be dead. You hardly knew me anyway and I wasn't too much of a mother,' she stopped, looked down at the table and shook her head, this time the tears came freely, she had no say in the matter. Anton gently squeezed her hand.

'You were young,' he said.

'I'm sorry Anton, I'm sorry,' was all she could say. She cried some more, shaking as she did so, Anton holding on to her arm. In the silence that followed he realised he could leave now, turn his back, and say goodbye. The truth was out, it was done. Perhaps it was best to let her be, let things lie and just walk away. He also wondered *What must it have been like? To be her at that point.*

Whatever else, she was his mother and surely it was worth some time to find out a bit more about her.

'Drink some tea,' he said, gently, taking his hand away from her arm, letting her lift her head, 'its good tea in here,' she looked at him, her eyes red and tired, tears still coming but she was putting a smile together. He lightly brushed her cheek with the palm of his hand. She lifted the tea and took a sip, then nodded in appreciation. He smiled at her, 'Good?' she nodded, he sat back, waited a moment, and said, 'So, where did you go?'

Later that night, in the quiet of his room, in the safety of his home, he lay on the bed and went back over the story she had told him of her life, jobs she had taken, places she had moved to and from and the other child she had, a girl, in her teens now, due to leave school that year. He wondered what she was like, what she looked like, whether she looked at all like him. His half-sister. He didn't want to talk about it, not with Malcolm or with Neville but he was happy just being with himself for now, knowing all this. Inside he was richer at the end of a long day, there was more to him now than before.

34

As Kirby's fight approached, the nervous energy around him reached a peak. It was only on the Thursday, two days out, that he found out who his opponent would be.

'He's called Jay Duro,' said Barney.

'Duro? Where's he from, is that Spanish?' asked Dave who was part of the regular morning briefing Barney conducted, where duties were assigned for the day.

'I didn't know, but I looked him up,' Barney was obviously not happy with what he'd discovered, 'he's a pro, a proper one, seven fights. He lost one which is encouraging but that was at the start. Since then, he's won five on the bounce, one on points, the rest knock outs or technicals.' No-one spoke, they could see there was more coming, Barney had a way of working up to things.

'And its eight rounds.'

'We've planned for six,' said Anton.

'No point in getting on my case, I know what we've been working towards but now it's changed, that's what happens. We've done a lot of work on his stamina so he's not out of it.' He looked around at them.

'Even so,' said Dave, 'eight rounds with a seven-time pro., whatever happened to easing him in?'

'We're not in that world, we take what we're given,' said Barney. 'Right, who wants to tell him?' No-one spoke.

'Thought so. I will then, but we all stay positive, right? Alright?' They nodded but no-one moved for a moment, all just taking it in.

Eventually, Anton said, 'Yes, of course. Come on, we need to get going.'

Somehow Barney managed to talk up the change of plan with Kirby, make it into a great challenge, one where Kirby could really impress, and they knew he would, his team were all really up for it, they were sure he'd have no problem with eight rounds, just need to think a bit more about pacing, this would maybe even play to his strengths in some ways. Kirby didn't look rattled by it, Anton looked for signs, but he didn't look at all bothered by the change. Of course, he didn't really have a lot of choice.

Saturday came round fast for most of them although Anton had a feeling that for Kirby it took an age. He slept in the car the night before, same as always despite offers of a proper bed from everyone who had a spare.

The locker room back-of-house at the old hall was infused with the smell of ageing timber and disinfectant. It was clean but had decades of history embedded in the benches and across the floors, countless scars, scuffs, and little gouges filled with the dark dust and grease of years gone by.

Barney arrived early to get things in order, Anton joining him shortly afterwards and helping by trailing round after him, putting Kirby's things out and taking notes of the names of the officials in charge, all the while being introduced all over the place by Barney who seemed to know everyone.

'Oi, oi, it's the Barnster,' a shiny suited man a few years younger than Barney and a couple of inches shorter, walked in without knocking and warmly greeted them.

'Bill… how long has it been?' Barney shook his hand but not over-enthusiastically, 'I want you to meet Anton, Anton Matheson, he's one of our key men back at the ranch, in fact he's re-opening the ranch, we're relaunching he's the new boss. Anton, this is William Barrowland.'

'Bill,' said Barrowland, putting his hand out. Anton took it and shook it, adding a friendly smile,

'Bill,' he said.

'Great card this evening,' said Barrowland to both of them, 'your boy, Kirby is it?'

'Kirby, yeah,' said Anton.

'Is he any good? Can he make a fight of it?' Anton looked at Barney and went to speak but Barney stopped him,

'He'll do a good job,' he said.

'Good, appreciate it,' said Barrowland, 'it's always tricky, you know that… undercards, making sure they're worth turning up for.' He gestured toward the door, 'It's all about the beer sales, we need the people here to make sure they happen.' He moved towards Anton and put an arm on his shoulder,

'Here's the score Anton, this is all just a big pub with a boxing ring attached, if I bring in lots of people, they ask me back. It's good to meet you Anton, until the next time, eh?' He was shaking hands again, eager to move on, other business to conduct, 'Barney, keep on staying one step ahead.'

'I will. See you Bill,' and he was gone. When the door had fully shut, Barney explained to Anton, 'Promoter. He's got one of the headliners I think, and he has Duro on his books too.'

'What was that about making a fight of it?'

Barney stood for a moment then looked at Anton, 'You get it, don't you? Duro's on a path, they're clocking up victories with him, making his record look impressive. We're not meant to win.'

'You're not saying-'

'-No, I'm not saying nothing. It's a proper contest, nothing funny but Duro is a long way ahead of our boy.'

'So, we're back with George's losers?' Barney took a moment to consider his reply then said,

'I don't know where you picked that up but no, we're not back in those times. Having said that, Kirby is going to lose and it's no shame.'

'What are we supposed to do?'

'Pick up the pieces, tell him he's a warrior, and tell him that his day will come; make sure he doesn't get hurt too much, patch him up and make sure he trains on. He'll have his day. Come on, we need to crack on.'

'Barney,' Anton put his hand out to stop him, 'I need you to tell me there's nothing dodgy about this.' Barney stopped and turned and got close to him,

'No. I don't do dodgy; I wouldn't have anything to do with it if it was. It's just a little undercard contest that's been set up to suit a lad called Duro, the conditions are a long way in his favour, okay?' Anton nodded to say he understood but in truth, he didn't really feel okay at all.

The others started to arrive, Barney had arranged passes for Dave and Franny as well as Keith who brought Kirby and insisted he wouldn't be watching but would just wait out back for them all to return. Kirby looked good.

'Sleep well?' asked Anton.

'Yes, all good,' he saw Anton looking at him intently. 'What?'

'Nothing,' said Anton, 'you're looking good mate, looking trim.'

They were second on the bill. Kirby spent the time during the first fight on the massage table, Barney working his muscles, loosening him up, getting him warm. The others went up top to see the opening contest, a lively six rounder at featherweight that went the distance for a points victory for the blue corner, it kept their minds off things for a while.

'We've got ten minutes,' said Dave as the victor's hand was raised and a few cheers came from the far side of the room. By the time they reached the changing room, Kirby was sitting up and Barney was getting ready to glove him.

'Better take a piss,' said Barney.

'Good point,' said Kirby and disappeared out of the door into the corridor.

'What's it like out there?' Barney looked at Dave.

'About half full.'

'Not bad. It's still early.'

When the call came Kirby was more than ready, he couldn't keep still, and Barney did his best to calm him.

'Easy, easy, easy… hold it in, keep some back, good lad.'

It was his first ring walk, his first as a pro. Barney thought he needed telling, have it pointed out to make sure he took it in and enjoyed the moment. Anton assumed he was just trying to distract him.

Now the place was more than half full, people were arriving all the time, Anton knew his side had been pushing tickets all over the place with everyone they knew, the gym was getting a small cut after all. It looked like Duro's team had done the same.

The noise seemed to build all the time or maybe they were just walking deeper into it. Out there somewhere were Malcolm and Neville. He couldn't see them, but he believed they were there. Anton felt the nerves now, like he was the one about to fight. At any rate, it was personal. He fussed over Kirby, helping him into the ring, passing him a gum shield and taking his gown from him while Barney organised the corner. As he stepped away, he gave him a last pat on the shoulder and leant in to whisper in his ear,

'Do it champ, you know you can.'

Duro was shorter than Kirby, conspicuously muscled and tattooed all over his arms, chest and neck. He looked serious, a look you didn't want to catch, a look you didn't want looking at you. He knew it too and gave Kirby a stare that must have got him thinking. Anton tried to work out what his weak spot might be but couldn't come up with one, not yet at least.

The introductions drew cheers for both of them, it sounded like the entire hall had taken one side or the other. It gave Anton a chill. Kirby turned back to the corner, Barney said,

'Remember, take your time.' The bell rang.

Barney's note was a good one and it took the edge off him, he came into the round thinking, not just tearing into it. Round one was slow to start, both men working out what they were facing. Duro didn't look like he was taking anything for granted, he looked tough, seasoned and like he was concentrating. Kirby looked as good as he ever had, they had done the best they could for him. *He just has to keep it together,* thought Anton, finding it really quite difficult to do that himself.

Kirby kept his hands high for the most part, tempting Duro in, waiting for him to get close and looking for the counter punch, hoping to get a chance. As a tactic it worked to the degree that he landed a few although none with very much behind them. Duro found it easy to duck out of the way of his jabs and was patient. Kirby lined one up towards the end of the round but showed too much to Duro who landed one just below his right eye, it made Barney wince.

At the break, Barney was there, wiping his brow, in close, 'Keep your hands up, don't be impatient, your chance will come… he's ducking well so try a bit of up and under.'

The second round looked looser, they moved a little more, looking for space, looking for ways in. Duro carried on ducking away from Kirby's jabs but was getting bolder in the follow ups, moving in another step to make room for a body shot or two. That began to work for him, and Kirby's defences were stretched, he had to keep thinking where the next one was coming from, and it kept him from causing too much trouble for his opponent. Before round three, Barney encouraged him to use his height advantage,

'Keep swinging up and remember to follow on. When he ducks, he has to come back up, have another one ready for him.' Anton wondered how much of this Kirby was taking in.

Kirby held his ground better in the third, doing his best to throw a third or even a fourth punch when he had a chance, even at the cost of letting Duro land one or two along the way. From outside the ring this looked like an escalation of hostilities and the crowd began to yell. The fighters stood their ground, and it looked even. *At least for now,* thought Anton, who was wondering just how long Kirby could keep this up for.

With a minute or so to go, they were both on the attack. It was pleasing the crowd, but it was heart-in-the-mouth time for Anton who wanted to look away. Near the end of the round Duro connected with Kirby's right eye again and this time he cut him. Barney cleaned him up when they stopped and told him to do his best to protect it for a while, above all not to let him hit it again.

Kirby's response in the fourth was to go on the offensive, lead with his left and keep his head turned away, if Duro didn't counter he followed up with his right and kept going until he was blocked. The upping of his shot numbers kept Duro busy and back, focussing on his defence.

'He won that one, didn't he?' said Anton at the bell.

'Yeah, must have, he's done well,' said Barney.

In the fifth, Kirby tried to carry on where he'd left off, but Duro was getting wise to it and looked livelier than before, dropping away more quickly and letting Kirby punch a lot of air. Kirby began to look tired, Duro was drawing his fire and waiting for his chance. It came soon enough, he dropped below Kirby's attack again and started in with body blows which unbalanced his opponent, following up with an uppercut of his own which flung Kirby's head back. A left, then a right followed before any evasive action was possible and Duro's supporters began to shout louder, sensing their man was done with waiting. To Anton, it looked like Kirby had just forgotten whatever plan he'd had, perhaps everything he knew, and he was lost. At the bell, Anton breathed out, suddenly aware he'd been holding it in for very long time.

In the corner, Barney looked closely at Kirby's face, the cut below his eye had opened up again,

'Fuck, he must have caught it again, I didn't see it,' Anton passed a swab and Barney dabbed away at the wound. 'Let's just defend eh? Just keep those hands up and be patient, you've done amazing, alright?' Kirby looked at him, he was breathing deeply and didn't waste any precious air on talking. 'Just stay out of trouble for a round, okay? You okay to carry on?'

'Yes, yes,' said Kirby, *too quickly* thought Anton and it was obvious Barney thought the same. When the bell rang, he shouted in Anton's ear,

'We get ready to throw the towel in, okay? If he goes down or starts to wander…' Anton nodded but knew it wouldn't be easy to stop him, not now, not having got this far but Barney was the one who was supposed to know what to do.

Kirby's problem in the sixth was that Duro's team had correctly guessed he would stick with defending for a round and Duro was able to take advantage and relax his own defence to allow him to launch a barrage. Kirby kept his hands high and that worked, most of Duro's shots hit his arms and hands but it was exhausting and Duro didn't let up, he just kept it coming. Eventually the bell stopped him, but he didn't look as if he needed it.

'Can you see?' Barney was in front and up close to Kirby whose right eye was all but closed up. Kirby nodded. 'Not out of that one though eh?' said Barney, tending to him. Anton looked over at Duro's corner: their fighter was sweating, drinking water, and nodding vigorously as his trainer gestured and shouted at him. Duro flexed his hands, rolled his head to stretch his neck muscles and drummed the canvas with his feet. In contrast Kirby was statuesque, seated, arms resting on his legs, conserving whatever energy he had left.

'Protect the eye,' was Barney's only note as the seventh round started.

Anton put a hand on Barney's shoulder, 'He can't do two more rounds.'

'I agree,' said Barney, 'get ready then.'

The seventh was only a fraction slower than the previous round, Duro's movement was still impressive, he was able to stop Kirby from staying in one place and he kept him moving, his principal tactic now seemed to be to wear his man down. Kirby was almost fighting side on, leading almost exclusively with his left in order to keep his right side as far away from Duro as he could. It meant his attack was predictable and although he had a decent enough left it wasn't his strongest. Kirby's single-minded attention to protecting his eye left him open to Duro's body shots that came in twos and threes, Kirby only reluctantly dropping his hands to fend him off after he'd taken enough and really had to stop him.

Just over halfway in Kirby took a chance and surprised Duro with a right hook which landed cleanly on his chin, sending him back a couple of steps. Kirby followed up with a left jab which Duro had seen coming but it gave Kirby another chance at a right which he put his whole weight behind, catching Duro square on and drawing blood from his nose. The crowd noise rose further still and Duro looked unsure for the first time; he backed away and Kirby got a moment to breathe. Duro composed himself and got balanced again but he was wary now and just jogged gently on the spot, threatening to come forward but deciding not to for now, both of them happy to let the time run down.

At the bell, Kirby turned and ran to his corner looking like a man running down a hill, his legs not keeping up with him, he fell onto the stool and Barney covered his face with a cool, wet towel.

'That was something, that was it mate, brilliant. You showed him, showed them all,' he wiped his face and patted his shoulder, 'are we done?' Kirby shook his head. Barney looked up at Anton who stared at them both,

'He's not ducking,' said Anton; Barney looked at him, looked like he should shut up, but he said again, 'he's not ducking out of the way so much, there's a way through.' He wasn't sure if Kirby heard him, but Barney looked away, then back and shook his head.

Barney got into Kirby's eyeline and said, 'You have nothing left to prove, son, you're a hero. Let's stop.' Again, Kirby shook his head.

The bell rang and he stood, Duro too, looking for the first time like he might be getting just a bit tired as well. They came together in the centre of the ring, Duro jabbed with his left, Kirby pulled away and countered with a left of his own which caught Duro's mouth but not hard enough to stop him sending in a right-handed body shot, then a left followed by a powerful right hook to Kirby's head which caused him to stagger back.

Barney told Anton to pick up a towel, did it in such a way that it wasn't a request, his face said it all, they should be ready to call an end to it, but Kirby somehow stayed on his feet. Duro was slower coming forward now, but he was still able to accurately plant a left which caught Kirby's eye again, Kirby somehow jabbing back with his left as he stepped back. Anton had climbed the step by the ropes and Kirby glanced at him, saw him standing there. Kirby looked at him and mouthed *no*.

Anton could see Barney in his peripheral vision, about to climb onto the steps to take up a position next to him, Anton was sure he was getting ready to tell him to signal to stop the fight, so he kept his eyes forward, fixed on Kirby, watching every move. He saw Kirby step forward again, flex for an attack, saw Duro land a low shot below Kirby's slowing defence. Kirby bent over with the blow but didn't try to parry, instead he used his hands to throw a right, then a left hook follow through at Duro who stood his ground even when they connected. Duro jabbed again in response, causing Kirby's face to crumple and both eyes to close up for a moment but he stayed standing and jabbed with his right which pushed Duro back, then another, then a third on the same spot, Duro now off balance and not knowing where the next was coming from. Kirby followed on, swung hooks alternatively left then right, not stopping, his own legs unsteady, shaking but still holding him there. Duro stepped away and stood back up, stood straight and rebalanced. Kirby waited for a moment then stepped back himself, inviting him, drawing Duro in. Duro swung but Kirby saw it coming and leant away then countered with his right which had everything he had left in it, catching Duro full on in the face.

He fell onto his knees for a moment, then all the way down. Kirby watched him go down, staggered back and let the ropes take his weight as the count over Duro began. Anton watched the referee, counting himself, wondering why it was so slow, but Duro couldn't stand, he looked up and Anton saw the hurt in his eyes as he willed himself to stand but his legs wouldn't move. Finally, the referee stood back, counted him out and stretched his arms wide. Anton and Barney climbed through the ropes in time to catch Kirby and keep him upright as his legs gave way.

They took a side each, lifting Kirby's arms over their shoulders, his head slumped, legs no longer able to take his weight on their own. All around them the noise blanketed the air: cheers, applause, cries of joy, protest, and shouted opinions. Duro's team came into the ring and lifted their man to a sitting position then gently coaxed him back up onto his feet and slowly helped him away. The official was speaking but was hard to hear and the cheers just grew louder when he raised Kirby's arm. Kirby lifted his head and looked around, his right eye closed up, ears both red, and bruises starting now to come through all over; he was drenched in sweat. Someone had fetched Keith from out back and he climbed into the ring to embrace his son.

The crowd divided into two, Duro's friends and supporters and the neutrals had calmed and were talking to each other or heading to the bar, their interest in proceedings at an end. Kirby's side were still cheering and shouting to him, high on the moment, aware they had seen something they would remember.

Out in the crowd, Anton could see Father Mike who was standing on a chair and holding his arms high in the air while he clapped enthusiastically. Tyrone was nearby and looked as if he'd brought his whole family, Kirby was one of theirs now, part of the family and they celebrated accordingly.

Anton kept looking round to try and find his father, sure he was somewhere. Everyone was on their feet and moving around which made the task more difficult. He could hear someone calling his name, it sounded like Neville but there was another cry from the same direction, an ululation and whooping that could only have one source.

He strained to see out into the room, then saw Malcolm walking toward the ring, leading the way, Neville behind him, waving his arms in the air and turning now to high five the woman behind him: Franca.

The three of them reached ringside still punching the air and cheering and looking up at Anton.

He turned and hugged a sticky, sweating Kirby, patted him twice on the back of his head and almost kissed his forehead, deciding at the last moment to forgo that one. Keith was there and took one side of his son, Barney the other, to lead him slowly off. Anton stepped through the ropes, stood on the edge of the ring, and jumped down.

'Well done son, that's a brave lad you got there,' said Malcolm, opening his arms and hugging him, 'blimey, you niff.'

'It's not me, I got it off him,' said Anton, indicating the shuffling figure of his victorious fighter.

'I bought a guest,' said Malcolm, stepping out of the way to reveal Franca.

'Whoop,' she said, her arms in the air still high on the moment. He looked at her, her deep dark green eyes, that hair. She dropped her arms, tried to calm herself and looked back at him, her face flushed and with a grin she couldn't have stopped if she'd tried. For a moment they stood just gazing at each other, oblivious to everything else until Malcolm said,

'Is this gonna take all night? I need a drink.'

Anton took a step toward her, and they came together, arms outstretched, then wrapped tightly around each other in an embrace neither wanted to end. Eventually Franca leant back without letting go and looked at him.

'Try again?' she said.

He leant forward and kissed her, held her closer still.

He heard his dad say, 'We'll be at the bar then.'

Anton rested his head on her shoulder, gently kissed her neck and whispered, 'Yes.'

ABOUT THE AUTHOR

Simon Thomsett lives in London and has been writing for many years. *The Rules* is his first book to be published and is part one of a two-part story, the second part is planned for publication in 2025.

Printed in Great Britain
by Amazon

46674220R00218